The Turning Tides

Jane Fenwick

Copyright 1st Edition

Copyright © 2020 Jane Fenwick
The right of Jane Fenwick to be identified as the author of the
Work has been asserted by her in accordance with the Copyright,
Designs and Patents Act 1988.

First published as an Ebook in 2020

All rights reserved. No part of this book may be reproduced,
scanned, stored in a retrieval system or distributed in any printed
or electronic form, without the prior written permission of the
publisher; nor be otherwise circulated in any form of binding or
cover other than that in which it is published and without a
similar condition being imposed on the subsequent purchaser.

All characters in this publication are fictitious and any
resemblance to real persons, living or dead is purely coincidental.

A CIP catalogue record for this title is available from the British
Library.
ISBN 978-1-9161957-69

Cover design by Charlotte Mouncey

www.janefenwick.co.uk

For My Family

Also by Jane Fenwick

Never The Twain

My Constant Lady

Alnmouth, Autumn 1766

Prologue

A solitary bell tolled as Gabriel Reynolds showered soil onto the coffin lid obscuring the brass plaque. On Gabriel's left, Caroline daughter of the deceased and Gabriel's one time fiancée, added to that which he had dropped. From hand to hand the box passed around the grave from one black coated mourner to the next. At last it came to rest in the hands of a red-haired young woman on Gabriel's right. She removed her soft, kid glove and scooped up the last of the soil completing the task with a heartfelt sigh. Eleanor Reynolds squeezed her husband's hand before slipping the small, black glove onto her cold white hand. Grief stricken, Caroline leaned heavily upon her childhood sweetheart as the mourners processed slowly from the churchyard to their awaiting carriages, the light mizzle coating them in a cobweb of moisture. Thomas Hodgeson was dead.

1

Two months later

'I have to call at Caroline's on the way to the bay. There are more papers for her to sign.' Since her father's death, Gabriel had been helping Caroline with her business affairs. 'There's still much to sort out. She's never had anything to do with Thomas' businesses before. She hasn't a head for commerce like you my love.' Gabriel picked up his saddle bag containing his own documents.

'I should like to see how she does. I could come too as I've not had sight of her for some weeks. She still refuses callers.'

'I'm not sure it's a good idea to come today. Let me speak with her and introduce the plan. I agree it would be a help if you could assist her; you're good with accounts and the like. Perhaps she might talk to you about her loss. Two months is only a little time to come to terms with her father's passing. She's still shocked. The suddenness of his death was a blow for us all.'

Eleanor stood on her tiptoes and planted a kiss on his lips. 'Very well then. Speak with her and ask if I can be of help in any way.'

Gabriel made to leave.

'Try not to be late home tonight, remember we have guests this evening. I know you have a lot on your plate at the moment what with your own work and Caroline's, but try not to overdo it. You'll make yourself ill.'

'I'm fine, but I'll be late if you keep me talking any longer.' He rang the bell to ask for his horse to be saddled. He waited but no one came. 'Perhaps I might find Jax in the stables?' he said distractedly.

Eleanor called after him: 'I'll make a start on the accounts you brought home yesterday. I'll send them to the bay this afternoon when they're done shall I?'

'Thank you my love that will be a great help.'

Eleanor had been doing all she could to lighten his load and he appreciated it. Unusually his wife had run her own business affairs for years buying and selling shares in ships amongst other things. Being able to pass on some of the day-to-day matters of Thomas' business to Eleanor was proving helpful.

Gabriel knew Caro was struggling to cope, not just with grief, but with the business. She had no real interest in shipping; even when her father was alive she'd been more interested in fashion than frigates. Thomas had managed everything himself and now, with his death, she had inherited the shipping line and was under pressure to take the reins, at least until a factor could be found to take over.

Gabriel strode through the kitchen, the lingering smell of kippers hanging in the air, and out to the stableyard at the side of the house. Where Lisbet was he couldn't speculate. His manservant, Abner Boatwright, was possibly hiding in the smokehouse. Connie the new under cook was nowhere to be seen either.

'Jax I need Copper saddled,' he called as he marched across the cobblestones. There was no reply. 'Where is everyone?' he muttered under his breath beginning to be annoyed that his entire staff had gone missing. They had a habit of disappearing when they were most needed he noticed.

From the corner of his eye he saw a woman enter the yard. She was wearing a burgundy riding habit with a matching hat and muff. He recognised Caroline Hodgeson's familiar figure.

'Good morning Caro, this is a surprise. Have you walked here? I seem to have misplaced my staff; they're good at disappearing when work is required.'

'Yes I have walked. It suited my purpose today.'

He noticed her face was pale and impassive. 'I thought we'd agreed I'd call to see you on my way to the bay this morning. What purpose? I too have a purpose and that's to give my staff a sound thrashing when I find them.' He grinned.

Caroline took a step nearer although the length of the

yard was still between them. Gabriel, who had been about to unbolt the stable door turned and began to walk towards her. He watched astonished as she took a pistol from her muff and held it at arm's length pointing it towards his chest. The muff dropped to the ground and time stood still.

'This is my purpose Gabriel.'

Confusion swept over him. He couldn't believe his eyes, but saw she was deadly serious. He felt his face drain of colour.

'If your purpose was to humiliate me then you succeeded. First you jilted me after five years, and then to add insult to injury you marry someone else after an indecently short space of time. You and I planned a Christmas wedding; well one of us had one. Could you not have waited?' She took a step nearer. 'Not satisfied with this you then parade your new wife around Alnmouth to rub my nose in it further. Flaunting herself and being so proud to be "Mrs Gabriel Reynolds" while I'm to be pitied and humoured like a child. You have abandoned me and now Father has left me too.'

'Caro I'm sorry. Please, you look troubled, come inside. I'd no idea you felt this way.'

She ignored him and continued to point the pistol at his chest, her beautiful face strangely devoid of emotion, her eyes glassy. 'When you called off our wedding I told you I was humiliated.' Her face suddenly showed her distress. 'For years I waited for you and just as I had the winning post in sight you snatched away the prize. I hate you. How could you treat me so badly? I have done nothing to deserve this treatment.'

'Please Caroline put the gun down. You're upset. Come, we can talk about this.' He held out an appeasing hand and attempted a smile.

'There is nothing left to say. No man will ever look at me now, I'm second hand goods.' Her arm wavered slightly.

Gabriel raised his arms in supplication and hesitatingly stepped forward. He saw her tighten her grip on the gun.

'Stay where you are Gabriel. Keep away from me. I wish I'd never met you. Stop or I'll shoot.'

A solitary gull cried in alarm as the gun went off and Gabriel Reynolds fell to the ground.

ℛ

Dr Wilson Chaffer had examined the wound to Gabriel's thigh. The injured man sat on the settle by the kitchen range with his leg raised on a stool.

'It will need stitches I'm sorry to say. It's just a flesh wound but at least the bullet isn't lodged. Here, take this,' he passed the brandy decanter, 'you'll need it to numb the pain.'

Gabriel continued to explain what had happened for the benefit of Eleanor and his good friend the doctor.

Wilson began to thread a needle. 'I saw Jax enter the stableyard, Caro's back was towards him, but she must have sensed someone was behind her for she looked over her shoulder. The action of turning meant the gun was lowered slightly then, without a moment's thought for his own safety, Jax leapt forward and knocked the gun from her hand. It went off as it clattered to the ground. I remember the sound of the shot reverberating around the yard, then I fell backwards.'

'You're lucky my friend, the shot has only skimmed the outer edge of your thigh. Your groom's actions may well have saved your life.' Wilson began to sew the gash which had now stopped bleeding. 'You won't be able to put weight on it today; although it's only a surface wound you may start it bleeding again if you don't rest up.'

Eleanor, sitting opposite her husband, was chalk-white. She looked away when the stitching began. 'I was coming out into the yard when I heard the shot and saw you fall. All I could think was that she'd killed you. I saw the blood oozing through your breeches... '

'You can't get rid of me that easily my love.' He could see she was still rattled by the morning's events. 'I'll be up and about in no time, but it was the oddest sensation.' Gabriel took a slug of brandy then gritted his teeth as he felt the needle pierce his skin. 'All at once time slowed down, but at the same time seemed to stand still... I can't explain it. I saw Caro drop to the ground. I thought she was injured too but then I felt the pain and the warm blood seeping through my fingers.'

Wilson finished stitching then handed a glass of brandy to Eleanor. 'Here, drink this, you're in shock.' Eleanor screwed up her face.

'I know you don't like the taste of brandy, but swallow it down, it'll calm you,' Gabriel coaxed.

'Thank goodness Jax had the presence of mind to run for you Wilson.' She pulled a face as she sipped the brandy. 'It was exactly how you described it Gabriel. Time seemed to stop and I couldn't think what to do.'

Wilson bandaged the wound then tied it off. 'I'll go to see what can be done for Caroline if I may. Where is she?'

'I think Lisbet took her to lie down,' Eleanor said. 'Connie will show you the way.'

'How do you want to deal with this?' Wilson enquired. 'Surely the constable needs fetching.'

Gabriel was determined. 'No, this is my entire fault, I should have noticed her grieving had changed its course. Perhaps she's had some sort of breakdown? Since Thomas passed she's been distracted, fragile. Judging by what she said she holds me responsible for her present misery, but that was just the ravings of a... I hadn't known that she felt this way.'

'Nor I,' Eleanor sighed, 'I thought she was taking up a lot of your time but felt perhaps she was grieving for Thomas and struggling to come to terms with taking over the business. I had no idea she blamed you or resented me.'

Lisbet, a headstrong and garrulous Geordie, came bustling into the kitchen. She helped herself to a nip of brandy.

'A'm in shock,' she said defensively as Gabriel raised an eyebrow at his cook's nerve. 'A left Connie in charge. A bin watchin' over Miss Caroline in case she suddenly produced another weapon and run amok.'

'Hardly likely Lisbet.' Gabriel frowned at the woman who had all but raised him. Abner, never one to miss an opportunity, limped in and following Lisbet's lead downed a glass of brandy himself.

'That's my best brandy,' Gabriel warned, but his servants knew they were on safe ground under the circumstances.

'She's gone off her head if yer ask me.' Abner topped up his glass.

'Just as well no one is asking you then is it not? Take Jax a glass, he possibly has more need of it than you. If you'd been about earlier all of this might never have happened.' Gabriel winked at Eleanor and turned to address the doctor. 'Perhaps a sedative may help Caro?'

When the doctor had left the room Eleanor asked her husband: 'What did you mean when you said her grieving had changed?'

'I didn't think to mention it to you, but the last few

times I went to see her with papers to be dealt with she showed no inclination to look at them. I know she's not really interested in the business, but still... She seemed suddenly bright and cheerful and pleased to see me. I thought perhaps she was coming to terms with Thomas' sudden passing, but now I'm not so sure.' He traced the line of his jaw with his thumb. 'She seemed to want to talk about everyday things, things she remembered about her father. I presumed she was a little sad and lonely and needed to forget her troubles with an old friend. I thought it her way of grieving.'

Doctor Chaffer returned. 'I've given her a sedative. She seems calmer now, almost detached from reality; it's as if she doesn't know what she's done. I've known Caroline for years and it saddens me to see her in such a poor state. When I saw her last she seemed composed enough under the circumstances. I'd no reason to think she was suffering anything other than grief as she hasn't called on my services professionally, not since Thomas passed that is. I only saw her once just after he died. When I called at Eastshore last week the footman said she wasn't receiving visitors. I thought nothing of it as we all grieve in different ways. I just imagined she wanted to be alone.'

'This behaviour is certainly out of character.'

'It may be a case of delayed shock.'

'Grief is a terrible thing. It can creep up on you at the

strangest times.' Gabriel hung his head. 'Sometimes I can be having a perfectly happy day and then I remember my father is dead and that I'll never see him again. Caro's grief is still new and raw. She needs to take care of herself. *We* need to take care of her.' He looked to his wife who nodded. 'Perhaps she's suffered some sort of mental breakdown?' Gabriel offered.

Wilson agreed and said: 'She needs rest I think.' He waved away the brandy bottle Gabriel proffered. 'Perhaps she needs medical help from a specialist?'

'Has she gone mad do you think?'

'It's most likely the result of the sudden shock from her father's death which has temporarily unbalanced her mind.'

'But that was two months ago. Would she still act this way because of his death? She seemed to be blaming Gabriel for her troubles,' Eleanor said looking sceptical.

Dr Chaffer tried to explain. 'His heart stroke was very quick and unexpected. He waved her goodbye at breakfast and was dead by midday. Just collapsed and died right there in front of Gabriel.'

'It was some shock to me too.'

Gabriel remembered the day his father's old friend had died. He saw again Thomas' frightened, agonised expression as he slumped to the floor of his office. There had been no warning, save for Thomas saying he had indigestion, but Gabriel had known him to complain of the condition all his life and so thought nothing of it. He still felt guilty, although he knew in reality there was nothing he could have done to save the man who was like a father to him. He still saw the helpless look that Thomas gave him as the light faded from his eyes. It had all happened so quickly and so unexpectedly.

'I think Caroline should stay here with us tonight Gabriel. There's no one at Eastshore to care for her besides the servants. I could send for her maid to bring her what she needs. What do you think?' Eleanor's hands were trembling despite the brandy he noticed.

'Yes by all means. Perhaps that would be for the best so long as you don't mind my love.'

'Of course not, she needs our help. I'll send a note with Jax.'

'Do that, but don't say what's happened. If word gets out all of Alnmouth will know about the shooting by supper time.'

When Eleanor left the room Gabriel looked to his friend. 'Eleanor is a strong woman, but this has been a shock to her too. I know Eleanor and having something to do will help take her mind off things.'

'Do you think Caroline is jealous of Eleanor? Are you not worried to have her in the same house after what she said?'

'She can hardly take a pot shot at her when she's sedated, but you're right I suppose, I shouldn't like to leave my wife alone with her until we see how she does.'

Wilson shook his head and looked resigned. 'Who would have ever thought Caroline was a dangerous woman?'

'Given the right circumstances all women can be dangerous Wilson. I thought you would have known that.'

'Lottie's tame,' he laughed mentioning his intended's name, 'though she does have her moments.'

'Eleanor can still surprise me even after all this time. She has an unpredictable side that rears its head when I least expect it.'

When Gabriel had brought his new bride to Alnmouth less than a year ago he'd known that the situation would be difficult for both women. He realised the usurped lady would possibly feel it most. When Gabriel had called off his engagement to Caroline she had assured him she was not in love with him either; it seemed they had outgrown each other. Gabriel would always be fond of her, they had played together as children, grown up together, but he realised he didn't love her in the way he expected to love a wife. Caroline was a good woman, indeed she was a beautiful woman who possessed traits and accomplishments most men would admire. She was also an heiress so had no shortage of suitors, some more desirable than others, but to Gabriel she was more like a sister than a lover.

After the broken engagement and a visit to her aunt

to avoid the gossips, she had returned and had appeared to be happy enough. Then her father, whom she doted on, had died suddenly leaving her alone. Gabriel realised she had suffered greatly recently. He felt he should have done more for her.

When Caroline's maid arrived Eleanor told her a version of what had happened, a version that simply said her mistress had been taken ill and collapsed.

'Miss Caroline is to stay here at Westshore until she's recovered. It would be helpful if you could stay to attend her.'

'Of course, I feared something of the sort might happen. Over the last few weeks she's suffered greatly with her nerves. She's scarce eaten anything substantial and she can't seem to sleep. I wanted to send for the doctor but she wouldn't countenance it. All she said was "if he can mend broken hearts then by all means send for him".' Ellise looked at her sleeping mistress. 'She was so close to her father. His loss has been a great shock to her constitution. Taking over the shipping empire has been weighing heavily upon her, she never had much of a head for figures, but she didn't want to prevail upon you sir more than was necessary.'

'I wish you had told me then I could have helped. Perhaps I might have convinced her to rest or see a doctor.' Gabriel wasn't angry with Ellise but he was frustrated he'd misread the signs.

Eleanor said: 'My maid, Charity, will show you

where everything is and I'm sure she'll sit with Caroline while you take some rest and your meals.'

Despite a feeling of disquiet Gabriel rested for most of the day, but couldn't concentrate on anything other than his newspaper. He knew Eleanor was trying not to fuss about him; she knew his life wasn't in danger, but they both knew he'd had a close call.

ℛ

It had been a long day and they were both happy to have an early night. Gabriel needed help but only to climb the stairs. His thigh was stiff and sore but apart from that he had suffered no ill effects from his ordeal.

'Does it not seem strange that Caroline is under your roof this night? Do you feel the oddness of it?' Eleanor talked to his reflection as she sat at her dressing table. Their bedroom was softly lit.

'*Our* roof my love, not mine. Yes, I suppose it does although I'm not sure where else she could have gone, we could hardly have sent her back to Eastshore to an empty house with just the staff to care of her.'

'I agree. I'm so lucky to have a large family, but I miss them especially at times like this. Poor Caroline only has her aunt now.'

'There's a cousin who lives... I'm not sure where now; I think he's recently married. In any case her relatives aren't close by.' She watched as Gabriel lit more candles. 'I think he lost an arm in the war with

Spain.'

'Poor man,' Eleanor said wrinkling her nose. 'It will be wonderful to see Tomas and my parents at Christmas, I love it here in Alnmouth, but I miss them so much, and Whitby too of course.'

Eleanor was close to her twin brother and this was the longest time she had been apart from him. She'd tried to explain to Gabriel about the special bond she and her twin had, but as an only child Gabriel found it hard to imagine though he sympathised with her.

Christmas Eve would also be their first wedding anniversary. Eleanor's aunt, uncle and cousin from nearby Warkworth were also to join the celebrations.

'Can I ask you something, something personal?' Eleanor watched her handsome husband untie his stock and drop it on a chair. He could still make her tummy flip.

'You can ask, but I'm not sure I'll be obliged to answer if it's *very* personal.' Gabriel winked at her. 'You know I can deny you nothing.'

'Very well then I shan't ask.'

'Eleanor, I think I know my own wife well enough to understand what you would ask me. You want to know if I ever went to Caroline as I came to you in Amsterdam before we married, when we anticipated our wedding vows.'

Eleanor saw him smile at the memory while she continued to brush her hair.

'The answer is I did not. I think I told you that at the

end of our relationship I didn't think of her in that way. She felt more like a sister to me.'

'But you must have thought of her in *that* way at some point.'

'That's true of course, but then we were so young... and chaperoned. She wouldn't have compromised herself and I shouldn't have let her, from a practical point of view that is. If there had been an accident she would have been shamed. It's as you always say, different for women.'

'Yet you compromised me?' He came and rested his hands on her shoulders and kissed her neck.

'That's also true, but it was different.'

'How different?'

'Well for one thing we'd agreed on a short engagement so if you'd found yourself with child then we could have married in haste. And secondly,' he ran his fingers through her hair, 'I couldn't deny you; I knew you wanted me passionately.'

She tapped him with her hair brush and chuckled. 'You have a high opinion of yourself sir. Were you not just as eager?'

Eleanor smiled remembering the night in Amsterdam when he'd come to her room before they were married.

'Did I not demonstrate how I felt?'

She turned and rested her head against him. 'Poor Caroline, we're so lucky. Do you suppose she will get well again?'

'I hope so, I feel responsible for her. I once promised Thomas I'd always look out for her and I meant it. I hope this doesn't upset you, but it's as though she's my unmarried sister and I have to protect her. She has no one to look out for her. Caro isn't like you, she isn't strong and capable. She's always been the centre of Thomas' world and wanted for nothing.'

Eleanor knelt to help Gabriel remove his breeches to ensure the bandage on his thigh was secure. 'I'll try to be more of a friend to her if she'll let me although I've found it awkward sometimes when we've met socially.' They climbed into bed and Gabriel blew out his candle. 'Does your leg pain you still?' Eleanor asked.

'I'm brave and can stand it,' he joked. Eleanor loved his dry sense of humour. 'Just so long as you don't decide to take up arms against me too.'

She kissed him lightly and turned to blow out her candle. They lay side by side, their eyes gradually becoming accustomed to the dark.

'When I think of what might have happened this day. She could have killed you. How would I live without you?' She turned to look at his profile in the dark. His hand stroked her face and found it wet with tears.

'Hey what's this? Don't cry, I'm here and safe. You can't think that way.'

Eleanor rolled onto her side and tried to draw nearer to him, but was worried about hurting his wounded leg.

'I know,' she sighed deeply, 'there aren't many men who would house their would-be assassin. You're a very special sort of man my love.'

'And there aren't many wives who would allow their husband's past love to be under the same roof after she tried to shoot him.'

Eleanor felt the rasp as she stroked his stubbled cheek. 'I think Caroline's more troubled than we realised and I'm ashamed to admit I'd begun to feel a little jealous of the time you were spending with her. I thought she was trying to win you back, trying to steal you away.'

'I had no idea. Why did you not say anything?'

'I did try, but you were doing your best to be helpful, trying to support Caroline in her hour of need. I thought she was taking advantage of your good nature. Trying to... You didn't suspect her motives? I imagined she was trying to manipulate you somehow. You know her better than I of course and it seems I was wrong and I feel guilty for it now.'

'She's not devious. I saw how alone she was and I pitied her as I would anyone in the same situation. I wanted to help, that's all, of course the business can't run itself.' He stroked her arm. 'You must know I have love only for you. When I loved Caro, if ever I was truly "in love" with her, which I now doubt, we were children. I've only ever loved one woman and that's you.' Gabriel pulled her into his arms and kissed her.

'And I've only ever loved one man... Bendor!'

'Very amusing my love.' He tickled her.

They lay in silence for some moments.

'Wilson says he'll try to get professional help for Caro and we too must do what we can, although I'm at a loss to know what to do for the best. I'll have to write to her aunt in the morning. We can only try to support her.'

'Yes you're right.'

'Man alive!'

'What?'

'You've never said that I'm right before, you really must be suffering shock.'

She snuggled in closer and smiled into the darkness, thankful he was alive.

2

Christmas Eve would be Gabriel's and Eleanor's first wedding anniversary. It had been an eventful first year of marriage. There had been heartache and loss, but also love and a coming together; a close bond brought about by adversity and mutual respect.

When Gabriel Reynolds, head of the second largest shipping line in Alnmouth on the Northumberland coast, had married Eleanor Barker, an independent minded redhead from Whitby, it had been a love match *almost* from the start. They had met under unconventional circumstances but soon came to see they couldn't be apart.

At the time, Gabriel had been engaged to Caroline Hodgeson and Eleanor was betrothed to William Seamer, a whaling captain; neither of them loved their intended. They had met, indirectly, when her father had been commissioned to build a new ship for the handsome ship owner. Gabriel had been keen to expand the business after his father's premature death leaving him sole heir to a shipping fortune. After events first conspired to keep Gabriel and Eleanor apart, they had finally married at St Mary's church by the side of the ruined Abbey, one hundred and ninety nine steps high above the harbour town of Whitby on a crisp and frosty Christmas Eve.

Eleanor was looking forward to this, her first Christmas in her new home. She hadn't seen her parents and twin brother since her wedding day and was excited to be seeing them again. All her immediate family, except her older sister Atalana and her husband Obed Coffin, were travelling from Whitby to stay at Westshore, their wonderful light-filled house on the seashore. Her sister Atalana, and her husband, wouldn't be joining them as they were strict Quakers and kept Christmas quietly. Eleanor would miss her precious niece and nephew, also twins, as they wouldn't be allowed to visit either. They were six years old and she was sad to think she was missing out on them growing up.

Also joining them would be her Aunt and Uncle Brown and her cousin who lived at Warkworth. The town being only a few miles away from Alnmouth she had seen them often since moving to Northumberland; it was a comfort to her to have some family close by. She got on well with her cousin as they were a similar age. Eliza too was recently married but her husband, a naval officer, would be at sea. Sir Bendor Percy and his wife Grace, along with Cora, Grace's unmarried sister were also to stay for the festivities. Bendor was Gabriel's oldest and closest friend; they were like brothers.

A ball was planned for New Year's Eve and much excited preparation had already gone into making the ball as grand as it could be. They were expecting upwards of seventy guests and Lisbet and Eleanor had spent many happy hours planning the menus and the arrangements. It was to be the first ball for many years at Westshore and the first one of Eleanor's married life. Eleanor was a great organiser and had compiled copious lists; she wanted nothing left to chance. She was looking forward to it all, especially the dancing.

Gabriel's wound was healing quickly so that he only limped a little in the mornings. The stitches were expected to be removed when he came back from Newcastle where he had been overnight on shipping business. Eleanor sat at breakfast, a troubled look about her as she stirred her coffee. Last night's events threatened to spoil her mood.

When Eleanor was younger and had lived at Sandsend two miles or so outside Whitby, she had been in the habit of stealing out to the beach alone at night. The beach was her favourite place; she felt at peace there. Since moving north she had given up the habit, after all she now had a handsome husband to occupy her. However, when he was away from home she allowed herself the luxury of a stroll on their secluded beach at Westshore. There was something magical about the beach at night, especially if there was a full moon trailing a silvery pathway along the sea. She sometimes roused her whippet Slate and took her along for a midnight saunter.

Last night it had been a moonless, frosty night, but she'd had the urge to venture forth. She had wrapped up warmly and was about to leave by the kitchen door, having woken the sleeping dog, when she heard the sound of hooves plodding through the stableyard. At first she'd been alarmed and pulled back from the small window in the scullery. Then she recognised first the horse, it was Ned, and then the man leading him, it was Abner Boatwright their old retainer. The horse was weighed down by a tea chest on either side of his saddle.

Eleanor had returned to her bedchamber with a disgruntled dog following behind her. 'We can't go out now. That can only mean one thing,' she told the dog as she got back into bed. Slate, who was never allowed on the marital bed when Gabriel was at home, curled around her mistress' feet and cocked an ear. 'If I'm not much mistaken that be smuggled tea,' she whispered trying a piratical accent.

ℛ

The next evening Gabriel strode into the drawing room where Eleanor was reading before a roaring fire. He rubbed his hands together before bending to kiss her full on the lips. She dropped her book as he pulled her to her feet and wrapped his arms tightly around her waist.

'You feel like a warming pan. Man it's freezing out there.'

'I've been compared to nicer things,' she said as he squeezed her. He kissed her again. 'You should go away more often if this is the attention I get on your return.'

Abner came in bearing a tray with brandy. 'You'll be wantin' this to warm yer up A expect, 'tis blitherin' owt there.' He put the tray down and made to leave.

'Thank you, I will. What would I do without you and your spy glass knowing my every move?'

Eleanor sat down as Gabriel poured himself a brandy. 'Are you alright my love? You seem... distracted. Did a letter come from Caroline?'

She was relieved the conversation about Abner's nocturnal wanderings could be put off a little longer. She wasn't even sure whether Gabriel was involved. She knew French run brandy and claret sometimes found its way into their cellars, but that was common practice with all who lived on the coast, high born or low.

'Her aunt has written saying Caroline has arrived safely in Scarborough. Mrs Grant hopes Caroline will soon be up to writing to us herself.' She bent to pick up the book she'd dropped.

After the shooting Caroline had gone to stay at her aunt's house. She had stolen away early the next morning without speaking to either of them. She had left a note saying how deeply sorry and embarrassed she was by her behaviour. She hoped that in time they would forgive her.

'Good, let's hope she recovers soon.' He swirled the brandy around the glass. The amber liquid came dangerously near to spilling over the rim. 'Was everything alright while I was gone? You didn't take a lover for the night to keep you warm?' He smiled and settled back contentedly in the chair opposite.

'When I find one to match you my love I'll let you know.'

He was amused at her flattery. A companionable silence fell between them then Eleanor took a deep breath and summoned up her courage.

'Is there much in the way of smuggling around these parts? And before you make a joke, no I'm not thinking of setting up a run.'

'We live on the coast, of course there's smuggling. Why do you ask? I sense this isn't just light talk?'

Eleanor bit her lip thoughtfully. 'I once told you when I was in Sandsend I came across smugglers on father's land. Contraband was being hidden in our barn by a steward. He was paid for turning a blind eye until that is, I put a stop to his lawlessness. Father wouldn't have approved. Would you ever consider hiding run goods here?'

'In my line of business, certainly not! As someone who imports from Holland, France and the Baltics I can't afford the customs men sniffing around. Why are you asking me this? Has something happened?'

She shuffled uncomfortably in her seat. She knew Abner had been with the Reynolds family for many years and that Gabriel trusted him implicitly. She didn't want to be the one to break the bad news, but she couldn't ignore it either, not if, as Gabriel now confirmed, he had nothing to do with the trade. She had contemplated speaking with Abner before Gabriel returned home, but had rejected the idea as she didn't want to appear to go behind Gabriel's back.

'Last night I heard a noise outside, hooves in the stableyard.'

'From the bedroom? You have good ears.'

'From the kitchen. It was about midnight and then I saw the horse was Ned. He was being led by Abner.'

Gabriel said: 'And you think he'd been on a run? He would be on his way back from The Hope and Anchor I imagine; he sometimes takes Ned in the winter as his leg troubles him in the cold weather - rheumatism.'

'With two tea chests on Ned's back?'

'There must be some mistake. Are you certain it was Abner?' Gabriel sat back thinking. 'I remember Father once told me that when he went out one morning Ned was lame and looked like he'd been ridden in the night. He found a half anker of brandy at the back of the stable. Someone had commandeered Ned to carry contraband without asking and whoever it was had left payment in kind. My father was furious.'

'It was Abner. There was no mistaking his limping gait.'

Gabriel looked positively livid. 'Damn him. How dare he? After my run in with the law last year this is unforgivable.'

He was half way to the door when Eleanor called after him: 'Where are you going? Think first my love. Don't act in haste and say something you may come to regret.'

'I'm going to see if there's stuff hidden.'

'There is. It's behind the stable covered in a tarpaulin. I checked this morning to convince myself I hadn't dreamt it.'

Gabriel came back and pulled the bell by the fire place. 'I won't say how I know of this to Abner, but I must speak with him now. I will not have this going on under my roof.'

Eleanor saw anger on Gabriel's face the like of which she'd never witnessed before.

Abner limped in.

'Were you about last night, at the ale house? What time were you abed?'

'Aye, I was at The Hope and Anchor. As well as A can recall A was abed before eleven A should think.'

'So not out in the stableyard unloading tea chests from Ned's back?'

'Ah well, now that A think on...'

'Don't lie to me. What's wrong with you man, after my ordeal with the law last year you bring contraband tea onto my land. Are you short of money? Have you not had a pay rise every year for the last twenty odd years? Do I keep you short of anything?'

Abner hung his head but didn't reply. He had a surly look about him. Eleanor knew this defiance, this lack of respect, would upset Gabriel.

'How long has this been going on? Years I expect. Does Lisbet know of your law breaking?'

'A suppose she do. You knows how it is round here, everybody's a finger in the pie. You've turned a blind eye to stuff yerself.'

'I have yes, but not to things happening on *my* land. I've known when a drop was intended around the bay and closed my curtains and ears to the mule trains going by. That's different because they're poor people who need the money to put food into their children's bellies. If the King is stupid enough to keep taxes high then what does he expect the poor to do? They won't stand by and starve. But you... you have no need. Your belly and pockets are always full. Man alive, no wonder you're never seen without your spy glass.'

Eleanor felt like an obtrusive bystander. Gabriel walked to the window and back, a look of scornful agitation on his handsome features.

'Shall I tell you the worst of this situation?' He didn't wait for a reply. 'It's that all these years you've been a trusted servant, a member of our family almost and this is how you repay me. I can hardly believe it.'

He rang the bell pull again and strode on long legs to the door, his limp gone. He held it open as Lisbet appeared.

'A cannot spare long the meat needs a bastin'.' She saw the look on her master's face and stopped talking abruptly. She stood by Abner and cast a worried, sidelong look at her common-law husband.

'As of now you are both no longer in my employ. Go and pack your bags and get out. Now, this very night.'

Lisbet, alarmed, looked to Abner, her eyes wide and her chins trembling. It was clear she thought Gabriel had run mad. She looked to Eleanor who sat grim faced but silent.

'What's goin' on? A don't understand Mr Gabriel.' she said twisting her apron in her fat fingers.

'Abner will explain as you pack. I'll make your wages up to the end of the month, though God knows you don't deserve it. I should throw you out now as you stand.' He rubbed the stubble on his chin. 'I'll just say this Lisbet; I'm especially disappointed in you. You knew what Abner was up to and yet you did nothing to stop him or to alert me. I thought you honourable and trustworthy. You have both betrayed me. It's beyond belief. I'm only glad my father isn't here to witness this state of affairs. You should be ashamed of yourselves.' Lisbet's chins began to wobble all the more as the penny dropped. 'Get out of my sight both of you before I report you to the constable myself.' For once Lisbet had the good sense to stay quiet. As they reached the door Gabriel stopped them. 'I've just had another thought. Does Jax know of this? Does he play any part in your lawlessness?'

'No,' Lisbet sobbed, 'don't take it out on the lad, it were just him, the great lummox.' She hooked her thumb towards a sullen looking Abner. 'A telled him it weren't worth the risks, but he wouldna listen to me the dunce.'

'Then more fool you for letting him drag you into this.'

The door closed and they were heard to go upstairs to begin to pack.

'My love are you sure about this? Could you not get him to take the tea away and give them both another chance? They've been here so long and are quite old to find posts elsewhere. It's as you say, they have known and cared for you man and boy.'

'Then they should have thought of that before.' Gabriel slumped in the chair. His face was ashen. 'This is unbelievable. I've never doubted their loyalty. They've had free reign here always. Lisbet has ruled the roost until you came, now I feel betrayed, let down. She should have come to me. Since my mother died when I was seven years old she raised me, looked after me, loved me, or so I thought.'

Eleanor stared into the fire. 'I think you're being over hasty my love, don't act in temper. Lisbet possibly just went along with Abner's runs knowing as you say how most on the coast have dealings with smuggling.'

'I can't condone his actions. If the preventative men were to find contraband goods on my land who do you think they would charge? Not Abner but me! Possession is nine tenths of the law.'

Eleanor's mind was racing ahead. She was only glad she had hired an under cook to learn from Lisbet. Now Lisbet was sacked, without Connie they would starve. A thought suddenly occurred to her; what of Christmas and the ball? She knew Gabriel was too angry and upset to worry about such practicalities now, but the facts would have to be faced and soon; as would the disposal of the contraband tea.

'What shall you do with the tea?'

'I don't know. I don't want it on my land yet I don't want to get caught moving it either. I should make them carry it out of here on their backs.'

Eleanor rose and placed her hand on Gabriel's shoulder. 'I'll go and inform the rest of the staff as they'll need to know. Their work load will be greater now of course.'

The remaining servants stood in the kitchen as Eleanor addressed them: 'Mrs Cotter and Mr Boatwright have been dismissed. I know this will come as a shock to you all but there it is.' Jax, who had known them longest, looked visibly distressed. 'I won't go into why they have been let go, but needless to say there will now be more work for you all. You will of course be recompensed for this. Tomorrow I shall set about trying to find replacement staff so you won't be over-burdened for too long hopefully.' She took a breath. 'Connie if you could finish supper and serve it at the usual time Mr Reynolds and I would appreciate it.' Connie nodded her head but kept silent. 'Joe, you shall perform Abner's duties until further notice please.'

Joe was a recent addition to the household. Gabriel had recently come to realise Abner, at his advancing age, should not be performing heavy work and so the younger man had been engaged. So far he had proved himself willing and able. He was a strong, wiry young man with a quiet demeanour and a good attitude.

Eleanor turned to go.

'Mistress Reynolds have they gone already or can A say goodbye?' Jax shuffled forward.

'Come with me, *you're* not in trouble Jax.' He followed her through to Gabriel's study where her husband was making up the final wages for his errant staff.

'Jax this is a sorry business. What do you know about Abner's activities? You used to sleep in the hayloft so you must have heard him moving about at night. You surely heard him taking Ned out?'

'Aye, A did. A knew that he hid stuff from the preventative men, but A thought you telled him to do it so A never thought nowt about it.'

'I knew nothing of this. It's against the law and you know that. I'm disgusted and disappointed with Abner's behaviour for he's not poor and starving, but that doesn't concern you now. If anyone approaches you asking you to take part in a smuggling run in any capacity you need to tell me straight away and I'll deal with it. Do you understand?'

'Aye but,' he hung his head in misery, 'A can't think what to do wi'owt Lisbet. She's bin like a mam to me. Can A at least see her afore she goes? Where're they goin' to go?'

Eleanor watched as her husband drew a deep breath.

'Here, take their pay to them and say your farewells.' He passed two purses to the lad. 'I feel for you Jax, I know you're an orphan and without family and you've flourished under Lisbet's love and guidance. I know this is hard for you, but after the trial last year, especially *because* of the trial, I cannot have law breaking in this house. Abner not only put *me* at risk he put you in danger too. Colonel Bird could have thought you involved in the smuggling also. Even if you denied dealings with the trade you could have been implicated, you couldn't have proved otherwise. You're becoming a man and you may be tempted by talk of high rewards with little risk, but don't chance it Jax. You have much to lose. If ever I found you meddling in the trade you've seen what would happen to you. I'll not hesitate to turn you off my land, much as it would grieve me to do so, as it does now with Lisbet and Abner. I don't act lightly in this matter believe me.'

Jax shuffled on the spot. 'Just so yer know the tea chests have gone. Captain Trencher's men came earlier.'

Gabriel grimaced. 'Well at least they're off my land - that's something I suppose.'

Jax went to say his goodbyes.

'Gabriel... '

'Leave it Eleanor I won't be swayed.'

'But... '

He marched from the room leaving her alone.

Later as Charity was helping Eleanor dress for supper she thought about the problem of having family and friends for Christmas and hosting a ball for near on a hundred guests without a cook.

Charity interrupted her thoughts. 'The staff are that troubled by Lisbet and Abner's sacking, Jax in particular is upset bless him. Lisbet's been close to the lad. She can be cantankerous, but she's a heart as big as the ocean.'

'And as unpredictable as one too. There's nothing to be done about it I'm afraid. Perhaps in a day or two Gabriel will change his mind, but I doubt it. When my husband digs his heels in he won't be moved. He feels they've let him down, which of course they have. What though are we to do over Christmas without Lisbet's culinary skills?'

'Connie had a fit of the collywobbles when she realised she might be put in charge of the ball. She's not got enough experience surely?'

'Oh Lord poor Connie, I must pacify her. If she walks out on us we'll be in an even worse predicament. Send her to me now and I'll speak with her, try to reassure her, but what I'm to say to put her mind at rest I've no idea. If the worst comes to the worst we'll have to scale down the festivities.'

As she waited for Connie, Eleanor suddenly had an idea.

Supper did not pass pleasantly. Gabriel was much affected by what he rightly saw as Abner's disloyalty. Eleanor could usually talk her husband around, but she sensed it wasn't even worth trying. She knew from past experience not to push too hard.

At length Eleanor thought to raise the subject of engaging more staff to replace the pair. She knew Gabriel was distressed at what had happened but nonetheless they needed replacements as soon as possible. Finding *any* servants at this time of year with Christmas just around the corner would be hard. It had seemed to her an impossible task that staff of any calibre could be recruited, but then Eleanor had thought of a possible solution she hoped would save them. After edging around the subject she took the bull by the horns.

'With the ball and family coming to stay we can't manage without an experienced cook, you do see that don't you my love?'

'I will not change my mind Eleanor.'

'Understandably... ' Eleanor knew Gabriel had a stubborn streak and wouldn't be reasoned with until he'd calmed down. 'At any other time it wouldn't be such a dilemma; Connie could look after the two of us without a hitch. I've had an idea, a temporary solution to the problem at least.' Gabriel raised an eyebrow questioningly. 'What if I were to write to Caroline's aunt and ask her if Caroline would loan us the use of her cook while she's away? After all they're presumably idle while she's from home. If we could also borrow a footman then I daresay we could manage with the extra staff Lisbet has already booked for the festivities.'

Gabriel pushed his plate away irritably. 'Mrs Madison is an excellent cook and she's been with Thomas almost as long as... Lisbet has been with us. It would be an excellent solution although I'd feel bad bothering Caroline when she's ill. As you say it would be kinder to approach her aunt and see how she feels about broaching the matter with Caro.'

The letter was written and despatched immediately after supper. Within a few days a reply was received from Caroline offering as many of her staff as was necessary, greatly putting Eleanor's mind at rest.

When the new staff arrived at Westshore the atmosphere suddenly felt different; the footman, Ribble, was quietly efficient and Mrs Madison soon took charge in the kitchen. It was also agreed Thomas Hodgeson's old manservant, who had been performing other duties since his master's death, should be employed on a trial basis to do for Gabriel.

On the day of the manservant's arrival Gabriel sauntered into Eleanor's dressing room. 'I'm not sure how I feel about having a young man dress me. Abner always just laid out my clothes. It may feel intrusive, awkward somehow. If it does I can send him back I suppose, though it would seem ungrateful.' He shrugged.

Eleanor knew Gabriel wasn't a vain man, but she also thought he could perhaps do with a little tidying up from time to time. Her husband was the kind of man who oozed effortless elegance no matter what he wore, but with a little extra trouble he could look dashing.

'He's a lot younger than I expected and quite handsome,' she said as she looked at Gabriel to gauge his response. 'I'd have thought Thomas had an old crusty looking after him.'

'Old crusty indeed!' Gabriel grinned. 'Handsome is he? I'd not noticed. Hobbs did for Thomas until he thought to retire him despite the man's protests; he must have been ancient when Tomas pensioned him off. I would think they'd been together as long as Abner and my father.'

'Well I for one will look forward to seeing you turned out as neat as a pin and with a freshly shaved face every day. Walters will have you licked into shape soon enough I expect; you'll wonder how you ever managed without him.'

Gabriel moved swiftly, grabbed her hands then rubbed his unshaven chin over them making her recoil.

'Ouch.'

'Are you complaining? I was thinking I might grow a beard.'

'I think not! If you do you'll be banished to your own room.'

'We both know that's not true.' He pulled her to her feet. 'Are you seriously saying you can resist me?'

Eleanor pursed her lips to stop herself from laughing at her husband's audacity. 'With you all smartened up and with a smooth face I'll be powerless to refuse you! Now let go I have a ball to organise.'

3

On the twenty third of December the Barker family were due to arrive from Whitby. Eleanor and Gabriel were preparing to go downstairs to break their fast when Eleanor put her hand on her husband's arm.

'Wait a moment I want to talk to you.'

He smiled indulgently. 'You've been talking to me since the minute you opened your eyes this morning, I can see how excited you are.' Gabriel too, was happy to be hosting Christmas and was looking forward to sharing his home with her family. It had been a long time since there had been a proper family Christmas at Westshore.

'It's so long since I've seen my family, but it's regarding them I would speak with you now, before they arrive that is.' She took a deep breath. 'Gabriel I'm with child again.' For a second there was a stunned silence. 'I want to tell my family and can't do so of course until I've told you. I think I'm three months gone.'

The last time his wife had told him she was pregnant it had led to a misunderstanding and weeks of anguish. Now Gabriel looked excitedly at his wife.

'This is wonderful news but last time you were sick in the mornings. I haven't noticed you've been off your food.'

'Nor have I been so far; I've not even felt nauseous. After Christmas I'll see a doctor to have it confirmed, but I'm certain I'm expecting. I even have a small bump I think.' She laid her hand on her stomach.

'A summer baby! Possibly June? This is the perfect Christmas gift.' He drew her towards him and kissed her softly then continued to hold her close as she laid her cheek against his chest.

'You must take especial care this time. I know you don't care to be idle but after last time... '

'I know. No riding astride from here on, I'll take care. You don't have to worry; this baby is much wanted although it can never replace the one we lost of course.'

He knew Eleanor was determined to carry this child within her to term. He already had a son, but Steven was on the other side of the world. Gabriel and Eleanor had found out after their marriage that his mistress had given birth. Even though he had ended the relationship before his marriage, it had caused anguish and heartache all round, doubly so when Eleanor miscarried the baby she was expecting soon after. Gabriel had met his son just once before Libby had emigrated with him for a better life in America.

'I desperately want to give you a child, but I also long for one for myself. This time all will be well I'm sure.' Each was lost in their own thoughts.

'It will,' Gabriel said, 'and this child will be the first of many.'

By late afternoon the family had arrived and Eleanor was especially pleased to see her twin brother; she had never been apart from him for so long. Gabriel watched cheerfully as they laughed, teased and chatted with each other. He knew she missed him. They exchanged letters but Tomas was a poor correspondent and so they had much to talk about.

Eleanor had suggested to Gabriel they should share their news before the rest of their guests arrived on the following day. They agreed to tell the family after supper. The meal over, Gabriel stood at the head of the table and raised his glass.

'I should like to propose a toast.' His in-laws raised their glasses, smiling and happy. 'To my beautiful Eleanor who one year ago made me a very happy man by becoming my wife. This first year of our married life hasn't been the easiest, but we have battled through and are all the stronger for the travails we've experienced. We have both learnt to appreciate we have a lot to be thankful for.' He looked at Eleanor who had a tear in her eye. 'In June, Eleanor will give birth to our child or, with this family's pedigree, could that be *children*? If it is twins they will be more than welcome.' He looked at her adoringly.

Happy chatter broke out before John Barker seconded the toast adding: 'To Eleanor and Gabriel. I think I can say on behalf of your mother and brother that we are so very pleased and happy for you and for us too. More grandchildren are most welcome whether they come in ones or twos.'

They recharged their glasses. Eleanor's mother, Anne, squeezed her daughter's hand, then the two of them retired to the drawing room, no doubt to discuss the happy event.

ℛ

The rest of Christmas went off well. Mrs Madison was an excellent cook, although Gabriel said no one could cook a goose like Lisbet, but he had to concede her puddings were irresistible.

It was late evening when all were replete with food and drink that Eleanor found herself in the library alone with her twin brother. They looked alike although Tomas was fairer, not a redhead like his sister. He was learning the shipping trade from his father who owned one of the largest boat building businesses in Whitby.

They had been chatting amiably for a while when Eleanor asked: 'Are you still fancy free or has some maid or other captured your heart? Isn't it about time you started to think of marrying and producing an heir?'

Tomas looked a little thoughtful. 'I've been hoping to get a quiet word with you on just that matter.'

43

'Have you someone in mind, are you caught at last?' She indulged him now where she had so often argued with him for the louche way he treated women. He had been an irrepressible rake in the past.

'There is someone, someone who caught my eye at the very same time of year these twelve months gone. You know her so I hesitate to speak. She's courteous to me, friendly, but I think perhaps she looks on me as one might look upon a brother; I don't want to make a fool of myself or embarrass her if I speak my mind.'

Eleanor laughed loudly. 'I can't even think who it is you talk of, but it's clear this is not your usual flirtation. My goodness you're lovelorn I do believe. Who is it? Tell me before I burst with curiosity.'

Tomas scowled not wanting to be the butt of her joke. 'I'll give you a clue when I say I haven't set eyes on her for a year until recently and am just as captivated now as I was then. She's witty, pretty and above all intelligent.'

Eleanor was astounded. 'Who is this paragon? You say I know her?'

'Indeed, she's under your very roof as we speak.' He flushed a little.

'Cora or Jane? It must be Cora as she has the readiest wit, she always has some clever remark or ironic observation. Is it true? Am I correct?'

'It is and you are. But I, who can usually read women like a good book, am unable to see whether she likes me or is merely being polite as I'm your brother.'

Eleanor could see he was serious, he'd never appeared love struck before. She stopped teasing him.

'These last few days since she arrived I've talked with her for quite some time and find I like her more and more. We rode out together today and it was most enjoyable. I know she's a little older than me, but she's so clever, entertaining and to me, beautiful.'

'I don't know what to say. I can see your predicament, but nothing ventured nothing gained as they say. If you speak with her and she rejects you at least you don't run in the same circles all the time so you won't see her all that often, although family gatherings might be trying. But why should she turn you down? You're moderately good looking,' here she nudged him playfully, 'rich and equally have a ready wit and boyish charm. I'm sure she would take you without a moment's hesitation.'

The next day, fortified with port and brandy, Tomas managed to get the lady alone. He posed the question and was indeed accepted without indecision. As her mother, Lady Beadnell, was expected for the ball it was proposed they should wait to announce their engagement until Tomas had asked for permission to marry her. He could not however, resist telling Eleanor and swore her to secrecy.

R

Gabriel climbed into bed beside his wife. 'You look like the proverbial cat. You look decidedly pleased with yourself my love.'

'I feel like her too.' She was resting back against her pillows and rubbing lanolin into her hands. Gabriel often wondered how she managed to handle her horse, a huge black gelding, with such delicate hands.

'I have news but it's a secret and you're not to betray the confidence.'

'As you're about to do?'

'Well, yes but I can't wait to tell you... Tomas is to be married.'

'Man alive I thought he'd never give up his carousing.'

'I'm sure he'll refrain from now on for he truly loves the lady.' She was waiting for him to question her further but he held off knowing she would succumb when she became frustrated with him.

On cue she burst out: 'You can be extremely vexing Gabriel! Are you not going to ask who he's to marry?'

'I wasn't going to as firstly, I know you're dying to tell me and secondly, I shan't know the lady as you're the only Whitby wench I know.'

She frowned trying to be cross with him but not quite succeeding. 'That *sir*, is where you're wrong for you know her exceedingly well, better in fact than I and better than Tomas come to think of it.'

Gabriel feigned intrigue. He took pleasure in thwarting Eleanor for the fun of it.

'Have a guess, I'll help you. She's here in this very house. He has been conducting a love affair under our noses and we've all been blind to it.'

'It must be Cora then I assume.' Gabriel put his arms behind his head and lay back triumphantly.

'How did you guess? I didn't and I'm much more perceptive than you, especially where my twin is concerned.'

'I think I'm insulted by that remark, but never mind.' He enjoyed the banter and the easy way they were with each other. He looked over at her as she began to snuggle under the covers.

'I know,' he said turning to face her and leaning on his elbow, 'because he told me after supper.'

'But he swore me to secrecy until he has asked her mama.'

'He told me because I know the lady well and he thought I'd be pleased, which I am. I've long thought Cora a good woman. He also said, and here we had a small wager, that you would spill the beans as you can't keep a secret, so he may as well tell me himself.'

Gabriel tried not to look too smug.

'A wager. What was the bet?'

'He wagered you'd tell me in the morning after struggling all night with your conscience while I bet you wouldn't be able to sleep until you'd told me what you know.'

He could see Eleanor was a little annoyed, but too happy to be properly cross. 'Well aren't you Mr-

Know-It-All. How much have you won?' She rolled on her side to face him and smiled.

'Ten guineas. Thank you my love, if only all money was so easily come by.'

He kissed her before he began to persuade her to be seduced; she didn't need much convincing.

ℛ

The day of the ball began with a howling gale and Eleanor had convinced herself half their guests would be put off from coming. She set about getting the last minute instructions to Mrs Madison and made sure the extra staff hired in from the local area had arrived, before she went to her dressing room to prepare.

She rang the bell for her maid, but Charity didn't appear. In her stead the scullery maid, a timid little thing called Ivy, arrived looking flustered.

'Sorry Mistress Reynolds but Charity's been taken bad, she looks summat awful and sed as she's not the strength to get up.'

Eleanor's maid had been with her for years; she was more a companion than a servant. Eleanor went to check on her and soon saw she was indeed indisposed with a feverish cold. It wasn't in the maid's nature to shirk her responsibilities, especially on a big occasion such as today. She was loyal and was distressed she wouldn't be able to dress Eleanor for the long awaited ball. It took all Eleanor's guile to make her maid stay in bed.

After arranging for her to be checked on regularly, Eleanor addressed the newly arrived staff to ascertain if any of them had experience as a lady's maid. One girl spoke up.

'I have Mrs Reynolds. I can dress a lady and make a reasonable job of dressing hair.'

She was a tall, willowy girl with conker-brown hair. She did indeed look more like a lady's maid than a general servant, being young, clean and well presented.

'Very well, could you please come and help me first? My maid is unwell. You can come back here when I'm dressed.'

Back in Eleanor's dressing room the girl said her name was Bryony Swift and explained she was recently moved to the town from Embleton.

'I was lady's maid and companion to a lady who died from consumption and so I'm looking for a position. I'm trying to pick up any work I can in the meantime,' she explained.

Bryony was quick and efficient dressing Eleanor's hair and when she had finished it was different to how Charity usually did it, but Eleanor had to admit it looked elegant nonetheless.

There was just something about the girl's manner which Eleanor couldn't like; she seemed a little arrogant somehow. Perhaps, Eleanor thought, the girl was nervous and this bravado went some way to covering her discomfiture. She gave her the benefit of the doubt.

By the time the first guests began to arrive the wind had blown itself out and a morose, mauve sky was teetering on the edge of rain. As family and friends assembled, Eleanor looked over to her husband who was just welcoming Wilson Chaffer. Gabriel looked so handsome, more groomed now that Walters, the new manservant, was dressing him. Gabriel's normally unruly curls had been tamed and his face, always prone to stubble, was shaved close. She smiled to herself and couldn't believe how happy she was and how much she loved and was loved in return; she noted there was no better feeling in the world. She moved to stand beside her husband.

'I know this is an awful imposition Wilson, you being a guest and all, but my maid Charity is taken ill. I think it only a chill but I shouldn't like it to turn more feverish. She's red hot to the touch. Might you look in on her and see how she does please? I should be in your debt.'

'Of course Eleanor, I'll pop along now if that's agreeable.'

Eleanor called for Ivy to show the doctor to Charity's room. He was not gone long and sought Eleanor out to reassure her. 'I've given her a draught to make her more comfortable and I'll check on her again later. As you say, possibly she's caught a chill and will be fine in a day or so.'

The ball had been a great success. Eleanor was dead on her feet when later she entered her dressing room. She had danced and talked and enjoyed herself so much. She had asked Bryony to help her undress and unpin her hair. She was eager to get to bed before she fell asleep sitting up.

The maid knocked lightly on the dressing room door and entered before Eleanor had time to utter the words "come in". Charity would usually wait, after all she was a married woman and at bedtime Gabriel may have been in the room in who knows what state of undress. She was too tired to mention it and in any case Bryony would not be here after tonight.

The servant made a slight curtsy but didn't smile. She moved over to where Eleanor sat at her dressing table.

'Can you please unpin my hair first; it's stayed in place all night, you obviously secured it well. My mother complimented me on the new style.'

Eleanor kicked off her slippers and wriggled her aching feet. The maid began to undo the hairstyle pin by pin. Eleanor removed her rings and rubbed lanolin into her hands. 'Did you get supper? Mrs Madison is an excellent cook is she not?'

'Yes ma'am.' She paused before adding: 'Thank you.' There was an uneasy quiet. Eleanor, usually bright and chatty, felt a strange restraint in the girl's presence. Perhaps they were both tired?

Gabriel poked his head around the door to see his

wife having her hair brushed. 'Man alive, I'm beat.' He flung himself on the sofa and lay flat looking up at the ceiling.

'Then go to bed, don't fall asleep there.' She shook her head and smiled at Bryony through the mirror, but the maid missed the look. She was staring quite blatantly at Gabriel.

'That's enough brushing thank you. Get me out of this corset before I burst.' Eleanor stood wearily.

'You shouldn't lace as tightly in your condition.' Gabriel propped himself up on his elbow.

Bryony watched him from behind Eleanor's back, while her fingers loosened the corset. She looked at Gabriel under her lashes thinking Eleanor couldn't see her, but the mirror gave the game away.

Eleanor stepped out of the beautiful turquoise gown and it slipped to the floor.

Gabriel addressed the girl: 'You can go home now thank you.' He got up and stood by his wife's side. 'I can manage the rest.' Eleanor smiled up at him. She knew what was on his mind.

The maid suddenly smiled sweetly at Gabriel and dropped a curtsy.

'Thank you Miss Swift,' Eleanor said. She slipped a silver coin in the girl's hand as a reward for the extra work she had done that evening. Bryony Swift merely mumbled under her breath as she left the room.

Gabriel knelt at his wife's feet, untied her garter and slid the stocking down her smooth leg and gently peeled it from her foot. She leaned on his shoulder to steady herself as he performed the same manoeuvre on the other leg. He stroked her naked thigh before flinging the stockings aside. Passing her night gown over her head he lightly brushed his hands down the side of her waist making her shiver.

'Well one of us could raise a smile from the girl,' Eleanor said. 'Before you came in she looked positively sullen. I expect she's tired too. She told me she was a lady's maid and her employer has died. She's from Embleton and is looking for work. Perhaps she's not used to fetching and carrying as she's had to do tonight, it must be a come down for her. In addition to her kitchen duties she's had to do for me too. I hope Charity gets a good night's sleep. Wilson has given her another draught and says he'll call again tomorrow. I just went in to see her but she's sleeping thank goodness.'

'I know my seduction is being batted away with chatter but it'll take more than that,' he said following her into the bedroom.

'I thought you were tired?'

'I'm never *that* tired,' he said. 'Did all go to plan? It seemed to from what I could see. You're such a good hostess - I'm proud of you.'

'Thank you my love.' She kissed his cheek which was already becoming rough with stubble. 'All seemed to go as we'd planned. I hope everyone enjoyed themselves.'

Gabriel sighed. 'I just wish Lisbet could have been here to see it all. The house looked magnificent. It really lends itself to entertaining. Lisbet put a lot of the hard work into the planning I know.'

'She did. You miss them, but you'll get used to life here without them soon I'm sure unless... you could still prove a point and make an example of Abner, but re-hire Lisbet. You've known them all your life but it's as you said, they let you down. You had no choice but to let Abner go, but Lisbet played no part in the business.'

Eleanor knew Gabriel had been wrestling with his conscience.

'I'm too tired to think about it now. I need a sober head to make important decisions.'

They climbed into bed and Eleanor blew out her candle and sighed with relief to have the weight off her feet.

'I'm exhausted.'

'Well you would dance almost every dance. What do you expect? Cora looked happy, I'm pleased for her. Bendor has offered them Dunstanburgh for the wedding party... Did you hear me?'

Eleanor was vaguely aware of her husband's voice as sleep began to overtake her. She felt Gabriel place an exploratory hand on her thigh which she studiously ignored.

'You looked so beautiful tonight. I do love you.'

He rolled nearer. She felt his arm encircle her. She

breathed in the familiar scent of him as she snuggled closer. A sense of safety washed over her and tipped her down into a warm slumber.

'Are you asleep?'

There was no reply.

4

Charity recovered from her chill quickly but was no sooner back in post when another problem befell her. She had news her father had taken ill suddenly and was not expected to survive. Eleanor insisted she return home to Whitby to be with her family. As Eleanor's parents were on the point of leaving, they offered to chaperone her back to Sandsend. Eleanor was only glad Charity didn't have to make the journey alone. She knew it would be a trial to her under the circumstances.

As Caroline had taken her own maid to her aunt's, another loan was impossible. Eleanor's only choice was to employ Bryony Swift on a temporary basis until Charity's return. Both were in need so Eleanor hoped the arrangement would work out.

Eleanor set about trying to train Bryony in the ways she would like things done. The young girl was a good maid although she was often dour and not at all talkative. Eleanor knew this was how "proper" maids behaved, but Charity had been different. She had been one of the village girls her mother had wanted to help. Consequently she had never been formally trained.

Eleanor, never a task master, had been sixteen when Charity began doing for her. Being so close in age, Charity had been fifteen, they were on friendly terms rather than mistress and servant. Eleanor had been used to gossiping and exchanging news with Charity and although she carried out all the tasks a lady's maid should undertake, Eleanor also used her as a confidante. Before she was married she shared all her girlish secrets with her. Charity had saved Eleanor's hide on more than one occasion when she'd been on one of her many nocturnal escapades back in Whitby.

Before her marriage Eleanor had thought nothing of helping with the mending and the tidying. Chatting also helped to pass the time, especially if she was having her hair dressed for a special occasion which seemed to take much time. She missed her maid, but since coming to Westshore, Eleanor's priorities had changed; she had more responsibilities now running her own household, yet she still had time for Charity. She was grateful she'd agreed to come to Northumberland with her. It had made the move easier having a familiar face about Westshore.

Eleanor had never stood on ceremony with staff and had tried to engage Miss Swift in conversation but all to no avail. The maid would reply but with the minimum effort and no obvious interest. Eleanor had also tried to remind Miss Swift to knock and wait before entering her bedroom or dressing room. Gabriel was often about and sometimes in a state of undress.

After all they were relatively newly married and enjoyed each other's company. Yet the maid seemed determined to knock and enter regardless of the times Eleanor had asked her not to. Only that morning, when she and her husband were alone, Eleanor had been forced to shout "Not now" as Miss Swift had entered their bedroom unannounced.

Gabriel had laughed, but Eleanor didn't see the funny side.

'Miss Swift, Bryony, can you please remember to wait after you have knocked? I realise in your last post your mistress lived alone and so you weren't going to disturb anyone else by walking straight in, but here it's different.' She tried not to sound exasperated but it wasn't the first time she'd raised the issue. For his part Gabriel couldn't have cared less, but Eleanor didn't relish being found *in flagrante delicto*.

'Yes, sorry Mrs Reynolds.' She didn't look sorry.

Besides this and more provoking, Eleanor also began to notice how Miss Swift's demeanour changed when Gabriel was in the room. At first Eleanor thought she was being over sensitive, by comparison she was now growing in size and felt unattractive when standing next to the tall, slender maid. But she watched Bryony carefully and each time Gabriel came into the room the maid's manner became light and cheerful. If she'd almost finished her task she would suddenly find a reason to remain and would surreptitiously look at Gabriel from under her lashes. Eleanor didn't trust her.

By late January, Charity had not returned from Whitby. Her father had rallied and failed several times until at last he'd succumbed and died. Eleanor had written sending her condolences and telling Charity to take as much time as she needed. She knew now the main bread winner in the family had gone there would be sorrow, but also anxiety. Eleanor enclosed money to ease their immediate needs.

The mistress of Westshore was still not enamoured of Miss Swift, but she had to admit she was efficient and good at her job even though she was surly, abrupt and unfriendly. Eleanor missed Charity who always had something to talk about, some observation to make, some remark to make her smile.

Miss Swift went about her work with an air of resignation, as if she had better places to be, unless of course Gabriel was in the room. Then she burst into life and bestowed smiles and comments like confetti at a wedding. The transformation was not lost on Eleanor.

R

As Gabriel rode back from the bay, it was a bright but freezing cold January day. The wind seemed to bite into his bones making him pull his great coat about him tightly. Heavy bellied clouds jostled one another out of the way. There would be rain before dark.

As he entered the stableyard, he noticed Joe and Jax

leaning on the wall by the kitchen door. Joe was trying to light a pipe and he had his hand cupped about the bowl. Bryony appeared behind them smiling. Jax hurried forward to take the reins.

'Copper needs to be shod I think, can you take her this afternoon?'

'Aye, A'll take her in a bit when A've fed her. He led Copper to the mounting block. 'Has she gone?'

'Who?'

'Miss Swanky Drawers.'

'By that I expect you mean Miss Swift?' Gabriel grinned. 'She's not to your liking I take it. I'm surprised Jax, she's a good looking girl.'

'She's too full of herself and any road she's got her eye on Joe. She's just asked him to tek her to The Hope and Anchor. He's petrified of her. She's a fearsome look sometimes when she doesn't get her own way. That pretty face of hers can turn milk sour.' Gabriel laughed. 'She said she'd show him how grateful she could be later if he took her for a night out.' Jax winked at his master.

'Did she now. I'm surprised Joe isn't interested; I would have thought her a distraction. She'll not be here long so if he tires of her she won't be hanging about like a bad smell.'

'She's bin after him for weeks but he's got his eye on somebody else. Somebody without her airs and graces. She's too forward fer his likin' or fer mine.'

'I see. You're not interested in his cast offs then?

Young men today are fussy are they not? I would've thought he could, well you know, enjoy himself while she's here.' Gabriel suddenly felt old. He dismounted.

'If the mistress heard you talkin' like this she'd have yer guts fer garters.'

'You're right of course, she most certainly would. Don't forget to take Copper to the farrier.'

Gabriel strode across the yard where Miss Swift immediately turned her bright smile upon him. He was getting used to her overly familiar ways. He found it amusing. Gabriel carried his saddle bags towards the kitchen.

'Good afternoon Mr Reynolds, he's a fine looking horse.' She nodded towards where Copper was being led away.

'He is a "she" Miss Swift and yes, she is.' He swept past into the kitchen. She followed close behind him.

'Is my wife at home?' He carried on walking through the kitchen towards the dining room.

'She's gone to Warkworth and said she would be home before dark, she's taken the carriage. Mrs Reynolds also said she won't need me later.'

Gabriel had forgotten Eleanor wouldn't be at home. Now she had agreed, somewhat reluctantly, that riding was not a good idea he had bought a carriage and pair so she need not be confined; he knew how she loved to be out and about. The carriage would also be useful when the baby arrived as it would enable Eleanor to go out more freely with the baby and a nursemaid.

'I've just some mending to do until Mrs Reynolds returns. Can I be of assistance to you in any way sir?'

Gabriel noticed she was very good at making innocent statements sound provocative. She stood before him looking demure and innocent.

'You can bring me the brandy please,' he said over his shoulder. He stashed some papers in his desk drawer then picked up the newspaper and sat by the fire to read. Gabriel looked up at the maid. He noticed she had the most glorious chestnut hair. He noticed women's hair; it was what had first drawn him to his wife. He guessed Bryony knew she was comely and lingered as if tempting him to make an advance.

'Tell Mrs Madison I'll eat as soon as she's ready to feed me.' He drank some of the brandy and turned his attention to an article about rising taxes on the front page of the newspaper. Bryony nodded and raised her eyebrows a fraction as if surprised she'd not been appreciated more. Gabriel smiled to himself and carried on reading.

After he'd eaten his solitary meal he was reluctant to leave the house again. It was raining heavily and he'd enough to occupy him at home. He returned to sit by the fire. He thought for a moment how he'd missed Eleanor at dinner; he'd become used to sharing his meals with her. Today felt like the old days before he was married when most of his meals were taken alone. He told himself to cheer up - she would be back later and then they would chat about their day.

He rang the bell. Ivy hovered inside the door looking like a frightened rabbit. 'Can you please ask Mrs Madison for more coffee?' Ivy nodded and scurried away. Moments later Bryony sashayed across the room, hips swaying. The effect was not lost on him as he looked up from reading about a local shipwreck. He was at ease and his legs were comfortably crossed in front of the fire as she placed the coffee pot on a nearby table.

'Look at the fire! Dear me it will soon go out.'

Before he could say he would deal with it himself, she had dropped to her knees and set about carefully placing coals on the fire with the tongs. He watched as she leaned forward. She was angled in such a way he had full view of her figure, as was the intention. She painstakingly placed the coals one by one. Her cheeks flushed with the heat of the fire and her dark eyes shone. She finished the task, but remained sitting on the rug at his feet. She looked up at him a playful smile about her pink, full lips.

'That's better. Is there any other service I can render you? As I said, I'm not too busy to spare you some time.' She looked at him brazenly. Their eyes met and she offered him a beguiling smile. She seemed confident and self-assured as if she were used to men admiring her.

'Some men who have wives in the family way can be grateful for the attentions of a young, undemanding maid I'll bet.' She smiled. 'I would imagine a virile man such as you would be grateful to have entertainment laid on in his own home. I can assure you of my discretion.'

The door opened and Eleanor burst into the room, a bright smile upon her face.

'Lord it's freezing! I thought you wouldn't be home until supper - '

She stopped abruptly, both in speech and movement, as she took in the scene before her. The maid didn't leap to her feet, but stayed exactly where she was. Then Gabriel watched as she raised herself elegantly, dropped a silent curtsy to him then swept past Eleanor with blatant disregard.

Before she got to the door, Eleanor turned towards the maid and with a voice that was measured and sweet said: 'Miss Swift I have good news. My maid is returning tomorrow so I'll have no need of your services after that. I know you're eager to take up a more permanent post and so I will prepare your wages. I expect you will be happy to be on your way. In the meantime I've asked Joe to start filling my bathtub and I'm sure he would appreciate a helping hand.'

Bryony nodded and with a look that could kill, left the room.

Gabriel let out a roar of laughter.

'I didn't know Charity was returning? That's fortuitous.'

'Fortuitous my foot.' Eleanor advanced like a ship in full sail. She tore the newspaper from his hand and glared at him. 'I cannot have that woman in the house a minute longer. She's transparent. Did you see how she didn't get up until I had noted the scene sufficiently? And you... are you blind? Do you not see what she's about?'

Gabriel laughed again. 'Sit down, calm yourself. Do you think me mentally deficient? Of course I know what she's up to. You of all people should know I enjoy the chase, for I chased you hard enough, all the way to Holland as I remember.' He looked at her sullen face and almost laughed again, but decided not to provoke her further. 'I don't like things handed to me on a plate. I should never have been interested, especially as she's an employee.' He knelt at his wife's feet. 'Rest assured I wasn't about to ravish her. I have eyes and energy for one lady only.' He winked. 'Go and bathe and I'll come and show you who I really desire.'

Eleanor searched his handsome face. She was putty in his hands - he hoped.

When Gabriel came into the bedroom, the bathtub was steaming but Eleanor was still dressed. 'Do you need help? Have you rung for Miss Swift or are you worried you will be tempted to drown her in the bathtub?' He grinned.

Eleanor sat on the chaise at the bottom of their bed. 'I've gone off the idea now, I'm too... agitated. Why not take a bath yourself? It's a shame to waste the hot water.'

Gabriel looked at the steam rising and decided he would. 'You can talk to me while I soak.'

Eleanor poured sandalwood oil into the tub as Gabriel lowered himself in.

'I can't remember the last time I bathed indoors in hot water. It's either the sea or the pump I favour as you know.' He sank back, closed his eyes and sighed. 'I could get used to this. I think I'm getting soft in my old age.'

As Eleanor struggled to kneel by the tub, her belly threatened to overbalance her. He knew she was convinced she was having twins, she was so big. She picked up the jug and began to pour water over his hair before rubbing soap into his scalp.

'I should do this more often.' He smiled up at her. There was a peremptory knock and Bryony Swift sailed in. She stood stock still at the sight before her.

'Thank you Miss Swift but I decided against bathing. I can manage for the rest of the afternoon. Please don't disturb us until I ring for you.' Gabriel could hear the suppressed laughter in his wife's voice. The maid dropped a curt nod and fled the room.

'The sight of you naked has probably inflamed her passions all the more. It's as well she's leaving in the morning.'

'You'll be glad to have Charity back I know. How's she getting here?'

Eleanor had the good grace to flush slightly. 'It's not been arranged yet. The note I received this morning said she was hoping to return next week sometime.'

'But you said... '

'I know, but that woman made me... I wanted rid of her.'

'So you will have to manage with Ivy! Is that not cutting off your nose to spite your face?' Gabriel sat up and took the soap from her hand.

'You're more than enough for any man, I want no other. I know you feel unattractive because of your growing size, but nothing could be further from the truth.' He traced the line of her breast with a wet finger. 'There are advantages to you getting bigger.' He smiled hoping to reassure her. 'There's more of you to love is there not?'

After supper Gabriel rang the bell in his study. Ivy came and he asked her to send Miss Swift to him. He hadn't told his wife what he was about to do; he suspected she wouldn't approve.

ℜ

Bryony had just finished packing her meagre belongings in her battered tapestry bag when she was called to the study. She knew this was Mr Reynolds' domain and wondered what he could possibly want. She smiled to herself as she checked her appearance in the mirror. She knew *exactly* what he wanted. She had seen how he looked at her earlier. A man like him had needs. She would rejoice in fulfilling those needs, in fact nothing would give her more pleasure. She knew that if they hadn't been interrupted earlier he would have been persuaded to seduce her, but then Mrs High and Mighty had swanned in and spoilt their fun.

Perhaps now, before she left his house, he was going to ask her to be his mistress, and set her up in a nice little place close by. Make her an offer, an offer she wouldn't refuse. He was so good looking, rich and in need of that something only a mistress could provide. She pinched her cheeks to put some colour in them. She would be content to be his mistress... for now at least.

She tripped down the stairs full of hope and expectation, things were looking up. With his support, her life would at last take a turn for the better. She knocked and waited until she heard him bid her enter. She composed her face.

'Good evening Mr Reynolds.'

He looked grave, not at all the look of a man about to engage a mistress.

'Mrs Reynolds asked me to make up your wages for the morning, but I thought to speak with you before you leave.'

She ventured further into the room, her face expectant, then smiled her most becoming smile. Bryony Swift had never had trouble attracting men, quite the reverse in fact. She knew her coppery-coloured hair and slim, willowy figure made men look twice and she liked it that way. Up until coming to

Alnmouth she'd had no shortage of offers from men. Some were from older gentlemen wanting to make her their mistress. She hadn't fallen for that. She knew old men could be grateful, but hadn't been keen enough on any one of them to take up their offers. Some admirers were love-struck boys who wanted to walk out with her. These were too young, too inexperienced or too poor... or all three. Then there had been a baronet who had visited her late mistress. He'd had the best potential. He was rich enough for certain and best of all, he was unmarried. There was only one problem; he was the most unattractive man she'd ever set eyes upon. He made her flesh crawl. She wasn't desperate. She could do better for herself in time, after all she was still only eighteen.

Alnmouth, she soon realised, was full of men, mostly seafarers and men involved in subsidiary trades; chandlers, rope makers and other merchants always to be found in a coastal town. She had to fight off the whalers; they were well off enough but hard drinkers and coarse. She had higher expectations than them.

She'd set her sights on a naval officer, but he'd been scarce once he'd tasted the goods. Then she'd met a man who had turned her head; he fitted the part much better than the others. She suspected he had something to do with the smuggling trade. The captain was dashingly handsome, fun loving and keen. He'd even left her with money to spend after his last run, but as he'd been gone for months she'd run out of funds and had been forced to take casual work.

Still, now she had found her eye roving to the master of Westshore and he was a fine looking man and much, much richer. With his wife expecting, Bryony was sure she could convince him to keep her close. She had been somewhat shocked to be dismissed so suddenly. She'd been hoping to have a little more time to ingratiate herself into Gabriel Reynolds' thoughts, and ultimately his bed. Now was her last chance. She stepped closer to her prey and looked up at him demurely, but provocatively. She tucked a stray lock of coppery hair behind her ear.

'My wife tells me you're a good lady's maid. She says you are quick and efficient. You are particularly good at dressing hair, even I've noticed the new styles.'

Bryony looked pleased and relaxed visibly. This was obviously some polite preamble before getting to the crux of the matter. Gentry were strange sometimes.

'However, there is one aspect of your work that leaves a lot to be desired.'

The words were like a slap in the face. She immediately bristled. This wasn't what she had been expecting.

'Both myself and Mrs Reynolds have noticed you seem to have one face for her and quite a different one for me. I find this disrespectful and disloyal. My wife has shown you nothing but kindness.' She felt her cheeks flame. 'Above all else, we expect loyalty from our staff.' He continued to speak seemingly unaware her head was spinning. 'My wife and I have treated you well, paid you above the usual rate and you have repaid my wife, in particular, with a sullenness bordering on the insolent. We are not the types of employers who expect our staff to tremble when we enter a room, but we do expect some sort of civility. Because of this impertinence I'm not minded to give you a reference. You, I presume, have a glowing report from your previous employer, who I understand was an elderly lady, so it will not be such a hardship. You will be attending my wife in the morning and I hope your attitude will be respectful and solicitous as is her right to expect. I suspect the reason for your behaviour, but I can assure you no lady will want a maid who behaves as you have done over the last months. I only regret I didn't speak sooner. Mrs Madison will furnish you with your wages at ten in the morning. Good evening Miss Swift.'

Stunned, Bryony was about to speak, but then thought better of it and bit back the words which might get her ejected on the spot.

How bloody dare he! She was livid, seething. She summoned all her reserves and dropped a brief curtsy, turned on her heel and with head held high left the room.

You'll regret dismissing me in such a manner. Who do you think you are? The nerve of the man. Bryony guessed *she'd* put him up to this. I'm not sure how yet, but just you wait Mr Gabriel Reynolds. I'll have my revenge.

Bryony Swift slammed the bedroom door then threw herself on the bed and stared dry-eyed at the ceiling.

5

Caroline, having returned from her visit to her aunt's, knew she had a letter to write. She wasn't looking forward to it but could put it off no longer.

Thinner, but no less beautiful, she sat at her desk and rang for Ribble, now back at Eastshore, to deliver her missive. It was the most difficult letter she had ever had to write.

Once the letter had gone she felt restless, but knew she couldn't go out; she expected a visitor. She knew once the recipient of the letter had the time he would come to see her. She knew he would *make* time, even if he was busy. He may come today, or he may come tomorrow, but either way she knew Gabriel would come as soon as he could once he'd received her apology. Even without her apology, she knew he would come to see her once he knew she'd returned to Alnmouth.

She didn't have to wait long. After an hour or so, Ribble showed Gabriel into the conservatory. Caroline had been trying to occupy herself with a little pruning.

Gabriel smiled warmly, took her hand and kissed it lightly.

'Let me look at you.' He took both her hands and stood back to gaze at her. 'Thinner I think, but it suits you. Other than that you look well. Why do you look so anxious? Don't trouble yourself on my account Caro, it's all water under the bridge. It's forgotten. Are we not old friends?'

'I have no concealed weapon about me I can assure you,' she said trying to conquer her feelings of guilt and embarrassment. 'You must think me a mad woman. Perhaps I was... am?'

'Don't berate yourself. You were suffering from grief, I expect you still are. One doesn't get over losing a father overnight. I speak from experience.'

'You're good to come to see me, I don't deserve your visit.'

'Not at all, we've missed you. You returned yesterday?'

'The day before. Thank you for sending my staff back.'

'Thank you for the loan, they've been a godsend I can tell you. Christmas couldn't have happened without them Eleanor says to tell you.'

They moved to the morning room to take tea. Caroline was pleased to have something to do with her hands. She still felt the awkwardness. She began to cry as she passed Gabriel a dish of tea.

'Hey come on now, don't upset yourself. Have we not known each other all of our lives? You were ill, you weren't yourself.'

'I could have killed you, and the things I said, cruel, vindictive things. I didn't mean them. Eleanor must think me a bedlamite! I never thought I could hurt you. I have thought a lot about that day as you can imagine, the shame, the... '

'Well, is it not time to stop going over it? What good can it do? No long term damage was done, it was a matter of a couple of stitches and I don't even have a scar.' He smiled sympathetically. 'Eleanor knows you were not yourself. She doesn't know you as I do but she knows I wouldn't have been engaged to a lunatic.' He was trying to make light of the situation.

'I don't like to make excuses, but I saw a doctor in Scarborough who said my actions were the result of the strain on my nerves following Father's death. He said I've had a breakdown, a sort of reaction to the suddenness of it. It was such a shock.'

Tears slid down her cheeks. Gabriel moved to sit beside her and put his arm about her slender shoulders. 'It was a shock for me too. I don't blame you, I never could blame you.'

'I shall of course apologise to Eleanor, if she will let me that is? I hurt her also with my wickedness.'

'You don't have a wicked bone in your body. Of course she forgives you, forget it ever happened. Eleanor wants to get to know you better and be your friend. She asked me to tell you to call anytime.'

'Thank you, but I don't deserve such kindness.'

Gabriel returned to his seat and helped himself to

more tea. 'Come to dinner soon. You need the distraction possibly?'

Caroline wiped her eyes. 'I couldn't come until I've seen Eleanor privately, to apologise, then I might. I have to stop feeling sorry for myself and get on with my life. Self pity is ugly is it not?'

She smoothed her dress and looked at the handsome man opposite her. 'Before I went away I was thinking what I would do about Father's business affairs. I'm not a son and heir,' she half smiled, 'and I've never had more than a passing interest in any of his concerns. I'm not a businesswoman. You know I'm not cut out for it. I know you have kept a watchful eye and I thank you for it. Possibly the best thing to do is find a factor, a steward, to manage the shipping. I couldn't let that go, but everything else I thought to sell off. What do you think?'

'It was mostly Eleanor who kept your father's business concerns afloat. She's a shipbuilder's daughter and deals with her own affairs as you know. She's quite the businesswoman herself.'

Caroline noticed how proudly he said this.

'Eleanor knows how to balance the books, though I've overseen and authorised any decisions beyond the day-to-day of course. I've been at full stretch with the new stud farm so my wife has been a great help.'

'I will thank Eleanor when I see her. I had forgotten about the stud. Is it up and running?'

'More or less, but we can talk about that at a later

date. Caro don't make hasty decisions about your affairs. Yes, getting a manager is a good plan and I can help you with that. Saul Coates can advise you if you do decide to sell the other concerns, but it's still early days yet. Thomas was a good businessman and he's left his affairs in good order. There's much wealth accumulated in these other concerns, they shouldn't be dismissed lightly in my opinion. You're a wealthy woman, but we can talk of this another time when you feel up to it.'

'Oh I'm sorry, I'm keeping you from *your* business.'

'Not at all, you misunderstand me. I only mean it's probably a good idea to wait a while before you make up your mind. Don't rush into offloading all your assets. The shipping line is doing well and so is everything else, especially the rope makers, but you might want to wait to see what kind of factor you hire. He might be able to run all your affairs if you appoint the right man.'

'Thank you for the good advice Gabriel. I'm considering going abroad for a few months, see the sights. My second cousin Emma has said she will come with me as my companion. I'll take your advice and wait until I return before making any big decisions, see how I feel then.' Her eyes welled up with tears again. 'You know I always loved this house, but now it's so full of memories, full of Father and all his things. It's such a large house. Now I'm alone here it feels so empty, I can't seem to settle as yet.'

'I understand. Westshore felt the same when my father died. In time you'll be able to live here happily again. You'll remember his old habits fondly, his mountains of books and charts and how much he loved you.'

Tears once again spilled down her cheeks.

'I'm sorry Caro, I'm upsetting you.'

'You're right of course, but it's still so raw, so painful.'

Gabriel looked at her wistfully. 'When Father died every room I entered, every drawer I opened had something of him to remind me he'd gone. Clearing away his belongings was one of the hardest things I've ever had to do. Yet I, and indeed you, can't keep everything; you can't live here and keep it as a shrine. If and when you're up to it I can assist you if it would help. Deciding what to keep and what must go can be very difficult. Lisbet helped me. She would find something in a pocket or a drawer and ask me what I wanted to do with it. Once she brought a gold snuff box to me, it was in one of Father's waistcoat pockets. He never took snuff as you'll remember, but it belonged to his grandfather. He always kept it with him.' Gabriel put his hand in his waistcoat pocket. 'Now *I* carry it as a reminder of him and as you also know, I detest snuff. I'm a sentimental fool am I not?'

'And now you have Eleanor to help you. That must be a comfort. She has filled the void your father left.'

'It is a comfort, but no one can entirely replace a

father. Who knows, on your travels you may well find someone to comfort you. You have a lot to offer Caro.'

'So I've been led to believe. That's another reason for removing abroad.' She smiled for the first time since he arrived. 'I've had six cards left already today.'

Gabriel looked confused.

'Cards left by gentlemen callers, or possibly their mothers!' Caroline explained further: 'There's nothing like an heiress to bring the cockroaches scuttling out of the skirting boards.' She named the men whose cards had been left.

'Man alive Caro, you can do better than those poor specimens. Bland must be close to sixty. I see there are drawbacks to being an heiress too. I suffered a similar plight when it became known I was a single man after our broken engagement. Every mother with a single daughter to marry off arrived on my doorstep, it was hell I can tell you.'

When Gabriel had gone, Caroline thought about her lost love. In her heart she knew they would never have made each other happy. She also knew he would always hold a piece of her heart. She would always love him. Not passionately, but warmly, tenderly, affectionately. He had been part of her life for as long as she could remember. He was a good man, a kind man. Eleanor, she thought, was a lucky lady to have his love and respect.

Caroline knew he had moved on from their

childhood romance. He had an attractive, intelligent wife and a thriving business empire. She knew now she had to move on too, and make a life for herself. It is what her father, and Gabriel would want for her. All she had to do now was be brave enough to take the first step. Alone.

6

Aweek later Gabriel and Bendor were invited to take dinner and play cards at Lord Acton's house in Alnwick. They had been invited once before and Bendor had enjoyed himself tremendously despite losing heavily at the tables.

Lord Acton usually provided after dinner entertainment for his largely male guests. Several rooms were given over to card tables and roulette. Gabriel, not one for gaming, only went to keep his eye on Bendor although he did enjoy the fine food and wine. His friend often lost large amounts of money convinced as he was at every turn that his luck was about to change. Gabriel knew without his watchful eye any gains Bendor made would soon be lost, especially when drink had been taken.

They had decided against riding to Alnwick and had taken the carriage as it was a wet and windy night. Gabriel half wished he'd stayed at home by the fire with his wife. He shivered as the coach rumbled along the potholed lanes. As he sat opposite his old school friend, he offered him advice.

'Set yourself a limit Ben and when you've reached it,

stop playing.'

'When I've lost all my coin do you mean? Man I intend to win. I feel lucky tonight. You're so tiresome sometimes Gabe.'

'Tiresome! Thank you for that. I hope you win, but you never seem to be able to quit while you're ahead. That's the trick as I see it.'

'Over cautious that's you. We shall have a good dinner, fine wine and then some good sport.'

'Lord Acton certainly keeps a good table and cellar I have to agree.'

'And a stable of fillies as I remember that are *not* of the equine variety.' He winked roguishly at Gabriel.

'Are we not happily married men?' Gabriel reminded him. 'Our days of philandering are over my friend, thank the Lord.'

'Indeed we are married, but there you go again. Dismal Johnny. We may well be spoken for, but it doesn't mean we can't admire from afar.'

'You're in a singularly odd mood my friend. Were I not your best friend I'd be hurt by those comments,' Gabriel chided as Bendor passed him a hip flask of brandy. 'So long as you only admire from a distance all will be well. I think I'm getting old,' Gabriel moaned, 'I never used to feel the cold so much.'

Bendor raised his eyebrows and looked down at Gabriel's feet pointedly. 'Thank God you have your boots on. I thought you would be wearing your slippers. Do you wear your nightcap under your tricorn? You're turning into an old man.'

The rain was still falling when they arrived. They sprinted from the carriage to the main door where two liveried footmen relieved them of their wet cloaks. They were shown through to the drawing room where two dozen or so gentlemen stood about in groups talking and drinking. After a while the dinner gong sounded and they went through to eat a lavish meal.

Lord Acton stood to make an announcement, his guests were replete with food and wine. 'Gentlemen, there will now be the usual entertainments - should you wish to be entertained that is?' He smiled a crooked smile and some of the gentlemen made loud appreciative noises. Lord Acton was well known for his wine cellar and some of his guests had already over indulged and were on the verge of being rowdy. 'There will be the usual gaming tables so please enjoy yourselves. The ladies will be arriving shortly, ah perhaps that's them now?'

Two footmen opened the double doors into the games room and a dozen or so "ladies" stood about decoratively awaiting their pleasure. There was a round of applause, muttered lewd comments and whistling.

'What should you like to try your hand at first Gabe? What about the blonde filly by the piano?'

Gabriel ignored the jibe. 'If you mean what should I like to lose at first, then the answer is something where no skill is needed, for I have none where cards are concerned as you well know. Hazard I think.'

They took their seats and two of the "ladies" came to stand by their chairs.

'Good evening gentlemen, are you feeling lucky this evening?'

'I most certainly am.' Bendor looked up at the blonde who introduced herself as Claire. A dark haired beauty moved to Gabriel's side.

'I could be your good luck charm.' She laid a hand on Gabriel's shoulder proprietarily and smiled down at him.

'I usually need more than a charm to make me win,' Gabriel quipped as he was dealt his first hand. He lost the first three games. Bendor on the other hand, won the first three and grinned broadly.

'Stay right where you are ladies, your charm seems to be working for me.' Bendor was enjoying himself. It wasn't long before Gabriel was twenty guineas down. He stood to leave the table. Bendor, who for a change was up, decided to take his winnings and try his hand at the faro table. Gabriel joined him, and so did their two companions.

Again Gabriel lost. Disgruntled, he played a while longer and although he made up some of his losses he was still eighty guineas down. He took his own advice and threw in the towel.

Bendor, still winning, watched his friend leave the table. 'Had enough? Try your luck on the roulette wheel, that takes no skill.' Gabriel moved to the refreshment table followed by the dark haired girl. Bendor winked at him.

'Your consolation prize sir.' The girl smiled seductively as she handed him a glass of claret.

'Thank you.' Gabriel looked at the girl properly for the first time.

'My name's Ruby. I can be very consoling if you have the need to be cheered.' She laid long, slender fingers on his arm. Ruby was buxom with black hair and dark eyes. She had a look of Libby, his mistress before he married he noted, but this girl was much younger.

Gabriel drank the wine. He noticed Ruby's friend Claire was sticking to Bendor like fluff to a jacket; she whispered continually in his ear. His friend smirked at whatever it was she was saying. Gabriel looked about him. He had lost eighty guineas and didn't intend to throw good money after bad. He thought about what Bendor had said about him being boring. Perhaps he should give the roulette wheel a spin? Gabriel could see Bendor was quaffing down claret at an alarming rate. He let out a shout as he won again. Claire refilled his glass and giggled as she bent to kiss his cheek. No doubt she would be keen to claim some of Bendor's winnings. She encouraged him to play on.

'Are you sure you wouldn't care to spend some time with me... alone? We could take a stroll or go upstairs?' Ruby roused Gabriel from his thoughts.

'Thank you Ruby, but I'll soon need to restrain my

friend over there. I expect his luck will turn shortly, then he'll become over confident he can win it all back and lose the lot. That's the usual pattern with him.' Gabriel saw Bendor's eyebrows knit together in deep concentration. 'He has a very speculative nature, but sometimes his common sense leaves him altogether, especially when he drinks too much, as he's doing now.'

'You're a good friend to watch over him so diligently. Very well, I shall take a turn about the room while you rescue him. Who knows you may appreciate me more from a distance.'

She moved off with a sway of the hips. As she fanned herself she cast a last provocative look over her shoulder at him. Gabriel watched as she sauntered away. She was, he noticed, a very comely girl.

Another shout went up and Bendor collected his winnings.

'Well what do you say to *that*? I've cleaned up. Eight hundred and fifty guineas!'

Gabriel slapped his friend on the back. 'That makes a pleasant change but do *not* go and lose it all again as is your usual trick.'

'There you go again, killjoy. I don't intend to. Did you not have any luck?'

'Not a bit, but I'm pleased you did. I'm lucky in love and that's all that matters.'

'I noticed you old rake. Not lost your touch with the ladies eh?'

Claire came to join them. 'It's the custom to tip your good luck charm sir. I can be very grateful.' Before Bendor could reply she put her arm through his and kissed his cheek again. He passed her a handful of coins and gave his old friend a sideways look as if to warn him not to interfere. He shrugged his shoulders.

Gabriel was reminded of their younger days when they were rakish together. They had quite the reputations before they were married. They had often drunk too much and womanised too frequently, but now Gabriel and indeed Bendor, were reformed characters.

Ruby returned having completed her circuit of the room. 'Seen anything to take your fancy sir? I haven't. You've been my first choice from the beginning.' She stood closer than was seemly. The woman, like all high-class harlots, was good at flattery. She continued to flirt, making Gabriel smile despite himself. He drank more claret as he laughed at Ruby's observations. She was whip sharp, good fun, amusing. As Bendor and Claire wandered off, Gabriel began to enjoy himself.

The evening wore on pleasantly and after more teasing Ruby leaned in closer and whispered in Gabriel's ear. He raised an eyebrow at the suggestion and laughed.

'Really! I must say I'm sorely tempted, but I find I need my bed. Thank you for your company this evening it's been very, erm, stimulating.'

'I too am in need of a bed. I said earlier I can be discreet. I can follow you up. We don't have to announce our intentions to everyone in the room if you'd rather not.'

'Thank you for the kind offer, but I see it's sleep I'm in need of above all else.'

With that Gabriel bowed and went to rescue Bendor before he lost all his winnings. He needn't have worried, his friend was sprawled on a sofa leaning against his good luck charm. He was almost asleep. He shook Bendor who grumbled at being roused.

'Come on, time for bed.' He helped his friend into the waiting carriage. Bendor slumped in his seat and instantly began to snore loudly. As they trundled along Gabriel mused on life. Perhaps I am a dullard, but I know myself to be a fortunate man. I have a beautiful wife at home and soon I'll have a child. No one but my own wife can please me these days and if that makes me boring then so be it. Gabriel smiled to himself.

'You're such a rogue Ben. The ladies aren't safe with you around!'

R

At breakfast the next morning Eleanor stared at her husband trying to assess if he had overindulged the night before. Sometimes when he and Bendor got together they returned to acting like schoolboys. He looked remarkably fresh-faced she decided. She trusted him, but men were unpredictable creatures and when in their cups made errors of judgement - or at least she thought they did.

'You say Lord Acton provided entertainment last night. By that I presume you mean women. Women with loose morals?'

'I don't remember them being loose. If I remember rightly they were firm in all the right places.' Eleanor rolled her eyes. Her husband continued to goad her. 'They were high-class if you must know. A little too much powder and paint for my taste, but good to look at. One of them, her name was Ruby, took a shine to me.' He smiled hoping she would rise to the bait he was dangling. She was determined she would not. 'She had a beauty spot just there.' He reached over and laid a finger on the swell of her breast.

'Probably to cover a pock mark,' Eleanor said matter of factly. 'Would you pass the coffee?'

'She also had a black velvet ribbon around her long, slender neck.'

Eleanor pierced him with a look. She hoped the look told him he was walking on thin ice.

'She had good hair and at least she smelled pleasant, honeysuckle if I remember rightly.'

'Are you trying to provoke me Gabriel? I know your game and I won't be played.'

She changed the subject knowing quite well that if he was telling her about this woman, he'd done nothing more than look, and possibly appreciate her looks.

'Did you win at cards or is that a silly question?'

'Of course it is. I lost about eighty guineas and then gave up in disgust at my own ineptitude.'

She saw him shift in his seat; she knew he hated not being good at something.

'Ben however was a different story, for he won eight hundred and fifty guineas. Can you believe it?'

'Goodness. Did he do his customary trick and lose it all again?'

'This time I managed to stop his usual recklessness, but I bet he has a sore head this morning for he drank excessively.'

'I'd wager he was popular with the women after that. I imagine they were round him like bees around a honey pot.'

'One in particular - Ruby's friend Claire. He said she'd brought him luck so he tossed her a few coins as a reward.' Gabriel shrugged.

'What's the saying,' Eleanor asked rhetorically, 'a fool and his money are soon parted?' She looked carefully at her husband who suddenly seemed deep in thought.

'Do you find me boring?' he asked looking decidedly sheepish.

'Boring? What a strange question.'

He poured more coffee. 'Bendor called me tiresome because I tried to caution him about losing too much at the tables. When he's in his cups he throws caution to the wind. Last night he won, but if I'd not been there he would have probably lost some, if not all of it.'

'He can afford to lose, but so long as gambling is all he's tempted by then all's well.'

'He's besotted with Grace as you well know. Claire was whispering in his ear, trying to lead him astray, but he fell asleep on the carriage ride home. Our days of chasing women are over.'

'I'm relieved to hear it. So long as you look but don't touch.'

'Oh yes, we both looked.'

'In answer to your earlier question Gabriel you aren't boring, but you are in danger of becoming a bore on this particular topic. Perhaps we should change the subject.'

ℛ

'Connie, has Mrs Reynolds passed through the kitchen? I've searched the house for her, but she seems to have disappeared.'

'A think she went through to the scullery sir. At least that's where she said she was goin'.'

Gabriel made his way there. He noticed his wife leaning over the stable door that led into the yard. She hadn't heard him come in so he decided to creep up and surprise her. He took a few steps then saw what had caught her attention. Joe was stripped to the waist with his head under the pump. Gabriel watched as the groom's muscle-bound torso twisted and turned under the torrent of water. Eleanor continued to watch, her chin resting on her hand.

'There you are.'

Eleanor jumped as her hand flew to her heart. 'I didn't hear you come in. You startled me.'

'You were otherwise engaged were you not?'

'I came looking for... oh it doesn't matter.'

'I can see what you came looking for. He's a fine figure of a man.'

'Joe? I suppose so. I didn't come looking... I hadn't really noticed.' Her cheeks pinkened at the lie.

'For someone who's not really noticed you seemed quite distracted. So much so you didn't hear me come in.'

'Well alright I admit he does have a good physique and a handsome face.'

As Joe began to dry himself and put on his shirt Eleanor turned to her husband. 'As you said about the whores at Lord Acton's, it does no harm to look.' She glanced at her husband and grinned.

'I see.' Gabriel's face was deliberately devoid of emotion. 'So if I'm about the house and Charity has her bedroom door open and she's in a state of undress, it's quite alright for me to ogle her is it? As you say it does no harm to look.'

'Of course that's not alright. How could it be?' She saw the trap he'd led her into. 'It's different for men.'

'Ah the old refrain. How so?' Gabriel kept a straight

face. He was enjoying watching her squirm. 'Is this not a... what's the phrase you use? Ah yes a "double standard"? The master of the house can't look at the kitchen maid, that would be wrong, but the mistress can gaze at the groom and that's acceptable?'

Eleanor was on the verge of losing her temper he could tell. He could see she knew she'd been hoist by her own petard, but didn't intend to admit it.

'Charity is a lady's maid. I don't have the time for chatter,' Eleanor said haughtily. 'I only came to get this.' She picked up a box of kindling. 'Are you not going to be late?'

Gabriel seeing he'd won the round grabbed his wife by the waist and fastened her hands behind her back. She tried to struggle free.

'Let that be a lesson to you Mrs Reynolds for next time you lecture me on how things aren't equal between the sexes.' He sniggered and tried to kiss her.

Eleanor wriggled trying to pull away. 'You think you're so clever don't you? Let go, I have things to do.'

Gabriel continued to keep hold of her. 'What things? When does Walters take his ablutions? Is he next on your list?'

His wife failed to see the funny side. 'Ha ha, very droll. If you're going to be childish Gabriel... '

He let her go. 'Very well then have it your way, but think twice in future before you get on your high horse.' He undid the stable door and went out into the yard. He turned to close the bottom half of the door, took two steps into the yard then called her name over his shoulder.

'What?' she snapped.

'I think I'll take a wash under the pump... Would you care to watch or is your husband not enough for you?'

She threw a piece of kindling at him. He ducked clear chortling.

R

A week after the meeting with Gabriel at Eastshore Caroline decided she must face Eleanor. She had put off the meeting for far too long. Before he'd left, Gabriel had told her Eleanor was with child and this had affected Caroline more than she had expected. Somehow it made her feel even more alone. Since her father's death she realised she felt cut adrift, vulnerable. It was going to be a difficult morning. She would need all her courage. She dressed carefully and asked Ellise to take especial care with her hair.

Although it was spring, the north wind was a cold one and by the time Caroline reached Westshore she felt chilled to the bone. However there was a warm welcome waiting for her as she entered the familiar morning room; a blazing fire in the grate and a smiling Eleanor received her with something close to affection. Caroline looked at the woman who had replaced her and noticed her pregnancy was more advanced than she had imagined.

'Come and get warm, the wind is biting is it not?' Eleanor, her hand on her bump, advanced to meet her. 'How I envy you your trim waist. I fear I'll never see my feet again.'

Caroline took the outstretched hand. The ice was broken. The two women sat face to face as tea was brought in.

'Thank you Ivy, we can manage for ourselves.' The young maid looked highly relieved as she scurried from the room. Caroline's mouth felt dry. She swallowed hard.

'Thank you for agreeing to see me Eleanor I - '

'Before you speak Caroline please let me say I don't want or need your apology. Gabriel has told me about your meeting last week and I hope we can draw a line under the unfortunate business. Let's all be friends for no good can come from dwelling on the past.'

Caroline sighed with relief and said: 'You are too kind, both of you. I'm embarrassed by my conduct and will endeavour to make amends somehow.'

'Do you take milk?' It was clear Eleanor was prepared to move on. Caroline decided to try to do the same.

'Gabriel tells me you plan a trip abroad.' Eleanor passed her a dish of tea. 'I'm quite envious. Where do you plan to go?'

'We plan to go to France initially then on to Italy and Portugal. She outlined her itinerary and then asked about Eleanor's forthcoming event. She felt herself relax a little as she sipped her tea. 'When is the baby expected? You look well.'

'The middle of June or thereabouts. I feel fine, just a little tired by suppertime. I need to take a rest after dinner, but I'm always busy, I hate to be idle.'

'As do I. We don't expect to return home until late summer so we shall still be abroad when you are confined. I hope you have an easy time, if there is such a thing.'

Caroline thought Eleanor looked a little anxious now they were talking about the birth.

'I'm a twin, did you know? I have a brother, Tomas. There are many sets of twins in my family.' Eleanor stroked her bump. 'I'm sure I'm having twins even though the doctor assures me I'm not. I would like twins. Get it all over and done with at once if you see my meaning?'

'Gabriel will make a good father, he loves children. It must be difficult for you I expect with your family living in Whitby. I should imagine you miss the support of your mother at this important time?'

'I do.' Eleanor explained she had some family in Warkworth. 'I also hope to make friends here in Alnmouth. I hope when you return from your travels you won't be a stranger.'

'You're very kind. I should like that very much.'

'If there's anything I can do whilst you're away please let me know. I'll be happy to help.'

Caroline had been fretting over one thing in particular and decided to ask for Eleanor's assistance.

'There is one thing, a small thing, but important to me nonetheless.' Eleanor inclined her head and waited for her to continue. 'I ordered a headstone for my father's grave, but it won't be ready before I leave next week. Could you please let me know when it is... ' Caroline swallowed hard, 'when it's erected? Could you write and tell me how it looks? I know it's foolish, but when I went to his grave yesterday to lay flowers it looked so forlorn and uncared for.'

'Of course, it will be my pleasure, well perhaps pleasure is the wrong word, but I'll place flowers every week for you too if that would ease your mind.'

'Again Eleanor, I'm in your debt. Thank you, it will be comforting to know he's not forgotten.'

'I met your father only a handful of times. He was kind and courteous to me. It can't have been easy for him what with his expectations for you and Gabriel, but I can safely say such a generous gentleman will long stay in the memory. Gabriel misses him so much I know. I'm sure he'll join me in tending Thomas' grave.'

Caroline could feel herself becoming overwhelmed. Any mention of her father soon brought tears to her eyes. She blinked them back and stood to leave. 'You're very kind, especially under the circumstances.'

'Please Caroline let's part friends. I wish you well

and hope you enjoy your trip. Use it to think about what you will do in the future perhaps and come back to Alnmouth rested and recharged. The old cliché about time being a healer may well be true, but time can also hang heavy sometimes can it not? I think it a good idea to go abroad; a change of scene will do you good. I hope you'll find much to distract you whilst you're away. Don't worry about Eastshore and the business, Gabriel and I will take good care of both.'

'Thank you, I hope for distractions too.'

Despite her initial reservations, Caroline was pleased she had made the effort to meet with Eleanor. Although she was uncertain whether she would ever be firm friends with Gabriel's wife, she would no longer feel awkward in the woman's company. They had little in common it seemed, but Caroline was grateful for the kindness she had been shown this day. On her return she would make a point of including Eleanor in her gatherings with her other lady friends. It was the least she could do.

7

As the date for the birth came closer, Eleanor grew restless and tired and not a little irritable. The nursery was prepared, a midwife booked and Gabriel had organised his work so he should not be away from home.

'Have you decided about Wilson?' Gabriel knew that although his friend had been attending Eleanor, she wasn't keen to have him at the delivery.

'I'm to book another man - Wilson recommended him, a Doctor Sharpe. Wilson knows how I feel and understands the reason; as we're often at table together I shouldn't want him in the delivery room. It would be well... embarrassing. Perhaps not for him as a doctor, but for me it would feel strange.' Her face crinkled into a mischievous grin. 'I've been told sometimes women often blaspheme like sailors during childbirth.'

Gabriel smirked. 'You must vent as you see fit my love, I know nothing of the birthing process except I'm glad I'm a man. I've heard your outpourings when you think no one's listening. I suppose your ripe language is a result of your misspent youth stowing away on ships.'

Eleanor changed the subject, she was trying not to think about the actual birth too much.

'Abalone fed Bea herself, that is she didn't hire a wet nurse. We've written about this over the past months. I've decided after all she's told me about the benefits for mother and baby I'll do the same myself. Abalone says it's common practice in Holland now amongst the fashionable.'

'It's a fashion!' Her husband looked askance. 'So what are the benefits?'

Eleanor shifted her bulk. She was finding it hard to get comfortable. 'It's said the baby bonds more with the mother and that the nourishment which is passed from mother to baby is better than that passed from a wet nurse. The baby grows stronger. I talked to Wilson about it and he's all for the idea. He says that a mother's milk is best for her own child.'

'I know nothing about it, but am content so long as you're happy. I trust your judgement.'

Two days later Bendor came to dine at Westshore. Eleanor and Gabriel were showing him how the new garden was progressing when Eleanor felt a dull ache in her lower back. After a while she excused herself.

'I hadn't realised the wind was so chilly, I should have brought a shawl. Will you excuse me I think I'll return to the house?'

'Of course, unless I can fetch one for you my love?'

'No no, don't bother Gabriel. You can show Bendor the new mermaid statue.' A sharp pain made her wince. The men were looking at a fountain which had been finished only a few days ago so didn't notice Eleanor grimace. They continued their tour of the garden.

Once inside, Eleanor began to climb the stairs thinking to lie down to ease the pain. A shocking spasm ran through her body as she clutched the banister. Charity, who happened to be in the hall, saw the situation and helped Eleanor to her bed. After another half hour, the midwife was sent for and the doctor called.

Gabriel flushed and anxious was soon by his wife's side. He was more than a little agitated but trying not to show it. 'I leave you for five minutes and look at you!' He let go of her hand and scraped his fingers down his cheek. He was nervous, excited and fearful in equal measure.

'I know, I can't be trusted it seems.' Another pain racked her body making her scream out.

'Curse all you like Eleanor. Do as you must, I shan't mind, curse me as this is my entire fault.'

'There's no fault Gabriel I was as willing as you.' The contraction eased as she lay back bathed in perspiration. The midwife bustled into the room and efficiently expelled Gabriel, but not before he'd told Eleanor he loved her whilst kissing her and stroking her hair.

'I don't want to leave you but I can't bear to see you in pain.'

Eleanor knew his fear of the childbed having lost his mother and brother there. She knew she had to be positive for the both of them. 'Go and talk to Bendor, I'll do my best to be quick about it.' She tried to smile though the next contraction was swelling.

After twenty long hours the crying of a baby could be heard in the hall where Gabriel had been pacing. He flung open the bedroom door as Charity, carrying soiled linens, was leaving. Eleanor smiled up at him as he stood by her side.

'Let me introduce you to your daughter.'

Gabriel was speechless. The look on her husband's face was priceless; a mix of joy, awe and gratitude.

'I still can't believe there's only one baby,' Eleanor said feeling slighted. 'All through my pregnancy I've been sure there would be two despite what Wilson said. It's always twins in our family.'

'But not in mine.' Gabriel found his voice. 'How do you feel? Are you well?' Gabriel was still concerned she knew.

'I don't think I'll ride out later, but apart from that, I'm tired but so pleased and happy.' She was doing her best to allay his fears. 'Do you want to hold her?'

Gabriel carefully took the baby in his arms and looked at the pink, wrinkled face. There was a downy fuzz of golden hair on her head.

'I'm so proud of you. She's going to be a redhead and that can only mean trouble. Shall we stay with the name we chose? I think she suits it don't you?'

Eleanor agreed. 'Yes, Alice it shall be after your mother, with Rose for her second name.' Eleanor could barely keep her eyes open.

'Or do you think it sounds better the other way about, Rose Alice?' It was the last thing Eleanor heard as she fell sound asleep.

ℛ

Alice Rose Reynolds was christened at St Waleric's on Church Hill across the estuary at Alnmouth Bay. It was not to be a lavish, grand affair. Gabriel was not a church-goer, but he'd given into his wife's wishes for a christening on the understanding it would be a small occasion.

Charity was to dress the baby in the christening gown which Gabriel had worn when he was baptised. It was a little large for her, but it was beautiful nonetheless. Eleanor watched as Gabriel held their daughter in his arms. He had his back to her and was oblivious. He rocked her gently from side to side and sang softly:

> *My hat has three corners,*
> *Three corners has my hat,*
> *And had it not three corners,*
> *It would not be my hat.*

Eleanor watched as he put Rose gently in his

upturned tricorn as if he were placing her in her crib. Her scrawny little legs dangled over the edge of the hat. She watched as Gabriel, whose face was full of love, bounced her up and down.

In that moment Eleanor knew she had never loved her husband quite so much. She moved to Gabriel's side and laid her hand lightly on his arm. 'So our daughter is to be christened in a hat?' She smiled. 'Where's Charity and where's the christening gown?'

'Ah, there's been a slight accident. Her Ladyship has been sick down it already which isn't an impressive start. Charity has gone to see if it can be righted.'

At that moment the maid arrived back. 'It's fine, no harm done. Shall I take her and try again?'

'Thank you Charity. You're good with her.' He handed his daughter to the maid. 'We'll no doubt be hiring a nursemaid soon, I'm only surprised one hasn't been hired already.'

Rose began to cry loudly in protest at leaving her father. He held onto his daughter's tiny hand. 'She's so perfect; I can't stop looking at her.'

'Even a doting father can't be impressed with the noise she's making. That sound is ear-splitting, it must be love.'

Eleanor glanced at her maid who smiled as she struggled to dress the screaming, squirming baby. Once the gown was fastened, Gabriel took back his daughter and held her in his arms. Eleanor noticed how small she looked next to him. Rose quietened immediately.

'Whenever I leave Westshore it's as though I'm leaving my whole world behind. You and her, here together; I can't bear to be apart from you both.'

Eleanor beamed at her husband. 'You'll become used to it, it's all very new at the moment.'

'Perhaps next time it will be twins. You expected two when this little mite was born. I should like twins,' Gabriel mused.

Eleanor saw Charity raise an eyebrow. 'There now Charity, if the man of the house has his way your workload will increase before you know it - we'll be late if we don't set off for church soon.' Eleanor turned to leave the nursery. 'Aren't you forgetting something my love?' She looked over her shoulder. Gabriel looked confused. He stared at his daughter a look of bewilderment on his face. Eleanor sang:

And had it not three corners,
It would not be my hat.

Gabriel picked up his tricorn and followed her laughing.

R

Although it was June, the wind was chilly as the small party arrived back at Westshore. Alice Rose had behaved perfectly throughout the church service.

Eleanor had found the ceremony strange; being raised a Quaker she had only ever been to one christening before, that of her goddaughter Beatrice. She'd wanted some sort of ceremony to mark the birth of their first born, and Gabriel had given way without protest. Content with his life, he would have granted her anything.

'I was surprised to hear the vicar christen your daughter Alice Rose.' Wilson sat next to Gabriel. 'I always hear you refer to her as Rose. Was he in error? As her godfather I wondered if I should have put him right.'

They were in the drawing room having just dined on cold meats and salads, strawberries and jellies. A few guests, including Bendor and Grace who were also godparents, were sitting in small groups or admiring the baby who continued to be remarkably docile.

'She's Alice after my mother, but for some inexplicable reason we always call her by her second name, Rose. Eleanor loves roses and the first time I met her she smelled of roses... but that's another story.' Gabriel smiled to himself.

'When do you leave for Whitby? Eleanor's parents will be keen to see their new grandchild I expect.' Wilson sipped his wine.

'We leave next week although I think it's too early to be travelling the country with a newborn, but you know what Eleanor's like when she has her mind set. Nothing and no one will change it. I know she wants to introduce Rose to her family, but there's another reason also for the visit, a sentimental reason.'

Gabriel and Wilson were close friends now. They had come to know each other when the doctor had first attended Gabriel's father before his death. He had also proved to be a good friend when Gabriel's stable hand Jax, had been abducted and defiled by a French sea captain. He'd not only helped the boy to get over his trauma, but had supported Gabriel when he'd stood trial for the manslaughter of the villain who purported the crime.

Gabriel explained: 'When I ordered my new ship to be built by Eleanor's father they told me about a custom they have in Whitby of blessing new ships when they're launched.'

'I remember. Did you not go to last year's ceremony?'

'It was two years ago believe it or not. It was over the period of that visit Eleanor and I became close. That's the other reason for going to Whitby next week. Not only is it the annual Boat Blessing, but my ship is built and will be blessed in the ceremony. Of course we don't want to miss it. It will be some occasion.'

'So your empire grows. Shall you sail her back to Alnmouth?'

'She's to sail straight from Whitby to the Baltics with a cargo of timber. I'd planned to sail out on her myself, but now with the baby and all... '

'Eleanor will not want to spare you so soon.'

'And I don't want to leave them either even though you assure me all is well with mother and baby. There will be time enough to go gallivanting around the globe when Rose begins to cut her teeth. I hear from Bendor that babies can become very grizzly then.'

'True enough. What is the ship going to be called, have you decided?'

'We had thought of a name. Eleanor, for reasons I won't go into wants her to be called "My Constant Lady" but I've instructed her father's sign writer to name her something different, something more in keeping I think. I hope when Eleanor sees the new name she'll still be talking to me.'

ℛ

Bryony Swift had been looking for work for weeks. She had been offered the odd day or two helping out in one of the big houses when they had guests and needed extra staff, but nothing which had led to anything more permanent. She was becoming despondent. What she was really looking for was to be a lady's maid again or a companion, but there was nothing to be had in Alnmouth. She was reluctant to move towns again now that she'd settled here.

Bryony had thought there would be plenty of work in Alnmouth and she was right, there was work to be had, it just wasn't the sort of work she was looking for. There was any amount of work to do with fishing;

gutting fish, mending nets, sewing sails, but this type of work was beneath her and besides the pay would be poor and the hours long. She would end up smelling like a fish wife. She couldn't countenance *that*. There was also servile work, but again it was below her standards. If something didn't turn up soon however she would have to think again.

One night as she was taking a stroll by the bay she heard a voice calling to her. At first she'd thought it just some amorous sailor chancing his arm. She often attracted men with her looks and tall, slender body. Then she recognised the man's accent and smiled to herself. Her captain had returned.

Bryony had first met her Irish captain when she was newly arrived in Alnmouth. He was one of the reasons she wanted to stay in the vicinity. Now he was back and was as pleased to see her as she was to see him it seemed. She meant to enjoy herself with the handsome rogue if at all possible; there had been little comfort since being forced to leave Westshore so abruptly. She was tired of counting every penny and going to bed hungry. Slender suited her, scrawny did not.

'Well my lovely, don't you look grand.' He bowed his dark head and kissed her hand. As he rose he winked at her. 'Aren't you just the sight a man wants to see on his first night ashore? I hoped I'd find you. I'll be ashore for a week or so, what say we have some fun like last time?'

Bryony knew better than to run into his arms. She

decided to play hard to get. 'And what makes you think I've time for the likes of you? Do you think I sit here pining away in your absence?' She tilted her chin and turned to move off.

He caught hold of her hand. 'I should like to think so, but with your looks you'll have a queue of admirers around the town I expect. I took the chance... I hope you don't mind but I've bought you a little token of my esteem.'

He took a diamond necklace from his pocket and dangled it before her. It sparkled in the half light, but she was no fool; she was certain it was paste. Nevertheless it was pretty and made her eyes light up. Doubtless he would have presented it to the first woman he'd come across who looked half willing, but she wanted it, and him. She liked nice things, she deserved them. She was tired of scrimping and going without. She knew with a little coaxing he could be generous, very generous she hoped.

'You think I can be bought with trinkets? I thank you sir, but you misunderstand me.' She pocketed the necklace.

'You and me are two of a kind my lovely Bryony. I seem to remember on my last visit you were, shall we say, appreciative of what I had to offer. Have I really got you so wrong?'

He pulled her towards him and kissed her ferociously taking her breath away.

Over the next week they spent an enjoyable time

together. He was attentive, generous and a good lover. Bryony didn't altogether trust him, but he was a welcome break from what had become a dreary existence. He knew how to make a woman feel special. He bought her ribbons, a pretty shawl and presented her with a piece of fine French lace, enough to trim the new dress he'd bought for her. She would miss him when he returned to sea. She would miss the square meals he bought her more.

'How long will you be gone and where are you off to this time?' Bryony lay in his arms in the small, shabby room she rented down by the bay.

'I'll be gone until I return.' He laughed enigmatically. 'Who knows what shores I'll pitch up on? I might get blown off course or then again,' he rolled her naked body towards him and nibbled her neck, 'I might be back before you've chance to miss me. I've a fair yearning for your charms my lovely colleen.'

When the captain sailed, he left Bryony with assurances and with enough coin to tide her over until she could get work, or so she hoped. She meant to try to hang onto this man so she didn't press him for a commitment; she knew that was the one way to lose his favour. He was a charmer but he wouldn't be tied down, well not yet at least. He had a zest for life and money to spare and for now that was enough for her. He was free and easy with his coin too, unlike some men she'd met in the past. They had both enjoyed themselves while he'd been ashore. They'd dined well and drunk the finest wines. She could get used to the good life. She pushed aside thoughts he might not return. For now she was content.

He had been evasive about his exact line of work, but unless she was very much mistaken he was involved in smuggling, possibly in running goods from France. It was a dangerous business and it meant he was often gone for weeks at a time. She thought him quite the buccaneer, but Bryony wasn't hoodwinked. He might convince himself she was his one and only when in the throes of passion, but she wouldn't be taken in so easily. She wasn't born yesterday and he wasn't the type to settle for a life with just one woman to warm his bed, of that she was certain.

He had a wandering eye and a girl in every port quite possibly. She knew his type well enough, but he made her happy, for the time being. Who knew when her luck would turn and she'd meet the man who would provide her with the security she craved. She was confident her looks would net her a more suitable, reliable beau. Her sights were set higher than a pirate, but he was fun and he made her feel cherished.

After her paramour had sailed, Bryony tried once again to get work. She still had the coin he'd left her, but she intended to keep tight hold of it. She needed it to give her a breathing space. She was sure she would soon secure a good position and at the same time meet a *real* gentleman. Perhaps the relation or friend of a new employer would take a shine to her and despite her servitude would offer her marriage and then she'd have the life of ease of which she had always dreamed. The money the captain had left her was welcome, but she had to find respectable work - and soon.

She shivered on the thin mattress and pulled her shawl tighter around her body. The candle was guttering, but she wouldn't light another. She cursed the name of Reynolds. This was his fault, his and his snooty baggage of a wife. Losing the work at Westshore had cost her dear. She knew the position was never permanent, but if she'd had more time to work on him things might have turned out differently. Pregnant wives presumably cut their husbands' rations and then he'd have come begging her for favours, favours she would have granted, at a cost. If he'd taken her as his mistress, set her up in a place of her own, she wouldn't be in this situation now; she'd be living the high life. She wouldn't have to take a job where she had to curtsy to some spoilt, little madam or be a drudge to some crinkly old woman who smelled of piss and powder.

She'd never been cast aside before, never been spurned. Men chased her and she was used to picking and choosing her suitors. She resented Gabriel Reynolds and not just for turning her out. She hated him for not wanting her. He would pay. One way or another she'd settle the score. The candle guttered and went out.

'You wait Gabriel Reynolds,' she said to the darkness. 'Do you think you can toss me aside like yesterday's broadsheet? Well think again.'

8

The journey by land and sea with a small baby was difficult to say the least, but eventually Eleanor and Gabriel arrived at Mulgrave House to a warm welcome. Rose was fussed over and admired and Eleanor was looked after by her parents as if she was the only woman ever to have borne a child. Gabriel was slapped on the back like a returning hero.

'Who would have guessed all this would have come to pass and we should all be here together? You two married and with a babe in arms.' John Barker, Eleanor's amiable and doting father, was admiring his latest granddaughter. 'And you came into the world all alone without a brother or sister to help you,' he told the sleeping infant. 'Like you Eleanor, your mother and I were convinced it would be twins.'

'I was so surprised; I was waiting for another to show itself.'

Tomas, Eleanor's twin brother, took hold of the baby and looked the proud uncle. 'She's a beauty but then I expected nothing less with her pedigree,' he said beaming at his sister.

After the family had dined a footman announced

Ginny Jenkins was waiting to see Eleanor. She left the family to go to the morning room.

'Ginny, how lovely to see you again, I'm so glad you could spare the time to meet me. Have you seen Charity yet?' Ginny was Charity's younger sister.

'Not yet, I just got here. She's well I hope only when you sent a message I thought... '

'Oh I'm sorry, how thoughtless of me. She's well, very well. She doesn't know I've asked to see you or why for that matter. I didn't want her to know until I'd spoken to you myself.' Ginny looked confused. 'I'm not making any sense am I? Sorry Ginny. Please sit down and I'll stop beating about the bush.'

Ginny sat on the edge of the chair and looked daunted by her surroundings.

'Would you like to be my daughter's nursemaid? Charity says you're good with babies and children and I know you two miss each other. I wondered if you'd be prepared to move to Westshore. She's a good baby and you would of course live in like your sister.'

Ginny's eyes opened wide. 'I can hardly believe it. I never expected such a thing when I got your message. I'll have to ask Mother of course, but yes, I'd love to be a nursemaid to your daughter. Charity wrote saying what a sweet nature the baby has. Thank you ma'am for thinking of me.'

Ginny and her family were poorer since their father had died and Eleanor knew that Ginny having work would help all the family. There were another three younger children still at home.

'If your mother agrees you could return with us in a month's time. I haven't spoken of this with Charity just in case she got her hopes up and you declined the offer. I'm so pleased. Perhaps you would like to take Charity back home with you now, I shan't need her tonight. She's keen to see you all.'

Eleanor returned to her family to tell them about the new appointment.

'That's good news.' Eleanor's mother Anne was especially pleased. 'They've struggled since Charlie died. He spent a lot of time at The Hart, but he always had regular work and looked after his family. Charity will enjoy having her sister close. You know, of course, that Ginny's young man joined the navy and so she ended the relationship. She told him as much before he took the King's shilling, but I think he didn't believe her. He soon found out differently.'

'Another strong minded Yorkshirewoman in the house, I'm outnumbered already,' Gabriel said. 'With a headstrong mother and nursemaid, Rose will grow up to be another Boadicea at the very least.'

ℛ

As Ginny's mother had agreed to her daughter's new job it was decided the young woman would start taking care of Rose while they were still in Sandsend. She and Rose could get to know each other before returning to Alnmouth. So on the morning of the Boat Blessing it was she who looked after her new charge while Eleanor, Gabriel and the rest of the family rode down to Whitby Harbour.

It was a warm summer's day, a few high fluffy clouds scuttled across the sky and a pleasant breeze ruffled the waves.

'I remember the last Boat Blessing we attended,' Gabriel mused as he rode by his wife's side, 'with you in your green riding habit telling me what to expect at the ceremony and *not* telling me you had just thrown over your fiancé.'

'And you telling me of your broken engagement to Caroline. A lot's happened since we rode this path before.' Eleanor's face crumpled. 'And not all of it good.' She half smiled at him. He knew she was thinking of the miscarriage they'd suffered. It had knocked them both for six when it happened.

Before the marriage there had been two broken engagements; one to his childhood sweetheart Caroline, and Eleanor's to a philandering sea captain, William Seamer. Then Gabriel had chased her to Holland to convince her to marry him, not an easy task when she found he'd kept a mistress in the past. It was something she'd found hard to forgive. Returning home, Eleanor had been injured when her ship was wrecked on Whitby Rock. Not wanting to be apart for a day longer than necessary, they'd married in haste and had a Christmas wedding in Whitby. Eleanor had then found herself with child, but before they'd had chance to get used to the idea of a baby, there had been a miscarriage. They had both taken the loss badly. Just as they were recovering from this, another bombshell had landed; Gabriel's ex-mistress had given birth to his son and taken him to America. It had truly been an eventful time.

'I can't imagine now why I ever agreed to marry William. What was I thinking? It seems I was just a child then, with childish ideals. My life would have been very different with him as my husband.' She shuddered.

Gabriel looked across at his wife. 'Life is good at the moment, in fact perfect now I come to think of it, everything is changed. You have a beautiful daughter, a handsome, attentive husband and I have the two most precious gifts a man could wish for - a new ship and plenty of money!' He grinned at his wife who rolled her eyes.

Gabriel had also changed. Gone were the black moods which used to engulf him. Now he liked to refer to himself as a born again optimist.

'Modest as ever I see, but yes, we're lucky. And I do love you more each day, though now you risk a fall as your head will get even bigger and you'll topple from your horse,' she said teasing.

He shot her a look. 'And I love you too, my love. Can you just try to remember that when you see the ship?'

'Why? I don't understand your meaning.' She raised an eyebrow. They were almost at the harbour now and Gabriel was a little anxious. Would she approve the name change of the ship? He hoped she would, no he knew she would.

They gave their horses to the grooms and began to walk towards the impressive collier. She was magnificent to Gabriel's eye. He had waited so long for this day. Eleanor with her family about her looked up at Gabriel's proud, smiling face.

'Well, are you pleased?' his father-in-law asked. 'I can see you are.'

'Excessively pleased, yes, well done John she's magnificent, my newest baby.'

It was then Eleanor noticed the ship's name written in flowing, red script. At the same moment Gabriel saw her see the name change.

'Oh Gabriel, I'm overwhelmed. I love it, you're so thoughtful. Of course I don't mind the name change, how could I?' She stood on her tiptoes to kiss him.

'What's all this?' Tomas was laughing at the show of affection.

'Look at the name Tomas. We'd agreed on a name, but Gabriel has changed it.'

'Has he? Brave man! I didn't know that.' He and the rest of the family looked up at the stern of the ship.

"The Eleanor Rose" was emblazoned for all to see.

R

Eleanor was enjoying being back in her home town of Whitby and spent many happy days seeing old friends and showing off her daughter. Her parents organised teas and dances and Gabriel too, was enjoying family life. For so long it had been only himself and his father so it was odd to be part of Eleanor's large, sociable family, odd but good.

Gabriel noticed Eleanor smiling to herself as she sat up in bed rubbing lanolin into her hands. 'That's an enigmatic look, what are you smiling at?' He climbed into bed beside her.

'I was just thinking how it still feels risqué having you in my bed in my old bedroom.'

He raised his eyebrows in surprise. 'Risqué?'

'Not risqué exactly but... strange. For so many years I lay in this bed dreaming of what my life would be like. I dreamt all my childish dreams in this room.'

'And planned all your girlish adventures?'

'Something like that yes. Of course once I was engaged to William I never expected to live anywhere else but Whitby. How things change. I'd expected to live in the house he'd had built for us along the coast road. It's a beautiful house with commanding views. Tomas says it's never been lived in. Did I ever tell you about it?'

'You didn't, but I did know of its existence. Tomas told me the day I came to dinner here when I unmasked you. He told me you were engaged and I remember feeling angry about it.'

'Unmasked! That makes me sounds like a highwayman.'

'You'd make a good one. I can just imagine you with your face hidden behind a mask and your hair blowing in the wind as you held up a coach and demanded - '

'Why did you feel angry?' Eleanor cut off his fanciful talk.

'I thought you a tavern wench remember. Then I saw you were a grand lady and I was thrown into confusion. There had been an attraction, obviously, when I first met you, but then I found you here only to be told you were soon to be married. I was uncertain how I felt about you. I never thought to see you again after you ran out on me at the tavern and then I found you but couldn't have you. You were engaged to someone else.' He snuggled under the covers. 'But now I have you and you can't escape. You're right, it does feel strange to be here, in your bed… in fact it feels... ' He made a lunge for her and tried to grab hold of her hands. She pretended to fight him off, but her hands were slippery with lanolin and he lost grip. They curled up together happily.

'Do you suppose he intends to put a new bride in the house?' Gabriel asked.

'Who knows? I care not. Tomas says he hasn't a lady at the moment. Perhaps he'll sell it.' She twisted a curl of Gabriel's hair in her fingers. 'I'm exhausted and Rose will be demanding a feed in two hours no doubt. Good night my love.' As an afterthought she added:

'There's been a lot of water washed up on the beach since we first met. All I know is I made the right choice in marrying you Gabriel. I love you so much.'

'And I you. Come here and I'll show you how much.'

ℛ

There was to be a party held in Eleanor's and Gabriel's honour at Ingram Eskdale's house on West Cliff. Eleanor had known the shipbuilder all her life as he was a good friend to her father. Gabriel had met Eskdale early on in his relationship with Eleanor and they had done a little business together. It was to be a party to celebrate their daughter's birth, a sort of second christening party for family and friends who hadn't made it to Alnmouth.

'So Gabriel, you have a new baby and a new ship? The latter is on her maiden voyage to the Baltics with timber I understand. When did she set sail?' Eskdale asked.

'Yesterday. We all went to wave her off as though she was a pleasure craft.' Gabriel smiled proudly. 'She'll return with her cargo to Alnmouth in six or seven weeks, depending on the weather of course. One of my longest serving men is captaining her, but I must confess I shall be glad to see her return safely.'

'Aye, shipping is a hazardous profession. I lost a ship some ten year back. It was devastating. Not just

123

the cost, like you I owned her outright, but the loss of life was a bitter blow. It was the captain's first mission and I often wonder if he made errors in judgement, but who can say. All hands went down in the icy waters of the Davis Straits. A sorry business it was. Many families left widowed and orphaned. The guilt! I still feel it now.'

Gabriel was about to reply when a young man came to join them.

'Good evening Mr Eskdale. Thank you for inviting me this evening, I'm very grateful to you.'

The young man, possibly slightly younger than Gabriel, had a confident air about him.

'Good evening Captain Turner, let me introduce you to Mr Gabriel Reynolds. This is Captain Padraic Turner, he's new to Whitby.'

'Good evening Captain, is that an Irish accent I detect?'

'It is sir. I'm a Dublin man, but am removed here to take up a new post. I used to be a soldier, but in peacetime I decided to try my hand at whaling.'

The man had dark, curly hair which was cut shorter than most men favoured. He was smartly dressed in his uniform which made him look quite dashing. Gabriel rarely made snap judgements, but something about the captain irked him. The man was cocksure, over confident. He had quite the swagger about him. Self doubt was obviously a stranger to him, pride an old acquaintance.

The captain looked about the room assessing the company. He talked at length and proudly of Dublin. It was more of a monologue than a conversation.

At last he changed the subject. 'Mr Eskdale can I be very forward and ask who is the young lady over there with the glorious red hair? I would swear she's of Irish descent with her colouring. She's a grand filly and she's certainly drawn my attention I can tell you.'

Ingram Eskdale smirked and glanced at Gabriel conspiratorially.

'She is your new employer's daughter, and she certainly isn't of Irish descent I can assure you of that.'

'Mr Barker's daughter is she? *That's* interesting. Not Irish you say; well, I won't hold that against her. She's a most attractive girl.'

Gabriel could hold his tongue no longer. '*Girl* Captain? That's my wife and the mother of my child of whom you speak.'

Captain Turner smiled easily. 'Forgive me sir, I'd no idea. You're a lucky man and I envy you.'

Gabriel's outburst was soon quietened, but he still felt rankled. 'I'm aware of my good fortune Captain Turner. Now if you will excuse me.' He strode over to Eleanor's side and protectively placed his hand under her elbow.

'What is it my love, are you hungry?' Eleanor smiled up at him. 'Supper will be called soon I hope, I'm starving.' She turned back to speak to Ingram's niece just as supper was called.

Gabriel felt unsettled and was further irritated to see that Captain Turner had been seated to Eleanor's left at supper. As was the custom, Gabriel was sat apart from his wife on the opposite side of the table and higher up. He'd often asked himself who did the seating plans at these events for he seemed to spend most suppers talking to some crotchety old widow or doddery old colonel, while Eleanor was usually placed next to handsome, young studs. He could feel his irritation scratching away at his reason.

Throughout the meal he kept a wary eye on Captain Turner. The courses were endless and it spoilt Gabriel's enjoyment of the food, seeing his wife with her head close to the captain laughing and clearly enjoying herself.

He had felt jealousy before, but that was before their marriage. He knew Eleanor well enough to trust her, but he didn't trust Captain Turner. Of course he didn't know the man, but what he did know he didn't like. There was something about him which made Gabriel wary.

After supper and when the men had taken their port and cigars, the orchestra set up and the dancing began. Gabriel took up a position standing guard by Eleanor's side. He knew he was being foolish but he couldn't help himself.

'Have you saved a dance for me?' Gabriel asked surveying the room for the captain, his usual sunny countenance gone.

'For you, why would I? You hate to dance. I can squeeze you in if you really want, but I'm not up to dancing every dance, I've just had a baby remember.' She raised a perfect eyebrow in astonishment at his request.

'Who are you to dance with first?'

Before she could answer a young man, the son of another local shipbuilder, came to escort her onto the dance floor. She smiled sweetly at her husband as she was led away. Gabriel watched her dance, she moved lightly and elegantly. He told himself to grow up. Didn't she deserve some entertainment with her friends and family? He knew she missed Whitby and her friends though she never complained. After she had danced two dances with the young man, she returned to his side.

'What's the matter? You're hovering by my side like a herring gull following a coble. You don't usually stick by me.'

'Can a man not be with his wife?'

'Of course he can, but not all day and all night. Are you bored my love? There's Tomas and his crowd, why not go and enjoy the company of the young people? I see Peter Eskdale is home on shore leave. I don't believe you've met Ingram's nephew?'

He felt like a small child being dismissed by its mother for being troublesome. 'Are you wanting rid of me?' he snapped back, 'I only thought you may become overtired and need me.'

Eleanor wasn't fooled. 'For goodness' sake Gabriel I may have had a baby, but I'm still capable of making rational choices without you standing over me. If I feel tired and want to go home I'll say so.'

Gabriel took a deep breath, bit back a bad tempered response and strode over to where Tomas and his friends were getting quietly inebriated.

ℛ

Captain Turner watched the interchange with amusement. He watched as the redhead's husband stormed off leaving her chatting animatedly with a young woman. She clearly wasn't as upset as he was by their discussion. She laughed at something her acquaintance said and her face lit up the room. The other woman was handsome enough, but Eleanor outshone her easily, her red hair gleaming in the candle light. Tendrils of coppery red had escaped their pins and framed her freckled cheeks. He knew freckles weren't fashionable, but they reminded him of the girls back home in Ireland. You could keep the pale insipid English rose, give him a fiery redhead any day. He also liked her figure, not too bony; her well-cut gown displayed her ample charms.

He knew he was on Eleanor's dance card for two dances hence, but thought to move into her sight sooner. He also knew if he joined her group, her husband would descend like a great protector which

128

would defeat the object. He thought about how to manoeuvre himself without looking too obvious. He sauntered over to where her father was holding forth with an older man. He began to talk to him keeping a watchful eye on her as he did so.

After a while, John Barker unwittingly helped him out. 'Have you met my daughter Captain Turner? There she is, come let me introduce you.' Before the captain could explain they'd already met, John Barker moved off expecting him to follow. Padraic smirked to himself as he followed his new employer across the room.

'Eleanor my dear, let me introduce you to Captain Turner. He's the newly appointed captain of The Whitby Lass, I told you about the appointment do you remember?'

'Yes Father I remember. We sat together at dinner, did you not notice?' The captain kissed her hand again although it wasn't strictly necessary. The three continued in conversation until it was time for him to lead her to dance the first of the dances he'd bagged.

He was looking forward to dancing with her. She'd been an entertaining dinner partner and now he would get the chance to hold her in his arms. He knew she danced well, he'd watched her with another young man earlier. He also knew he danced well too. They'd make a strikingly handsome couple.

Padraic Turner saw her husband watching them from across the room. He could see the sullen look on the man's face. He didn't blame him for sulking; if Eleanor were his wife he'd keep a close eye on her too. She seemed the type of woman who liked to flirt and tease. She had a ready wit and clearly liked to lead a man on. She was most unlike the usual married women he met on such occasions and by all accounts she'd just had a child; perhaps her husband was neglecting her?

'You dance well Mrs Reynolds.'

'Thank you. I love to dance but I haven't had the opportunity for a while.'

'Do you entertain much in Northumberland?'

'As much as we're able. Any excuse to dance.'

As they separated, he watched her weave gracefully in and out of the other dancers; she cut a fine figure. He was not the only man in the room to admire her he noticed. He made sure to hold her close each time they came together. When at last the dance was over he led her towards the terrace.

'Perhaps later you'll allow me to take you for some refreshment? You can tell me more about your business interests. It's unusual for a lady such as yourself to be interested in shipping.'

'Not just shipping Captain Turner, I have other business interests. I also lease a hat shop would you believe?'

'Does your husband not object? If you were my wife I think I'd feel neglected. A man wants to be the centre of his wife's life.'

'My husband knows me well and knows I'd be bored if all I did was my embroidery, I'm not good with a needle,' she joked and suddenly looked younger. 'It's fortunate sir that we aren't married, for I don't like to be dictated to by anyone. I like to be my own mistress and choose how I spend my time. I know most men think a woman's place is in the home, but my husband and I think alike on this subject. We suit one another.'

'I like a lady who knows her own mind. I imagine you can be quite a force to be reckoned with, in the home or out of it.'

Padraic Turner liked a bit of spirit in a woman, such a pity she was his employer's daughter. He led her to a quiet corner of the terrace. 'Tell me about Whitby. Are all the ladies here as attractive as you?'

R

Gabriel glared across the room. He watched like a hawk as each time they danced back together Turner made some little speech that made Eleanor smile. He hated the fact she was smiling at this young whippersnapper. He could feel his temper begin to simmer. He tried hard not to let it boil over.

'What's Turner's background?' Gabriel and Tomas were watching the dancing. Tomas looked over to where his sister was dancing with the captain.

'He was in the military... the Irish Guards or some such outfit. He's a brave man according to his letter of recommendation. Father was pleased to secure him for The Whitby Lass. He fought well in Spain I believe and these days with pirates marauding about the high seas it's good to have a military man in charge. Before that I think he sailed out of Ireland to America, importing tobacco or was it cereals?' Gabriel continued to scowl. 'Terrible big head though,' he added, 'likes to talk about himself and his exploits.'

'Exploits? He's a womaniser do you mean?'

'Possibly, but I meant his war record. Seems it's his main topic of conversation. He'll possibly bore Eleanor to death with his talk of battles and warfare. She's a pacifist at heart remember, her Quaker upbringing has seen to that I think.'

Gabriel was in no mood to be placated. He watched as the dance ended and Turner led Eleanor towards the terrace. This was too much. He fought to stop himself rushing over and putting himself between them. He managed to hold off, but kept a vigilant eye until they stepped out onto the terrace and out of sight. He grabbed a glass of wine from a passing footman and took it down in one draught.

'Steady on, the night is young. Have you and Eleanor had a tiff? You seem out of sorts,' Tomas asked concerned by his brother-in-law's scowling face.

'Ignore me, I've taken a dislike to Turner for some reason. It was something he said earlier.'

Gabriel told Tomas about the remark Turner had made about his wife.

'It's the sort of thing I'd do, always putting my foot in it. You aren't jealous of him? You should be proud he was complimentary about your wife. We Barkers are a good looking crew are we not?' Tomas nudged Gabriel trying to lighten the mood. 'I hope my sister has better taste in men than him. He's handsome and all, but he's a reprobate I'd wager. Even I've noticed how he eyes up all the ladies, though I concede he seems to have his eye firmly fixed on my sister at the moment, not on when he knows her to be a married woman. Even I draw the line when the lady is married.'

'What of Captain Seamer? He was her choice and look how he treated her. He betrayed her with a rich widow.'

'She was younger then, and had no one to compare him with. Now she's married to you I'm sure she's just having a little fun. She always was a flirt. He might be a rakehell, but Eleanor knows how to handle herself. Did I ever tell you about the time one of my lecherous school friends came to stay and made a play for her? She ran him down with her horse the next day and damn near broke his arm.' Tomas grinned proudly.

Tomas introduced Gabriel to a young lady who had joined their group. 'This is Miss Katherine Craig, she's Lord Mulgrave's niece.' Gabriel remembered his manners and became more sociable. He talked for some time with the young lady, who he noticed was strikingly beautiful with blonde curls and dimples. She was, he thought, not only attractive but intriguing. He found she was interested in horses and as he and Bendor were trying to get a stud farm off the ground he found they had a lot in common; indeed she may have contacts that would be useful to him. He began to regain his composure and calm down.

'My wife and I are in Whitby for two more days. Would you permit me to come and look at the brood mare of which you speak? I should be interested in your uncle's set up.'

'Of course, come tomorrow, in the morning if you can.'

From the corner of his eye, Gabriel noticed Turner was once again leading Eleanor to the dance floor. 'Would you care to dance Miss Craig or are you already spoken for?'

'It seems my partner is remiss. Thank you sir I'd like to dance.' He led her out and saw Eleanor raise her eyebrows and smile at him. He wasn't inclined to smile back and childishly pretended he'd not noticed her.

The dance was the kind of dance where at times, Gabriel's and Eleanor's paths crossed. Eleanor glanced at him as she swept by.

'You look cross. Surely you aren't still annoyed with me for shooing you off earlier?' The next time they passed she said: 'Are you alright?'

Gabriel continued to frown. 'Why wouldn't I be?' They drifted apart again before coming together once more.

'I have no idea but you look - ' the dance pulled them away from each other before she could finish the sentence. They didn't pass again for a few minutes, Eleanor and the captain having reached the end of the line.

'Are you cross with me?' she said when at last they passed again.

'Why, have you done something to make me so?'

Eleanor looked exasperated and turned her attention to her partner for the rest of the dance, purposefully looking away from Gabriel. This made him even angrier than before.

The dance ended and Gabriel led his partner back to her friends and thanked her. He knew he'd been rude; he'd barely noticed the lovely Miss Craig throughout the dance. He would ask her forgiveness when next they met.

He glanced about the room looking for Eleanor, but couldn't see her or Turner for that matter. He took another glass of wine and drank it off. He excused himself and made for the terrace. She wasn't there and neither, he thought mutinously, was Turner. He went back inside and looked in on the refreshment room. No sign of her there either. He could feel himself becoming frustrated. Again he tried to reason with himself. If she were with any other man than him I wouldn't care he thought, but there's something... Anne Barker was standing in front of him. For a second he was thrown. His mother-in-law looked less than amused.

'Gabriel we're leaving now. Eleanor said she didn't want to get back late because of Rose. Are you ready to leave or shall we send the carriage back for you?'

'I'm ready. I was looking for Eleanor but I can't seem to find her.' Gabriel scanned the room.

'She's waiting in the carriage with John. Come, let's be off then shall we, the air outside is chilly. We have thanked our host on your behalf.'

The carriage ride home was conducted in an uncomfortable silence. The sense of tension was palpable between husband and wife. When they arrived at Mulgrave House Gabriel went straight to the nursery where he found a fractious Rose crying bitterly.

'How long has she been like this Ginny?' He took the screaming, red faced baby from her arms.

'She's slept soundly until five minutes ago would you believe. She must have known her mama was on her way and is calling for her feed.'

Eleanor had disrobed down to her shift to feed Rose. She readied herself on the rocking chair by the fire and lifted her arms to take the baby from him. She opened her shift and Rose began to feed. The room fell silent. Eleanor made soft noises to her daughter. She studiously ignored him he noticed.

He stood watching, transfixed. He was awestruck every time he saw the two of them together like this.

His heart melted and the anxieties of the evening evaporated into thin air. Eleanor continued to disregard him.

Suddenly tired, he turned and went to their room where he washed and undressed. The drink he'd taken earlier was making his eyelids droop. He was on the verge of sleep when the bedroom door was flung wide open.

'What the hell was all that about? Your behaviour in front of my family and friends was embarrassing. What the hell came over you?'

Gabriel sat up bleary-eyed at the rude awakening.

'*My* behaviour? What about yours? I hardly saw you all night. You dismissed me quickly enough so you could spend time with that young - '

'Grow up Gabriel, stop acting like a child. First you hung about me like a gaoler, then you stood glowering at me from a distance watching my every move, it was infantile and uncalled for.'

'What do you expect? You clearly preferred someone else's company to mine. Walking alone with him in the garden! What am I supposed to think?'

Their voices were raised and both their faces red with anger. Gabriel leapt out of bed and stood in front of his wife towering above her. She looked up at him, not cowed and not silenced.

'That's just it - you clearly didn't think. I was on the terrace actually, not in the garden, as were lots of other people, my mother included. If you did stop and think you would have seen you were making something out of nothing.' She folded her arms and tilted her chin defiantly. 'So I talked with a charming, handsome man, I danced with him and took some air outside. Credit me with some sense Gabriel. If I intended to bed him I should have been a little more discreet than that. I'm hardly likely to start a liaison with you and my parents looking on.'

She almost spat the words out. Gabriel's normally deep voice also rose in pitch. 'Bed him, liaison, the thought had crossed your mind then! Do you know how it made me feel to watch him fawning over you? Do you expect me to stand by and be cuckolded?'

He shuddered and moved away to stand by the empty fireplace. He placed his hands on the mantel shelf and hung his pounding head; he had drunk far too much too quickly and the effects were now making him feel nauseous.

They hardly ever argued, and when they did it was usually over something trifling and it soon blew over. Gabriel's possessiveness tonight had maddened her he knew and he was sorry now. Sorry, but not apologetic. The image of Turner pawing at his wife was still too hard to bear. She knew he had a jealous streak so why did she taunt him? Then the thought struck him. Surely he trusted her? Of course he did. He was a fool to think she'd betray him.

When they were in company she often danced with other men, but Gabriel never minded as he didn't care for dancing himself. She often flirted, it was her nature. The thought surfaced again. There was something predatory about Captain Turner he couldn't stomach. The fault lay with Turner not his wife. He would apologise to her. He turned and held out his hand.

She ignored it. 'I'm tired and expect to be roused by Rose for another feed shortly.' Eleanor hurled the statement at him. 'I think you should sleep elsewhere then I won't disturb you further.' She climbed into bed and blew out the candles plunging the room into darkness.

Gabriel stood for a moment thinking what to do. If he were at home he would have stormed out and gone to his own room, but he wasn't in his own house. He could hardly go up and down the corridors at this hour looking for a room that was made up. What he dearly wanted was to get back into bed and lie by the love of his life and tell her he was a fool and was sorry. But his pride was injured. She'd dismissed him again.

Bed him, she'd said! That cut deep. He saw in his mind's eye his wife in the arms of another man. *That man.* He saw her face as it looked when she was aroused. He marched out of the bedroom slamming the door behind him. His only option was the chaise in the dressing room next door.

R

The next morning Gabriel woke with a crick in his neck and a sour taste in his mouth. Last night he had abandoned the chaise after a few minutes, he was far too tall to be comfortable on the delicate piece of furniture. He had spent the night on the floor with a small round cushion for a pillow. He felt chilled as he stretched. It was still early, but it being August the sun was up and it looked like it was going to be another hot day. The sky was a periwinkle blue. He pulled on his breeches and stole down the servants' stairs and out of the kitchen door. He sprinted down the sloping cliff side, gaining momentum as he stumbled and tripped on the loose rocks. On the beach he removed his breeches and threw himself into the bitter cold sea. After half an hour's strong swimming in the gentle waves he felt revived.

He knew when he returned to the house he would make it up to Eleanor for his bad behaviour. He hoped she'd forgive him. He would sweet talk her and she'd rebuke him, but then relent as she always did. The making up would be sweet.

He hadn't thought to bring a towel and so sat on a rock staring out to Sandsend Nab to dry off. There was heat in the sun already. He thought about the events of the previous night. What was it that he didn't like about Turner? Could it have been what he had said about Eleanor when they first met? His initial admiring comment about her was just an error of judgement like Tomas had said; a schoolboy error. He should have been flattered that someone besides himself admired his wife. But there was something else, something he couldn't quite put his finger on. He didn't trust the man, but why exactly he couldn't say.

He shook his head to rid his ears of sea water. He thought himself a good judge of character usually, and he judged Turner's character to be dubious. He ruffled his curly hair with his fingers and stared out over the sea that glinted green in the summer sunshine.

He wasn't proud of himself for how he'd behaved. It was as Eleanor had said, childish. The more he was annoyed, the more he drank and the more unreasonable he'd become. He realised he felt more protective of his wife now they had a child. He hummed to himself as reason began to reassert itself. Eleanor could take care of herself he knew. She was a woman with a strong character. He pulled on his breeches and began the climb back up the cliff. He felt ready for his breakfast and ready to apologise for embarrassing her in front of her family and friends.

R

After a disturbed night, Eleanor was at breakfast when a footman announced Captain Turner. She imagined he was here to see her father. Everyone else, with the exception of Gabriel, had finished eating an hour ago. She thought he was still sulking. She'd lingered over breakfast enjoying talking with her father as they used to do before she was married. He had just left the breakfast room.

'Show him in here Sykes and tell Father that Captain Turner is here to see him.'

Captain Turner strode into the room confidently, looking fresh faced and handsome in his uniform.

'Good morning Mrs Reynolds. I'm sorry to disturb you so early, but I need to see your father before I set sail.'

Eleanor was about to reply when her father bustled into the room. 'I am sorry Turner, I meant to send these papers down to the dock last night, but it went clean out of my head.' He handed over the documents. 'You cannot sail without them, it's a good job you noticed the oversight. Please, sit down and have some coffee now you're here.'

Eleanor poured coffee for Turner and was about to pour one for her father when he was called away by the second footman; his wife had need of him it seemed. John Barker bid Turner farewell and wished him a safe trip before leaving them alone.

Although Captain Turner had the documents he required he seemed in no rush to leave, Eleanor noticed.

'I hope you enjoyed yourself last night Mrs Reynolds, I most certainly did.'

Captain Turner's soft Dublin drawl appealed to Eleanor. She noticed again he had a slow, smouldering smile that certainly would appeal to most ladies. He sipped his coffee and looked her straight in the eye and without waiting for a reply he continued: 'As I said last night you dance well, I enjoy dancing when the lady in question doesn't step on my toes.'

Eleanor noticed how his eyes roamed over her blatantly. In the light of day he was still handsome, but far too familiar. Did he forget he was her father's employee and she a married woman?

'Last night was the first chance I've had for quite some time to dance, so yes, it was very enjoyable Captain. It was kind of Mr Eskdale to entertain us.'

'Do you come back to Whitby often? Does your husband's business bring you back?'

Eleanor was unsure what business it was of his where she spent her time, but answered politely enough. 'We don't come back as often as I'd like. I miss my family very much. My sister has twins and I miss seeing them especially as I used to see them every week. They grow so quickly,' she said wistfully. 'It is I who has the business connections here however, not my husband, although he has some dealings with Mr Eskdale. My family were Quakers until a few years ago and it's common practice for women to be treated equally. My grandmama left me shares in her will and that gave me a taste for buying and selling. I have quite a portfolio.' Eleanor folded her napkin in a dismissive gesture which the captain didn't seem to notice.

The Irishman looked surprised at her comment. 'I

remember you telling me of this a little last night, but what puzzles me is... '

Eleanor was tired and wanted to get to the nursery so interrupted him mid-sentence. She knew what he was going to say. 'How do I retain control over my business dealings when I'm a married woman?'

'Well yes, on marriage your assets pass to your husband surely?'

'My husband is a wealthy man in his own right Captain, so he has no need of my assets.'

He smirked cockily. She knew he'd taken the statement the wrong way.

'But still a man can't have too much money or too many assets I'd wager?'

Eleanor bit back a rebuke. 'My husband is a very singular man Captain Turner. He knows me well and knows what makes me happy. I think I said as much last night. He has my best interests at heart at all times, we're partners in every respect. "What's mine is his and what's his is mine", as they say. We're a modern couple I think.'

Annoyingly, the captain smiled languidly at her sharp rejoinder. Perhaps his approach worked on tavern wenches, but she was beginning to find his arrogance off-putting, his questioning bordering on the impertinent.

'You are indeed very modern. However, I think your husband's quite the jealous type is he not? He seemed none too happy when we two were together last night.

Not that I blame him, I should keep you close.'

'Would you indeed! I think you forget yourself Captain. You're mistaken about my husband sir; he trusts me and my judgement in all things.' Eleanor became defensive. She wouldn't have this man criticise her husband, even though he was correct in his assumptions. Eleanor was devoted to Gabriel even when, as now, she was furious with him. 'If you will excuse me Captain, I have to go to my daughter.'

'Would you deny me your company so soon? Won't you sit with me awhile until I finish my coffee? Won't you give me something to remember you by Eleanor? It'll be a long, lonely trip without something to keep me warm.'

Eleanor thought a slap across the face would warm him, but managed to keep her temper in check. She was now firmly of the opinion Captain Turner was truly full of himself. His arrogance in thinking she'd prefer *his* company to that of her daughter's, or her husband's, was spectacular. She was about to deliver a stinging retort when Gabriel, dishevelled and in a loose linen shirt and riding breeches, entered the room.

Gabriel stepped over to his wife's side and placed his hand lightly on her shoulder. He kissed her cheek then took the seat opposite the pair.

'Good morning.' He looked at the other man sitting comfortably by his wife's side. 'Captain Turner, what a surprise to find you here. I thought the tide waited for no man.'

Gabriel picked up a butter knife and began tapping it lazily on the table.

'Papa forgot to send the passports down to the ship last night and Captain Turner has called up for them before he sails on the next tide.'

'How thoughtful of you Captain.' Gabriel's tone was light, amused. 'In your shoes I think I'd have sent an underling to collect them... unless of course I was hoping to catch sight of someone.'

Eleanor scraped her chair back with a look of suppressed anger on her face. Gabriel guessed she was still annoyed with him.

'Goodbye and safe passage Captain Turner.'

Gabriel couldn't fail to notice the icy look she threw his way as she left the room. She was going to need careful handling if the rest of the visit was to pass uneventfully.

Gabriel was secure and unperturbed. His torment from the night before was but a distant irritation, after all, this man was off to the Arctic for two months for God's sake. He was no threat to his marriage. Gabriel felt better now with a clear, sober head. He saw how lucky he was. He appreciated his wife, his daughter and his Whitby family.

'I hope you have everything you need Captain,' Gabriel said amiably.

'I believe I have, thank you.'

The younger man finished his coffee and stood to leave. Gabriel ran his finger lightly down the knife blade.

'You've a long arduous trip ahead, I don't envy you. The sea can be a cruel mistress. You'll need all your wits about you, these days pirates roam the seas wantonly, as I'm sure you're aware.'

'It'll be an adventure. I'm looking forward to the challenge.'

Gabriel lounged back in his chair and looked up at the man. The captain was handsome and, it had to be said, had a certain charm about him. Gabriel could see how women could be attracted to him; he was a buccaneer, an adventurer, a renegade.

'Goodbye Captain Turner, I hope you have a safe and prosperous trip.' He held out his hand, he could afford to be generous. The younger man took it, but looked more than surprised it had been offered.

'Goodbye Mr Reynolds, I'm sure I shall.'

The footman showed him out as Gabriel rang for his breakfast, he was suddenly ravenous.

Gabriel was still eating when his mother-in-law entered the breakfast room and sat opposite him. She nodded to him then rang for more coffee.

When they both had steaming full bowls before them she asked: 'Did you sleep well Gabriel?' She could guess the answer to the question having just left her daughter in the nursery and been apprised of where he had slept.

'I've had better nights.' An embarrassed smile played about his lips.

'I can imagine. I don't want to be the interfering mother-in-law, but would you listen to what I have to say Gabriel?'

'Of course Anne, I value your opinion, but I already know I was in the wrong.'

She tilted her head in acknowledgement then came straight to the point and said: 'I know my daughter. I know her good points and her faults. In the past, as I'm sure you are aware, she has made errors of judgement. Impulsive decisions which sometimes got her into bother. She can be headstrong, wilful, especially if backed into a corner. She has her father's stubborn, tenacious streak.' She poured more coffee. 'Since meeting and marrying you I have seen how she's blossomed and matured under your love and care. I may not see her as often as I would like now she lives from home, but she writes in glowing terms about her marriage and how thankful she is to be a mother.' She sipped her coffee. 'Eleanor has many good points as I'm sure you are aware, one of which is loyalty. If there is one trait my daughter possesses in abundance it is faithfulness. She would never, I would stake my life on it, betray you with another man my dear. She loves you too much. I saw the look on your face last night when she was dancing with Captain Turner, I also saw the look on hers in the carriage on the way home.' She speared him with a flinty look.

'I'm sorry you and John had to witness my crass behaviour last night. I respect you both and want your good opinion. I know all you say is wise and true and I'm ashamed of my conduct. I don't know what came over me. My only excuse is that I love Eleanor so very much and feel so protective of her, and Rose too of course. I feel the responsibility.'

Anne Barker, who had just witnessed her daughter's distress, was not going to let her son-in-law off the hook so lightly. 'Protective or possessive Gabriel? There is a difference. All women want to feel cherished and loved and as a new father, I know you want to do right by your family, but if there's one thing that will push Eleanor away from you, it's if you appear over-bearing. She needs space to grow into her new role. She's anxious to be a good mother, especially after the miscarriage last year. She told me yesterday how large she felt throughout her pregnancy. She's still not the confident young woman I'm used to seeing. After giving birth a woman has to have time to adjust, she still has baby weight and is conscious of it. No doubt last night she was responding to attention because it gave her ego a little boost, nothing more.'

'I've been at pains to assure her she's beautiful to me no matter what size she is.'

'I do hope you worded it better than that Gabriel.' She teased him.

He smiled and rubbed his knuckles down his unshaven chin. 'I had already resolved to make it up to her. I'll go now and speak with her.'

'Why not go and make yourself a little more

presentable first and give her temper time to subside.' Anne took his hand in hers and squeezed it affectionately. 'Women are complicated creatures Gabriel. You're both young and have a happy future together if you can learn to see the other's point of view from time to time. Don't try to restrain her too much, she will only come to resent it. I know this from experience.' She shook her head and smiled. 'John tried to control me early in our marriage and he soon came to regret it.'

'Thank you for being so understanding Anne. Not having a mother myself I appreciate I don't have that wisdom to guide me. I know little of how a woman's mind works, but I'm willing to learn. I hope you'll always feel you can put me on the right road if you see me straying off the path.'

'You have a wife who, under normal circumstances, is perfectly able to do that for you. I speak to you as one who means to help, not lecture. Now off with you and let's hope when I see you next you don't have a black eye. Eleanor has a good right hook... ask Tomas.'

R

Eleanor rocked gently as she fed Rose in the nursery. The baby's eyes were closed and Eleanor marvelled at her daughter's long lashes and tiny hands. She began to doze herself.

150

Ginny gently took Rose from her mother's arms. Eleanor roused herself and stood for a few moments, watching Ginny tapping the tiny bundle's back to wind her. The door opened and Gabriel shaved, groomed and in his riding clothes, approached shamefacedly.

Eleanor still wondered at how handsome he was. Her heart gave a small lurch as she looked at him. She hoped he would always have this effect on her even though she was still infuriated with him.

'I said I'd go over to Lord Mulgrave's to look at his brood mare today.' Gabriel stroked the top of Rose's head with his crooked finger. 'His niece, Miss Craig, told me about her last night and I thought to see the horse before we leave. Would you care to ride over with me?'

Eleanor considered the peace offering.

'I'd intended to ride as it's such a lovely day so I could accompany you I suppose.' She didn't intend to forgive him just yet.

As so often happened, as they rode together they addressed the problem. Gabriel had already apologised and had tried to explain his irrational jealousy by telling Eleanor he trusted her, but not Captain Turner.

'But that makes no sense to me. If you trust I'll rebuff any of Turner's advances then he becomes impotent surely?'

'That's perfectly rational, but last night I didn't feel logical. When you were out of sight I imagined him touching you, trying to kiss you. *That*'s what was making me angry. The thought of him taking liberties made me uneasy.'

'A man suffering an overactive imagination! Is that not what women are usually accused of? Oh Gabriel, you are foolish. I would no sooner take up with Turner, or any other man for that matter, than fly to the moon. You should know that. You were trying to be gallant, but it felt more like possessiveness. Do you understand what I mean?' She looked at Gabriel's puzzled expression.

'I do. Forgive me I was an imbecile.'

'Well let's forget about it now and enjoy the rest of the day. Perhaps I should be jealous of Miss Craig. She's quite beautiful from what I saw of her last night.'

'It's her uncle's dam I'm interested in,' he said ignoring her provocation. 'If we could get some of the bloodstock in our line at the stud we may be onto something.'

After looking around Lord Mulgrave's stable of thoroughbreds and discussing the possibility of using the dam, Eleanor and Gabriel headed back home. The cliff top ride would be a pleasant one in the early August sunshine. The following day was to be their last before returning home to Alnmouth and they wanted to make the most of it.

Eleanor looked at the sea glittering in the midday sun. 'I love Westshore and Alnmouth, but I do miss Whitby. It's been so wonderful to be here.'

Gabriel agreed: 'It has, and when Rose gets older I'd like her to know Whitby and her cousins too, of course.'

During their stay Eleanor had seen her twin nephew and niece almost every day. 'I'll miss Harriet and Edward, they grow so quickly. I've noticed so many changes since our last visit, not just in how they look but in how they act.' She sighed. 'I agree Rose must know her Whitby family. Perhaps the twins could come to stay with us in Alnmouth?'

'Your sister seems very different to you. Has she always been so serious or is it shyness, I never can tell? Does she have a lighter side?' Gabriel tipped his tricorn back from his forehead and wiped the sweat from his brow. The sun was high in the sky and scorched all it touched. They had come into a declivity and were sheltered from the breeze by the cliffs on either side.

'Attie wasn't always so, although she's never been what you might call light-hearted, but since she married Obed... '

'I hope you won't be offended, but I can't like him. He's such a dour man, so straight laced. I don't have much time for religion as you know. I think each to their own so long as they don't rub my nose in it, but he's a zealot. I like to think I'm a tolerant man, but he seems narrow-minded and pious.'

'Gabriel! I never heard you speak so ill of anyone before, well except Captain Turner possibly.' She enjoyed teasing him. 'I agree with you, but Obed does have some good points I believe.' Eleanor laughed when Gabriel pulled a face. 'I know what you mean though. They only come to family parties now, so severe have they become in their Quaker ways. I fear for the twins somewhat. Perhaps they wouldn't let the children come to stay with us? I know Obed thinks as an aunt I'm a bad influence on his children. Did you see the way he looked when I encouraged Harry to have more pudding? It's as if I was leading her into temptation. Attie doesn't seem to notice. She's always been shy, reserved if you like, but now she seems to have no opinions other than her husband's. Mama sometimes jokes she's not her daughter.'

'Perhaps I married the wrong sister.'

'Perhaps you're right. I can't imagine my sister making Obed spectacularly jealous by flirting.'

'Don't joke; it's not a pleasant feeling, jealousy. It worms its way into the gut and makes me feel less of a man somehow. I feel not in control of my emotions.'

'It's unpleasant. Worse than that it's corrosive, it's harmful when it gets out of control, but you have nothing to worry about.'

'You say that now, and I know it to be true, but last night... ' He let the sentence drift off.

'Last night you'd been drinking, much more than you should perhaps. The drink feeds the green-eyed monster do you suppose?'

'Even before the drink, I hated the way he looked at

you, especially the way he pawed you.'

They were back on this subject again. Eleanor thought they'd done with it. She thought to take the heat out of the conversation. 'You know I'm a flirt, you know I like to tease, and it's just harmless fun. You know there's no danger of me doing more than a little playful vamping.' She glanced over at Gabriel's stern face. She pressed her point home. 'It's not only you who can feel jealousy. I've felt the same with you, only I don't reprimand you about it.'

'I'm not telling you off, I'm explaining how I feel.'

Eleanor looked sceptical.

'When have you felt jealous of me? What have I ever done to make you green-eyed?'

'At the risk of swelling your head, I've felt it on more than one occasion. You're a very handsome man my love. I've seen how the ladies admire you when you turn on the charm. You have a way with you. You look as if whoever it is you're talking to is the only person in the room. It can turn a girl's head... and I should know.'

He covered his embarrassment by wiping the sweat from his forehead with his handkerchief. He wasn't a vain man; not like one she could mention.

'How can you be jealous about something I'm not aware of doing? Give me an example of where I've overstepped the mark.'

'Just one? I can name half a dozen.' She smiled at his discomfiture. Gabriel didn't smile back. 'Last time we were at Bendor's, I was sitting with Grace and you were across the room with a group. I didn't know them, they were out-of-towners, but amongst them was a lady whom you singled out for special attention. Even Grace commented.'

'You mean Bella Glade?'

'You remember her? I'll agree sometimes you're naive shall we say, you don't always see you're being manipulated. You're susceptible to flattery I dare say, like most men.'

'Am I being manipulated now?'

Eleanor ignored him. 'You were *extremely* flirtatious, joking, and almost whispering in her ear. She put her hand on your arm more than once. If you noticed at all, you didn't stop her from *pawing* you. I admit my hackles were up for a time.'

'I'm being accused of double standards again I think? I concede the point.'

'I'll make a modern man of you yet.'

'What then brought your hackles down may I ask?'

'I was placated because all at once, while you were talking, you looked over and saw me. You suddenly remembered I existed and smiled at me. It wasn't a "Man alive, I'm in trouble" sort of smile, but an "Oh look there's my wife and I must go and talk to her" and you did. You brought Lady Glade over and introduced us. It was then I saw the poor woman had all her hopes dashed.'

'You've lost me. Dashed, how so?'

'It was clear to me she'd no idea you were a married man or if she had known, she didn't know your wife was in the room. Her face showed her displeasure when we were introduced, though she was quick to hide it. She was definitely giving you the glad-eye up until that point.'

Gabriel looked thoughtful and said: 'The difference with our behaviour as I see it is you consciously flirt, whilst I do not. Granted you flirt a lot with lots of men, young and old.'

'It's just banter, just my way.'

'I know, but here's the rub, I see you banter, flirt whatever you want to call it and when it's with some gouty old friend of your father's, I haven't a jealous bone in my body. I know when you're *vamping* as you name it, there's no threat, no chance you mean what you say. But when it's someone like Turner, there's every chance you might mean what you say. What's more, he might act upon it.'

'*I* would never act upon it. We all look at other men and women from time to time and admire, but I know when I'm well off. Again at the risk of making you big headed, I know you could have any woman you wanted if you did but know it, yet I couldn't hope to have every man.'

'Are you fishing for compliments? You turn heads and you know it.'

'Perhaps, but I'm not beautiful, not like... ' Eleanor wished she hadn't ventured down this path and stopped speaking abruptly.

'Like who?'

'Well, like Caroline I suppose. She has a classic beauty. She was born to be revered.'

Gabriel let out a loud laugh. 'You amaze me; I never thought you compared yourself to other women.'

'Show me a woman who doesn't.'

'I've said it before, I know little of what goes on in a woman's head. Having no female relatives has me at a disadvantage I think. Rest assured Mrs Reynolds, you're the most beautiful woman in the world to me. How can you think yourself not beautiful? You're incomparable.'

'I'm not being falsely modest, I know I'm not a witch,' she chuckled, 'but do you remember when first we met?'

'I do and it was my undoing,' he said in jest.

'You said you thought me a gypsy; gypsies aren't known for their classical beauty. At best with my hair dressed and a touch of artifice I'm attractive, not beautiful.'

Gabriel smiled the smile that had been known to melt her heart.

'Beauty they say is in the eye of the beholder.' He pulled her horse's rein towards him so the two mares were close. 'I behold you and want to hold you,' he leaned in towards her and lifted her hand to his lips, 'now and forever.'

Bryony was getting desperate. There was no respectable work to be had anywhere in Alnmouth. She had been forced to stoop low and take a job as a barmaid in The Schooner Inn on Northumberland Street. She had run out of money as well as options.

It was a rowdy place when the whalers were ashore. The landlord was known to keep an unruly house, so the better elements favoured The Crown and Anchor. It was a low paid position, but came with a small, cramped room up in the rafters. As part of the job she was allowed free meals, but the food was poor and not what she was accustomed to.

'Beggars,' she told herself, 'can't be choosers.'

Sometimes the whalers were generous with their tips. They appreciated a good looking woman after their months at sea and the extra coin helped supplement her meagre wages. Some offered her more if she would take them to her room. She wouldn't lower herself still further, she wasn't that desperate. One man, a pock marked giant of a brute with a livid scar on his cheek had been reluctant to take no for an answer. There had been a scuffle when another sailor had intervened and rescued her from his attentions. At first she'd been grateful, until she realised her rescuer meant to have her for himself. Just in time the landlord's wife had urged her lazy husband to intercede and disaster had been averted.

The money from her captain had finally run out and she'd heard nothing from the last two positions for which she'd applied. She was frustrated and despondent. Wenching in some grubby little tavern was beneath her dignity, but if her captain were to return she wanted him to be able to find her. If she moved on she might lose him. She told herself the job was a stop gap, something to tide her over until he returned or she could get a proper, respectable position.

'Hey Bryony, stop yer day dreamin' and get the men over there a drink. They're fair dyin' er thirst.' She shook herself as she carried the jug of ale over to a table of newly arrived sailors. They made lewd comments and one of the younger ones made a grab for her, but she was too quick for him. Since the last incident she'd learnt to be nimble on her feet.

A naval officer entered the tavern ducking his head to avoid the low beam. For a moment Bryony's heart missed a beat, she thought it was *her* captain but she was mistaken. Her shoulders sank. She had time to notice however, that he was a fine looking man. She turned on the charm and asked him what he would like to drink.

'I'll take rum,' he said moving to sit by the fire. She placed his drink before him and watched him closely as she served the other tables. She moved provocatively, swaying her hips, but it was all to no avail.

She tried another tack. 'Is there anything else I can get you sir?' She smiled beguilingly.

'I think not.' It seemed he was immune to her wiles. Was she losing her touch? 'Tell the landlord his rum is watered and I'll not be paying for it.' With that he pushed his way through the crowded bar and left the tavern.

Bryony picked up the empty glass and considered throwing it after him, but then at the last moment thought better of it; she needed this roof over her head. She was beginning to fear the worst. If she wasn't very much mistaken she would soon be showing signs she was with child and then what was she to do? She was hoping the father would have returned by now, he'd been gone far longer than she'd anticipated. For the time being she thought, I'll just have to lace my stays tighter.

9

Eleanor and Gabriel now home in Alnmouth were standing at the quayside. The Eleanor Rose was due back any day from her maiden voyage and Gabriel was anxious to see her return safe and sound. Not that he had any real fears, the anxiety was borne from the fact it was the first big decision he'd made to have her built since his father died. He knew he was being over cautious, but still it would be a relief when she was safely home.

As they wandered into the town, Eleanor recognised a familiar face. 'Is that not Bryony Swift in the blue dress?' She nodded her head in the direction of Pease Street.

'Yes it is, but she looks different somehow.'

Eleanor noticed too, but unlike Gabriel she could see the reason for the difference in the girl's appearance; her clothes looked shabby and threadbare. Of course when she was at Westshore she wore a uniform so always looked smart. In her own clothes she was not so well turned out. 'It's months since we saw her. She seems to have put on a little weight too. Her face looks the same, but she has a thicker waist I think.' Eleanor wished, somewhat sourly, the maid had been a little fatter when she'd been in her employ. It had been comparing her pregnant self to the lithesome Miss Swift which had led to some of her loss of confidence. Bryony was too far distant to acknowledge and Eleanor was glad, she had never really got on with the girl.

That same evening Wilson Chaffer was expected to supper. He'd asked if he could bring a guest, a lady friend. Eleanor was keen to meet her as she'd heard a lot about Charlotte Lambton.

Wilson had told Gabriel he'd been thwarted in love when a lady he was interested in was sent away as her father didn't want her to marry a lowly doctor. The lady had now returned and as her father had died there was no obstacle to their meeting.

Now that Caroline was back in Alnmouth, her servants had been returned, all with the exception of Mrs Madison who had decided to stay at Westshore much to Eleanor's delight. Ransom, the new butler, was one of two new servants to start work at Westshore. The other, a footman named Carver, was young and eager to please whereas Ransom was older, steadier and more experienced.

Ransom showed the doctor and his lady friend into the drawing room and introductions were made.

'This is Miss Charlotte Lambton.' Wilson presented his lady to Eleanor and then to Gabriel.

'We've met before, but it's some time ago I believe.

You're still friendly with Caroline I expect?' Gabriel asked.

'I am, but I'm just returned to England so haven't seen her since her father's sad demise.'

After the exchange they went out to the terrace where the late evening sun was casting shadows but it was still warm enough to sit outside. Drinks were poured and when everyone was seated Eleanor said: 'I was sorry to hear about your father Miss Lambton. You too have suffered a loss I believe.'

'Thank you, yes. Mr Lambton was my stepfather. We were never close. He married my mother when I was thirteen and I was away at school for most of the time, until I was eighteen in fact. I think he wanted me out of the way.'

'I see. A stepfather can make life difficult for daughters sometimes I understand, but at least he didn't stint on your education. You must be grateful to him for that?'

'I am, but when I finished school and he found out Wilson and I were becoming close, he decided to send me to France to be finished, to separate us you understand. I wasn't so grateful then. I'm sure Wilson has told you the story, but now there's no reason we can't be together, unless we tire of each other of course.'

Gabriel exchanged a look with his wife at this forthright statement. Eleanor had a glint in her eye; she recognised a kindred spirit. Charlotte insisted they call her Lottie and throughout supper the talk flowed easily.

Eleanor found she liked Lottie very much. She was elegantly dressed, even though she was still in mourning; not all women looked well in black, but Lottie Lambton could carry it off. Her raven-black hair seemed to add to her striking appearance. Her dark eyes seemed to dart from one speaker to the other as they chatted. She had a mischievous smile and an infectious laugh. She was tall but fine boned, aristocratic looking. She was lively company and seemed confident and at ease with her new acquaintances. More importantly, Eleanor could see she was intelligent and had a sense of fun.

'Shall we be very modern Lottie and *not* leave the men to their port?'

'Should you mind gentlemen? Or do you want to talk about us?' Lottie asked smiling at Eleanor. Gabriel and Wilson led the ladies back into the drawing room where they continued to talk about current affairs, business and baby Rose.

'Wilson knows I'm not fond of babies. I don't want one of my own if I can help it.'

Gabriel looked scandalised at this outspoken statement, but Eleanor only laughed.

'Good for you Lottie, not all women want to breed.'

'But will you not want a son and heir Wilson? How is that to be reconciled if your relationship advances?'

'Gabriel! That's an impertinent question and none of

our business,' Eleanor remonstrated.

'Forgive me,' Gabriel looked abashed, 'I spoke without thinking - perhaps the ladies should have retired. Forgive me Lottie.'

Lottie assured him there was nothing to forgive.

'We'll cross that bridge when we come to it,' Wilson said not at all put out.

'Did you see The Eleanor Rose came in yesterday Wilson?' Eleanor deftly changed the subject to spare her husband's blushes.

'Back safe and sound from her maiden voyage.' Gabriel looked relieved to be on safer ground. Wilson explained the significance of this statement to Lottie.

'Your father is a shipbuilder Eleanor, is that how you two met?' Lottie looked from one to the other expectantly. Gabriel and Eleanor exchanged glances.

'In a manner of speaking yes.' Eleanor tried not to smile.

Although the couple had met when Gabriel was in Whitby to order his new ship, he had met Eleanor in a tavern where she'd been acting the role of a serving wench; this was in her younger days when she was sometimes reckless and headstrong. She had mellowed somewhat since her marriage.

'We met in unusual circumstances,' Eleanor offered. 'Perhaps when we know each other a little better I'll tell you about it.'

R

Over the next few weeks Eleanor began to see quite a lot of Lottie Lambton. She was younger than Eleanor by a couple of years, but Eleanor liked her breezy personality and her easy, light-hearted nature. She, like Eleanor, could be outspoken but she also had a similar sense of humour and Eleanor was glad to have a new friend with whom she could talk.

One day they had been shopping when again Eleanor saw Bryony Swift. This time she was much closer and coming out of the haberdashers. They were close enough for an exchange.

'Good morning Miss Swift,' Eleanor said trying to sound pleased to meet her. She needn't have bothered. Bryony tilted her chin in the air and breezed on past, snubbing her previous employer.

'Oh how rude!' Lottie said. 'Who is that?'

'She worked for me when my maid Charity had family problems. Her name is Bryony Swift. She was always a strange girl.'

Eleanor told the story of how she came to work at Westshore and how she had left under a cloud.

'Oh dear, she doesn't sound the sort of woman one would want around a new husband. In a few years time when Gabriel is becoming tiresome perhaps you could re-hire her to ease your burden.'

'Lottie you're outrageous. I shall never tire of Gabriel, how could you even suggest it.'

'Wait until you've been in the family way every year for ten years then tell me you aren't tired of him.'

'You're cynical for one so young,' Eleanor said without rancour, 'are you of a mind to marry Wilson, for if you are babies are usually the inevitable result.'

'I told you I don't like babies over much. I do love him, but I'm not keen to enter into marriage just yet. I'm young and I like my own way too much.'

'Does Wilson know how you feel?'

'About marriage? Of course, we've talked about it, he's a very modern man you know. He wants to marry me, but sees how as an heiress, my fortune which isn't so very big, might mean I have other choices.'

'Other choices? Do you mean other men? Men of higher rank or position?'

'Lord no, I told you I love Wilson. He's a sweet man and very clever, we get on, but I'm only just reached my majority and I might want to travel.'

'That sounds exciting. Where should you like to go?'

'I'd like to do the Grand Tour, like a man. I've the funds and the time so I'd thought to take a companion and see the sights.'

'Will Wilson wait for you to return?'

'He says so. In fact he's thinking of going to London to medical school to learn about the brain. He's interested in mental afflictions.'

'I'm envious of your travel plans, it sounds very exciting. Is this a pipe dream or do you mean to do it?'

'I mean to do it of course. Life is for the young and for living.'

'How long would you go for? I should be loath to

lose you now we've become friends.'

They had reached the path where they should part company.

'Perhaps three or four months. I thought to go in the spring, March or April perhaps. Have you travelled much?'

'I've been to Amsterdam, twice. I must tell you about it some time. We didn't have much of a honeymoon as Gabriel had the business to run. We would both like to travel, but now with a baby - speaking of which I need to hurry back or Rose will be screaming the house down.'

The two friends parted, arranging to meet again soon.

After supper Eleanor and Gabriel were sitting by the fire, Gabriel with a brandy and Eleanor drinking a cordial.

'I hope Lottie is good for Wilson, I think she is, but if what you say transpires and she goes traipsing around Europe, poor Wilson will be left alone again. He was quite miserable when he thought he'd lost her.' Gabriel cared about the welfare of his friend Eleanor knew, but she didn't share his point of view.

'*Poor Wilson*! You make him sound like some lovelorn schoolboy. It will be different this time. He'll know she's coming back to him and if he's to study in London, then they will both be fulfilled. They can stay in touch by letter.'

'*If* she comes back. Sometimes I find her flighty.

What if some Italian Lothario takes a shine to her fortune? She may have a roving eye.'

'She might and who can blame her. Every gentleman who's done the Grand Tour I bet had more than a roving eye.' She looked at Gabriel provocatively. 'Do you know there's a book published every year to inform *gentlemen* of where the best brothels are to be found in the major cities of Europe? The journal even goes so far as to inform the reader what services each whore performs.' Eleanor saw the shocked look on her husband's face and sniggered.

'I did know, but I wonder how you do? You amaze me sometimes.'

'There's something else I meant to tell you too, speaking of wanton women. I saw Bryony Swift again today. She must have found employment in Alnmouth somewhere for her to be seen about twice. She does look different, more careworn somehow. Down at heel.'

Eleanor told her husband how the woman had cut her dead.

'It doesn't surprise me. That girl had some chip on her shoulder.'

'She's not a woman's woman if you understand my meaning. She's the sort of woman who needs the attention of men.'

Eleanor thought about how the maid had behaved when Gabriel walked into a room; it was in stark contrast to how she'd acted with Eleanor.

'Speaking of lovelorn men, do you know there's one living under our very roof? I'm guessing that's the reason Jax is taking especial care with his appearance and disappears to Boulmer whenever he can.' Gabriel smiled to himself.

'He has a girl? That's nice, I'm pleased for him. After his ordeal it shows he's feeling better. Do you know who it is?'

'No, I broached the subject, but he blushed scarlet and made some excuse to go back into the tack room. I'll try again sometime. I'm curious who it can be, there are only five or six families living in the hamlet and they're all fisher folk.' He stared into the fire and kicked a log sending sparks flying. 'There's one big house that belongs to a grain merchant, perhaps it's his daughter? If it is Jax will have done well for himself.'

'Gabriel you are foolish.'

'Thank you my love. Foolish, why?'

'Never mind. Just see what Jax has to say.'

No one knew exactly how old Jax was, perhaps he was sixteen or he could be eighteen. The groom didn't even know when to celebrate his birthday. One thing that was obvious, however, was that he'd grown tall and filled out over the past twelve months. He was no longer the scrawny urchin who had turned up at the bay three years ago. His voice was deep and resonant, his shoulders broad and his hair streaked with blonde by the sun. Good food and Lisbet's care had made a man of Jax. A few days after his talk with Eleanor, Gabriel found the opportunity to quiz his stable lad about his love life.

'Jax have you got a moment?' Gabriel didn't want him disappearing again.

'Aye, is summat up?'

'I just wanted to ask how you are. I've not had the chance to talk with you much lately with being away in Whitby and all.'

'Fine as always. The horses are all good, aside from old Ned who has a touch of rheumatics.'

'It's you I'm asking about, not the horses.' They walked to the paddock and Gabriel sat on the low wall crossing his ankles and stretching his long legs out in front of him. He folded his arms. 'Do you have a girl Jax? Is that why you're away to Boulmer whenever you can? You're not in trouble, go where you like when the work is done, you know that.'

Jax sat on the wall and stared at his feet. Gabriel and Jax were usually easy in each other's company, but the lad looked uncomfortable, bashful. Gabriel knew Jax as a friend as well as an employee. Since he rescued Jax from the French captain there had been an unspoken bond, a friendship between them that meant confidences were often shared. Gabriel knew Jax looked up to him, he knew there was nothing Jax wouldn't do for him.

'Well spit it out man, are you courting?'

'Well aye, as a matter of fact A do have ma eye on somebody. Do yer know Mr Crannock, him that lives at the big house in Boulmer?'

'The grain merchant? I do. He has two daughters and a son I believe. Which of the daughters is it? Meg is the eldest; she's a pretty little thing.'

Jax guffawed loudly and looked at Gabriel as if he were mad.

'Not the daughters, one o' them fine ladies wouldn't look at the likes of me. It's his under cook. Sarah's her name. She sneaks me the odd morsel out of a night.' He winked at Gabriel.

'Does she now?' Gabriel sniggered and slapped Jax on the back. No wonder Eleanor had called him foolish. Gabriel realised his mistake. 'And how far is this courtship progressed? How old is she?'

'She's sixteen and we've been walkin' out since the spring. She's an orphan an' all like me.'

'Well I'm glad you're happy, especially so after what happened to you. If you ever need to talk you know where I am. Do you know about the birds and the bees Jax?' Gabriel smiled as the young lad blushed.

'A reckon A know me way around a filly,' Jax joked back.

'Speaking of which, it looks like Sir Percy and I will have the stud farm up and running early next year. I talked of it with you before. It's been on my mind to offer you a job there, though I would be sad to lose you from Westshore. It would be a promotion, more responsibility and more money you understand. We're looking to hire a farm manager and you would be his right hand man. What do you think? You would learn a lot and it would be a step up. Joe can hold the fort here until we find a replacement for you.'

'A should be keen, but A don't read and write well you know that. How much of that would A need to do?'

'A fair bit eventually, but only when you've done the hands on practical training. Mrs Reynolds is keen to teach you. She said when she gave you lessons last year you were a quick learner. If you and this girl, Sarah, are serious it would be a good move for you. You'd be quite a catch for her.'

'What even more'n now?'

'Well give it some thought. It would mean having lessons on top of your work here, then moving to the farm and learning the job from the bottom up. If all goes well it will be a great opportunity for you.'

Jax looked at Gabriel, a smile on his handsome face. 'A don't need to think about it, when can Mrs Reynolds start learnin' me?'

'Teaching Jax. She will teach and you will learn.'

Jax frowned. 'Whatever yer say master,' he said cheekily.

10

Eleanor was looking for Jax for his first lesson. She had tried the stable and was about to go into the tack room in search of him when she saw a bent old woman by the scullery door. It was a gypsy.

'Buy some lucky heather ma dear,' the old crone said, as she held a piece of the purple flower towards her. 'Cross ma palm wi' silver an A'll tell yer future.'

'I already know my future.' Eleanor smiled but not in a dismissive way. The gypsy, wearing a dusty purple dress, edged closer.

'There'll be more to come.' The gypsy looked knowingly at Eleanor's waistline which still showed signs of baby weight. 'Three mebbe four.'

Eleanor slipped her hand into the pocket of her skirt and drew out a sixpence. She handed it to the woman.

Once, in Whitby, Eleanor and her sister had met gypsies on the moors, their brightly painted caravans waiting to go to the yearly fair in the town. They had both had a reading. They'd laughed uproariously on the way home at what she'd told them. It had all been nonsense of course. The gypsy had never mentioned Eleanor would meet a handsome, rich ship owner and remove to Northumberland, nor had she mentioned that Attie would meet and marry a Quaker. Today, Eleanor liked the idea of a little distraction, a little entertainment.

The old woman peered off into the distance dramatically. 'There be one lost and one to replace... ' the woman began. Eleanor swallowed hard thinking of the child she had miscarried and the baby in the crib inside. She kept her face expressionless, neither confirming nor denying the statement.

'There be four more to come, but not all by your labours.' The gypsy took hold of Eleanor's hand and peered at it myopically. The two hands were in stark contrast; one white and smooth, the other gnarled and olive. 'Twins could be... there'll allus be bairns any road... can't not be wi' that man a' yorn.' She smirked lasciviously. 'Tek care of wild vines, red berries can poison. Trustin' doctors isn't allus the way... Careful of that puddin', it might be sweet but the taste can linger.'

Eleanor tried to make sense of the woman's ramblings and screwed up her face quizzically.

She continued: 'There be a horse that's lucky fer yer an' a black dog that's not lucky fer anybody, but don't trust the rover; he means to harm and to separate but not 'til he's had his fun in every port from here to Cornwall.'

Eleanor hoped she'd be able to remember the gypsy's prattle later to tell Gabriel. He would dismiss it as rubbish she was sure.

'The tall dark un hasn't allus bin true, but when the change comes, and come it will, he'll not flinch. If yer want to live long and see yer grandchildren grow up then keep away from strong drink, an' him an 'all.'

Eleanor suppressed a giggle. Perhaps the old woman was a Methodist, but then the gypsy narrowed her eyes and gripped Eleanor's hand tighter.

'There be small coffins, but fer you an' not fer you, o'er in another place from here... Back where yer come from first.'

Eleanor shuddered involuntarily and tried to pull her hand away. She'd heard enough, but the woman's speech rolled on like an encroaching tide.

'The bairn that turns up next will be parted from yer by the sea. The black crows are a sign. Watch out! The sea's a heartless mistress. She's wild an' untameable an' when the tides turn so shall yer luck.'

She dropped Eleanor's hand abruptly, signalling she'd finished. 'May the luck of the Irish be forever at yer door.'

Eleanor's mind was trying to hang onto the speech, but thought this a strange parting shot as the woman had a strong Geordie dialect, not Irish at all. Captain Turner came to mind. She wouldn't mention this last part when she told Gabriel about the reading. She didn't want to rake up old jealousies.

Jax appeared from the tack room and sauntered over to where the gypsy stood. 'Buy some lucky heather - '

Eleanor interrupted her rehearsed speech. 'My stable lad has neither the time nor money for a reading, thank you. Good day to you.'

Jax followed Eleanor into the house to begin the lesson. 'Did she tell yer future, were it good?'

'She told me a load of old rubbish. I don't know why I bothered. Let's get started, I hope you haven't forgotten your letters from last time?'

Later at supper, Eleanor was telling Gabriel the story of the gypsy's visit. 'When I got to the study while Jax was reading I scribbled down what she'd said in case I forgot later. You know what my memory's like of late.' She drew a scrap of folded paper from her pocket and began to read from it.

'Your food will go cold, you don't believe all that twaddle surely?'

'No, but I might keep it to see if any of it makes sense to me at a later date.' She read out the part about the small coffins, her face serious and sad.

'You know I've always thought my brother-in-law's surname odd. Coffin. Obed Coffin. I'm glad it's not my name.'

'Gabriel! Small coffins could mean Harriet and Edward?' She looked perplexed. *'They be fer you an' not fer you.* What does that mean I wonder?'

'I've no idea. Did you smell strong drink on her breath?'

'No I didn't, but she did warn against *a tall dark 'en* taking too much to drink if he wanted to live to see his grandchildren, so go steady with the brandy,' Eleanor warned.

The next evening, Ransom entered the drawing room and handed a note on a tray to his mistress. It was addressed to her husband. Gabriel was away for the next two nights on business in Berwick. She read it hastily.

'O Lord,' she said without thinking. 'I must go to the bay at once. Tell Jax to saddle Jet. Send Ginny to me and tell her to hurry, oh and tell Jax he'll need to come with me.'

The note was from Nathan Pearson, one of her husband's captains. He can't have known Gabriel was away from home. The message said The Whitby Lass had been forced to take safe harbour at Alnmouth on her way back from her mission in the Arctic. She'd been attacked by a French frigate. There were no other details, but Nathan had said he thought Gabriel would want to know as the ship was owned by his father-in-law.

The October night was cool and windy as Eleanor and Jax galloped the few miles to the bay. She located the ship after leaving Jax with the horses. Nathan was waiting at the bottom of the gang plank.

'Gabriel is away from home so I've come in his stead. What's happened? Are there injuries? Is there damage to my father's ship?' Eleanor came straight to the point.

'Seven have been pressed, two are injured, though

not seriously, and Captain Turner's been shot in the arm. The ship has sustained some damage.' Nathan was equally succinct.

'Dear God, where is the captain? Seven pressed! Oh the poor things. What will their families do? Wait until Papa hears.'

Eleanor's thoughts and tongue were racing.

'The captain's in his cabin. I've sent for Dr Chaffer, but have just received a note sayin' he's attendin' elsewhere and will come as soon as he can.'

'Oh no! Lead the way Nathan; I'll see what I can do.'

Just then Captain Turner, his arm in a makeshift sling, came towards her.

'Mrs Reynolds, this is a pleasant surprise. I hadn't expected to see you.' He glared at Nathan.

'My husband is away from home and Captain Pearson sent a message saying The Whitby Lass had been attacked. How is the arm, are you in much pain?'

'I think it's but a flesh wound, no more. It seems to have stopped bleeding at any rate, but I've lost seven of my crew which is more alarming to me than my arm. There's also damage to the hull which needs attention.'

'Tell me the names of the men lost. I'm bound to know them and their families.' Eleanor bit her lip. She was almost in tears. Being Whitby born and bred she had grown up with this sort of tragedy, but it never got any easier. Turner told her the names.

'Not Ethan Thirsk. He and his wife have just had a son, I saw Meg only last month before I came home.'

Eleanor knew it would do no one any good if she broke down. She tried to think what to do next. She saw several sailors whom she knew. She talked with them and assured them she would send provisions and a message to her father to let their families know they were safe. She then turned her attention to the captain.

'Dr Chaffer has been sent for, but he's out on another call. Would you care to come to Westshore Captain Turner? I'm sure you'll be more comfortable there; he can attend to your arm when he's free. There's little to be done for the ship tonight.'

'Thank you Mrs Reynolds, if you're sure it won't be any trouble. I know my arm isn't going to cause me any great bother, indeed I've suffered worse in my time in Spain, but still it won't hurt to receive the attentions and the sympathy of an attractive lady.'

Eleanor scowled at the inappropriate nature of Captain Turner's remark. Under the circumstances she thought him callous, unsympathetic, wanting in respect. He gave instructions to the first mate telling him of the arrangements then followed her ashore.

'Jax, Captain Turner will ride Ned and we can ride together. Jet can easily take both our weights.' Jax helped her mount then sat behind his mistress, but was reluctant to put his arms about her.

'Hold on tight Jax or we'll have another injury.' They set off for Westshore and as there was no moon they took their time.

'We've a good haul aboard so at least that's some consolation.'

'Nothing I know will make up for the pressed men. My father will be most alarmed. At least because you were armed they didn't get more men, though seven is bad enough.'

John Barker, her father, had been a Quaker until he'd been disowned some years ago for deciding to arm his ships. The Quakers of Whitby had long been at the forefront of shipping and were pacifists; therefore he went against the doctrine by taking up arms. He was thrown out of the Friends because of it. He'd been grieved at the decision, but his conscience was clear; he would not risk the lives of his crew. In recent times they had become more and more at risk from pirates. Eleanor knew he would be troubled over the loss of his crew who may never see Whitby and their families again.

'We managed to put some holes in the other ship, and I managed to pick off half a dozen before I got hit myself.'

'I'm sure my father will be grateful.'

'I hope so. No owner wants this trouble brought to his door and this is my first mission for your father. Let's hope it's not my last.'

Eleanor was at pains to assure him her father was a fair and respected owner and was sure he wouldn't hold the incident against him. They were soon home.

'Jax, tell Ivy to make a fire in the blue room and ask her to find bandages and boil water. Then see to the horses please.' She slid from her horse, then led her unexpected guest into the drawing room. 'Should you prefer whisky or brandy Captain?'

'Whisky would be grand.' He waited for her to sit.

'The last time we met did we not dispense with the titles Eleanor?' She saw he meant to risk trading on their last meeting where she had agreed to call him by his Christian name.

'Yes we did, but tonight's events have been quite shocking.' She poured herself a glass of canary; the sweet wine would calm her nerves she hoped. They sat either side of the fire, Padraic in Gabriel's usual seat.

'Are you alright Eleanor? You look a little pale.'

'Yes, thank you. As I said, tonight has been a little unsettling what with men press ganged and you injured and The Whitby Lass damaged.' She looked across at him. His handsome face was smiling at her.

'Have another drink it'll calm you, allow me.' He refilled her glass.

It felt strange sitting opposite this man, who had flirted and flattered her when last they'd met. Unbeknown to him, he'd been the cause of an argument because of Gabriel's irrational jealousy. Was it irrational? The thought suddenly surprised her. Padraic Turner had something that drew her to him like a moth to a dangerous flame. He appealed to her reckless side. Now she was a happily married woman with a baby, her usual bold nature had been naturally subdued, her adventurous streak curtailed, he awakened something in her that had been dormant.

She wondered about the captain. He was a war hero by all accounts. He'd travelled and seen the world. No doubt he'd left a trail of broken hearts in his wake. He was carefree and exciting, charismatic and dangerous. She suspected he was one of those men that couldn't help but flirt, whether the woman was old and double chinned or young and buxom. It was in his Irish blood.

She realised that was where he differed from her husband. They were similar in colouring and both handsome, but her husband was charming rather than a reckless flirt. When she'd first moved to Alnmouth, she'd seen how women looked at Gabriel. Young and old adopted a different stance when he deemed to pay them attention. Behind their fans she saw them hide smiles of pleasure and something else, especially in the case of the younger ladies. Yet Gabriel didn't tease and lead them on as the captain most certainly would. Her husband was respectful and respected. Men trusted their womenfolk in his company. They would not trust Padraic Turner.

'Is your Christian name Gaelic?' Eleanor said suddenly realising he was watching her closely.

'It is. It's the Irish equivalent of your English name Patrick.'

Wilson Chaffer's arrival put an end to their exchange. Eleanor asked him to escort her guest to the blue room which was ready and waiting to accommodate him. Eleanor finished her drink and went to the nursery. Rose was due her feed. She settled herself in the rocking chair as Ginny brought the baby to her.

Eleanor thought of the consequences of tonight's events. She would have to write to her father first thing in the morning. She knew he would be saddened to hear what she had to report.

Dr Chaffer wasn't long with his patient. Before he left, he told Eleanor that as the captain suspected, the arm had suffered nothing more than a surface wound. Unlike Gabriel's gunshot injury, Wilson was unable to sew it back together as the ends were frayed and not straight enough to join. He explained there was a greater risk of infection as the wound would lay open. He left instructions to keep it clean and covered, lest it should turn angry-looking which was a sign that it was infected. If the instructions weren't adhered to, he pointed out, the captain could lose his arm.

ℝ

Early the next morning, Eleanor dressed in a simple gown of madder red, was once again in the nursery attending to Rose's early feed. The door of the room was ajar, Ginny having just left to take the soiled cloths away. Captain Turner stood concealed by the angle of the door and watched. Eleanor's eyes were down and fixed on the child. She was unaware she was being observed.

The captain held his breath as the woman he'd thought about so much over the last seven weeks, unlaced the front of her dress and revealed her breast for the benefit of the hungry baby; how he wished she were unlacing for his benefit and not the brat's.

She began to sing a lullaby as she rocked gently by the fire. Her hair was restrained and tied back in a simple chignon. Her face, free from powder or paint, had a natural blush from the heat of the fire. She looked youthful, almost too young to be nursing her own child.

He wondered, not for the first time, what it would be like to lay with her. He would do his best on this unexpected visit to find out. What luck he thought that the arrogant husband was away from home. Perhaps tonight after supper he would make his move, test the waters so to speak. The thought of her had kept him warm many a night on the icy waters of the Davis Straits.

He hoped she was the type of modern woman who might be up for a little sport. The last time he'd seen her she was dressed in all her finery, and looked every inch the lady, but last night she'd looked so different. She'd arrived unexpectedly on deck, simply dressed and with her lustrous hair blowing free in the breeze. To his mind she'd been even more beguiling than before; it was rare for him to be so smitten with a woman. If you looked at Eleanor Reynolds closely she wasn't a classic beauty, he'd had many more beautiful women in his time, yet she was captivating, intriguing. There was some animalistic charm about her, something special which just begged to be ravished.

He was suddenly startled from his amorous thoughts.

'Can I help you sir?' A young maid had stolen up behind him, her presence muffled by the thick carpet. He turned and gave her one of his most seductive smiles.

'I'm sorry, I was looking for the breakfast room. I see now I turned in the wrong direction.' His explanation seemed to satisfy her. 'I'm Captain Turner and you are?'

'Ginny sir.'

The girl flushed and curtsied covering her confusion.

'Thank you Ginny.' If all else failed this pretty little thing would help pass the time while he waited for the ship to be repaired. The girl gave him directions.

'Mrs Reynolds will join you soon sir, but I'm sure she'll not want you to wait on breakfast. I'll tell her you've gone down.'

Padraic was helping himself to more ham when Eleanor joined him at the breakfast table. How he'd like to see her gracing his table every morning. Every morning after a night of abandoned loving he thought as he pulled back her chair. He allowed himself to imagine her naked and willing.

'Good morning, how is the arm?' Eleanor poured

herself coffee and offered the pot to him. He accepted a refill.

'Ah, it's grand, no bother at all. I'm sure a day or so of rest will see it mended.'

'Rest? I thought you would have much to do today Padraic?'

'I meant resting my arm. I'm about to leave to set in motion the repairs needed to The Whitby Lass. I can walk the short distance; the fresh air will do me good. It's a grand day by the looks of it.'

They chatted amiably whilst Eleanor ate. The captain would have liked to have sat for longer, but knew after a while he could tarry no more. He rose to leave.

'Please send me a note if you can join me for dinner Padraic. I eat about three. Gabriel isn't back until the morrow so otherwise I'll eat alone.'

There's an invitation if ever I heard one he thought. 'Thank you, I'll see if I can tie up all the ends of my business by then. It would be a pleasure to join you Eleanor.'

'I've written to my father to let him know some of what happened, but I'm sure you will be writing a more detailed report on the incident.'

'Of course. As soon as I get on board it will be my first job. As I said last night it's the last thing I want to do, tell an owner his ship's been attacked, but at least we didn't lose all the catch.'

He bent over her hand and kissed it as he rose to leave. Gabriel Reynolds was a lucky man indeed.

Back on board he gave instructions regarding the repairs and wrote the letter he'd been dreading. Early in the afternoon he sent a note to Eleanor. He regretted he would be unable to get away for dinner, he said he would hopefully return in the early evening in time for supper.

He had done all he could do to begin the repairs, but decided it wouldn't do to rush back to this attractive siren. He'd learnt a thing or two about women in his time and knew it didn't always pay to be at a woman's beck and call. A little bit of playing hard to get often reaped rewards he knew. Her call was strong and sweet, but he wouldn't allow her to draw him onto the rocks just yet. Besides, she was his employer's daughter. He knew she had written to her father with her version of events. It wouldn't hurt if she told her dear papa he'd been most assiduous in taking care of his crew and the damage to the ship.

He allowed himself a little fantasy as he lay in his hammock smoking a pipe. The dream was of supping and drinking well at Mr Gabriel Reynolds' expense and then taking the lady of the house in a way that would mean any other man she had after that would be a poor second best. He smirked to himself and looked forward to returning to Westshore and the lovely Eleanor Reynolds.

Then he remembered another temptress who resided in Alnmouth; he was certain she'd be pleased to see him. He leapt from his hammock and pushing his tricorn on his head set off along the quay to where a very pleasing and entertaining chestnut-haired beauty awaited him.

R

Eleanor thought she should make more of an effort with her appearance as she had a guest. Charity was dressing her hair.

'Don't do anything too fancy, I'm only at home remember. Besides I'm tired and can't be bothered to sit for long.'

She had selected a gown of the deepest blue which she knew suited her. She hoped it looked well, but not as if she was trying too hard to impress. She had some sympathy for Padraic's plight, but she hadn't forgotten his arrogance when last they met. She didn't want to encourage him.

'Captain Turner will be here soon and I want to be down before he arrives.'

Charity grinned. 'I should want to look my best for that gentleman. When Ginny caught him on the landing this morning he gave her such a look she said! Fair made her knees go weak. I was the same when I saw him in the yard yesterday. He's quite the buccaneer.'

Eleanor was not so much an old married woman that she couldn't share a gossip with her maid. 'You'd both better watch out, I'll wager he has a girl in every port.

I imagine there are lines of broken hearts he's left in his wake, but still you can dream.'

Eleanor knew what she'd suspected was true; the captain was a flirt and a heart breaker. 'You and Ginny should take care to lock your doors when you retire. You don't want an unexpected visitor.'

'Do we not!' Charity lifted her eyebrow. 'I imagine the captain wouldn't let something like a locked door stand in his way. Ginny was fair taken with him, I never seen her prattle on so much about a man before.'

While her servants dreamed of a liaison, she intended to play like a mouse while the cat was away. Just a little flirting would pass the time and lift her spirits she told herself. No harm could come of it. After all, Gabriel wasn't here to play the jealous husband and what the eye didn't see the heart wouldn't grieve over. She went down to await the arrival of her guest.

Supper had been pleasant. Padraic had a sense of fun and a way of telling a tale which made the mundane become fascinating. He was a typical Irishman and enjoyed "the craic". He explained the term to her: 'It means gossip, fun, enjoyable conversation. I find you "good craic" as we Irish would say.'

Eleanor was enjoying herself. She'd never met anyone quite like Padraic. For the moment she'd forgotten his self-importance which had irked her previously.

The evening was cool and they moved to sit by the

fire. Eleanor had drunk a little wine, but was now sipping a cordial. She knew if she drank more she'd become loose lipped, as Tomas used to say. Padraic had the whisky bottle by his side and was making free with it. The warmth from the fire was now making her pleasantly drowsy.

Padraic was just finishing a tall tale when he leaned towards her and took her hand. He was demonstrating a point from the story which involved one of "the little people", as he called them, holding hands in a particular way. He locked eyes with her as he stroked her palm with his finger. She suspected he'd been waiting all evening to touch her and had invented this fiction to that very end, but still she was amused and not a little flattered.

There was a tap on the door and then Eleanor heard a familiar voice.

'Eleanor, I'm sorry to disturb you so late. I told Ransom I would announce myself.' Caroline flounced in smiling. 'My horse has thrown a shoe - oh I'm sorry I thought you were... Gabriel.'

Because Lottie had long been a friend of Caroline's the three ladies had been meeting often and so now Caroline was Eleanor's friend too. It had helped Caroline and Eleanor to get to know one another better having a mutual female acquaintance.

Eleanor snatched her hand free from Padraic's and noted Caroline's surprised look. She introduced her friend to her guest and explained how he came to be at

Westshore.

'Dear me, how awful, I'm sorry to hear of your travails Captain Turner.'

Eleanor explained her husband's absence.

'Gabriel is in Berwick until tomorrow you say?' Caroline looked pointedly at her. Eleanor felt like a naughty child with her hand caught in the biscuit barrel. She sat up and tried to look alert; the company and the wine had made her mellow, but she now realised how it must look to her new friend. The captain lounged back lazily as if he belonged there not at all concerned about appearances.

Caroline was offered a seat. Eleanor noticed with chagrin that she chose to sit next to Padraic. It was clear she was intrigued by the roguish, good looking Irishman. Captain Turner angled himself towards Caroline and looked approvingly at the new arrival.

'My, if only I'd only known what beautiful women were to be found in Northumberland I should have moved here and not to Yorkshire.' He turned up the light in his dark eyes.

Caroline was cool, but Eleanor could see she was captivated by the captain. Padraic poured Caroline a glass of wine. As she sipped it she looked up at the captain from under her lashes. The three talked and flirted, each of the women vying for the captain's attentions.

Then Eleanor realised the absurdity of the situation and allowed her friend to take centre stage. After all, poor Caroline had had an awful time of it recently. She deserved cheering up, and besides, Padraic looked too self-satisfied, the old arrogance had reasserted itself. No doubt he felt himself more than worthy of the two women's attentions.

After a while, Eleanor arranged for Ned to be saddled to take Caroline home. She realised if Caroline stayed longer she would have to ride home on her loaned horse in the dark. Reluctantly her guest rose to leave.

'Thank you for lending Ned to me Eleanor. I'll get my groom to return him in the morning. Good night Captain Turner it was a pleasure to meet you, I only regret it was in such tragic circumstances.'

She didn't look regretful. Indeed, Eleanor smiled to herself, she looked as though she would be rewarding her horse with a carrot for becoming lame and allowing her to become acquainted with this handsome man.

'If ever I'm pillaged again I hope it will be in Alnmouth so that we can all meet once more.'

As Padraic bowed and kissed Caroline's hand Eleanor wondered at his choice of the word "pillage". The double meaning was not lost on the two young women. Neither blushed, but both tried to conceal their amusement.

After Caroline had left they settled down to resume their chat. Padraic refilled his empty glass.

'Miss Hodgeson is a very attractive lady, I expect

she has suitors lining up for her attentions.'

'Inevitably,' Eleanor said smiling. 'Caroline and I have become firm friends despite the fact she was once engaged to Gabriel; they were childhood sweethearts.' Eleanor watched with amusement as Padraic's eyebrows shot up.

The captain smiled broadly. 'Is that a fact? Your husband has a fine eye if you don't mind me saying so.'

Eleanor wasn't sure if she did. 'Miss Hodgeson, Caroline, has recently lost her father. She's been abroad for her health.'

'She looked well enough to me, the change possibly did her good. She lives nearby?'

'She does. This house is Westshore and Caroline's is Eastshore, it's a couple of miles distant. Gabriel's father and her father, Thomas, were very close, but the match was made when they were young; they both outgrew the attachment.'

'Luckily for you Eleanor,' he said smirking. 'Does Caroline have brothers and sisters to console her now her father has gone?'

Eleanor couldn't decide if Padraic was showing too much interest in this woman he'd barely met, or whether he was just being respectful. Was she rankled because he'd changed his focus of attention from her to Caroline? On reflection she thought not.

'She hasn't any close family, just an aunt in Scarborough and some cousins too I think. One cousin, I think lives not far from Whitby. I seem to think he was a military man.'

'There aren't a lot of us about anymore. I still think of myself as a soldier. Soon there will be another war and we shall all re-enlist I hope.' He talked for some time of the campaigns he'd been involved in and the wounds he had suffered.

Eleanor, never one for the finer points of military campaigns, grew weary and a little bored.

'It's getting late and I expect my daughter will wake me at some ungodly hour wanting to be fed. If you'll excuse me, I'll wish you a good night Padraic.' She got to her feet and shivered. She noticed for the first time it had turned chilly.

'Last night the good doctor suggested my dressing should be changed each day so the wound didn't become infected. Could you please arrange for some hot water and clean bandages to be brought to my room and I'll endeavour to change it.'

'Oh dear! What a terrible hostess I am, I'd quite forgotten his instructions.'

Eleanor felt genuine remorse at her neglect. Had Wilson not said Padraic could lose his arm if it went bad? She summoned Ivy and ordered what was needed to be taken to the blue room.

'I'll change the dressing for you, you can't do it one handed. You won't be able to secure the bandage.'

'Are you sure Eleanor? Would it not seem improper? What would the servants think if they saw you coming to my room?'

She knew he didn't care what the servants thought. She imagined he was trying to show a little pretence wouldn't go amiss.

'My servants know better than to gossip, and anyway they know you can't fend for yourself. I think if I asked Ivy to help you she'd faint. Gabriel only has to glance in her direction for her to blush crimson.'

Eleanor gave the captain a few minutes, then knocked on the door and entered. She saw Padraic sitting up on the bed, his legs outstretched. He'd removed his shirt and sat bare-chested. She noticed the flat stomach and the well muscled torso. Unlike her husband, his chest was smooth and hairless. She acknowledged he had a good physique, but preferred Gabriel's equally muscled, but hairy chest. She loved to run her fingers through the dark mass.

She perched on the edge of the bed and began to unwind the bandage from Padraic's strong arm. She knew he was watching her. She took the sponge and washed the wound. It didn't appear red and angry looking so she presumed it wasn't infected.

'Does it hurt?'

'It just stings a bit, it's bearable. You're very gentle.'

'I've had good practice.' She dried the wound and before she could stop herself began to tell him the story of how Gabriel came to get shot at by Caroline. She had indeed become loose lipped.

'What! His ex fiancée tried to kill him? The demure

young lady I just met?'

'Well, we're not sure she wanted to kill him, but she meant to do him some harm at the very least. She was grieving, it wasn't her fault.'

She began to re-dress the arm, winding the bandage and securing it with a knot.

'I never would've believed it. Does your husband rouse such passion in all the ladies hereabouts?'

'I expect so,' Eleanor said. 'But Caroline was suffering grief as I said, she meant him no harm. All is forgiven now. He bears her no grudge I can assure you.'

Eleanor felt the need to correct the balance. She felt she'd been disloyal to her new friend.

'There, all done.' She remained sitting on the edge of the bed.

'Thank you Eleanor, you're a good nurse.' He looked up and smiled at her. She saw how easy it would be to succumb to him. 'The least I can do is thank you for your attentions.' He leaned towards her and lifting her chin with his forefinger thanked her with a tantalising kiss. It was a mere fleeting, brushing of the lips. It was soft and sensuous, but could have been passed off as affectionate if she were to accuse him of taking liberties.

Eleanor swallowed hard. She remembered a time when she had found herself in a strange man's room at The Fleece Inn in Whitby before she was married. She had been reckless and had risen to a challenge. She'd got herself into a tricky situation and it was only because the man in question was honourable that she'd escaped with her honour intact; the man had been her future husband. She knew given the slightest encouragement this man wouldn't act so gallantly.

She stood, picked up the bowl of water and held it in front of her like a shield. She smiled innocently. 'I've all the thanks I need knowing tomorrow you'll be well enough to resume your journey and will be able to reassure my father you did all you could in such tragic circumstances to secure the safety of his crew and cargo. Good night Padraic, sleep well.'

She slipped quietly out of the room.

ℛ

Was that a smirk he saw playing on Eleanor's pretty lips? He knew he'd been out-manoeuvred this time, but that meant he wanted the woman all the more. She'd merely whetted his appetite. He lay back on the bed contemplating his next move like a soldier planning his next campaign.

He couldn't have arranged it better when she'd agreed to come to attend him in full sight of her servants. She'd given herself the excuse she needed to come to him. All servants gossiped in his experience, but if they did in their master's hearing Eleanor had given herself the perfect alibi. But she hadn't been powerless to resist as he'd expected, much to his disappointment.

She was indeed a tease and needed seducing he was certain of it. He'd heard gossip when he was in Whitby, rumours that before she was married she'd been unconventional, a little wayward. He liked the idea she was headstrong and wilful. It boded well for future meetings. A woman like her would surely not be satisfied with just one man's attention. She was no light woman, but she could have her head turned for the right inducements he was sure. He was content to wait to be her lover - for now.

Who knew what might develop when she'd tasted illicit love? The world was a big place. If she decided to run away with him there were a thousand places they could hide and never be found. It would be a singular pleasure to take her from the odious Gabriel Reynolds. In fact it would add a certain frisson to the affair knowing he'd taken the thing the man prized above all else. He'd seen the jealousy, the sense of ownership and entitlement, that night in Whitby.

Eleanor Reynolds was the type of woman who was quick to arousal in his experience. He could of course have pressed her harder, teased her like she'd teased him. There was no doubt she wanted him as much as he wanted her. If it had been any other woman he'd have taken her. They both wanted it, he knew it. They were consenting adults and if her husband was stupid enough to leave her alone what did he expect? A woman like Eleanor would enjoy the sport. She didn't strike him as the sort to stick to her wedding vows when there was fun to be had.

It was a damn shame her father was his employer. That was all that was holding him back if truth be told. He couldn't risk John Barker's wrath. He needed this captaincy. Had he misread the signals and she'd told her father he'd tried to have his way with her it wouldn't bode well, not on top of the bad luck he'd had with The Whitby Lass.

He lay staring at the ceiling. Other opportunities would turn up. She would come willingly next time he knew. Chances had a strange way of turning up when he least expected them. It was the luck of the Irish. Please God he wouldn't have to wait too long. It was most unlike him, but he was strangely infatuated with this flame-haired beauty.

ℛ

It wanted twenty minutes to four and Eleanor yawned as she fed Rose. It was still dark. She was in her usual place by the fire which was all but out. She smiled to herself as she thought of the handsome captain laying frustrated down the hall from the nursery. She recalled the look on his face as she'd slid out of his grasp and out of the room.

He was amusing, fine-looking and keen to take a tumble with her that much was certain. All she had to do was steal into his room, pull back the sheets and…

She laughed out loud causing Rose to hiccup and dribble milk down her chin. She mopped up the milk and rubbed Rose's back to wind her.

She'd enjoyed the fiction, for that's all it was. It had been a pleasant interlude while Gabriel was away. She'd basked in the light of the captain's flirtatious attention, but she saw Captain Turner for what he was; an unprincipled womaniser. Yes he was good company and had the knack of making a woman feel special, but he also had a high opinion of himself. His arrogance, she realised, was the one thing she found off-putting. She knew there would be others who would succumb to his shenanigans. He would seduce a grandmother if she'd let him.

Eleanor had enjoyed deflating the ego of this philanderer, but she would never be another notch on his bedpost. Eleanor knew she'd never cheat on her husband, but she'd enjoyed being admired. Not that Gabriel didn't pay her enough attention, he did, but this was different. It was a little trip down memory lane, back to a time when she was young and free and not a little reckless.

She would tell Gabriel what had happened, after all they had no secrets from one another now. She hoped he would see it for what it was, just harmless fun.

She lay Rose in her crib and looked on as she slept peacefully, then kissed her plump cheek and padded barefoot to her own room. She stopped and listened. Was that a noise? It was the almost inaudible sound of a door down the landing being closed stealthily.

Once in her room she locked her door. She hoped the girls had remembered to lock theirs too. She was certain Padraic was a sleep walker, or that would be his excuse if he was discovered wandering about at the dead of night. Before she knew it Captain Padraic Turner would be gone, gone on the next tide to Whitby leaving just a pleasant memory behind him. She yawned as she climbed into bed. She wished Gabriel was home. The huge bed felt empty without him.

ℛ

Bryony Swift rolled onto her naked back. She was pleased her captain had returned. Her joy at his arrival was tempered when she'd seen his injury. She'd been alarmed at first when he'd turned up at The Schooner wearing a sling on his arm, but he'd assured her it was nothing but a scratch. He couldn't stay long this time he'd said, as he was on the morning tide, this being an unscheduled stop due to an incident with his ship.

Still, she was pleased he'd found her and not just because he was a good lover. Although she now knew for certain she was going to have his baby she decided to wait to tell him. She was still hardly showing so she needn't rush at him. She knew his temperament and feared he'd abandon her if she failed to handle the situation sensitively. He was the type to feel trapped if she wasn't much mistaken. He would be gone again

203

sooner than usual so she wouldn't have time enough to work on him on this stopover. She would wait and plan and bide her time.

He told her about his recent escapade and how he'd rescued his ship single-handed from the clutches of French pirates. He bragged about his prowess and how he'd managed to bring the ship into safe harbour. He told her it was the thought of seeing her beautiful face again which had made him reckless, but ultimately triumphant.

Bryony listened enthralled at his buccaneering. Although she didn't doubt his bravery she did suspect the story was embellished for her benefit, but still he was exciting.

'Why don't I come with you to Whitby? We could enjoy ourselves for longer then.' The words burst from her unchecked. She hadn't meant to sound so eager. He stroked her hair absentmindedly. He was on the edge of sleep. 'I can't seem to find suitable work here, but perhaps I'd be luckier in Whitby. It's a bigger place is it not?' She was cross with herself for appearing needy. She knew this was the one way to lose him, but her condition was making her anxious, reckless.

After a long moment he roused himself. 'I'm not sure I'll be staying in Whitby after this latest upset. My employer will blame me for the incident with the French frigate I imagine and I may be given the old heave-ho. I'll send for you when I know what's happening. Or I might come back for you if I'm let go. Don't worry my beauty I know where to find you, didn't I find you soon enough today?' He kissed her fingers idly and smiled his most dazzling smile which made her weak at the knees.

'I know you, you're a rascal and mean to keep me here to your own ends, but as you can see from my present circumstances I'm in dire straits. Who would ever have thought I'd be forced to stoop so low as to take work in a tavern! I'm ashamed. I deserve better than this surely?'

'Worry not my sweetheart, I've money to spare. As you say this place is beneath you. I don't want to think of that rabble downstairs chasing after my lovely colleen when I'm away. Tomorrow I'll be gone and you can tell the landlord where he can put his lousy job.' He leaned over the edge of the bed and handed her a pouch of coins. It felt pleasantly heavy. She was roused as he reached for her and she forgot about her troubles for the time being.

'Now show me how grateful you are.' He pulled her towards him.

Bryony smiled with happiness. She'd known he wouldn't leave her in this cesspit. She was placated. When she was with him all her fears disappeared in a puff of smoke, she was content, satisfied. As he made love to her again she knew he wouldn't forsake her. She just had to be patient a little while longer.

Padraic Turner had been lucky at the card tables. Again. It seemed he could do no wrong on this trip, which was just as well if he was going to be out of work soon. He'd played the gaming tables since he was a boy back in Dublin when he'd watched his father cheat the regulars at the Shamrock Inn out of their earnings. He'd a quick eye and soon picked up the sleight of hand moves that helped him palm cards niftily. Cheating at cards had kept him afloat between jobs for as long as he could remember.

Back on board The Whitby Lass his thoughts returned to Bryony. He'd thought her different to all the other women in his life, but it seemed he was wrong. He was disappointed. The last thing he wanted was another woman in his adopted town. He had Milly to service his needs in Whitby and she was proving to be entertaining enough.

Bryony was a lovely looking woman and her slender figure was filling out nicely. She now had delicious curves where before she was all angles. He liked a woman with a bit of meat on the bone, but then if she was going to become demanding, frankly he could do without the hassle. There were always more ports and more women waiting for a handsome fella such as himself.

Time, he thought, to drop anchor and sail on to new horizons. Once he'd bedded Eleanor Reynolds that is.

And besides, another more lucrative woman was on his mind; this other woman, this blonde beauty would surely reap rewards.

Miss Caroline Hodgeson was stunning, an heiress and best of all was without a father or brother to disapprove of him. He would do his utmost to further this alliance. She was surely one of the most beautiful women he'd ever seen *and* she was rich. He'd have to move fast if he was to secure her. An heiress with her looks wouldn't be on the marriage market for long.

When Eleanor had told him the heiress had once been engaged to Gabriel Reynolds he could hardly believe it. Did everything fall into that man's lap? But why would he give up Caroline Hodgeson's fortune he ruminated? It was surely beyond reason to give up both beauty and riches. Eleanor was an attractive lady, but in the cold light of day even Padraic knew she wasn't so unconventional as to leave her husband and child for a life with an Irish rover. It had irked him to admit it, until that is he saw another opportunity had opened up. He knew a dalliance was the best he could hope for with Eleanor, but what a dalliance it would be. Caroline however, was a different proposition altogether. She was single, landed and he could tell from experience, she liked the look of him. Her sweet face floated into his head.

He half dozed and mused on the situation. Perhaps Eleanor had brought the bigger dowry? Who knows? All he knew was that he'd have to move quickly where the heiress was concerned. All he had to do now was find a way to meet her again. Eastshore, that's where she lived, perhaps he'd take a stroll and see what type of property and land she had. It was about time he had a more permanent place to lay his head.

A lot now depended on whether John Barker was the fair man his daughter thought he was. If the man gave him the push he'd soon be looking for work - again. But then there was always the trade to fall back on. He could always do a run or two to France, smuggling was always profitable. Yet he was tiring of this uncertain life. Perhaps it was time to try his luck away from the card table and free trading, attempt a life less precarious. Somehow he knew everything would work out just the way he wanted. After all didn't he have the luck of the Irish?

R

Eleanor had always been an early riser, but since Rose's birth her sleeping patterns had become erratic. The morning after Caroline had borrowed Ned, Eleanor was up and dressed, but hadn't broken her fast when a visitor was announced.

'At this hour,' she said crossly startling Ivy.

'It wants forty five minutes to eleven ma'am.'

'I suppose you've been up since day break; so have I in reality. I imagine it feels late in the day to you.' Ivy scurried off like a mouse back to her hole.

When Eleanor arrived in the breakfast room Caroline was waiting. 'I'm sorry to keep you Caroline, I've not broken my fast yet. Rose is very demanding. Her Ladyship's needs have to be met every four hours. She's like clockwork.'

'You look tired, it can't be easy, but why do you not employ a wet nurse?'

Eleanor explained her reasons. Caroline raised a shapely eyebrow. Eleanor liked Caroline, but realised she was quite conservative in her views. She noted how her friend changed the subject to a more respectable one.

'I've returned Ned, thank you for the loan.'

'I'm only glad I could be of assistance.' Eleanor began to eat. She was ravenous.

Caroline leaned forward and in a low voice murmured: 'Where is your house guest?'

'I expect he breakfasted at the usual hour. I haven't seen him this morning. He'll have sailed by now I should think.'

She noted the wistful look on Caroline's beautiful face as she loaded her plate with ham. She also noticed how Caroline looked fresh as a daisy and well rested. She envied her.

'He's very easy on the eye,' Caroline smiled, 'what a pity he's gone. He's mighty handsome and amusing, and his accent I found most engaging.'

'Is that a twinkle in your eye Miss Hodgeson? I agree he's rather handsome in a rakish sort of way.

However, I think him the type to have a girl in every port. The lady who pins him down, if such a one exists, will have her hands full. He's the type who's best admired from afar I think. He's a heartbreaker if ever I saw one.' They giggled like schoolgirls, but Caroline wasn't so easily deflected.

'He has a military background he said. My cousin, Arthur, the one who lives near Whitby, also served in Spain. I wonder if they knew each other. I expect not.'

'And now he works for my father, but I got the impression he misses the heat of battle and would prefer to be soldiering still. He seems a man of action. He'd some tall tales to tell of his time fighting in Spain.'

'I bet he looks dashing in his scarlet uniform,' Caroline ventured.

The two women had never been on such easy terms before. Eleanor was pleased Caroline felt relaxed enough to share confidences.

'I do believe you're quite taken with Captain Turner,' Eleanor said teasingly.

'For all the good it will do me,' she replied longingly. 'Why is it all the interesting men live elsewhere? At every gathering in Alnmouth there are the same men; old, gouty or bald.'

'I have a feeling we haven't seen the last of the intriguing Captain Turner. I think he's the type to turn up when least expected.'

'I can but hope. At this rate I shall die an old maid.'

'I hardly think that likely. You can have your pick surely.'

'Oh yes how true. My pick of the old, the gouty and the bald.' Caroline rose to leave. 'I'll leave you to your baby duties. You must already be behind hand in your tasks.'

'I always am it seems since Rose arrived. If you can wait I can ride into Alnmouth with you, I have an errand to run.'

'I'm sorry Eleanor I must be off. I have... an appointment with my, erm, dressmaker. I'll see myself out.'

ℛ

On her way home Caroline just happened to be riding by the bay when she noticed The Whitby Lass was still moored. What luck. She walked purposefully along the quayside to where one of her own ships was berthed. Another stroke of good fortune was Captain Turner's ship was berthed next to her own.

She heard an Irish voice call out: 'Ahoy there.'

She looked up to see the very man she had hoped to see. When Eleanor had said he intended to catch the morning tide she thought she would have missed him. She was pleased to see she had not. He came down the gang plank towards her at speed and grinned broadly.

'Good day Miss Hodgeson.' He kissed her hand as he bowed low. 'I'd not thought to have the pleasure to

211

see you again so soon. The repairs I'd hoped to be finished have taken longer than expected and I've missed the tide. I don't think I'll be able to catch the evening tide either, so I'll be ashore another night by the looks of it.'

'I'm sorry to hear you're inconvenienced sir. What a pity. I'm just on my way to see the captain of my ship, the Alnmouth Girl. She was my father's pride and joy and now she is mine.'

'You, I take it, are the girl the ship's named after?' When he smiled his eyes twinkled and his handsome face lit up the grey morning. 'Mrs Reynolds told me the sad news of your father's death. May I offer you my condolences? You must feel it most keenly.' His countenance suddenly turned sombre. He had an animated face.

'Thank you. As you can see I'm out of mourning now, but I still miss him terribly.' She hoped she wouldn't shed a tear but if she did it would be comforting to weep on the captain's broad shoulder.

'I can imagine. You have no near relatives to help you I understand. It's a sad situation.'

'My nearest relatives are in Scarborough, although my cousin Arthur who served in Spain lives with his wife near Whitby.'

'Arthur Hodgeson... ' Captain Turner furrowed his brow trying to think whether he knew the man. 'No, I don't recall the name.'

'Arthur Ansley. He's a relative on my mother's side

of the family.

'Captain Ansley! Well would you believe it? I do know him. We served together. He's well now I hope? He was shot and sent home before me and we lost touch, I'm pleased to hear about my old friend and comrade at arms.'

'Sadly he lost his lower arm which was worrying for everyone. He's always been such an active man, a brave man, but I think he's adjusted remarkably well. Other than that he's in good health. I saw him last Christmas as a matter of fact.'

'It's a small world as they say. I'm glad to hear he made a good recovery. He was a courageous soldier and a good friend.'

The captain then spent some little time telling her about a skirmish they'd both been involved in where he'd helped save her cousin's life. Caroline was secretly pleased they had this family connection as it meant she could further their acquaintance. A sense of propriety could be maintained if she dared ask him to sup. She was never forward, it wasn't in her nature, but when might she see this attractive man again? She didn't want this opportunity to slip through her fingers. A picture of old, gouty, bald men flashed before her. She screwed up all her courage and took a deep breath. 'If you are to be ashore this evening Captain I could give you supper. I could not of course ask you to stay. It would not be seemly.'

'That would be grand Miss Hodgeson, you're too

kind. I shall look forward to it.'

After giving him directions to Eastshore, Caroline parted from the captain. Just in time she remembered she was supposed to be on some fictitious errand to the Alnmouth Girl. She went aboard and was greeted by her captain. He was more than a little surprised to see her as she had never before graced him with her presence. She made some excuse and left quickly to ready herself for her charming, handsome visitor.

11

Later that day Gabriel arrived home and found his wife and daughter in the summer house. After greeting and kissing them both he sat down and yawned. Then he saw how tired his wife looked and felt guilty. She'd never had dark circles under her eyes before. He was tired from the long ride home, but at least he'd had a full night's sleep. He wished she'd relent and hire a wet nurse.

He'd come from the north so hadn't passed through Alnmouth; he knew nothing of the fate of The Whitby Lass and her crew. Eleanor told him what had happened. Gabriel listened and asked questions as the story unfolded.

At last he said: 'Your father will be much put out, it's a growing problem for all of us.' He shook his head in dismay. 'Those poor families, their loved ones and their livelihoods lost.'

'It's so unfair, all the men want to do is make an honest living but it seems any ship is fair game these days. Their poor wives and children; I don't envy Papa having to break the news to them.'

They sat together each with their own thoughts until

Gabriel suddenly said: 'So you had a house guest? Is there anything you want to disclose? Should I be worried?'

'You should always worry about me Gabriel. You know how impulsive I can be.'

She nudged him playfully then told him everything that had happened... well presumably everything? As she included the part where she'd gone to Turner's room to re-dress the wound he knew she was telling him all there was to know. He trusted her even though he didn't trust him.

Then she told him how the man had kissed her.

'He did what? I knew he was a blackguard, did I not say so? In my own house he tried to seduce you when we had given him shelter. I'll have him horse whipped.' He was furious.

'Lord Gabriel, I wouldn't have told you had I known you would turn green again. Nothing happened; it was the merest brushing of lips.'

Gabriel snatched a breath and considered what she'd told him. If ever he saw the rake again he'd let him know what he thought of him, let him know he knew what he'd been about. He'd a good mind to set off for Whitby this very night. He tried to calm his agitation. He knew if he lost his temper Eleanor wouldn't listen to him and he needed her to see the error of her ways, see the danger she'd put herself in.

He turned a calmer face to his wife. He knew she would call him patronising if he didn't phrase this speech correctly. 'That's all very well Eleanor, but you were alone with him, in his room. Had he pressed his case would you have been able to fight him off? I think not.'

He saw the look on her face. It was one of defiance tinged with the thought that perhaps, just maybe, he could be right. He took both her hands in his. 'At the very least you should have taken Charity or even Ivy into his room if you had to dress the wound yourself. Lord knows Ivy standing guard would have cooled his ardour.' He tried to make her smile. He could tell she realised she'd been too trusting, though she'd ever admit it of course.

'Before you accuse me of jealousy again, I'm not speaking in anger, but out of concern for your safety. You put yourself at risk Eleanor, do you not see that? It doesn't bear thinking about what the devil might have taken without a moment's thought.' He shuddered and watched as she took a deep breath.

'I never think people may take advantage. To my way of thinking it's just a game. I once accused you of being naive, but perhaps it's the other way about and I'm the gullible one.'

'I don't mean to appear condescending my love, and it's over now and you weren't compromised thank God, but have a care in future. I never thought I'd say this, but perhaps he's not the rake I had him down for. At least he didn't force himself on you. He could so easily have overpowered you.'

They sat in silence for a long while. Gabriel saw the look on his wife's face and knew she agreed with him.

'I always think I can take care of myself, but now I'm a mother perhaps I should think twice.'

'Don't ever change my love, but try to curb your impetuous nature just a little. Man alive I sound like your father! I don't mean to nag, but you still have the power to shock me it seems.'

'Shock or surprise?' She gave him a wry smile. 'We've had this debate before. I'll always be impetuous, but I'll think twice in future, I promise.'

Then Eleanor surprised him again by telling him about Caroline's visit and about her apparent infatuation with Turner.

'Are all women under his spell?'

'She was quite taken with him. She returned Ned herself. I think she was hoping to catch a glimpse of him again this morning otherwise she could have sent her groom over with Ned.'

'Caroline has better taste in men surely?'

Eleanor smiled mischievously. 'Are you sure? After all she was once engaged to you remember.'

'As I said, she has good taste in men.' He smiled at his wife. 'Turner however, is a "wrong un" as Abner used to say. It's as well she'll not see him again. I'd feel just as uneasy if he were sniffing about Eastshore.'

'Sniffing about! You make him sound like a dog.'

'Exactly! Like a rabid dog.'

'I know how you feel,' Eleanor chuckled at his description then looked serious, 'but I like him. I believe most women would be attracted to his handsome good looks and fine physique, and he could charm the bees from the honey pot, but I've a bad feeling about him now. The gypsy said, nothing sensible, I'm being silly. It's just a feeling of, oh I don't know. He feels... dangerous. That's part of his attraction too I suppose but with hindsight you're right. I shouldn't have been in his room alone.'

'Yet you were alone with him all evening. At supper you were unchaperoned, but let's not start that again. I only wish I'd been here.'

'I locked my bedroom door and told Charity and Ginny to lock theirs too. I didn't trust him not to sleep walk.'

Gabriel looked puzzled. 'So you did have some sense of self-preservation. You amaze me.'

He was keen not to start lecturing again so instead made a flippant remark. 'He would have met his match with you my love. Since your encounter with the gypsy you've turned into a soothsayer. What have you seen in your crystal ball?'

She narrowed her eyes at him. 'It's nothing, just a feeling that comes over me like when a cloud passes in front of the sun. When he's in front of me I don't feel it, but it's like he's cast a spell, it's when I think about him later that I feel uneasy, on edge.'

'In that case I command you to stop thinking about

him. Now go and have a lie down for an hour, you look done in. When was the last time you had a full night's sleep? Are you sure you won't hire a wet nurse my love?'

'I am sure, but I'll go and have a nap, I'm exhausted. Not only did I have a broken sleep feeding Miss Greedy-guts, but when I did get to bed I lay awake for ages thinking about those poor press ganged men. However will their families cope?'

'Would you like me to send for Wilson to give you something to help you sleep?'

'Thank you but no. I'll feel better after a nap, I'm sure I'll not need rocking.'

When Eleanor had gone inside Gabriel sat and stared out to sea. The tide was coming in, rushing up the beach like a trespasser intruding on his land. The sea would come right up to the garden, to the very edge. If it hadn't been for the defences they'd put in, the garden would be washed away. The sea would encroach, make inroads on his land then retreat just as urgently. High tides could destroy everything in their path, defences were essential.

He'd thought that with marriage all his troubles would be over. Now he had a wife and baby to protect and he felt the responsibility of it weighing heavily upon him. He knew Eleanor had been impulsive and headstrong before they married. He'd not realised she was still so rash, so precipitate. She wasn't a foolish woman, but she was perhaps more susceptible than he'd imagined. She always acted so capably, so mature, yet he realised she was still young. Despite having more life experience than many women, she had more to learn about life and about men in particular it seemed. He vowed to take better care of her. He realised, and knew Eleanor realised it too, that she'd had a narrow escape. An intruder had sought to invade, but thankfully this time the interloper had retreated like the tide. Gabriel watched as the waves lapped against the defences and thanked his lucky stars.

Later after supper they were both tired. It was Eleanor's turn to yawn.

'I think I'll have an early night.' Gabriel's eyes lit up, but she'd already left the room and didn't see the glint in his eye. He was glad to be home. He'd missed her. By the time he arrived in the bedroom, Charity was leaving having readied her mistress for bed. Eleanor looked her husband up and down. Was that a glint in her eye too he hoped?

He undid his neckcloth and removed his waistcoat watching as she slipped her nightgown over her head. Eleanor stood in front of him pulling open his linen shirt.

'Last night when Padraic was laid on the bed - '

'Padraic is it now. First name terms eh?'

'When he was laid on the bed,' she continued, 'I noticed that besides him having well defined muscles,' she paused for effect, 'he also had a completely hairless chest.' She ran a hand through the mat of dark hair on his chest. 'And I thought to myself do I prefer a hairy chest? Real men have hairs on their chest to my mind.' She grinned at him and he kissed the top of her head.

'So are you saying he's not a real man?' Gabriel smirked.

'Well I'm sure he knows his way about the bedroom, but you once told me that we choose with our eyes first. I think I've made the right choice choosing you my love.'

'You only think?' They kissed long and hard before he lifted her roughly and carried her to the bed. He smiled and wondered how Captain Turner would feel if he knew he'd been relegated to second place because of the lack of hairs on his chest.

Later Gabriel was drifting off to sleep when Eleanor suddenly piped up: 'The chances of Padraic turning up here again when I'm alone are slim are they not? But you're right, I did take an unnecessary risk with him.' Gabriel took her hand under the covers and waited. He knew there was more to come. 'Earlier Charity told me he flirted with her when I was from the room. She also said Ginny caught him outside the nursery supposedly looking for the breakfast room. You're right. He is a chancer. They both locked their bedroom doors, something they've never done before. It seems it was a good job too as Ginny says she heard someone try the door handle in the early hours. Ginny isn't taken to being fanciful so I expect when he got nowhere with me he thought to take advantage elsewhere.'

'The man's a tomcat.'

'Make your mind up,' Eleanor scoffed, 'earlier you called him a rabid dog.'

'Whatever he is he's not to be trusted.'

'Charity and Ginny aren't silly schoolgirls they're strong Yorkshire lasses. He would have got more than he bargained for if he tried to mess with either of them, but I take your point. He's a scoundrel. I'm so glad I warned them to lock their doors.'

'And yet you say Caro was taken with him.'

'He's a charmer and a flatterer. He knows how to wheedle his way into a woman's affections I should think and Caroline is susceptible at the moment. Don't go rushing to her aid. His ship has sailed so she'll possibly never see him again, even if she wanted to.'

ℛ

The nights were getting longer as autumn turned to winter and Eleanor and Gabriel spent many of their evenings quietly at home enjoying each other's company. Sometimes they liked to play backgammon and although Gabriel wasn't a fan of gaming he'd started to enjoy this game to which she'd introduced him. It was a different type of challenge to cards and one in which they were equally matched.

'I must say I'm mighty envious of Lottie doing a

Grand Tour of sorts. I've always wanted to travel.' Eleanor's voice was dreamy.

The couple had finished supper and were sitting by a roaring fire. 'I know you have my love and I only wish I could have spared the time and taken you abroad for our honeymoon. I was so busy with the business at the time. Next year is a possibility, we might go then.'

'Really, that would be marvellous. I should love it if we could.' Eleanor flung her arms around her husband's neck making him spill his brandy. He wiped it from his hand with his handkerchief.

'When Caroline talked of the places she'd seen I thought Italy sounded especially interesting. And Venice, we must see Venice.'

'I've seen Venice but you're right you'll love it and Italy. Florence I haven't seen so we could add that to the itinerary.' Gabriel beamed at the look of anticipation on his wife's face. It pleased him to see her enthusiasm.

'Oh but what about Rose? I couldn't leave Rose for months.'

'Nor could I but she will be almost two by then. We can take Ginny. It won't be an insurmountable problem, what would present a difficulty is if you fell pregnant again.'

'You say that as if you had no input in the matter.' Gabriel was amused at her turn of phrase. 'As it happens there's news on that particular subject. There will soon be the patter of tiny feet.'

'What! I never guessed. Why then are we discussing going abroad?'

'You wouldn't guess for it's not me.' She looked down at Slate asleep next to Scrabble in front of the fire.

Gabriel huffed. 'For a minute there... I thought she was getting fat. I thought her belly the result of all the scraps you feed her from the table.' Gabriel touched Scrabble's flank with his foot. 'Well, you old rascal Scrabble, I didn't think you still had it in you.'

Scrabble sat up and cocked his head to one side. He had very expressive eyebrows for a dog.

'I think she can't be far off her time although I don't know how long puppies take to cook.'

'Cook! About a couple of months I think, not long at any rate. Man alive, what *will* they look like? A terrier and a whippet cross. On a more practical note what will we do with all the puppies? She could have eight or nine. We'll be overrun.'

'Oh, don't even think of it.'

'I could no sooner drown a puppy as hold back the tide, you know me better than that my love.'

'Yes I know. You're as much an old softy as me - we'll have to find homes for them. Does The Eleanor Rose have a ratter?' she asked.

'One of the pups could go there I suppose and a couple to the stud farm. Perhaps Scrabble should be retired. He's getting soft in his old age, so another could go aboard the Alnmouth Boy if that were the case. We can keep a bitch and a dog for, well you know.' Gabriel couldn't say the words out loud, he was far too sentimental.

'For when these two... I can't think about that.' Eleanor rubbed first Slate's ear and then Scrabble's. 'On a similar subject, I can't wait for the first foal to be born at the stud.'

'All this new life. We're so lucky and hopefully the foals will make money for us.' He kissed her hand.

'They'd better do after all the time and effort you and Bendor have spent there.'

'It's not a hobby my love, of course we'll make money.'

'Are you sure it's not a pastime, you both seem to spend an inordinate amount of time at the stud.'

'Oh ye of little faith, just you wait and see. We'll become one of the most renowned studs in the North of England, supplying horses to the King.'

'So I should hope. How is Jax doing, does he like his new role at the stud?'

'He's doing well although it's tough for him as he's still struggling to learn his letters as well as his new job. He's a hard worker and I've every confidence in him. I'd thought to give him one of the cottages on the stud farm when he marries, a sort of tied cottage that he would have while ever he works for us. That should set up the newlyweds nicely.'

Eleanor snuggled up to him and kissed his cheek. 'You're a good man Gabriel Reynolds and I love you for it.'

'Do you care to show me how much?'

'When we've booked our trip I'll show you just how much. In the meantime let me show you another way to bear off. We could finish the game we started last night?' His wife moved to the backgammon board.

'I'd hoped for a "baring" of a different type.'

'Winner takes all?' she replied as she sat opposite him a determined look in her eye.

'I've a feeling I'm going to enjoy this game,' he said. The stakes were high.

12

Eleanor and Gabriel had finished their Christmas shopping when they spotted Bryony Swift coming out of the butcher's shop. She was across the road so they didn't have to acknowledge her. The last time Eleanor had tried to speak to the girl she'd been snubbed. She wasn't going to risk the insult again.

'She's still attractive, but seems less eye-catching in my opinion; she appears to have lost her lustre.' Gabriel watched as Bryony looked in the baker's window.

'She does.'

Eleanor noticed she wasn't as lithe as before, but didn't think it kind to say so despite the fact she disliked the woman. She felt a little sad for her. She'd clearly come down in the world. She said as much to her husband as they continued down Crow's Nest Street.

'Well whose fault is that? Her attitude possibly makes her unemployable. She has some chip on her shoulder.'

'It's just as well I don't have to earn my living by waiting on others as I'd possibly have a worse attitude

228

than her. It can't be an easy life.'

Gabriel squeezed his wife's arm. 'You're right there my love. I fear anyone trying to tell you what to do would get short shrift.'

She nudged him with her elbow for his cheek.

Later that same day Eleanor was at her accounts in the office she shared with Gabriel when the door opened. Gabriel stepped in looking unkempt and in his shirt sleeves.

'Don't come traipsing mud in here wi' them mucky boots,' Eleanor said in her attempt at a Yorkshire accent. 'When I was a girl that's what Bessie our old housekeeper used to say whenever she saw me.'

Gabriel stopped dead and looked at his mud-caked boots. 'In that case, look in the second drawer down of my desk and hand me my penknife my love.'

Eleanor opened the drawer and rummaged around. As she expected it was a mess of papers, twine, used sealing wax and broken quills.

'Oh look! How did that get in here?' She smoothed a piece of wrinkled paper with her own handwriting on it.

'What is it?'

'Do you remember when the gypsy came? I wrote down what she'd said knowing I'd forget otherwise, I was teaching Jax his letters at the time. I wondered where it had got to.'

She began to read it.

'Eleanor. Penknife if you please.' Gabriel shuffled

from one foot to the other impatiently.

'Sorry it doesn't appear to be here.'

'Try the next drawer down, I was sure it was in there.'

Again she searched. This time she was successful. She handed the knife to her husband and he put it in his breeches pocket.

'My reward?' She looked up at him and put her arms around his neck.

'I'm glad I don't employ you, the remuneration would be costly.' He began to kiss her then stopped suddenly and taking her hand he led her through the house. 'I want to show you something.'

'I've fallen for that line before.' She tried to wriggle free and planted her feet firmly. He tugged harder and she was forced to follow.

'You'll like what I have to show you,' he said laughing over his shoulder.

In the corner of the tack room amongst saddles, bridles and surplus hay bales were two hurdles; both were leaning at precarious angles. Gabriel cut twine with the penknife and secured the hurdles to two rings in the stone walls so when fastened together they made a pen.

'Come and look.' Gabriel proudly showed Eleanor his handiwork. She peered over the hurdle to see Slate and her puppies contentedly lying in a bed of straw.

'Despite what you say we can't keep them in the parlour. They're not house trained and there'll be accidents. Eleanor tried to interrupt. 'Yet I know you don't want them outside. Is this not a good solution?'

Eleanor leaned over and stroked Slate's head. 'It is but,' Eleanor frowned, 'I see how it contains the puppies so they don't wander off and get lost, but what about Slate? Is she not a prisoner?'

'Stand back my love.'

When they stepped back Gabriel shouted: 'Slate come.' She jumped the hurdle with ease. 'I already put her to the test as I didn't want to waste time making the pen if she couldn't get out.'

Eleanor tugged Slate's ear. 'I'm glad I didn't have to jump hurdles after I'd just given birth.' Having received praise Slate returned to her puppies. 'I'm pleased she only had five pups,' Eleanor leaned into the pen to admire them, 'now they're all assured a home.'

'The only bitch is the grey one so I think that one and the black one with the rough coat are the two we should keep at the house.'

'I agree. I want to call her Pebble. You can name the dog, that's only fair.'

'Very well, I'll call him Scrabble.'

'You can't call him the same name as his father.'

'Why? It'll avoid confusion. He'll be Scrabble Junior just like when we have a son he'll be Gabriel Junior.' He pulled Eleanor towards him as she looked askance trying to fathom his reasoning. 'So where's *my* reward?' He bent to kiss her but she dodged out of the way nimbly. He grabbed her again and ran his hands down her body. She tried to wriggle away.

'What?' Gabriel smiled and was about to kiss her again when she pushed him away.

'Stop it. I haven't yet regained my waist after the birth, I don't like you feeling my - '

He nuzzled her neck. 'Curves? I told you before I love your curves. If a woman doesn't go in and out in all the right places a man may as well not bother.' Gabriel let her go, but only to shoot both bolts on the tack room door. 'What was that about a prisoner?' He pushed her gently back onto the hay bales and lifted her skirts. 'Now, let's think about adding a son to our family shall we?'

R

Christmas at Westshore was a quieter affair than the year before. Eleanor's parents had arranged to visit but at the last minute Atalana and the twins had been taken ill with colds so her parents had decided to stay in Sandsend and look after them. Eleanor, not for the first time, wished she lived closer to her family. It was ironic Gabriel had no family in Alnmouth to worry about, while most of her closest relatives were miles away.

When Lottie heard that Gabriel and Eleanor were not to have visitors for the festive season she'd invited them for Christmas dinner. The name of Lottie's family home, Wooden House, made Eleanor smile; she hadn't known there was a place called Wooden. It was a hamlet above the estuary. The house was named after the place not the building material, which in this instance was stone. Lottie had also invited Caroline, but she had plans to stay with her aunt and her cousin Arthur.

It was just as well Eleanor's parents weren't expected as the mild winter suddenly turned ferocious. The snowy roads were closed and ships were embayed for most of the festive season. Luckily for Caroline she had set off before the weather had changed.

Gabriel ever mindful of the fact his wife had grown up a Quaker, showered her with gifts. Amongst the various presents of jewellery, a beautiful gown of bronze watered silk and other trinkets was something a little more unusual.

'An architect's plan. Oh my goodness, it's for a conservatory. It will look beautiful and will be warm in the spring and autumn so we can still enjoy the sea view.'

'It's a gift for us both I suppose, but I know how you love to be in the sunshine. In a conservatory you can look out to sea and be warm too.' Eleanor was excessively pleased. 'The building will begin around February if the weather's not too bad so if all goes to plan it may well be in use by late spring.'

'When I mentioned the idea I never thought you'd act on it my love. I'd thought you'd forgotten about it.'

'I never forget anything you tell me Eleanor, you should know that.'

𝓡

Caroline, dressed in a gown of deep burgundy velvet, was escorted into dinner by Captain Turner. It was not such a surprise to her he was to spend Christmas as Captain Ansley's guest for it was she who had secured him the invitation after all.

Back in late summer after he had supped with her, they had kept in touch by way of some very poetic letters. She'd not imagined he could be so eloquent, so passionate. A romance had soon blossomed.

He had told her he'd parted company from John Barker and his ship, The Whitby Lass. He said he hoped to move closer to her as he "couldn't bear to be apart from her". She too was keen for him to move north. She was sure she could find work for him on one of her ships if he really wanted work, but she wasn't keen for him to go on dangerous whaling missions which would take him away from her for months. She meant to persuade him to stay on dry land. He'd told her not to worry as he had plans afoot. He assured her they wouldn't take him away from her side for long.

'You're off to Ireland in the New Year?' Arthur Ansley asked when the men were enjoying their port and the ladies had retired to drink tea and nibble biscuits.

'I am, but I would be obliged if you didn't tell your cousin just yet. I shouldn't want to spoil the festivities for her. She doesn't know of my plans yet.'

'I see. Is there an understanding between the two of you? As Caroline's nearest male relative I ought to know I suppose, though what I could do to stop her doing as she wishes is beyond me. She's of age and her own mistress.'

Arthur Ansley was the type of man whose main priorities in life, now he could no longer go to war, were gaming and womanising. He had married a timid, little woman whom he enjoyed baiting for sport. Behind closed doors he was a mean man and a bully. Once she'd provided him with an heir, he found he had no time or inclination for his wife except to take what was rightly his, but only when nothing better was on offer. The dowry she had brought was busy earning interest and she was content with the children so he felt at liberty to take his pleasures elsewhere and this he did. Often.

'There's no formal understanding, we've not met frequently enough for that to be a consideration, but I'm happy to see where this visit takes us. I must say I'm keen to secure her on the evidence so far. She's a very beautiful woman.'

'And a rich one. I daresay since her father died she's had suitors lining up at the door. Any man would be glad to have her, 'tis just a pity she's a cousin,' he slapped his leg with his one good hand and laughed, 'or I should have offered for her myself.' Ansley poured himself another brandy. 'You have business in Ireland?'

'In Dublin, yes. It may take a while to untangle but I hope to move to Northumberland by the spring.'

Arthur snorted. 'An entanglement eh? Will that be of the female variety? You were always one for the ladies as I remember. We had some fun in the war did we not? I miss those dark haired señoritas.'

Captain Turner refilled his glass and changed the subject.

13

February was a dark, dreary month. Eleanor always thought her spirits were at their lowest ebb at this time of year. It was a short month yet seemed betwixt and between; neither full winter nor spring. The work on the conservatory had begun, but today the weather had been freezing and so the builders had gone home early. The days were lengthening but spring could never come quickly enough for Eleanor. Today had been iron cold and the light had barely lifted at all. The sea, the sky and her mood were all dull and grey.

Eleanor sat by the fire in the library. Gabriel was reading on the sofa beside her. She was in a melancholic mood. 'Does it still make you sad when you look at the portrait of your mother?' she asked as she gazed at the alcove where there was a large painting of Alice Reynolds holding a two year old Gabriel on her knee.

'It used to do, when I was younger.' He placed a spill in the page so he wouldn't lose his place. 'She died so young; she was just seven and twenty.'

'It must have been awful for you and your father.'

'It was. My father was grief stricken for what

seemed like an eternity to me as a boy of seven.'

'I've never lost anyone close while you've had the misfortune to lose both your parents.' Eleanor continued to stare at the painting. 'Who painted the portrait? It's well executed, the jewels look almost real. Is it a good likeness?'

Gabriel put his book down. He knew he wasn't going to be allowed to continue reading, not that he minded. He liked chatting with Eleanor, especially about his family.

'I think so although such beauty is hard to capture. Her hair was very dark and thick, her eyes too were dark, almost black. To me as a child, they seemed to glitter when she smiled.'

'You have her hair colour but not her eyes; your eyes aren't so dark. I think Rose has a look of you at that age. Her hair seems to be getting darker don't you agree? Perhaps she'll be auburn-haired not red like me. Look at your curls in the painting, I know ladies who would kill for those locks.' Eleanor leaned into him.

'My father bought her the sapphires for an anniversary I believe. In the portrait she's wearing the necklace and the earrings, but there was also a bracelet and a ring. I remember her wearing that gown; she always wore the sapphires with that particular dress.'

Eleanor squeezed his hand affectionately. 'What a waste of life, one cut short and your brother's barely begun.'

'You questioned why I was worried when you told

me you were with child. Small wonder I feared losing you in childbirth. As you know I was convinced history would repeat itself.' Gabriel snuggled closer to his wife and put his arm around her. 'We're very gloomy all of a sudden,' he said shuddering.

'History didn't repeat itself. I'm still here and so is Rose.' They both knew what the other was thinking. 'Don't fret something bad will happen when I fall pregnant again, lightning doesn't strike twice in the same place. You told me your mother had a difficult time bringing you into the world because you were a big baby. It weakened her. Perhaps that was why she died and why your brother was lost. I had a relatively easy birth with Rose, there were no complications and she wasn't so big.'

He listened as Eleanor tried to reassure him. They both wanted to add to their family at some point in the future, but he couldn't help but worry. He had even more to lose now.

'You're right of course, for it won't serve to spoil what we have now by worrying about something which may never happen.' He kissed the top of her head. 'On another subject I wonder where her gowns went. I don't remember her things being got rid of, but I suppose they must have been taken away. There's a trunk upstairs that has some of her things in, but not clothes. The moths would have had them by now. Her diaries are in there, I remember reading them when I came home in the school holidays one summer.'

'You must have been missing her. How sad you must have been. Do you want to go and look?'

'No, but you're welcome to look if you have the time. I shouldn't mind if you read her diaries, it would let you see what she was like. She was beautiful and not just on the outside. I believe my father loved her as much as I love you.'

ℛ

Again the next day was cold and dreary, made worse by a gale which forced Eleanor to stay indoors. She watched as rain was hurled against the bedroom window. She sighed as she drew a heart in the condensation. She was restless and although she had plenty to do she couldn't seem to put her mind to anything for long.

Eleanor was about to go downstairs when she recalled the conversation with her husband from the night before. She walked along the landing to the room where Gabriel's mother's belongings were stored.

She hefted the heavy lid of the trunk and knelt down to see what was inside. Perhaps she would read the diaries. Eleanor carefully lifted out a fan, a pair of kidskin gloves wrapped in tissue paper and a bundle of sheet music. She laid them to one side. Next she uncovered some tapestry and needlepoint. Both were fine and expertly wrought; Eleanor could barely thread a needle. One of the canvases depicted a garden with beautiful summer flowers. She laid this apart from the other sewing, perhaps it could be made into a wall hanging, not by her of course, but someone who knew how to do such things. As her own mother was equally inept with a needle and thread, Eleanor would have to give this some thought.

The musty, dusty smell made Eleanor's nose itch as she reached down to find a stack of leather-bound diaries. There were seven in total. The dates Eleanor soon saw, started in the first year Alice Reynolds had come to live at Westshore. They continued to her untimely death.

Eleanor picked up the last diary and opened it at the latest entry. She began to read. The poignancy as she read the words, knowing as she did that a few weeks after this the poor young woman and her new born baby would be dead, was hard to bear. A single tear ran down Eleanor's face. Alice Reynolds was beautiful, loved and rich, yet had been called to her maker all too soon. Life and childbirth in particular, was indeed precarious.

The entry was written when Alice had been told by her doctor to take bed rest until her baby was born. She'd suffered sickness all through her pregnancy, yet not once in the pages Eleanor read did Alice complain. Eleanor would be vexed had she to spend two months in bed; vexed, impatient and irritable for certain.

Alice talked lovingly of her husband Jack coming to sit with her each evening and of the seven year old

Gabriel bringing her a toy boat he'd made with his father. She described Gabriel as "serious and quiet". He had, she concluded, been told by Lisbet not to overexcite his mother. She described how one evening Gabriel had fallen asleep in her arms and how Jack had later carried the sleeping boy to his bed.

Eleanor could sense her own mood turning melancholic. There was no wonder Gabriel used to get black moods. It was all so sad, this loss of young life. She selected the diary for the year Gabriel was born hoping it might be more cheerful. She sat back against the trunk and began to read at a page which had fallen open. It was an entry recording the day of Gabriel's christening. Before they'd left for St Waleric's church, Jack had given Alice the sapphire jewels.

'So it wasn't an anniversary present, but a gift for presenting Jack Reynolds with a son,' Eleanor said to herself as she smiled at the serendipity. When Alice Rose was born, Gabriel had presented Eleanor with an aquamarine necklace and bracelet which matched the ring he'd given her on their wedding day. Had he known he was carrying on a tradition his father had started she wondered?

She heard Ginny's voice calling from along the corridor. Eleanor stood and stretched and laid the diaries in a neat pile. She poked her head through the door.

'I'm here Ginny, do you want me?' The nursemaid appeared at the top of the stairs.

'You said to tell you when Rose woke from her nap.'

'I'll be along in a moment,' Eleanor called. She returned the items to the trunk with the exception of the tapestry and the diaries. 'I wonder,' Eleanor said to no one in particular, 'where the sapphires are now?'

R

'Who's the invitation from?' Eleanor asked over breakfast.

'Lord Acton.'

'The man who provides *entertainment* for his guests?'

'Yes, but I shan't go.'

'Is it always just men who're invited, besides the "entertaining" ladies of course?'

'I don't think so. Lottie Lambton was at one I seem to remember.'

'Lottie! Who was she with?'

'Not Wilson. They're usually the kind of party where young people drop in. Small groups come to play the gaming tables, if they've not been asked to dine that is. There's usually quite a crowd.'

'I should like to go if there are young people, I feel like an old married mother these days.'

Gabriel looked at his beautiful wife and smiled as he buttered a bread roll. 'Ah yes, you look like an old drudge. Why have I not noticed before?' He saw her smile despite herself. 'You wouldn't enjoy it my love,

243

you would be forever tut-tutting. It wouldn't make for a relaxing evening. I should never have a minute's peace.'

'Why should I not like it?'

'You would be complaining the girls were ill-used. It would be like the Warkworth wedding we attended before we were married where you went on all night about the man Ives and his lack of moral fibre.' He grinned at her as she was about to react.

Two days later Gabriel and Eleanor arrived at Lord Acton's party fashionably late. Rose was cutting a tooth and had been fractious so that they hadn't wanted to leave her until she slept.

Gabriel introduced his wife to Lord Harry. To his amusement she proclaimed her surprise at Harry's appearance.

'I'd imagined him old and he's not. I would bet he's no older than thirty and he's not at all good looking,' she whispered as Gabriel led her away.

Lord Acton was pale and bewigged and not overly tall. The portly peer wore a fine suit and a flamboyant peacock-blue waistcoat. His shoes had stacked heels; clearly he was trying to make himself appear taller.

'He's not at all what I'd expected.'

Gabriel lifted an eyebrow. 'You do amuse me. I can't be blamed if Harry doesn't live up to your expectations.'

'It's just that I thought... oh never mind.'

Gabriel watched as Eleanor glanced about her

appraising the guests. They were mostly young, fashionable men with the odd young lady sporting the latest London fashions. Amongst them, a dozen or so ladies of ill repute drifted between the gaming tables. They were easy to spot with their gaudy gowns and painted faces.

He knew his wife was quietly appalled but wasn't going to be predictable and say so.

'There's a lady playing at one of the tables, I think I'll play a hand or two.'

Gabriel was surprised.

'I often played cards with Father and Tomas, another reason my family are no longer Quakers.'

'I didn't know you could play?'

'There's a lot you don't know about me my love.' She slid into a vacant chair at the table and Gabriel stood behind her. 'I hope you're not going to hang around giving tips and advice.'

He moved to the opposite side of the table. 'Who am I to dispense advice about card playing? Will here suit you *your ladyship*?'

Eleanor sniffed and began to play. She won the first two hands. 'Beginner's luck,' she told the young man opposite her. She also won the next three hands.

Gabriel noticed her opponents looked none too happy at being beaten, possibly because it was a lady who was taking their money. Eleanor's luck ran out and she lost the next few hands.

Gabriel wandered off to the refreshment table and

poured himself a brandy. He returned to the table to see the young man, who was across from Eleanor, push his chair back and throw his cards on the table in disgust. Eleanor looked up at her husband and smiled sweetly. He got the distinct feeling his wife had hidden talents.

He sensed someone come to stand close by him. He turned to see Ruby.

'Good evening sir, I hoped you'd be here tonight.'

'Good evening. You look er, alluring.' She was wearing a scarlet gown which was cut daringly low. The dress set off her dark hair and eyes to best advantage.

'I've only just arrived, I was held up.' She put her hand on his shoulder to pick off an imaginary piece of fluff. There was no mistaking the double entendre.

'Is Sir Percy not here?' she said looking about her. 'Claire will be disappointed if he isn't.'

'He's away on business I believe.'

'I wonder if I can persuade you to hold me up later. I should like it if you did. You've been on my mind since last we met.' She moved closer so that her thigh brushed his.

'As I said last time, were I not a happily married man I'd be sorely tempted.'

She laughed softly. 'A change is as good as a rest they say.'

There was a sudden cry from the table and another player threw in his hand. Eleanor caught his eye and raised an eyebrow. He smiled at her then turned away and listened to something Ruby was saying. He was only half listening.

'Lady Luck seems to be with you this evening madam,' Gabriel heard the player on Eleanor's left say through gritted teeth.

Eleanor smiled beguilingly. 'She does indeed sir, but I'm of the opinion that one makes one's own luck.'

Two more players replaced the pair who had left as Eleanor dealt the next hand. Some of the men were a little tipsy and this made playing them easier he imagined; they didn't have their wits about them like his wife did. Eleanor was sipping a cordial, her head was perfectly clear. She looked to be enjoying herself. She wouldn't make a poker player, however, her face would give her away.

At last Eleanor cleared the decks. She had won the pot. She swept her winnings into a pile and put them in her reticule. She came around the table to where he was standing.

'Good evening Ruby and thank you for keeping my husband amused whilst I was busy.' Ruby looked surprised then disappointed.

'The pleasure was all mine,' Ruby said a touch of annoyance evident behind the smile.

Gabriel was amused. 'How much have you won my love?'

'Enough to know it's time to retreat, I shouldn't want to lose this amount - she tapped her bag. Would you mind getting drinks my love? I've worked up quite a thirst.'

Gabriel bowed and moved to the refreshment table.

'How do you know my name, have we met before?'

Gabriel was close enough to overhear the conversation. He listened in.

'My husband mentioned you after the last party here. We have no secrets from one another.'

Gabriel smirked at Eleanor's defensive response.

'I see. You're a very lucky lady and not just at cards. Your husband is a moral man, and a handsome one. The two don't often go hand in hand.' Gabriel felt a twinge of guilt for eavesdropping, but carried on regardless.

'As I've just said to one of my opponents, I think we make our own luck in life, if one is prepared to take risks the returns can be high.'

'I think it easier to make your own luck when you have the luxury of having a soft cushion beneath you, then taking risks is less uncertain. Without a buffer it's a different matter I believe.'

'I see you're probably right. It's harder to take a risk if one has a lot to lose. Tell me, I hope you don't think me impertinent, but how much money would you expect to make at such an event as this? Is it worth your time?'

Gabriel didn't know why but he was surprised at his wife's audacious question. She often said what she thought and asked questions that others avoided.

'Worth it? Worth my honour do you mean? Some of the gentlemen whose coin you've just taken will possibly now not be quite so generous,' she said ironically. 'A man spends more on a whore when his ego is high and he's just won. When they need consolation they generally drink more and tip less. In answer to your question however, yes it is worth it. Were I to work at the bay I'd have to ply my trade daily but this way I work only a few times a month.'

Gabriel returned with the drinks, thinking it expedient to interrupt.

'I'll try my luck at hazard my love,' he said not moving away when it was clear Eleanor didn't mean to follow him. Perhaps his wife thought the conversation much more entertaining than cards.

'Before this erm, line of work, what ambition had you?' His wife was still intent on interrogating the poor girl it seemed.

'Again, ambition is the province of the upper classes is it not? Unless of course you call surviving an ambition.'

'I'm sorry if I offended you, but I don't judge. If you knew me better you'd know I meant nothing by the remark. I'm over curious sometimes. It occasionally gets me into trouble.' Eleanor looked to him for confirmation. He nodded amicably.

'I'm pleased you don't judge Mrs Reynolds as you can't possibly imagine my life.'

Gabriel noticed Ruby's colour was up and her chin

jutted out proudly. She was trying to rein in her anger. Eleanor continued on blithely.

'If you had the choice, if you had a buffer that is, what would you be? What would you do with your life?'

Ruby laughed and Gabriel noticed she suddenly looked younger behind the red lips and the beauty spot. 'Before I was elevated to this rank do you mean?' Ruby tilted her dark head and smiled sardonically. 'I worked the bay from the age of fourteen. I've friends who work there still. I go back and see them sometimes, poor sods. It was a miserable existence. When I worked there I lived in what can only be described as a hovel, most of the women and their children still live in squalor, lots of men also it has to be said. I have no dreams, no ambitions unless you call netting a rich man and becoming his mistress an ambition. *That* would make for an easier life.'

Eleanor scowled. Gabriel sensed she was winding up for a lecture.

'People should always have ambitions Ruby. A few years ago in Whitby I met a young woman who like you, had a bad start in life. Even though the young woman was a sail maker by trade and worked hard, she still had to prostitute herself by night to make ends meet. She had a sister with two children to care for besides herself. Life was hard for them. She had a change of fortune and was set up in a hat shop. She's made a great success of it. If you had such luck Ruby and got the chance, should you give up this life altogether?'

Ruby chortled. 'In a heartbeat; not all the men I meet are like your handsome husband.' She smiled as they both looked up at him. He suddenly felt self conscious.

Eleanor held out her reticule to the woman. 'There's just short of one hundred guineas in there. Take it and make your own luck. There's your cushion.'

Ruby looked wary. She looked at Gabriel who shrugged. 'Is this a jest?' She didn't take the purse, but stared at it as if it would bite her.

Gabriel was astonished for a second time. His wife was truly full of surprises.

'No it's not a joke. I should never consider such a thing. If you'd like advice on how to invest the money come and see me. Perhaps you could begin as I did and put some of the money in shipping, that's usually a safe bet. I should like to help you to have ambition.'

Ruby took the purse, but then felt the weight. 'I can't take this. What will your husband say?' Again Ruby looked to him, but before he could speak Eleanor continued.

'Don't concern yourself about what my husband thinks Ruby.' She slid a sidelong look at him and smiled mischievously. 'It's money I didn't have when I came here this evening and as you rightly said, it's money that may have come your way anyway had I not won it from your potential... clients.'

'How do you know I'll not squander it, lose it over a

game of cards? Or drink it away... '

'Why would you? You would be stupid if you did, and you don't appear empty-headed to me. I don't believe for a minute you enjoy your work so why would you risk losing the money when it's possibly your one chance of getting away from this degradation.'

'Why indeed?'

Ruby allowed herself a smile.

ℛ

'I can't believe you did that.' Gabriel and Eleanor were on their way home. 'You gave a whore all your winnings.' Gabriel relaxed back in his seat and grinned. 'Why may I ask?'

'Her need is greater than mine and I felt like doing her a good turn.'

Gabriel snorted derisively. 'If you wanted to help her you should have offered to give her counsel, helped her invest it wisely. Certainly not hand it to her on a plate. I can't believe you just gave her all the money. Tomorrow she'll no doubt be spending it *unwisely* on fripperies and will never come and seek your advice, until it's all gone that is. Then she'll possibly come for another handout.'

Eleanor sat in the darkness of the carriage. It had started to rain and she thought of the poor women and children at the bay in their meagre, damp hovels. She thought of the babies, the children without food in their bellies. She thought of the poor women who had to stoop low to look after their children. Her anger suddenly flared.

'Another handout! Are you sure about that? If you are then perhaps you'd care to bet on it? You imagine women are like children who need the guidance of men to make sensible decisions. You think women are irrational creatures who can't fend for themselves without a man. You're infuriating sometimes Gabriel Reynolds.'

'I told you tonight wouldn't end well. I should have got your high horse out before we left home. I'll take you up on your wager, for while I admit you would do very well without me, a girl like Ruby hasn't the education or the capacity to think ahead, to plan for the future. The money will run through her fingers like water. What do you care to bet my little generous one?'

He ran his hand down her thigh. She knocked it away impatiently; she was in no mood for flirting. 'I'll think about it, but it will not, under any circumstances involve you know what.' She laughed seeing his disappointment.

'The winner surely sets the bar?' Gabriel argued.

'She does and as I'm confident I'll win you'd better watch out.'

The last comment had silenced her argumentative spouse. They were almost home when Gabriel broke the peace. 'I wonder how Rose will turn out. With your influence she could be quite an opinionated young lady.'

'So long as she knows she can be anything she wants to be I don't mind, although I'd like her to have some commercial sense so she isn't totally dependent on a man. She'll be lucky for she has a large soft cushion beneath her.'

'I'm still surprised you're content to be just a wife and mother.'

She glowered at him, piercing him with an icy look. '*Just,*' she tutted. 'I've my business dealings don't forget. I've also been thinking about the charity we talked about to help women. I'd like to invest time and money in such a venture as I think it a worthy cause. I once told you I shouldn't have married at all, had I not wanted children and a father for them of course. One has to make sacrifices.'

In the darkness of the carriage she suspected Gabriel couldn't see her face clearly. If he had he'd have seen she had a deliberately provoking expression about her.

'I'm a sacrifice am I?'

Eleanor kissed him stopping the tirade that was about to head her way. He was so easy to placate she thought. Men were simple creatures at heart.

R

A week passed and Ruby hadn't made contact. Over

supper Gabriel had been gloating. He was still confident he'd win the bet. Eleanor had been batting away his jibes light-heartedly all evening not at all concerned; she had faith in Ruby.

'I've been thinking what I'll demand when I win,' he said as he downed the last of his claret.

'That's a waste of time for you won't win. I've told you Ruby will come and I'll help her in whatever way I can. You're a man; you don't know women, well not all women.'

Gabriel huffed and got up from the table. 'No offence taken I'm sure but I was thinking for my prize I may - '

'Gabriel, forget whatever pipedream you've conjured up, you won't win my love.' She watched him shrug and leave the room smiling. He was sure he was going to win the bet, but Eleanor was equally confident Ruby wouldn't let her down.

The next morning Ivy announced a visitor.

'Who is it Ivy?'

'It's a, la - a visitor, says her name's Ruby. Mrs Madison saw her and told her to be off, but she said you'd asked her to call so A thought she'd better not be turned away.' Ivy's face was beetroot red.

'Show her in and ask Mrs Madison to bring tea. Don't let her send you with it Ivy. Tell her I want her to serve us.'

Ivy looked terrified Eleanor noted as she scurried from the room almost tripping over her own feet. She hoped Mrs Madison wouldn't take it out on poor Ivy for delivering her missive.

'Ruby, how nice of you to call, please take a seat.' Eleanor noticed the girl looked even younger without her powder and paint. She still had an edge to her that singled her out as not quite respectable. Without a doubt it was that to which Mrs Madison had taken exception.

Ruby was carrying Eleanor's reticule. 'I bet you thought I'd done a runner?' Ruby looked about her. 'The fact is that after the night when we met I had a spot of bother.'

The door opened and a tight-lipped Mrs Madison brought in the tea tray.

'Thank you Mrs Madison, will you pour for us please?' There was an audible sigh, but the housekeeper did as she was bid. 'Mrs Madison makes the most marvellous cakes Ruby, would you care for one? Mrs Madison please offer my friend a cake if you will.'

When tea was served and the housekeeper had left the room, Ruby said: 'Making a point were you?'

'Something like that.' Eleanor smoothed a wrinkle from her day dress. 'Now what were you saying?'

'Two nights after the card party, a gentleman who'd been at Harry's, Lord Acton's that is, looked me up as it were.' She shifted in her chair. 'When I refused him he got angry. I asked him to leave and after a very frank exchange he did, only to call on Claire. Sadly for her, he was in a vile mood when he got there and ill-used her quite badly. The next day I had to spend some of your winnings on a doctor for her. She was hurt quite bad, it's an occupational hazard I'm afraid. She's on the mend now, but I couldn't leave her. We're close Claire and me, we've been through a lot together; we watch out for each other. The rest of the money's still here.' She lifted the heavy purse. 'If it's alright with you I want to share the money with Claire. We've an idea, but it would possibly take two of us to bring it about.'

'I'm sorry to hear about Claire. As you say it's a hazard of the job, but no one should have to suffer at the hands of such brutes. Men can be such bullies.'

Eleanor could feel her temper rising. In truth she'd only ever known good men, kind men like her father and Gabriel. William had a side to him but she'd never seen the worst of it she suspected. Perhaps her mama had been right and William did have a cruel streak. She shuddered thinking of what might have lain in store for her had she married him and not Gabriel. She knew she'd lived a life of privilege and was grateful for it, but that didn't mean she didn't feel for Claire.

'It's your money to do with as you wish, tell me about your idea.'

Ruby sat on the edge of her seat. 'Down at the bay when a ship comes in, often ladies have taken a passage on a working collier or the like. There aren't many passenger ships plying the coast.'

'I know, sometimes my husband transports ladies who are perfectly respectable, but don't always have the means for another type of passage or, as you say, there's no passenger ship available.'

'We've seen how when these ladies come ashore they have little choice but to stay at one of Alnmouth's finest hostelries.' She laughed at her whimsy. 'We had an idea to set up a respectable boarding house for ladies, no men allowed you understand. Then perhaps they would feel safe. We would charge a little more than an inn, but the ladies would know the place was respectable. We would provide meals too if they wanted, employ a cook. Your Mrs Madison would suit us nicely.'

'What a good plan, I'm sure it would work. The main problem is acquiring a place big enough to make it worthwhile. You'd need at least ten rooms I should think to make a profit. As women can't buy property you would be forced to lease, unless you're prepared to trust a man to buy in your name. Do you know any trustworthy men Ruby?'

The irony was not lost on the girl. The two women spent the next hour discussing the proposed project.

'Just one more thing Mrs Reynolds,' Ruby said after they'd discussed the plan at length. 'Where I live it's unsafe to keep this much money. It's making me nervous stuffing it under the mattress so would you look after it for us until we've need of it? Then I should sleep easier.'

'Of course Ruby, I'll put it in our safe. I'll ask my husband about what we discussed regarding buying a property. He's without doubt the one man in the world you can trust. I can promise you that.'

'You said what? You want me to stand surety for two whores to run a boarding house. Are you mad! Perhaps you're being a little green my love? They're possibly intending to open a bawdy house and with my name attached I'd leave myself open to being prosecuted for running a house of ill repute.'

Gabriel was already reeling from the blow of losing the bet, now this was being presented to him as a fait accompli.

'It will be a reputable establishment. The girls want to be respectable, they're tired of being degraded.' Eleanor explained what had happened to Claire.

'I feel for the girls and I applaud the fact you're trying to help them, but as I've said before those types of girls are uneducated and seldom plan beyond the next... well you know what I mean. They probably earn good money when they ply their trade at places like Harry's, but do you see them saving for a rainy day? You do not.'

Eleanor frowned. 'How patronising you are. How do you know they don't have a nest egg? Besides, every day is a rainy day for a woman who has to sell her body to survive. Ruby and Claire are barely eighteen. I was shocked how young Ruby looked without her face paint.'

'We digress my love.' She could see Gabriel was eager to leave for the bay. 'You're good to try to help others, even though in this instance I think you're misguided.' He stood to leave. 'I love your altruism, but this time you've bitten off more than you can chew in my opinion. I also know if I come out too strongly against this proposition you'll dig your heels in even deeper. I know you.'

Eleanor was frustrated she was so predictable. 'There's one other thing,' she followed him into the hall, she hadn't finished with him yet, 'you owe me Gabriel. I believe I won the bet did I not?' She was trying not to gloat but not succeeding.

'I suppose you did.' He glowered like he did when he lost at cards. She tried not to preen.

'You're a sore loser my love.'

'Well how do you propose to exact your revenge?' He tapped his riding crop against his boot.

'Let me think about it.' She stood on tiptoes to kiss his cheek. 'I'm sure I'll be able to think of something.'

'I'm sure you will. One other thing, I've just remembered, Mrs Madison is threatening to hand in her notice. I meant to tell you earlier.'

Eleanor showed her irritation by using one of her favourite swear words. 'Why does she want to leave? We can't do without her.'

'Apparently it's beneath her to serve "the kind of company Mrs Reynolds has taken to entertaining".' He put his coat on, picked up his tricorn and headed for the door.

'Lord, she wasn't at all happy when I insisted she and not Ivy serve Ruby the other day, but she was being such a snob. For all her religious fervour she's not very Christian.'

'If I were you I wouldn't say that to her face, she's already indignant. I'll leave it with you, I need to set off - I'm late as it is.' He bent to kiss her. 'One last thing my love; if I'm deprived of Mrs M's puddings I'll hold you personally responsible.'

Eleanor sighed deeply and made her way to the kitchen. She wasn't looking forward to this interview. She knew her shortcomings and was aware diplomacy was not one of her strong points. Her short temper was also something she battled with especially now when she was getting little sleep. She took a deep breath as she entered the kitchen. She had thought to send for the cook and see her in the morning room, but then thought better of it and decided to beard the woman in her own lair.

'Mrs M. Good morning.'

'Ma'am.' The cook bobbed a small curtsy.

'My husband tells me you're unhappy.'

'Mebbe I am. I told Mr Reynolds I'll not stay here and serve the likes of *her*. I'll leave rather than have them sorts of women here at Westshore. I thought this a respectable house.'

Eleanor was livid. She didn't see what business it was of hers who the mistress of the house invited to tea but she knew to say so would only make matters worse. 'It's true Miss Ruby isn't the sort of lady I normally entertain, but there's a good reason for her to come here. Allow me to explain.'

Mrs Madison huffed but reluctantly conceded. Eleanor was certain that no matter what defence she offered, the woman would still be offended.

'It's not my job to serve the likes of her,' the cook spat out.

Eleanor was barely able to hold her temper. If it weren't for Gabriel's warning ringing in her ears she would have sacked the woman on the spot for her bigotry. And besides, Mrs Madison was an exceptionally good cook and good cooks were thin on the ground in Alnmouth. Even as she spoke the tantalising smell of biscuits filled the air.

'You and I are very lucky Mrs M in that we both enjoyed an upbringing where we had parents who loved and guided us.' Eleanor knew her cook was brought up in a Christian, law abiding house. She went to church regularly. 'We had a roof over our heads and food aplenty. Sadly, this is not the case with the two ladies whom I recently met. They had no guidance from loving parents, indeed both were mis-treated by their own fathers. They have been brought low through necessity, not by choice.'

'Necessity! There's many a girl dragged up at the bay by poor parents, but they don't offer themselves to men fer money. They have a choice. Look to Ivy. Her father was a drunk and as lazy as the day's long. He took his fury out on her mother with his fists most days when he were in his cups. Poor Ivy got out as soon as she could, but she din't go on the streets, she found herself a decent position. She made the right choice. She's a hard worker is Ivy and she takes pride in her work. Choices indeed!'

Eleanor was finding the interview unsettling. She hadn't expected an argument. 'You're right of course, but who are we to judge unless we've walked in another's shoes? It's my intention to help them out of their current predicament by finding them more respectable employment. I think that is a Christian thing to do, do you not agree?' Eleanor threw in the last sentence to try to appeal to Mrs Madison's religious beliefs. The cook seemed less than impressed.

'Happen as mebbe, but it's not right havin' painted trollops in the house. People will see them comin' and goin' and wonder what's goin' on. Jax and Joe made comment and you don't want them two gettin' ideas!'

Eleanor drew in a long steadying breath and played what she thought was her trump card. 'Did not Jesus entertain Mary Magdalene? All I'm asking is you try to understand that we need to be charitable to those who can't fend for themselves in the ordinary way.

From here on in, I'll ask only that you keep to your kitchen if she should call again. I will not ask you to lower your standards by waiting on her.'

Eleanor knew she needed to make the concession and considered offering the maddening woman a pay rise to tempt her to stay. Then she thought better of it. 'Surely you're aware of how highly you're prized by my husband and I Mrs Madison. We would be sad to see you leave us, but if you're unhappy then we quite understand your position and will of course provide you with the best of references once you have served notice.'

Eleanor had hoped all along the cook was calling their bluff, but if not then she had backed the cook into a corner. Her temper had finally got the better of her.

Mrs Madison took a tray of biscuits from the oven and Eleanor's mouth watered. Gabriel would be furious if the woman left. Mrs Madison's huge bosom heaved.

'Right then, I'll stay just so long as you stick to your end of the bargain, but I still wonder what folks'll say.'

Eleanor sighed with relief, but thought to leave the kitchen before she said something more to antagonise her cook.

'Thank you Mrs M. When you've a moment please send Ivy with tea and some of those delicious looking biscuits. I'll be in the morning room.'

Eleanor should have felt jubilant, but she didn't.

When Ivy brought the tea tray she asked the young maid to pour for her. She saw the poor girl flush scarlet and watched as her hands shook.

'Are you happy here Ivy?'

'Happy? Happen A am. It don't matter to me who A serve Mistress Reynolds.'

It was clear Mrs Madison had been getting at Ivy.

'You've been with us some little while now and I think it's about time you were rewarded for your loyalty.'

'Rewarded?'

'Is there something that you lack that might make your life a little easier?'

Ivy dropped the teaspoon; it clattered on the bone china saucer. Her face glowed redder than ever. Eleanor was mindful of what her cook had told her about the girl's upbringing. Eleanor wanted to make the girl's life a little better if she could.

'Do you lack anything Ivy? Should you like something for your room?'

'A dunno.' She thought for a moment. 'Mebbe a mirror? A dropped mine an' it smashed to pieces.'

'Oh dear, I hope you aren't superstitious.' Ivy looked blank. 'Come to my bedchamber in half an hour, I have just the thing.'

Half an hour later Ivy presented herself.

'Will this do? I've several mirrors, I'll not miss one.' Eleanor realised how condescending she sounded. 'I would also like you to have this.' She passed the maid a fine woollen shawl. 'It's light but warm. You could wear it on your day off.'

Ivy looked more suspicious than pleased Eleanor thought, but she ploughed on. 'There will also be more money in your pay from this quarter. I want you to be happy here at Westshore Ivy and I aim to reward loyalty and hard work. Always know you can come to me if there's anything amiss. I know Mrs M can be quite... intimidating, but don't let her bully you. Come to me if there's ever a problem.'

'Thank you Mistress Reynolds.' The girl, wide-eyed, bobbed a curtsy then tripped over a chair as she left the room.

Eleanor plonked herself down on the bed. She thought about the young girl who served them dutifully. She'd hardly noticed her, hardly knew anything about her until Mrs Madison had told her about her past. The only time she heard the maid's name was when the cook was complaining that she'd broken something. Poor Ivy hadn't asked to be born into poverty. Now all she had to look forward to was a life of servitude. Life was unfair, especially if you were a woman, there were few opportunities open to the uneducated she realised. She fully intended to do something about it.

14

Tomas and Cora's wedding was set for March and as it was to be held at Dunstanburgh at Bendor's invitation, Eleanor's parents had decided to pay a visit to their daughter and son-in-law on the way north. They were to come to Westshore for a month and as the Christmas visit had been cancelled, they were looking forward to it all the more.

The day of the wedding poured with rain. The sun resolutely refused to show itself and thunder could be heard echoing around the church.

After an enormous wedding breakfast, Gabriel sat beside the bride. 'Do you suppose it an omen there was a storm raging as you were taking your marriage vows?'

Cora quelled him with a look. The pair had always had an easy camaraderie. They enjoyed baiting each other but nothing could spoil Cora's wedding day. 'Do you remember when you asked me to elope with you Gabriel? I believe that too, was during a storm here at Dunstanburgh. I refused of course as I thought we would drown before the honeymoon.'

Tomas looked taken aback. 'What's this? Must I

fight a duel with my brother-in-law for your honour Cora?'

'Hardly! It was when I'd broken off my engagement to Caroline and Cora's family were playing matchmakers. They didn't care which of Grace's sisters I married just so long as I chose one of them. I was such a catch.'

Eleanor rolled her eyes and changed the subject.

'Your gown is exquisite Cora. Where was it made, surely not hereabouts?'

'As a matter of fact it was, although it was from a French design.'

'Don't tell Eleanor,' Gabriel joked, 'or she'll have the order book out.'

'Have you turned into a skinflint?' Cora asked. 'I never had you down for a miser.'

Bendor stoked the fire. 'The older he gets the more cautious he becomes. You should have a night playing the card tables with him; he's like a mother hen watching over me, always urging me to quit while I'm ahead.' The friends laughed at Gabriel's expense.

'I for one am glad of it,' Grace interjected. 'My husband would gamble the family fortune away when he's in his cups. Ignore them Gabriel you carry on watching over my errant husband. Bendor has a reckless streak sometimes. I fear our children will have nothing left to inherit if he has his way.'

'How is the stud farm doing?' Tomas asked. Gabriel was glad the subject had been changed. He could tell

Grace was getting herself worked up.

'We expect our first foals in early summer,' Bendor said. 'That's somewhere else where Gabe keeps a tight hold on the purse strings.'

'Again I owe you a debt of gratitude Gabriel.' Grace knitted her brows together.

Gabriel tried to deflect her. He knew she worried about Ben's gambling habit, but now was neither the time nor the place.

'I wish everyone would leave me be, if Ben had his way we would've bought every thoroughbred this side of Newmarket. A little caution with one's money is never a bad thing.' He looked pointedly at Bendor who was too merry to take the hint.

'Sometimes we have to take a risk, look how it panned out when I got us Falladore, she's the best mare we have in the stable. You said we'd over reached ourselves but wait until she foals. We'll be quids in.'

'There you go again counting your chickens before they're hatched!' Grace warned.

It was Eleanor's turn to change the tune. She looked to her sister-in-law and sighed. 'I envy you your honeymoon abroad Cora. We were to travel this spring, but with my parents' visit and your wedding it's been postponed. Also the stud farm is in its infancy so Gabriel can't be away for so long.'

'I'll take you abroad one day I promise.' Gabriel smiled sympathetically at his wife.

'But Eleanor, only if you're prepared to travel economically. I expect the first leg of your journey will be in one or other of Gabe's colliers.' Bendor punched his old friend on the arm and dodged the returning blow.

The conversation eventually took a lighter turn and the wedding party drew to a close.

On the journey home Eleanor was quiet.

'Are you tired?'

'Not especially. I was thinking about Grace.'

'What about her? I thought she looked well.'

'Oh yes she did, but she seems concerned about Bendor's gambling. Is she right to feel worried do you suppose?'

Gabriel thought for a moment before answering. 'I too was worried for a time, but I think he's managed to rein in the habit of late. I know he was playing the tables a couple of times a week and losing more than he was winning. I was worried he was getting in with the wrong crowd, but now with both of us spending such a lot of time at the stud he's too busy to be gaming.'

'You never said you were worried.'

'Ben and I have known each other for so long it feels disloyal to discuss him, to talk about him behind his back as it were. Even to you my love. Anyway, last month we had a frank exchange of views and I think I got through to him. Grace had asked me to talk to him, as you say she was concerned.'

'Poor Grace. She's obviously still vexed; to mention it so pointedly and in company too.'

'I blame myself. When you were dancing I took her to one side and told her I'd spoken with Ben. I'd meant to ride over to see her last week but you know how it is, other things got in the way. I think it put the matter in her mind again. She's just concerned for him.'

'Rightly so if he's spending so much time from home.'

'Bendor has a lot on his plate. The estate does well, but he works hard and likes to play hard. I think after our conversation he's got things back into perspective. He knows he has a lot to lose. Having such a large estate can be like having a noose about one's neck I'd imagine. He has good agents, but likes to be in control.'

'That sounds familiar.'

'We all like to know what's going on with our concerns... even you.'

'I'm glad you're no good at the card table.'

'Thank you Eleanor. What would I do without you to boost my confidence?'

ℛ

'It seems no matter how hard we try we can't find a property to buy or lease to start our new enterprise.' Ruby and Claire had come to Westshore to explain

271

their situation. Eleanor was sorry to hear their news.

'We'd found a building which was the right size and in a good location, but the gentleman who owned it decided to lease it to a man, rather than two women. I suppose that's hardly surprising.'

'Something will turn up soon.'

'I don't doubt it, but now we've thought of giving up this life we're eager for a fresh start. We can't give up our night work until we have other monies coming in. Otherwise we'd have nothing to live on.'

Eleanor noted her husband was correct in his assumption that the girls hadn't saved any of their hard earned money.

'I suppose you could find work but what you mean is there's nothing that pays so well. Have you thought of moving further afield to look for a property? The business could do just as well in Amble, Craster or Beadnell. Possibly they have more suitable properties to buy or lease?' Eleanor suddenly had another idea. 'I used to live in Whitby before my marriage. A town of that size would be perfect would it not? Why not give Whitby a look?' She was pleased with her suggestion. 'Mr Reynolds has The Eleanor Rose sailing for Whitby in a week's time, and I know he'd let you have a berth on board. He would waive the passage I'm sure.'

'We hadn't thought of a bigger location.' Ruby looked at Claire, a bright look upon her agile face. 'I believe you're right Mrs Reynolds. Perhaps there would be more properties to choose from in a bigger place.'

'I don't know, there may be a down side, prices might be higher too but I think it's worth an exploratory visit.'

Later that evening Eleanor told Gabriel of her idea.

'You appear intent on pushing me into the arms of harlots it seems. I can just imagine my crew's faces when they see who we're to transport to Whitby. Are Ruby and Claire to work their passage?'

Eleanor narrowed her eyes at his flippancy. 'They're to have free passage.'

'Eleanor, I'm running a business. If they're to become businesswomen then Ruby and Claire must realise they have to pay their way just like anyone else.'

Eleanor smirked. 'But you owe me my love; I won the bet and the passage will dispense the wager.'

Gabriel shook his head. 'I'm hoodwinked again. You should be the head of the East India Company; their profits would soar with you on the board.'

'Or perhaps I'll come too.'

'Travel to Whitby with two whores?'

'They won't be whores by then. I told you they're keen to be respectable.'

'Nevertheless you have responsibilities here do you not?'

'I suppose I do. They have to do this for themselves I think. Very well I shan't go, but I'll write to Mama and ask her to look out for suitable properties.'

15

June brought storms to the Northumberland coast. Waves crashed upon the shore, winds howled down the chimney and rain lashed against the windows. After a warm spring, early summer had taken a tumble. Rose, at almost a year old was growing and thriving and Eleanor was more tired than ever, she never realised a baby took up so much time. She had Ginny of course, but she preferred to look after her daughter herself whenever she could.

After the couple had breakfasted together, Gabriel looked with concern at his wife who still looked tired. 'I've some business to take care of at the bay, but I'll be back in an hour or so. Should you like to take a carriage ride if the weather stays fine? The fresh air will do you good.'

He thought perhaps all she wanted to do was go back to bed, but he knew she would agree to go. She possibly guessed he was trying to cheer her up. The poor summer was affecting her state of mind and this combined with being tired had brought her low. He wasn't used to this side of Eleanor and it disturbed him. It was something he'd not witnessed before.

'That will be nice, thank you my love. Are you sure you can spare the time?'

'I'll make time, it's the least I can do.'

Gabriel smiled to himself as he left the house.

Within the hour he'd returned but he wasn't alone. Eleanor was waiting for him in the drawing room. When the door opened, the look on his wife's face told him all his planning had been worthwhile.

'Abalone! What a lovely surprise, I'd no idea.'

Gabriel standing behind his wife's best friend was carrying Abalone's daughter in his arms.

'My how you've grown. You were just four weeks old the last time I saw you. I'm your godmother.' Eleanor lifted Beatrice from Gabriel's arms.

'Careful Eleanor she's quite a weight now.' Her friend beamed.

Abalone and Eleanor had been friends for many years, ever since Eleanor at sixteen, had stowed away on a Dutch collier heading for Amsterdam. She'd been spotted almost at once, but the captain, Abalone's husband, had taken pity on her and taken her to meet his wife.

Bartel and Abalone Visser were a golden couple, both were blonde-haired and blue-eyed. Eleanor had persuaded them to let her stay for a month and during that time they'd become firm friends. Eleanor fell in love with Amsterdam and with this unusual, artistic woman during her stay. Eleanor looked up to Abalone; she loved the free and easy lifestyle the couple enjoyed.

Eleanor had returned to Holland when she was trying to decide what to do when she had found Gabriel had a murky past. It was Abalone's influence which had helped heal the wounds and allowed Eleanor to relax her principles. Gabriel had followed her to Amsterdam and after a lot of heart searching and intervention from Abalone, they had come to an understanding. They had married soon after their return to England.

'Before you start to get in a flap my love,' Gabriel cautioned, 'the staff know guests are expected. Rooms are ready, my old crib has been brought out of storage for Beatrice and extra provisions ordered. You don't have to lift a finger.'

Eleanor was astonished. 'I don't know how you've arranged it all without me knowing, I'll have to watch you in future.'

The tea tray was brought in. 'What a good husband you have Eleanor, I knew he would make you happy. And this house, it is just how you described it, so light and airy and so close to the sea.'

Gabriel interrupted politely. He could see a cosy chat was on the cards. 'Will you please excuse me ladies. I still have business to which I must attend. Bartel is here too Eleanor, we're working together on a new scheme. We'll both be back for dinner.'

He left the two together to get reacquainted.

ℛ

Eleanor was so pleased to see her old friend; they were enjoying the visit, enjoying sharing confidences. Although they corresponded regularly, they both agreed there was nothing better than being in each other's company.

After a late breakfast the two friends sat talking in the newly completed conservatory.

'I have a gift for Rose for her birthday,' Abalone said. 'How quickly the time passes. Today she is one year old, I can hardly believe it.'

'Thank you that's so kind.' Eleanor opened the parcel and saw it was a sketch of her daughter playing with her favourite rattle. 'You're so talented Abalone, it's her likeness exactly. She'll treasure it when she's older I'm sure. Wait until Gabriel sees it, I know it will have pride of place in the library.' She stood back to admire the portrait.

They began to discuss motherhood and their daughters. After a while Eleanor mentioned something which vexed her. 'I'm for ever being asked when the next baby will be on its way. How rude old biddies are. What business is it of theirs when I have another child?'

'It is the same for me. It is annoying is it not when one is hoping and each month passes and there is still no baby. I dearly want Bea to have a brother or sister.'

'Gabriel would have a house full if he had his way, which is worrying as the house is quite large as you see. I, on the other hand, am content with what we have at the moment, there's more to life than babies. I've all sorts of plans swilling about in my head, for a charity as well as new business ventures.' Eleanor wrinkled her nose. 'Last week I made a particular effort to go to a shareholder meeting. It's a new company I've invested in and I wanted to attend to see the set up. When I got there I was made to feel most unwelcome.'

Abalone raised an eyebrow. 'Let me guess, they were all men who thought you had no reason to be there.'

'Exactly! Most men live in the dark ages. I forget not all men are like our husbands. Reluctantly the shareholders agreed I could stay, how kind of them. They spoke to me like a dim-witted child throughout.' She grimaced. 'I'll make a point of going to the next meeting just for the hell of it. I made one or two salient points I think. They were acknowledged but dismissed out of hand.' She shook her head.

'I encounter the same thing when I approach galleries sometimes, but things are a little more forward thinking in Holland. I have a new exhibition to mount, but this time I was approached by the gallery which made a refreshing change. Things are progressing a little, especially in the art world. I'm sure you would have been just as unwelcome at a shareholder meeting in Amsterdam. Shipping has always been men's work.'

'I know. Enlightenment is a long way off. I think I'll

take Rose next time. That should give them an attack of the vapours.'

Abalone chuckled and said: 'Not a good idea if you want to be taken seriously. Perhaps you should go dressed as a man?'

'I don't think I could carry it off these days.'

'Perhaps not, but we also need to keep our men on their toes, even Bartel needs a reminder from time to time that I am capable of more than looking after the house and daubing paint on a canvas. Yet going back to our earlier conversation, I still want Bea to have a brother or sister to play with, I am not getting any younger. We should count our blessings, I know we can't have everything and there are many worse off than us.'

Eleanor and Abalone decided to walk on the beach. It was a cool, windswept day, but the two friends were keen to be outdoors. The sky refused to brighten and gulls cawed mournfully overhead. A carrion crow swooped and added its voice to the gulls' discordant chorus. The sun wasn't providing the warmth it should have done for the time of year.

As they returned to the shelter of the garden, Eleanor pulled back the hood of her cloak. 'We could sit in the summer house before we return, or if you're cold the conservatory will be warm.'

'I would prefer to stay outside in the fresh sea air for a while longer.' The two friends linked arms and set off for the summer house.

Eleanor suddenly stopped dead. 'What's that I wonder, on the seat there?' From a distance they were both unsure.

'It looks like a crib; surely your nursemaid would not leave Rose outside unattended in this wind?'

'It's not Rose's crib.' They hurried to the summer house and peered inside where a basket containing a baby sat on the seat. An infant wrapped warmly in a patterned shawl slept soundly. The two women looked at each other in astonishment. They cast about them, sweeping the beach hoping to see someone who might have left the baby, but the beach was deserted. Then Eleanor saw a note attached to the shawl. After she'd read it she passed it to Abalone. They exchanged troubled looks. Eleanor felt her legs turn to jelly and her stomach turn over.

℟

Bryony Swift watched the scene unfold sheltered from the buffeting winds by the high dunes. She ducked as she saw the two women cast about, bewilderment written on their faces.

'That's taken the smug look from your face Mrs La di Da Reynolds,' she muttered to herself. 'Wait until your husband sees the note. Will he be believed when he tells you he knows nothing of the baby? I think not. At the very least it will put a seed of doubt in your mind. What's the saying about revenge being a dish best served cold? Consider yourself served Gabriel Reynolds.'

Bryony watched as Eleanor continued to look about her.

It gave Bryony no pleasure to give her precious child away, especially to a woman she hated, but what was she to do? The thought of Eleanor Reynolds taking care of her son gave her no satisfaction, but rich people such as the Reynolds didn't look after their own children she knew that much. They had a nursemaid.

Since the birth Bryony couldn't find work, what with a baby to mind how was she supposed to manage? Without a man to shoulder the responsibility her options were limited. At least now both of them would survive, even if they did so separately. Her captain seemed to have disappeared off the face of the earth so he was no use. He didn't even know he was a father. Would he care if he did?

Bryony had been watching the house for some weeks and had seen the young nursemaid out and about with the Reynolds brat. She at least seemed kind. By placing her beloved boy at Westshore she'd be able to keep her eye on him, or so she hoped. She stifled a sob. Her grief at losing her baby threatened to fell her. She never imagined she could love someone as much as she loved her son. She wrapped her arms about her thin body. Her insides felt they were being wrenched from her with hot irons. Her heart was breaking.

Bryony watched as she saw the blonde lady carefully pick up the basket and for a moment she almost ran out and snatched him back; who was this woman? But then she knew she had nothing to offer him, nothing but a mother's love and that wouldn't keep him alive. Giving him away was the only thing she could think to do. She had to put his needs before her own, no matter what the cost to herself.

Even from this distance Bryony could see Eleanor Reynolds' face had turned as white as milk. The companion carried her baby through into the conservatory and disappeared from sight. Eleanor followed, looking about her as if she expected someone to appear at any moment and lay claim to the boy.

Tears began to fall as Bryony got to her feet. She fought to gain control of her emotions. 'Crying won't get you anywhere my girl,' she chastised herself. She took a long calming breath and turned her back on Westshore.

You'll rue the day you treated me like dirt under your feet Mr and Mrs High and Mighty. How I wish I could be a fly on the wall now. Let's see what *that* will do to your oh so perfect marriage.

R

The four friends stared into the basket as a blissfully unaware baby slept on. When Bartel had seen his wife come into the room carrying a burden, he had done as any gentleman would do and got up to relieve her of it. Bartel put the basket on a table.

'Have you two been shopping?' the blonde Dutchman joked.

Eleanor, who was not usually the fainting type, sank to the floor. Gabriel leapt forward and caught her, then scooped her up in his arms and laid her on a sofa.

'Man alive what the... ?'

Eleanor recovered her senses quickly and stood alongside her friends and husband. They all stared at the baby. Gabriel read the note and looked at his wife who was chalk white. Bartel signalled to his wife and they made to leave the room.

'Please don't leave on our account. I want you to hear what I have to say. You're our friends and I have nothing to hide.'

Gabriel looked again at the note, disbelief written on his face.

'Eleanor my love, you know this is some mischief. You know this baby isn't mine. We have no secrets from one another. This is as much news to me as it is to you and I swear on Rose's life I'm not this boy's father.'

The note in his hand said the baby boy was named Gabriel after his father. It had asked the boy be recognised by him as his heir.

'Why would someone do this Gabriel, whose child is it?' He saw the look on his wife's face and his heart went out to her.

'How would I know?' Gabriel's frustration was evident in his voice. 'This isn't my son no matter what the note says. It's a work of fiction. I don't know why someone would accuse me; somebody is trying to make trouble. Why would I recognise him as my heir when I don't recognise him at all?'

Bartel offered a suggestion. 'Some poor woman quite possibly saw the fine house and hoped her baby would have a better life. I don't accuse you of course, but why would someone leave their baby with such an incriminating note? Perhaps the woman knows you, or of you?' He looked to Abalone. 'Did you see anyone while you were out on your walk?'

'When we saw the basket we both looked about us, but there was no one in sight.'

There was a heavy silence as everyone tried to process their own thoughts.

At last Eleanor looked at Gabriel. 'I don't know why this has happened, it's like a bad dream, but I do believe you Gabriel. I know we've had problems in the past, but I know you're loyal and honest, yet it doesn't explain the note. Had the baby been left anonymously then it would have been different. We would have thought it odd of course, but we'd have supposed some poor woman at her wits end had left the baby hoping we'd notify the authorities. We'd have supposed her unable to care for the baby, but the note is meant to harm.'

'And I'll say what you're all thinking - with his dark curls he looks like me.'

Eleanor let out a sob.

Abalone shook her head. 'Women, unmarried women, are forced to give up their babies every day. Some abandon them in the canals in Holland. They have no choice when the man casts them aside, but leaving the child, accusing you of being the father is done to damage your reputation as Eleanor rightly suggests. The mother may mean to force your hand to keep the baby or risk your good name by notifying the authorities. Perhaps she means to blackmail you?'

'Blackmail?' Gabriel paced the room. 'Man alive I won't be blackmailed. It's all speculation, none of us knows the answer, but what are we to do now? We need to speak to someone about this. Who should we notify?'

There followed a discussion about the short and the long term care of the unknown baby and what to do about him. At last all agreed, as the baby was clearly so young, perhaps only six weeks old, that someone must be found to feed the boy. For now, the baby slept on oblivious of the trouble he was causing, but sooner or later he would need feeding.

'Presumably whoever abandoned him had fed him shortly before discarding him.' Eleanor shuddered. 'How could she take the child from her breast and leave him to his fate. I could no sooner do that than - '

'But you do not know the woman's circumstances,'

Abalone interrupted, 'she may be heartbroken but thinks it is a sacrifice worth making if her son can be cared for by rich parents. This makes me think it is someone you know. It could even be a man, perhaps a father or a brother? The woman may have died in childbirth and he, possibly a working man, cannot care for a baby.'

Eleanor sank back on the sofa as Gabriel rang the bell.

'What are you doing?'

'The servants might have seen someone about earlier. I'll gather them together to see if they saw anyone acting suspiciously.'

Ginny came to say Rose was ready for her feed, so she was the first to be interrogated.

'Ginny did you go out earlier, did you go anywhere near the summer house?'

'Rose had her walk, but we haven't ventured out since this morning. The wind was that fierce.'

Eleanor reluctantly followed Ginny to the nursery.

Before all the staff could be gathered together, the baby woke and started crying. Abalone picked him up and tried to soothe him, then followed Eleanor to the nursery.

The staff lined up in the drawing room wondering what was going on. They couldn't imagine why they'd been gathered together like this.

Gabriel addressed them: 'I've asked to speak with you on an urgent matter.' The staff shuffled uncomfortably. 'Cast your minds back to earlier today and try to remember if you saw anyone at Westshore, a stranger perhaps. It may have been a man or a woman, possibly someone whom you didn't know. Did any of you see anyone in the garden or on their way to the summer house carrying a basket?'

There was a gentle murmur, but no one offered up any information. Ivy's face was blood red, but Gabriel knew the girl to be painfully shy and didn't see this as a sign of guilt. He suddenly noticed Joe was absent.

'Where's Joe, why is he not here?'

Mrs Madison spoke up. 'He's gone into Alnmouth sir, to the blacksmith. He should be back soon.'

'How long has he been gone?'

'He left not ten minutes ago Mr Reynolds sir, he said he meant to go this mornin', but time ran away with him.'

'Send him straight to me as soon as he returns Mrs Madison. If anyone remembers anything at all please come and see me immediately.' He ran his fingers through his hair. 'Thank you all. You may go about your business.'

Gabriel poured rum for himself and Bartel. 'I think the local magistrate should be contacted.'

'I agree. You need this sorted out as quickly as possible. Eleanor looked most upset.'

'Who can blame her? Lord, she must rue the day she married me.'

Gabriel sent off a message to Sir John Riddleston.

He knew Riddleston, a local land owner, but only ran into him occasionally at social events. He was generally well respected in Alnmouth. He had asked Gabriel, on more than one occasion, to consider the bench himself, stating the county had need of good men. Gabriel however was reluctant; after his own run in with the law where he'd been accused and acquitted of manslaughter he was loath to have anything more to do with courtrooms. Under the present circumstances however, he could think of nothing else to do but to contact the magistrate for advice.

'Eleanor, I've sent for Sir John. You've met him briefly I believe, he's the local magistrate.' Eleanor had fed Rose and she and Abalone had returned to the drawing room.

'Why has he been sent for?' Eleanor shot a flinty look at Gabriel.

'We must inform the authorities my love. What else would you have me do?'

'I don't know.' Eleanor looked dazed.

'We need guidance on what to do.'

'I suppose so.' She was in shock.

'This little one will need a feed soon I expect?' Abalone looked to Eleanor.

'I'm sorry Abalone this... this incident, this - oh God - this new calamity will have spoilt your visit. Every time Gabriel and I are happy something turns up to rock the boat.'

Gabriel took both his wife's hands in his. 'It's as you

say Eleanor, each time the sea calms a tempest erupts and threatens our course. I would spare you this if I could.'

'I know you would Gabriel, I don't blame you.' She still looked pale. 'I'm aware how this sounds,' Eleanor sobbed, 'but I want that boy out of the house and out of our lives.' Tears were threatening to fall as he reached for her and held her close.

The interloper continued to cry.

'I understand how you feel, but it's not this little *jongen's* fault. He is an innocent.' Abalone was the voice of reason.

The baby continued to bawl. Abalone made a suggestion: 'Perhaps if Ginny brings some sugar water I could try to pacify him for a while.'

Eleanor looked at her friend with startled eyes. 'Don't ask me to feed him Abalone, I know you think him hard done by, as do I, but I can't find it in me.' A tear slipped down her cheek.

Gabriel pulled her closer. He felt her pain.

'I would not ask you Eleanor, but if a wet nurse cannot be found today, this little boy will go hungry. I could feed him myself if need be.'

Eleanor's eyes opened wide, but she didn't answer. When Ginny came she gave the sugar water to Abalone who began to feed the solution with a teaspoon. The baby became quiet.

'There now my handsome boy, are you wondering where your mama is?' Abalone cooed to the child.

Ransom brought a note.

'It says Riddleston will call within the hour as he's to dine with Saul Coates so will be passing by.'

The hour passed slowly. Eleanor and Abalone drank tea, but the men had need of something stronger and more rum was drunk.

At last Sir John arrived. Introductions were made and the situation explained. The magistrate looked Gabriel in the eye.

'Well sir, this seems a rum do.' He accepted a glass of canary wine. 'The baby was left in your summer house you say?'

'That's correct sir. My wife and her friend here found him after their walk.'

Before the magistrate arrived the four friends had discussed whether to disclose the incriminating note. It had been agreed even though it was awkward, they had to tell the whole story if the child's mother was to be located. Gabriel handed the note to Sir John.

'Ah, this is embarrassing for you Gabriel. It cannot be easy for you either Mrs Reynolds.'

Gabriel saw Eleanor's stony expression. Gabriel knew Sir John thought there was no smoke without fire. He thought the boy was a by-blow it was clear. He watched as Riddleston gave his wife a pitying look. He knew to deny all knowledge of the baby too vehemently would only make him look guilty. He held his own counsel... just.

'I will alert the constable, but I do not hold out much

hope.' The magistrate took snuff to fill the awkwardness of the moment.

Abalone broke the silence. 'Mothers all too often abandon their offspring in a harbour town where sailors have their sport then leave the girls high and dry. It is the same situation in Holland, Sir John.'

The magistrate scratched an itch under his powdered wig. He looked into the crib as the child gurgled contentedly. 'Handsome little chap, doesn't look very old, but not a new born. Was he in this condition when you found him? He looks well nourished and cared for.'

'He was. We're eager a wet nurse is found for him Sir John.' Gabriel saw how his wife looked perfectly calm; only he, and possibly their friends, knew what she was going through. Her hands were clasped in her lap possibly to stop them from trembling.

'He will need feeding shortly. We have pacified him with sugar water, but his belly won't stay fooled for long.'

'The only thing I can suggest is I send him to the workhouse where wet nurses are two a penny. That will be the best solution I think.'

'The workhouse! I hadn't thought he'd go to such a miserable place. Is there no alternative?' Gabriel paced the floor.

The magistrate shrugged his broad shoulders. 'If you care to keep him until his mother is found, *if* his mother is found that is, that would be a temporary answer.'

Gabriel shot a look at his wife. 'I don't see we have a choice. I know you don't want the boy in the house Eleanor, but would you have him go to the workhouse? We can think again in a day or two. Who knows, as Abalone pointed out, a blackmail note may arrive.'

'Ah yes, blackmail. The thought had occurred to me. You would not be the first to be blackmailed Gabriel.'

It was clear from Riddleston's expression he thought Gabriel had been caught out with some servant girl or other. Again he wanted to set the record straight, but knew it was useless.

'I'm of the same mind as you. I can't send a child there.' Eleanor looked defiantly at Sir John. 'But what about a wet nurse, can one be sent here to Westshore?'

'I expect so Mrs Reynolds. It would be capital if he could stay here; as usual there is much disease at the poorhouse. Less risk for the boy if you could take care of him, difficult as it is for you my dear.'

Gabriel was beginning to wish he'd not called the man in. The magistrate's tone was condescending to say the least. He could see Eleanor was trying hard to stay calm and maintain her dignity. He knew she wanted to tell the magistrate to get out, but was sensible enough to hold her tongue. He too suppressed the urge to bite back angrily.

Sir John made to leave. 'I do not expect we will ever find the mother. Not unless she has a change of heart and returns for him, or as you say is intent on blackmail. You will have to come to terms with the fact there is nowhere else for the child to go I am afraid, save the workhouse that is, there is no foundling hospital hereabouts.'

When the man had gone, and before any more discussion on the subject could begin, Ivy brought the message that Joe had returned from the blacksmith. Gabriel asked her to send him in. He put the same question to Joe as he'd put to the rest of the staff.

'A never saw nobody, but then A was in the tack room all the forenoon an' in the barn this afternoon.' Gabriel knew it was a long shot but he'd had to ask.

'Thank you Joe, you can go.'

The groom turned to leave, but as he got to the door he turned and looked at Gabriel. 'It might be nowt but A did see one person on me way to the blacksmith now A come to think on it. Not exactly a stranger though. She were in front er me and in a hurry by the looks on it. It were windy, mebbe she were just wantin' to be out er it. A seen her about the dunes a bit lately.'

'Who was it Joe?'

'Bryony Swift. She were walkin' that fast A never caught up with her afore she turned off. Ned's lame, he's cast a shoe, so A was takin' it steady.'

Gabriel shot a look at Eleanor.

'Bryony Swift?' Eleanor's face flushed with anger.

'Dear Lord,' Gabriel was shocked, 'turned off where

Joe?'

'She went the back road to The Schooner. Jax told me she's been workin' there, bit of a come down fer her.'

'You're right Joe it is a bit of a come down from lady's maid to tavern wench.'

'It certainly is,' Eleanor agreed, 'you don't think... '

Before Eleanor had time to finish the sentence, Gabriel was asking Joe to saddle Copper.

Gabriel entered The Schooner via the tap room lowering his head to avoid an oak beam. It wasn't a tavern he was inclined to frequent normally, The Hope and Anchor being nearer to his work.

After ordering ale he started a conversation with the landlord. 'My wife hired a maid last Christmas. Her name was Swift, Bryony Swift. She was wondering if she was still available for work, our groom said she's been working here?'

'She were, but that were months back. Had to let her go. She thought herself a cut above, right little madam she were. Would've given the minx her marchin' orders sooner, but turns out she were in the family way. Men don't come here to look at what they've left home to get away from, if yer get my meanin', Mr Reynolds.'

'With child you say? Is she still in Alnmouth do you know?'

'The wife told her of a place down by the bay to rent. She lived-in here, room comes wi' the job. We needed her room fer the new lass who's a lot more accommodatin' than Bryony Swift A can tell yer. A think she must have had the bairn by now. Although A've not seen her about maself.' Gabriel looked thoughtful before downing his drink and thanking the landlord.

Ironically the area of the bay the landlord mentioned was where Gabriel, a long time ago and before his marriage, had kept a mistress. It seemed a life time had passed since then. He was a changed man now.

As he had no address for Bryony, he decided to knock on the door of Libby's old house and ask if anyone knew of her. It felt strange to be standing on the doorstep again. This was the house he'd helped Libby move from when he first met her. The house seemed even more derelict than he remembered. An old sack covered a broken pane of glass and the door barely fitted its frame. In the intervening years since Gabriel had been here, the landlord had clearly done little in the way of repairs. It was indeed no more than a hovel.

A young girl clutching an infant stared at him as she opened the door. She looked no older than fifteen.

'Is your mother at home?' Gabriel asked, presuming the girl was looking after her sibling.

'Ma died five year since, but A'm in the same trade and can accommodate yer. Come in.'

Gabriel was taken aback. 'I'm sorry you misunderstand, I'm looking for a particular woman.'

'Well whatever it was she did fer yer A'm sure A can do just as good.' She winked and beckoned him inside once more.

Gabriel felt strange emotions; shock at being propositioned by a child being the predominant feeling. 'I don't require your services, but if you can supply me with information I can pay you all the same. Do you know a woman called Bryony Swift? She has possibly just had a child. She's tall and attractive with chestnut coloured hair.'

'That's a first, come to claim yer son have yer.'

'Son, you know she had a boy?'

'A know nowt, but a know men don't want daughters. Yer wouldn't be lookin' fer a lass, what good are they?'

'Every bit as good as boys,' Gabriel said angrily.

The girl merely laughed in his face. 'A'm new round here. A don't know anybody, not by name any road. The woman who lived here afore me had a bairn an' looked comely, the baby weren't very old, A've only bin here a few days. Could be her who yer lookin' fer, A suppose.'

'Did she say whcre she was removing to?'

'She weren't one for chattin', just handed over the key an' left. Oh she did say one thing now A come to think on.'

'What was that?' Gabriel was hopeful.

'She said the roof leaks an A'm welcome to the damp.'

The girl grinned. The baby began to whimper and squirm. She jiggled her up and down on her hip. Gabriel handed the girl sixpence for her trouble and was about to leave when he thought better of it.

'Are you minding the child for someone?' he asked.

'She's mine.'

'Yours? You look so young. Have you no family? Is there a father on the scene?'

'You be full er questions! He's long gone if yer must know. The minute A told him about ma condition he legged it. Same old story. Sailor from Holland he were, probably got girls all over the place. A'm on ma own, no family left to speak of.'

Gabriel stepped nearer to the baby and looked at its wrinkled red face as it let out a cry of outrage. He handed the girl another, larger coin.

'Here, take this and look after your baby. You're all each other have it would seem. What do you call her?'

'She's called Hope, 'cause that's all we got left - Hope.'

Gabriel felt sorry for the girl, but what could he do? He imagined this was an all too familiar story. 'If ever you're in distress come to the Reynolds shipping office and ask for me. I'm the owner. Is this the only work you do? Can you not get respectable work?'

'Oh aye, there's plenty who'll hire a girl an' a bairn. Only last week A were offered a job at a big house in Amble.'

Her caustic reply brought Gabriel up short. The girl

went to close the door. She'd clearly had enough of him. Tight-lipped, Gabriel repeated his offer of help as he bid her goodbye.

He stared ahead at the grey, squally sea. He thought of the life Hope would have compared to that of his own daughter. The child had been born into poverty and no doubt would die in the same state. With a mother like that, what future had she to look forward to? Not that he blamed the mother; she was but a child herself. Her life would be one of misery and hardship and of trying to protect her daughter from the effects of poverty. Her life would be spent trying to fend off disease and malnourishment. Continuous hunger would grind her down all too soon. She would share her squalid living conditions with lice, mice, fleas and bedbugs. Men would ill-use her and break her body and then her spirit.

Gabriel pushed his fists deep into his overcoat pockets. An uneducated girl like her would have no voice, no rights and no way of getting out of this poverty trap that had ensnared her. Little baby Hope literally had no hope of a decent life. Both were set on a path of destruction.

Gabriel shrugged trying to unfasten the burden that weighed heavily on his shoulders. He could hardly return to Westshore with another baby - this time the baby would have a mother in tow.

His thoughts reluctantly turned to Libby, his onetime mistress. Through his misdeeds she had found herself in the same situation as this poor girl, though she'd found respectable work. The result of his liaison with her had been his son, Steven, whom she'd taken to America in the hope of rebuilding her life. Gabriel had only met him once before Libby had married a Quaker and emigrated to Nantucket Island. Gabriel wished he could see his son again. He thought about him every day. Although he now had Rose, whom he adored, he would like to see how Steven looked, know how he fared. He would never see his son again and the fact would be a constant pain for him for the rest of his life.

Eleanor was always telling him life was different for men and he knew her to be right. Hope's father was unobliged to provide for his daughter. She was just a load to be cast off along with the anchor when he left these shores without a backward glance.

By the time Gabriel returned home it was time for supper, not that he had an appetite. He changed quickly and went to join the others in the dining room.

'Any news?' Eleanor asked hopefully.

'Some, yes.' He told them what the landlord of The Schooner had said.

'Bryony with child!' Eleanor was astonished. 'I would have imagined she was far too clever to get caught in that way.'

'Perhaps she thought to trick someone into marriage?' Gabriel cast a sidelong look at Eleanor. 'She was a cunning piece if you remember.'

In his absence, Eleanor had told Abalone and Bartel

about Bryony's character.

'Well she certainly sounds a candidate for being the mother,' Bartel said. 'The note would make sense if you parted on bad terms Eleanor.'

'It was not just my wife with whom she parted on bad terms.'

He told them of his last interview with the servant. Eleanor was wide-eyed. 'You never spoke of this with me! I'd no idea this meeting had taken place but that seals it I think. He must be her son. She didn't like me, but after what you said to her I can't imagine her to be *that* fond of you either.' Eleanor put her knife and fork down, her appetite gone.

'There's nothing more we can do tonight. Was a wet nurse found? Is the child fed?' Gabriel too had little appetite and pushed his plate away.

'Yes, although Mrs M wasn't inclined to let her past the scullery. She was as neat and clean as any who've come from the workhouse, but our esteemed cook thought her below standard. I've arranged for her to have one of Charity's cast offs. The girl's name is Patience, I suspect she's from a Quaker family with such a name. She looks no older than seventeen. There seems a dearth of unmarried mothers and a surfeit of men not willing to face their responsibilities.' Eleanor's temper erupted. 'It's easy if you're a man to sail away without a care in the world and not a thought for what you leave in your wake.'

'Not all men are so inclined,' Bartel reasoned, 'but

you are right Eleanor. It is the woman and her child that are left to pick up the pieces. You and I Gabriel will possibly not let our daughters out of our sight until they are old and grey.'

ℛ

'You do believe me Eleanor, about the baby not being mine?' Gabriel stood behind his wife and looked at her reflection in the mirror.

'Do you think you would be here now if I didn't?'

'Well, no I suppose not. What a day it's been.' Gabriel sat on the edge of their bed.

'Men have needs I seem to remember you telling me before we were married.' She threw him a quelling look.

'I know I've been guilty in the past as we're both aware. When you're a young man, a young buck about town you tend not to think of the consequences. Selfish I know, but there it is.'

Eleanor bit back an acerbic reply. She was in no mood for an argument, especially one they'd had many times before. Instead she said: 'Patience, the wet nurse, is so young and from a good Quaker family. When she found she was with child she was dismissed from her job as a maid. It was her employer's son who'd taken advantage of her. When she told him about her condition he just shrugged. The next day she was let go without a reference. She went home, but her parents disowned her. She had nowhere else to go but the workhouse.' Eleanor banged her hairbrush down on the dressing table in frustration. 'How could her parents turn their back on her? I imagine the "young buck" had promised her the earth then when she told him she was to have his child he moved on to the next maid.'

Gabriel told her about the girl at the bay and about Hope, the baby he feared was doomed to a life of hardship. Eleanor thought for a moment.

'Patience had a difficult birth, then her baby died minutes after she was born. Can you imagine that Gabriel?'

'Dear God, some have it so hard. We're so lucky.'

'We are. We should try to think of a way of helping these women and their children. Not some fallen woman institution to reform them; they're not in need of reforming, it's the men who need educating. The girls have been seduced, lied to, badly treated and abused. They're victims of sweet talking callow youths in some instances or misused by their elders and betters in others. Something should be done for these girls to help them help themselves and preserve what they have left of their dignity. There are some too proud to take handouts, the workhouse isn't the place for them, and especially not for their babies.'

Eleanor got into bed. 'I had a bad feeling this morning, a feeling something untoward was going to happen.'

'The old gypsy woman has a lot to answer for, you've become superstitious. You never used to be so inclined. Come, let's try to get some sleep and see what tomorrow brings.'

'I can tell you one thing it won't bring.'

Gabriel raised an eyebrow questioningly.

'It won't bring a penitent Bryony Swift to our door. There are some who are beyond help.'

16

Bryony, dressed in her second best day dress, looked up and down the various wharves. She'd not realised Whitby Harbour was so much bigger than Alnmouth. She had searched for a particular ship and its captain and at last spied The Whitby Lass which was being provisioned. Thank God she hadn't sailed.

Bryony now free of her burden, her son, had paid passage on a lugger to look for her lover. She was sure once he saw her he would be pleased and would take care of her. She strode confidently towards a stevedore who was leaning on a barrel smoking a pipe.

'Is Captain Turner aboard?'

'Yer don't want to be bothering with the cap'n. I'm sure I can help a pretty thing like you.' The man gave Bryony an admiring look.

'When are you sailing?' she asked bluntly ignoring his leering.

'Day or two, 'appen. Will be 'ere tonight fer sure so we could 'ave some fun together, you and me.'

Bryony left the man in no doubt any fun he would have this night wouldn't involve her.

'Is he aboard or not?' She was exasperated.

'Not.' The man spat into the sea.

She walked up and down the quay hoping to catch sight of her man, but after attracting the wrong sort of attention decided on a different tack. She didn't know Whitby, save for what her captain had told her, but she knew when she saw Grape Lane what sort of area *that* was and knew to avoid it. She was in need of somewhere to stay. It had to be cheap but respectable. She had some money but not enough to squander on fancy lodgings.

She'd sold all her belongings knowing if she missed her captain, she might have weeks to wait before he was back ashore. Now she knew he hadn't yet sailed she was keen to see him before he did. One night at a tavern maybe all she needed she hoped.

She entered The Fleece Inn little realising she was following in Gabriel Reynolds' footsteps of years before, for it was in this very inn where he had met Eleanor Barker as she was then. Bryony was shown to a tiny room in the attic, the catchpenny room. She sat on the straw mattress and thought what to do next.

After an uncomfortable, flea bitten night at The Fleece, Bryony Swift was up early and striding down the harbour without breaking her fast. With any luck she would break it with her man. She had taken care with her toilette and was wearing a simple dress of Prussian blue that set off her newly rounded shape nicely. Since the birth of her son she'd lost her willowy figure, now she was more buxom than lithe. It suited her.

The harbour side was busy as she side-stepped the detritus of a busy quay. Ropes, ironmongery, barrels of fish; rough looking stevedores and handsome uniformed naval men jostled about. Ships were being loaded and unloaded, provisions were stacked high, and men were hauling cargo on and off all manner of frigates, luggers, schooners and colliers. Red faced women were already gutting herring from the early morning catch.

Last night Bryony had formulated a plan. She would go aboard The Whitby Lass and ask for the captain again. If he wasn't aboard she would wait, no matter how long it took, until he arrived. He had to turn up sooner or later she reasoned. He probably needed to supervise some of the loading if the ship was to sail in the next couple of days.

A cocky character dressed in a naval uniform cat-called as she approached the wharf. She lifted her pretty nose in the air and ignored his lewd suggestion. Berth ten... She counted in her head. Berth eleven... She carried on until she reached berth twelve. It was empty. Her heart missed a beat. Was she at the wrong place, had she made a mistake? She remembered distinctly the number... twelve. She looked about her, hands on hips. Berth twelve was vacant, empty. How could that be?

'Where's The Whitby Lass?' she called to an old sea dog who was watching her from his seat on the harbour wall. Her agitation knew no bounds. Tears sprang to her eyes; she feared the worst.

'Left on the morning tide me dear, she'll not be back in port this next two months I reckon.' Bryony knew that with the ship her hopes for a life with her captain had sailed. She cursed all men, especially the stevedore from yesterday who had lied to her.

ℛ

It seemed no one in the Reynolds household got much sleep that night. On rising, Gabriel rode over to see Sir John, he hoped news of the mother had emerged. He came back despondent.

When Gabriel entered the breakfast room Eleanor and the Vissers had just finished eating, but were still at table.

'It's as we expected,' Gabriel said, 'it's the workhouse or nothing for the boy. If the mother doesn't return to claim him there's no other solution.' After Gabriel had told them what Sir John suggested they all sat chewing over what else might be done.

'If a blackmail letter was coming it would have arrived by now,' Bartel suggested. 'They would have struck while the iron was hot.' He looked to his wife as if asking permission to speak. She nodded her head imperceptibly.

'Abalone and I have a suggestion, another option for the baby. We talked about it long into the night. We would consider adopting the boy, taking him back to Holland and raising him as our own son. We are unsure what we would need to do. We would not want to break any law, but we could offer him a good home. It is an idea is it not?'

Gabriel threw a look at Eleanor who appeared totally horrified.

'Why so shocked my dear?' Abalone dipped a sweet roll in her hot chocolate. 'We have twelve bedrooms and although we intend to have more children ourselves, we do not mean to fill them all. This child could have a good life with us and we cannot bear to think of him raised in the workhouse. The way you described the place to me last night made us worry for his very survival in such an evil place. If he came with us he would be wanted and loved. If he came with us he might at least survive boyhood.'

'I don't know what to say or how it could be arranged. This is an unexpected turn.' Gabriel looked at his wife who stared back in astonishment. 'Sir John will know how to proceed I should think. This is so sudden - though I admit the thought of adoption had crossed my mind, the workhouse is no place for an infant.'

'It had crossed your mind to adopt him?' Eleanor stared at her husband in disbelief. 'You never said. I'd thought the same thing myself.'

'Whatever has happened we can't condemn a baby to such a fate, the workhouse is a death sentence for him

I would think,' Gabriel said.

'But are you sure you want the responsibility Abalone? We know nothing about him.' Eleanor sighed.

'What is there to know? I prefer to go on instinct and my gut tells me to give this child a chance. We have so much. We have more than enough to share.' Abalone smiled at Bartel. 'We are very decisive people. We once trusted our instincts and took in a young English girl who stowed away on one of Bartel's ships. We have never regretted helping her.'

Eleanor smiled. 'Being the stowaway in question I'm glad you did. You have always had a generous heart Abalone and you too Bartel, but I don't know what to say. Perhaps you could think about it for a few days, and then speak to Sir John,' Eleanor offered.

'We are determined to take him back with us if at all possible, unless of course his mama reclaims him. If Bartel and I were to go and see Sir John he may tell us if there is a procedure? A lawyer might be needed to draw up a legal document. We should not want to take him illegally. Gabriel will you vouch for us if we have need of it?'

Gabriel who was as shocked at this turn of events as Eleanor said: 'Of course. My lawyer is a good man. If you like we can consult him I expect.'

R

Five days later the adoption was complete. Neither the mother nor the expected blackmail letter had arrived. It had been a tense few days. Sir John, still suspicious of the child's exact parentage, had nevertheless been conscientious and had, along with Saul Coates, drawn up the papers needed for the adoption. The Vissers were to leave for Amsterdam as a family of four.

'No offence Gabriel, but we thought we would change the baby's name. He will be raised as a Dutch boy so his name should reflect that.'

'Of course, it would be a relief to me.'

'We will call him Mats.'

Eleanor's cloak billowed in the breeze as she watched her friends board ship ready to sail back to Amsterdam. She would miss her dear friend, but what had started out as a pleasant visit had taken a sinister, unexpected turn. Eleanor had seen how Abalone had taken to the boy and worried the real mother would turn up on the eve of their departure breaking her friend's heart. In the end, her fears were groundless and she took a last look at the boy. Gabriel was right; he looked remarkably like her husband. She shuddered and pushed the thought away.

'Be sure to write when you arrive home.'

'We will let you know what sort of a sailor little Mats turns out to be.' Abalone cooed at the boy in her husband's arms. 'We are leaving England with more than we bargained for, but we have no regrets.'

When the couple were back at Westshore, Eleanor

became agitated. 'What if the mother does come back for him? What if she changes her mind and turns up here and finds him gone?'

'Do you think it likely after so long? It's more than two weeks since she abandoned him. No one seems to have seen Bryony recently. Perhaps she's gone away. Who knows? We don't know for certain the boy was hers in the first place. We may be doing her a grave injustice.'

'It's true, yet I can see her doing something like this. She was spiteful enough and after what you said to her she would want to get back at us. It's funny neither of us are the types to take against people generally, we tend to live and let live but she wasn't a nice person.'

'There was something in her character. She was as you say, selfish and vindictive. She would have come between us if I'd let her and not given you a moment's thought. She was a devious baggage.'

'She was aiming to be your mistress I'm sure of that.'

Gabriel scoffed and said: 'I know, how on earth would I have managed with you as my wife and her as my mistress? Man alive, my life wouldn't have been my own. I have my hands full with you my love.'

It was the first time he'd smiled in days.

R

Eleanor arrived at Eastshore and left Jet with a groom.

The house was larger than Westshore and was a Tudor brick building with later additions. She was shown into the large, imposing withdrawing room which was furnished with heavy, dark pieces of furniture. The latticed windows added to the gloom by not letting in much of the late summer sun. Eleanor thought it a cold, manly room. She shivered.

The one bright light was Caroline. Her blonde hair dressed simply and her plain, but elegant day dress made Eleanor feel dowdy by comparison. She had arranged to take tea with Caroline; now she was home from her travels, she was determined to befriend her. She thought Caroline may be in need of company, she must still be missing her father.

'What plans have you now you're home?' Eleanor took the seat she was offered.

'Nothing so very exciting I'm sad to say. What of you?' It was clear she wanted to deflect the attention away from herself.

'We've had a little too much excitement of late I'm afraid.' She told Caroline about the Vissers' visit and the abandoned baby.

'Dear me, Gabriel would have taken the accusation to heart if I know him. It must have been a difficult time for you too.'

'It was and not helped by the patronising Sir John Riddleston. It was clear he thought Gabriel the father of the child. I could have... anyway the boy is in Holland and thriving thanks to my friends.'

Caroline looked bashful. 'Sir John has declared an interest, in me that is. Indeed he made a proposal the day after my return.'

Eleanor's mouth dropped open.

'I know! He has to be fifty if he's a day. I should rather die than marry him. Didn't I say before I went away there's a dearth of eligible young men hereabouts?'

Eleanor screwed up her face in distaste. 'Poor you, as you say it would be scraping the bottom of the barrel. It always astounds me that these lecherous old men have the bare-faced cheek to put themselves forward. Caroline please don't give up hope, I'm sure there's someone out there for you who is - '

'Not old, gouty or bald.' Caroline chuckled. 'I sincerely hope so.'

After a while Eleanor returned to the subject of the abandoned boy. She told Caroline about Patience and about the young girl at the bay who already had a baby to care for when she was still a child herself.

'Since the Vissers left, Gabriel and I have arranged for the young girl and baby Hope to move to a lodging house. We're paying her bills and trying to find her work. The episode has shown me how vulnerable young women with babies can be.'

'It's something I'm ashamed to admit I've never given any thought to before. I wrongly assumed that girls who got into trouble had a father with a shot gun who persuaded the man to do the right thing. I see from what you say it's different in a seafaring town where sailors come and go. You're kind to look after the girl.'

'I've recruited Lottie to the cause, we're going to try to help these women. We plan to set up a charity to help them to help themselves. Find them a place so the girls can go there rather than the workhouse. Gabriel and I have taken Patience on at Westshore. We didn't really need more staff, but I couldn't send the girl back to the poor house, she's had such a terrible time.' Eleanor sipped her tea. 'If we can provide a place where the women and their babies are safe and can be helped, a place where they can go out to work, respectable work not selling themselves, and earn money then this will be a good outcome for all concerned. While their babies are cared for the girls can start again, try to live better, independent lives. The poor girl at the bay was forced into prostitution when her sailor abandoned ship, but now she has another chance. Had she stayed in the hovel where Gabriel found her neither of them would have lasted long.'

'It's a laudable plan, but it sounds somewhat ambitious. You can't change the world my dear.'

'Perhaps not, but we can at least try to change the fate of the girls hereabouts. In time we might add a school room to educate both the women and their children. It's quite daunting I agree and a big undertaking which needs careful consideration. We'll need good people to run it and those with means to support it. It will take a great deal of money and a lot of time and effort, but I feel it'll be worth it. Someone has to do something for these poor girls, no one else is stepping up, we have to at least try to help.'

'Lottie called yesterday. We were at school together did you know? Anyway she mentioned something about a new venture, but in all the years I've known her she's had some scheme or pet project on the go. I hadn't realised it was so big a commitment. Lottie will be quite an asset. Once she gets the bit between her teeth there will be no stopping her.'

'Just as I'd hoped. It is a big scheme. We will need to find a house of a decent size with lots of rooms for a day nursery, a laundry and perhaps a communal sitting room where the women can meet and support each other. Then it will need to be fitted out and maintained of course.'

'You sound as if you can't wait to get started. How are you to fit it all in with Gabriel and Rose to look after?'

'I don't intend to do all the work myself, although I want to be hands on initially. I was wondering if you might be persuaded to help? You know the ladies of Alnmouth better than I, having lived here all your life. Could you help me by giving me the names of ladies you think may be interested in making a donation? Or sitting on a committee perhaps? It would save me wasting valuable time by approaching those who'd back off from such a project. Not everyone thinks as I do about unwed mothers and illegitimate babies.'

'Of course, as you say there are those who would faint at the words *unmarried mothers*, but I'm not one of them. If you will allow me I'll donate both my time and my money.' Caroline poked the fire bringing it back from the dead. 'I daresay I have more time on my hands than you at the moment, so a worthwhile cause would be diverting.'

Eleanor noticed she suddenly looked tearful.

'Like Alice and Jack Reynolds my parents only had the one child... me. Both families longed for more children, but it wasn't to be. Father always supported children's charities in particular. He loved children. You can see why they were keen to put Gabriel and I together, without a son Gabriel was as near as Father got to having one.'

For a moment Eleanor thought Caroline looked embarrassed at her disclosure, but then she said: 'Father would think this a good scheme I'm sure and I'd very much like to help in his memory.'

'Thank you Caroline, that's tremendous. I should appreciate any help you feel you can give. When can you start?'

℟

Eleanor sat in front of her mirror as Charity put away the brush, comb and pins. She looked at the clock for

317

the tenth time in as many minutes.

'Thank you, go and have your supper now. You don't need to come back later, I can manage for myself. Have a pleasant evening with your sister and don't get into any mischief. I've seen the look in Joe's eye when you pass by.'

'Nothing gets past you does it.' Charity picked up the laundry and left her mistress alone. Eleanor knocked the creases from her dress and once again glanced at the clock. Their guests were due to arrive any minute and Gabriel was going to be late, *again.*

When he'd left for the stud farm that morning, which she'd told him was fast becoming his second home, he'd promised not to be late. It was a promise he'd failed to keep all too often lately. She was just about to go down when the door opened and a shamefaced Gabriel darted into their bedchamber.

'I know, I'm sorry. Five minutes is all I need to change and I'll be down.'

Eleanor was furious. 'Yet *again* I'll be left to greet our guests alone. You've broken your promise and not for the first time. Rose is asleep and you weren't here to kiss her goodnight. Again. Dear God Gabriel, why not take your bed to the blasted stud.'

'It's only Wilson and Lottie, they won't mind so much.' He pulled off his jacket and threw it on the floor.

'It's I who mind, but apparently I don't count.'

Before he could defend himself further Eleanor

stormed out, slamming the door behind her.

As Gabriel entered the library he greeted Wilson and Lottie. 'I'm sorry to be such a lousy host.' His guests weren't at all put out, unlike his wife who pierced him with an icy look. 'Has everyone got a drink?' Gabriel poured himself a brandy.

'We were waiting for you my love,' Eleanor said mulishly.

'Ah, well then allow me.' He was about to pour drinks when Ransom announced supper was served. Eleanor gave Gabriel a look which could have frozen water. They went through to the dining room and took their seats.

'I've become obsessed with this new enterprise, the stud farm, which Bendor and myself have recently set up. My other businesses are beginning to suffer from neglect I think.'

'Just as well you have good men to look after the shipping line then,' Lottie said as she sipped her wine.

'I told myself it was just the initial set up of the new business which was diverting, but now four months in, I'm finding it hard to let go. First there was the actual building of the stud farm, then finding and buying good bloodstock, and finally the hiring of a suitable stud manager. All of it has interested me. I know I need to give my attention to other things; including my beautiful, long suffering wife, but it's been a stimulating project. Add to this the fact Bendor is just as keen and it's meant we've *both* spent many hours from home and our day-to-day work. No doubt Grace is equally upset with her husband.'

'No doubt she is.'

Eleanor was still disgruntled. She knew he was trying to make up for lost time by shooting her his most winning smile but she wasn't so cheaply bought.

Gabriel continued: 'If I'd not had my head in the clouds I could have been down sooner. I keep forgetting I have a valet; if only I'd remembered about Walters I'd have saved some time by going straight to my dressing room. He's very efficient. When he saw I was going to be late he'd laid out my clothes ready. I'd have been dressed and standing by Eleanor's side to welcome you both had I realised. Again I apologise to all of you for my rudeness.'

Eleanor, being well brought up, didn't allow her anger with Gabriel to spoil supper with their friends. She was a good hostess and enjoyed the evening. Lottie and Wilson were always good, cheerful company. Wilson was such a clever, erudite man and Lottie could always make Eleanor laugh. The heiress was fond of playing up to her audience, she particularly liked to shock Gabriel with her views on marriage in particular.

It had become their custom when just the four of them supped not to separate afterwards. They were all moderns and didn't approve of the custom of the men sitting with their port while the women sipped tea, but tonight Eleanor had other ideas.

'Come Lottie, let's take tea in the library so I can tell you what a disagreeable husband I married.' She was only half joking.

The two ladies were served canary wine. 'So what's Gabriel done to make him so disagreeable? Is it only the stud farm?'

'Only! I hardly see him and when I do all he talks about is horseflesh.'

Lottie said: 'Well that's surely better than fleshpots. I'd at least imagined he'd taken to whoring or found himself a mistress. I never imagined you to be the limpet type Eleanor; I thought you liked your independence?'

'I do, but there's independence and feeling like a widow. Rose adores Gabriel and yesterday she called "Papa" for the first time and I so wanted him to be home before she fell asleep tonight. I hoped she would say it again. He promised faithfully this morning he would be home in time to see his daughter before her bedtime, but of course he was late again.'

'Ah I see, you feel neglected. You need a little diversion of your own, a flirtation perhaps. Are you to go to the Harpers tomorrow? I hear Lord H's nephew is to be there. He's quite dashing, quite the stallion.' Lottie finished her wine. 'He's a soldier; I do love a man in uniform. Perhaps he'll distract you from your woes.'

'It sounds like you have a dalliance of your own in mind.' Eleanor refilled their glasses. 'I'm sorry to be a drudge Lottie, you always cheer me up I'm pleased to say. I've never met the captain, but I've heard about his reputation with the ladies. Gabriel and I are supposed to go, but we'll probably miss most of it if Gabriel is late home again.'

The door opened and Gabriel heard the last part of the sentence. 'I'm still in my wife's bad books it seems. I'd hoped for a thaw.' He sat beside her.

'I was just asking Eleanor if we would see you tomorrow night at the Harpers? You're tardy in your time keeping sir.' Lottie defended her friend. 'If you were married to me you'd feel the lash of my tongue and know my bedroom door would be locked to you until you'd made restitution in the form of nothing less than diamonds.'

'Wilson take heed, perhaps it's not too late to run away to sea. I hear the navy are on the lookout for surgeons.'

Again Eleanor saw her husband cast a tentative look in her direction, but she assiduously ignored him.

'I hope in that case Lottie you've remembered I'll be unable to attend. I did tell you.' Wilson shrugged. 'It's the new hospital trust meeting tomorrow night. I can't miss it, indeed I wouldn't want to miss it, but I might be able to come along later.'

Gabriel looked shamefaced. 'I'd forgotten it was the Harpers Ball tomorrow, I too am expected at the same meeting.'

Eleanor's face flushed in anger, but before she could

reply Lottie jumped in. 'In that case Eleanor, I'll call for you in my carriage at seven thirty and we shall go as two single ladies. I'll fight you for Lord Harper's nephew.'

When their guests had gone home Eleanor, having said goodnight to Rose, went to her dressing room and prepared for bed. Gabriel had also called in to see his daughter.

'She's so beautiful when fast asleep and hopefully she'll stay that way until a reasonable hour.'

'You'll hardly be expected to get up and feed her so what's it to you?' she snapped back.

'I've said I'm sorry.'

'Sorry for what Gabriel? Sorry for being late the last half dozen times we've been engaged, sorry for missing the Harpers Ball or sorry for not seeing your daughter? Last night she called out for you for the first time.' Eleanor sat on the stool by her looking glass and began to take off her jewels.

'Oh did she really call my name?'

Eleanor could see he was upset and wanted to hurt him more, but she wasn't the type of woman to try to score cheap points. Suddenly she saw the funny side of what he'd said.

'Well actually no, although I know our daughter to be the brightest child ever born, she gets her brains from my side of the family naturally, even she can't at her tender age form the word "Gabriel".'

'You're being deliberately obtuse. I'm well aware

she's been trying to say Papa. I wish I'd heard her. I'll mend my ways from now on my love. The new man at the stud is well able to manage without me.'

'I should hope so, presumably that's why you hired him.'

'Yes it's time to stand back, I see that now.'

Eleanor watched her husband's reflection in the mirror as he stood behind her. He pulled the ribbon from her hair allowing her thick, red hair to tumble down her back. She knew she wouldn't be able to resist if he kissed her neck. He knew just the place she liked. He leaned over and let his lips brush the spot. In that moment she forgave him everything.

17

Eleanor welcomed Caroline into the morning room. When they were seated she handed a list of names to Eleanor. The list comprised of the ladies she thought might support the charity Eleanor hoped to found.

'My godmother, Susan Stubbs, is newly arrived at Lesbury. Her husband has passed away recently. I hope to persuade her to help with the cause too, she was married to a judge and has seen first hand how the world works. I also thought Saul Coates, Gabriel's man of law, would be useful. I'm sure he could be persuaded to do any work required in setting up the charity pro bono. His poor wife, Rosalind, who I'm sure you've met, lost two babies prior to Felicity and Mary so I'm certain children are a cause close to both their hearts.'

'Thank you Caroline, I've met Mrs Coates but I didn't know of her losses, poor woman.'

'If you would like I can write to the ladies, and Mr Coates. I'll invite them to a meeting so you can outline the plan.'

'Can I persuade you to sit on the committee? I know

both Lottie and I would be grateful.'

'I should be pleased to help, Lottie has already asked me as it happens.' Caroline looked keen. 'The sooner we can get started the better.'

The two women discussed the new venture until dinner. The time flew by then Eleanor asked Caroline to join her and they continued their discussion whilst they ate.

'Are you to go to the Harpers Ball?' Eleanor asked when they'd at last exhausted the topic of the charity.

'I'll miss it I'm afraid, I have another engagement.'

Eleanor was surprised. The ball was one of the grandest of the year. It was one of the highlights of Alnmouth's society calendar, anyone who was anyone would be there.

'I'd hoped we'd see you. Lottie and I are going together as Gabriel and Wilson are at a hospital trust meeting first. You're welcome to join us if you change your mind.'

'Thank you but my other engagement is, er - quite pressing. I shouldn't want to change my plans at this late date.'

Eleanor waited for Caroline to expand further, but frustratingly she did not.

'I'm surprised you would miss the chance to find a beau. Lottie tells me there's a particularly handsome man expected, apparently his reputation precedes him. I believe he's neither old, bald nor gouty.' She smiled at Caroline knowing she'd recognise the jest.

Eleanor was surprised to see a suspicious look pass over Caroline's face.

'Who exactly do you mean?'

Eleanor told her about Lord Harper's nephew whose visit was causing such a stir.

'Oh him. He's a well known rakehell. I met him in York once, he's handsome enough, but not to my taste. He's not the type to settle down I wouldn't think and worse than that he's a high opinion of himself I seem to remember. He's charming enough if you like that sort of thing.'

'I see. He's of no particular interest to me of course I only thought... Anyway you'll be missed. Even if he's not to your liking maybe there would be others to tempt you. They come from far and wide for the occasion do they not? Not just sleepy old Alnmouth. Are you sure you can't change your plans?'

Eleanor was burning with curiosity. Why was Caroline being evasive? Why was she missing one of the grandest nights of the year? Eleanor remembered her manners and let the matter drop.

Later, on the beach as she watched the waves roll in and out languidly, she reflected on her meeting with Caroline. She was pleased to have her on board. She'd already helped the cause with her connections. She could see Caroline was going to be an ally worth having.

She then thought about how they'd been in each other's company. Gone was the awkwardness brought on by the shooting. Eleanor realised they were becoming more than acquaintances, they were becoming friends and it pleased her enormously. She saw how Caroline seemed a different woman lately. She seemed more at ease than when they'd first met. She had a light in her eye and seemed happier, more content. Eleanor put it down to the fact she now had a purpose in life; she seemed happy to have something to take her mind from her bereavement. She hoped Caroline had turned a corner.

ℛ

Caroline left Westshore, gave instructions to her groom to drive her to an inn on the outskirts of Alnmouth, and was then shown into an upstairs room with a view of a small courtyard. Caroline had asked Padraic to book somewhere out of town. He had chosen well, this place was respectable but off the beaten track.

She watched as Padraic Turner handed his horse to the inn's groom. She smiled as she admired the Irishman's good looks and strong physique, he certainly was handsome. He had a swagger about him, a self confidence and a twinkle in his eye. Add to this his unpredictable nature and his roguish, unconventional ways and it was no wonder he made her heart beat faster; she couldn't wait to be alone with him. She wondered what Eleanor would think if she knew about this liaison. After all Captain Turner was neither bald, old nor gouty. She smiled to herself. Surely she would approve her choice; indeed she might even be a little jealous when she found out.

'I'm sorry I'm late Carla.' He took her hand and kissed it making her warm with pleasure. He'd taken to calling her this pet name as he told her the Irish name Caroline claimed descent from the O'Conners in Donegal where "Carlan" roughly translated meant "one who combs wool". She thought it amusing to imagine herself a spinner or a shepherdess.

He rang the bell and ordered drinks to be brought to them. 'Why are we meeting here? When I got your message to arrange this rendezvous I must say I was intrigued.' Turner looked at her, a mischievous look on his face. 'Not that I'm complaining you understand, it adds a sense of excitement don't you think?' He caught a stray curl of her hair in his finger and stood far closer than was seemly.

'It does I agree, but the reason for the subterfuge is simple; each time you come to Eastshore we seem to be interrupted. Some busybody or other is forever calling. I don't mean to hide you away forever, but I'm not ready for everyone to know my business yet. There are those who would, even though well meaning, have an opinion about my friendship with you.'

Padraic looked irritated. 'Friendship is it? I'd thought we'd moved on from that Carla.' He reached out for her making her heart miss several beats. 'Who is it you think would disapprove? Not Reynolds? What's he to you now? Nothing I should hope. Why on earth do you care about his opinion? I certainly don't.'

'I care because we're close, like family. He would only have my best interests at heart. Why is it you think he doesn't care for you? You never did tell me.'

'Let's just say there was a misunderstanding when I first met him and his wife at Whitby. He appeared easily riled and prone to jealousy I seem to remember.'

'Gabriel isn't the jealous type, or at least he wasn't in the past. Nor is he quick tempered. Perhaps you gave him something to be envious about. Did something happen to make him act out of character?'

'Carla my sweet, surely we're not here to talk about your old flame?' He leaned in for a kiss.

Caroline moved away deftly. 'The maid will be here shortly, let's talk of other matters for a while.'

He threw himself on a sofa and crossed his legs. He looked up at her leaving her in no doubt what he was thinking.

For a moment Caroline was flustered. She couldn't ever remember a gentleman looking at her in such a way. Gabriel never had she was sure of it. She also couldn't remember a gentleman sitting in her presence before he'd invited her to sit first. A strange excitement filled her. This rule breaker was a pleasant change from some of her regular suitors. He was making her reckless. She would never have imagined she would allow such liberties yet here she was alone and unchaperoned before there was any understanding between them. Here she was like a wanton, just waiting to be led astray. Her friends would hardly recognise her. She hardly recognised herself.

Padraic Turner told the maid to leave the tray and as she left the room he moved seats. He sat close... too close.

'I've missed you my sweeting, have you missed me?'

'Of course.' She felt his breath on her neck. 'I'd expected you back last week.'

He sat back in his seat dramatically. ''Tis the weather my love. The Irish Sea is a cruel mistress. My business was concluded quickly enough, but the rough seas held us up.'

'What business was that? You never said.'

'Just something I've been finishing up. Let's talk about you my sweeting. What have you been up to? Seeing off a line of suitors I expect. Are there any I need to call out?'

'I had to disappoint another who was far too ardent only yesterday,' she said. 'Seriously you would hardly believe it but I've been enjoying helping Eleanor and Lottie, we're trying to raise money for the charity I told you about. That's taken much of my time of late.'

'You're a good woman Carla, but now you need to give all your attention to me.'

He took the kiss she knew he'd been waiting to steal

since the maid left them alone. She was powerless to stop him even if she'd wanted to do so - which she did not.

'When I booked this suite I took the liberty of ensuring there was another room, another room where we would be more comfortable if you understand my meaning?'

He stood and held out his hand. She hesitated. Seeing her waver he pulled her to her feet and kissed her with an urgency that shocked and thrilled her. She knew she was at a defining moment in their relationship.

He drew back and looked her in the eye and smirked. 'Don't worry my sweeting, I'll take care. We both want this, but you needn't worry. I love you and you love me. There's nothing more natural than a man and a woman demonstrating that love. Come, let me show you what real love feels like.'

R

Eleanor and Lottie having arrived at the Harpers soon found their dance cards filling up. 'Are you to leave space for your husband? He doesn't care to dance generally I know.'

'What's the point? He quite possibly won't get here in time, if he makes it at all. I haven't danced in an age so I intend to enjoy myself.'

'Good for you. I might save a space for the good

doctor, he's not let me down as often as your unpunctual husband and when he does it can't be helped. As he never tires of telling me a body cannot decide what hour to die.' She looked about her and nodded to an acquaintance. 'How you can stay cross with Gabriel is beyond me, he's such a handsome man. If you ever tire of him be sure to let me have first refusal.'

Eleanor knew Lottie's sense of humour well and didn't take offence at the remark. Eleanor knew it was Lottie's character to flirt with every man she knew. They had similar natures in that respect.

'We reached a truce last night but only after I told him off again of course.'

'I'm glad to hear it. You two are such a perfect couple, I hate to see you at loggerheads.'

Lottie stopped mid flow then nudged Eleanor. 'Look, there's the handsome nephew, how rakish he looks. I believe he has a countess for a mistress. He is much in London and rumour has it he fought a duel there last year. The other man was injured and almost lost an arm it's said. Isn't that straight out of a romantic novel?'

Lottie was enjoying herself. If there was one thing she liked more than flirting, it was gossiping. Eleanor watched as the captain, a tall, broad shouldered, fair haired man took to the dance floor with Felicity Coates. The young girl looked pleased as well she might with half the room looking on enviously.

After Eleanor and Lottie had partnered several gentlemen Lottie noticed they were being watched. 'Don't look now, but we're being assessed. I wonder which one of us will be deemed attractive enough to partner him, if either of us comes up to the mark that is.'

Before Eleanor could answer Dolly Harper, along with her nephew approached. 'Ooh la la, here goes,' Lottie muttered under her breath. Eleanor had just enough time to snigger and reply: 'Behave yourself, are you not spoken for?'

The two ladies were introduced to Captain Andrew Harper. Close up he was every bit as good looking as he was from afar Eleanor thought. His piercing blue eyes appeared hooded giving him a sleepy, languid appearance. His fair hair was neatly tied in a queue. He had the strut and self-assurance of an officer; his uniform buttons and boots were highly polished. As they were introduced Lottie, to her credit, ceased her schoolgirl silliness and posed a question: 'What regiment are you with sir?'

He smiled a white toothed smile. 'The forty two of foot Miss Lambton. We're to begin training in Northumberland shortly so I shall have the pleasure of being stationed hereabouts for the next few weeks or even months.'

'That will be a treat for the ladies Captain, all your military men in their dashing uniforms will certainly liven things up I'll wager.'

Captain Harper swept a hooded glance towards Eleanor. By the look on his face he'd reached a decision regarding who he would ask to dance. 'Do you have space on your dance card for me Mrs Reynolds?'

'Certainly Captain, I have the quadrille free.'

Lottie's next dance partner came to claim her. She was swept off, but not before bestowing a knowing look at her friend.

'Will you excuse me my dear Mrs Reynolds,' Lady Harper asked, 'I have to mingle. I have just noticed a wallflower and I cannot have a wallflower spoiling the look of the room.' Without waiting for a reply she sailed off.

'Do you know my aunt well? She's quite a tour de force is she not?'

'Not well, but I know her by repute. She's a popular hostess, her balls are always eagerly anticipated and well attended.'

'I see that's true. It's a little overcrowded for my liking.'

Eleanor knew Gabriel would think the same if only he'd turned up.

'From where do you hail? My aunt tells me you're not from these parts?'

Eleanor explained and for the next ten minutes she felt as if she were being interrogated; one question after another was aimed her way.

'Captain Harper do you think me an enemy spy?

You will soon know me better than I know myself, all these questions.'

'How nice that would be. I have some interesting ways to get people to open up. My military training has been extensive. I should like to get to know *all* of you a little better.'

'Would you indeed? You are forward sir.'

Eleanor, a born flirt, was enjoying the attention. She glanced towards the door but there was still no sign of her husband.

'I should like it if you interrogated me Mrs Reynolds. I imagine you're good at negotiations.' He lowered his voice and moved closer. 'I should enjoy that very much indeed. Perhaps we could reconnoitre, explore the terrain.' He grinned wolfishly. 'Where's your husband tonight? He's negligent in his duty leaving you alone. Some unscrupulous gentleman might try to take advantage.'

'Do you know any? Most of the gentlemen here tonight I'm already acquainted with and I know them to be harmless, more's the pity. If I were a single lady I'd despair.'

Eleanor watched as Lottie took her place on the dance floor with a different partner. 'My husband is at a meeting, a doctor friend is trying to build a new hospital in Alnwick. They may be along later.'

'If what you say is true and dashing young gentlemen are in short supply it's just as well my men will soon be on manoeuvres.' His eyes glittered. 'We can't have you lovely ladies without excitement can we?'

'I'm sure the ladies will enjoy the sight of your men on parade. They're bound to brighten up the proceedings. Most ladies can have their heads turned by a man in uniform I'm told.'

After dancing the quadrille with Captain Harper, Eleanor looked about for Gabriel but he'd still not arrived. She liked the company of other men from time to time, but she liked Gabriel's company more. What with the stud farm and the shipping line, they'd spent so little time together recently. She'd hoped he would be here by now. She sighed.

'Am I boring you Mrs Reynolds? I'd hoped to divert you.'

'Not at all Captain, I was just thinking how hot it is in here. It is as you say, quite crowded. I would welcome a little air.' She wafted her fan which only seemed to move hot air about her. She looked for Lottie but saw she was dancing with Saul Coates.

'Allow me to escort you onto the terrace, unless you want to take supper?'

'Cool air first I think.'

Captain Harper led her onto the terrace where they found themselves almost alone as many had already gone to sup. Eleanor, never one for convention, didn't ask to be returned to the ballroom as she knew would be the proper thing to do. She thought about Gabriel's warning about her taking risks where men were concerned. She looked around the terrace and was reassured there were enough people about. The officer was hardly likely to compromise her in front of so many people she reasoned. However, she wouldn't let him take her into the gardens; there were braziers to lighten the darker recesses but she could see there were but a few couples about in the shadows, couples who quite possibly wanted to be alone.

Eleanor breathed in the cool night air. 'That's better.' She slipped the ribbon of her fan onto her wrist.

'You have the most beautiful hair Eleanor. Such a shade of red I never saw before.'

'Thank you Captain but,' she frowned a little, 'I don't remember giving you leave to call me by my first name.' She saw his uncertainty. He was wondering if she was serious. He sought to find out.

'From our conversation so far I didn't have you down for being a stickler for the rules. I thought you a modern lady who would welcome a little informality.'

'I'm a *married* lady remember Captain Harper. So long as that's the only liberty you take.'

'I intend to take more than that my dear. When will your husband be from home? From what you said earlier he has a new mistress, in the shape of his stud farm, though why he'd prefer horseflesh to your flesh I can't imagine.' He ran his finger down her bare arm. 'What silky, smooth skin. So white, so soft.'

'I can assure you my husband takes good care of my needs. It's a new passion which distracts him at present that's all.'

'Distracted enough to forget his wife? That should be a criminal offence. I feel *I'm* about to begin a new passion.' Again he touched her arm, but this time let the touch linger when it reached her fingers. He lifted her hand to his lips. 'If I were to call on you tomorrow? From what you say your husband will be from home for hours, time enough to educate you in the way the army moves. I could show you some action.' He stepped closer. 'I should like to feel you... skin on skin.' He undressed her with a sweeping glance.

Eleanor leaned in, looked up at him through her lashes and whispered: 'Is that so Captain? Then let me oblige you.' She stepped back a little and took aim, then slapped Captain Harper a resounding smack across the cheek. She looked up at his shocked countenance. 'Skin on skin. Is that what you had in mind?'

She turned on her heel and walked back towards the ballroom ignoring the astounded glances about her. She had barely taken half a dozen steps when she saw the tall figure of a man leaning nonchalantly against a pillar his arms folded across his chest. It was her husband.

'You've arrived. At last.'

'Just in the nick of time it seems.' He grinned. 'Do you need a hand or have you everything under control?'

'I think I've dealt with the problem thank you. Have you eaten? Shall we take supper together?'

He led her though the ballroom. Once they were seated in the refreshment room Gabriel looked admiringly at her.

'Would you care to tell me what all that was about?'

Eleanor explained.

'Ah I see, so your flirting has landed you in hot water... again.'

'*My* flirting! It's not my flirting that's the problem it's men who think they can take advantage of a lady and a married lady too. There are countless single ladies here this evening yet... '

'May we join you or would you rather we didn't?' Lottie and Wilson stood beside them cutting off Eleanor's diatribe.

'Of course you may.' Eleanor looked up at Wilson who she hadn't seen until now. 'Did you have a good meeting Wilson?'

'Most of the patrons for the new hospital were only interested in being charitable if their names could be seen to be attached to the project. Charity, it seems, is only desirable when one can be *seen* to be generous.' He shook his head despondently as he took his seat.

'Did Lottie mention we're to organise a ball for the women's charity we're trying to establish? If the great and the good purchase a ticket at say, fifty guineas, they can then congratulate themselves for being kind hearted publicly.'

The two men looked at each other in amazement. 'Why didn't we think of this scheme for the hospital fund?'

'You don't have ladies on your board. If you did I'm sure one of them would have made the suggestion. Men think they know everything, but as you can see they don't,' Lottie said trying not to look smug.

'Who will you invite?' Gabriel asked.

'Only people who can afford the entrance fee, the aim after all is to raise as much money for the cause as possible.'

'We could have a masked ball,' Eleanor blurted out in excitement.

'My love, won't that defeat the object of being *seen* to donate to charity?'

'Well not necessarily. No one ever keeps their masks on. Perhaps we could all officially *unmask* at a given time?'

'Now the militia are about it would be fun to invite some of the higher ranks, the ones with money that is,' Lottie added. 'Captain Harper for certain would draw the ladies.' She twinkled as she looked pointedly at Eleanor.

'My wife has already received all the charity she needs from that quarter as far as I'm aware.' Gabriel smiled at his wife as Eleanor's cheeks pinkened.

'Has she indeed. I thought he looked taken with you when I went off to dance. What have you been up to Eleanor? I swear Gabriel I did try to control her, but you know how wilful she can be.'

'Let's just say Eleanor made a donation of her own, and Captain Harper is now in no doubt that my wife is *not* as generous as he thought she was.'

18

A few days after the Harpers Ball, Lottie called at Westshore to see Eleanor. Rose had colic and had taken a lot of settling the night before so Eleanor looked tired as she greeted her friend. She could have left Rose to the ministrations of Ginny who was perfectly capable, but she preferred to tend to her daughter herself when she could.

'Well, is your tiredness due to extracurricular activities?'

Eleanor looked puzzled.

'Are you being tactful? You can tell me, I shan't breathe a word I promise.' Lottie was wide-eyed with curiosity. Eleanor still didn't understand what Lottie was getting at. Her tiredness was befuddling her brain.

'Did you take the good captain up on his offer? I'm sure he made a play for you judging by the look in his eye.'

Eleanor told her friend about what had happened on the terrace.

'You slapped him? I shouldn't have turned him down,' Lottie declared in a dreamy voice.

'Lottie you're scandalous!'

'I wish. If only I'd the opportunity, such a pity he chose you. I told you he was a knave. He went after you, a married lady, when he could have had me instead. Life can be so unfair sometimes.'

'As you say, I'm a married woman and would never dream of having an affair. I can see now why your stepfather sent you away. You're shameless.' She loved Lottie's brazenness.

'For all the good it did. All it served was to throw me into the paths of some very attractive Frenchmen. Ooh la la.' She giggled.

'Seriously Lottie, what about poor Wilson, I thought you cared for him?' Eleanor poured more coffee.

'I do love him dearly but,' she broke a biscuit in half and nibbled it daintily, 'there's more to life than marriage and babies. No offence my dear, but it's true. I told you I intend to travel and broaden my horizons before I settle down if ever that is, I choose to settle at all.'

Eleanor thought she knew Lottie well enough to ask personal questions. Her friend was unconventional and forthright so she wouldn't take offence, hopefully. That was one reason they got on so well.

'When you were in France did you have a *liaison* with one of your Frenchmen? You don't have to tell me if you'd rather not. It goes without saying anything you tell me is in confidence. I shouldn't tell Gabriel... promise.' She joked imitating her friend's comment.

Lottie smiled a sly, knowing smile. Her eyes

twinkled mischievously. 'I may have done.' She couldn't resist a gossip. 'His name was Armand. He was a comte, only a minor one, but still a count nevertheless. Had I married him I should have been a comtesse! It was just a... well you know. He was very discreet. The French are not so buttoned up as we English. It was interesting, fun. No one got hurt and I gained experience and then I came home when my stepfather pegged it.'

Eleanor nearly choked laughing at Lottie's irreverence.

'You're quite a girl.' Eleanor wiped her hands on her napkin and stood. 'I envy you your freedom, yet I wouldn't trade Gabriel and Rose for the world. Come, shall we ride before *madame* needs my services again?'

𝓡

'If we're to get good fancy dress costumes we need to choose what we want before they all get picked over.'

Gabriel was collecting his papers ready to leave for the bay. 'Costumes?' he muttered distractedly.

'For the charity ball.'

'I thought it was to be a masked ball.'

'It was, it is, but it's also a costume party. I told you.'

'Oh man, no. I hate rummaging about in the dressing up box for something to wear. I'll go as a ship owner.'

345

He cast a wry look at his wife.

'You won't be rummaging in any box. I thought we could go as a matched couple; Cleopatra and Anthony, Maid Marion and Robin Hood, something along those lines?'

'I'm not wearing hose Eleanor. I'll only partner you if I can choose. I'll not look a fool. Grownups parading about as monks and nuns, it's ridiculous and demeaning. It's all a bit odd, a tad childish to my mind. Can't I just make a donation and stay at home?'

'Don't be such a stick in the mud. I can't picture you as a monk somehow.'

'Or you as a nun for that matter.' He headed for the door.

'Well unless we pick our outfits soon we'll be going as Adam and Eve as all the best costumes will be taken.'

Gabriel grabbed his wife by the waist and pulled her to him. 'Now you're talking. We might be a little chilly however.' He nibbled her ear.

'Don't start getting ideas.' She pushed him away. 'I thought you were about to take your leave?'

'I was, but now I've an idea to take something else.'

Ransom coughed. They hadn't heard him come in. 'Mrs Madison asks if you will send down the week's menus ma'am.'

Gabriel shot the butler a brusque look.

'Tell her I'll do it now.' Eleanor side-stepped her husband.

'I'll be off then.' Gabriel cursed under his breath. 'When Lisbet and Abner were here we never got interrupted. Sometimes I feel my home isn't my own, he moves as if on castors.'

'I seem to remember you often complained Abner and Lisbet were never where they should be.'

Gabriel shrugged. 'I did, but I miss them. I wonder how they are? Do you suppose they managed to find work after they left here? I hope they did.'

'I don't know my love, but they must have moved from Alnmouth, I've never seen them about.'

'Me neither.' Gabriel pushed his tricorn on his head and headed for the hallway. 'No one could sew a shirt like Lisbet, not even my tailor. She'd have conjured up a well fitting costume for the fancy dress ball in no time. Something sophisticated and appropriate for a man of my stature, not something bordering on the infantile.'

Eleanor looked heavenward. 'Perhaps she would, she thought the sun shone from you.' She kissed his cheek. 'She might have made you an angel costume with wings and a halo. Angel Gabriel.'

'Very funny.'

'I'm sorry my love I know you miss them, but I did think you were over hasty at the time. Ask around at the bay, someone may know where they went.'

'I have. More than once, but they seem to have vanished. It's a mystery and anyway we couldn't take them on again. Can you imagine the carnage with

Lisbet and Mrs M sharing the same kitchen! But still, I'd like to know they're well, content.'

The night of the charity ball was a chilly one. All day it had rained and all thoughts of music on the terrace would have to be abandoned if it didn't stop. Lottie, Caroline and Eleanor had worked tirelessly to make sure everything ran smoothly, but sadly they couldn't command the weather. The ball had been a month in the planning and the three ladies had enjoyed themselves immensely.

At Westshore Eleanor was down first, even though Gabriel had been home early enough to be ready in time. He had been true to his word of late and reformed his ways. Most evenings he was home in time to see Rose before she was put to bed. Marital harmony had been restored.

Eleanor poured herself a glass of sherry and sat down to wait. She wondered what costume her husband had finally decided upon. All she knew was they were not going as any of her suggestions. He had chosen for himself. In secret.

Every idea she'd suggested Gabriel had vetoed for one reason or another. In the end he'd chosen his own costume, and told his wife it would be a surprise for her. She was hoping it would be a good surprise and that he'd chosen well. All she knew was he'd been allowing his hair to grow longer and had taken to wearing it in a queue, as he did when first they met. She thought it suited him. He looked handsome, dashing. She had high hopes.

The library door was suddenly thrown open to reveal a masked highwayman. He was pointing a pistol at her.

'Stand and deliver, your money or your - '

Scrabble, who had been asleep by the fire, decided there was an intruder to see off and hurled himself at Gabriel's leg. Luckily the riding boot took the worst of the bite before his master could remonstrate with the confused dog.

Eleanor burst out laughing. It wasn't the response her husband had been hoping for she guessed.

'Well at least you can rest easy knowing Scrabble will protect me should a trespasser break into the house.'

Gabriel, rubbing his leg, glared at the guilty looking terrier. 'That's not a good start.' Gabriel recovered his sense of humour.

'You look magnificent my love.' He noticed Eleanor's costume for the first time.

Eleanor, or Elaine of Astolat, a medieval lady from Arthurian legend, curtsied low to her husband. 'If only you would have agreed to be Sir Lancelot it would have been perfect.'

'I told you nothing would induce me to wear hose and a tabard.'

'You have good legs.' Eleanor looked him up and down. 'You can hold me up any time you choose dressed like this.'

Gabriel put his hands on Eleanor's waist. 'Temptress. What - no corset?'

'Medieval ladies didn't wear them apparently and for me to do so tonight would ruin the look I think. Besides in my condition it's a relief not to be laced up tight.'

Eleanor had told Gabriel a few days ago that she was with child again. They were both enormously happy.

'You not only look lovely, you feel lovely too.' He ran his hands down her body. She pushed him away laughing. 'You've done enough damage already, come on or we'll be late.'

Eleanor, Lottie and Caroline had sold all the tickets for the charity ball. They were looking forward to the dancing and seeing what costumes the guests had decided upon. It had finally been agreed the ball should take place at Wooden House. As it was a little way out of Alnmouth it was ideally located for most of the guests. Like Westshore it had been relatively newly built by Lottie's stepfather who had dealt in futures. The large imposing house had beautiful views over the estuary, and out to sea, and a pleasant garden and terrace which could be used should the weather keep dry. It also had a good sized ballroom for dancing.

'I'm dying to know who Caroline's companion for

the evening will be.' Eleanor faced Gabriel in the carriage as they drove to the ball. She was holding her conical headdress in her lap as it was too tall to sit on her head. Eleanor had asked Caroline if she would like to share their carriage to the ball, but she'd declined. 'I don't know why she would refuse the offer. After all we will be passing Eastshore on our way to Wooden House. She's been acting most mysteriously of late.'

Caroline had explained she had an escort for the ball, but refused to be drawn about who her partner was to be. Eleanor was itching to know, she hated mysteries. She was intrigued and irritated in equal measure.

'You'll find out soon enough.'

Eleanor piqued at Gabriel's lack of curiosity tutted. 'More than once I've called on charity business only to find her not at home. On one occasion I had the distinct impression she *was* at home because I'd seen Caroline's groom and he told me she had not long since come back from hunting. It was all very odd.'

'She likes her own company perhaps. She's had much to sort out of late. I know she's been clearing some of Thomas' belongings, not an easy thing to do.'

'It's not that, there's something else I know it. Tonight I hope to find out what's been taking up so much of her time, or rather who. Of course she's entitled to her privacy, but I can't think why the need for secrecy. I'm dying to see who her companion is.' She hoped Caroline had at last found someone to make her happy.

'Are you warm enough my love?' the highwayman opposite her asked.

'I am thank you, but shouldn't you be riding alongside not sitting comfortably *inside*? It looks strange travelling with you dressed like that.'

'I'm not risking getting soaked so you'll just have to get used to it, besides I think it adds a sort of derring do. You look like a damsel in distress, and I the roguish brigand about to dishonour you.'

'It's a bit late for that my love. Is this a secret fantasy of yours? "Help! Take anything you want but not my honour".' Eleanor clapped her hand to her brow dramatically. 'What an imagination you have Gabriel.'

Before he could answer, the carriage came to a halt. Eleanor put her hand on his pistol.

'Get off,' Gabriel sniggered, 'it might go off! Surely I should be taking advantage of *you*, not the other way about, you unruly wench.'

A footman opened the carriage door and let down the step.

'Is that thing loaded?' Eleanor grinned. The footman failed to see the funny side as they climbed down and entered the hall laughing like children.

Eleanor was gratified to see the ballroom was stuffed to the gunnels. There was every kind of costume from St George and a peculiar looking dragon, to angels and two cherubs. There were men decked out in togas and ladies with tall, elaborate headdresses towering precariously on their heads. One man had come as a tall ship complete with two masts and a spanker and all the rigging. Everyone had made an effort; the occasion was looking like a great success.

The guests had been asked to wear a mask. There was to be a grand reveal at midnight followed by fireworks. Of course, most people recognised each other instantly, yet there were still one or two cunning disguises.

'There's Caroline, I knew she'd wear something beautiful.' Eleanor pointed her fan in Caroline's direction.

'Is she a shepherdess? What a strange choice for a ship owner's daughter.'

'Gabriel! You can be so old fashioned. She's a woman in her own right, not simply someone's daughter. I'm your wife, but the role doesn't define me. Would you have me come as a ship owner's wife? Caroline is at liberty to choose whatever she wants to wear.'

Gabriel rolled his eyes.

'Who is her escort? Is he King Henry?' Eleanor peered across the room.

'It's too crowded,' Gabriel complained, 'I hate crowded ballrooms. I can't see Henry VIII. The man standing closest to her is a pirate. Blackbeard perhaps?'

'I'm glad it's crowded, the more guests we cram in means the more money we make for the charity. Remember this is to raise funds.' Eleanor looked over to where Caroline stood with her head close to the pirate. 'If he's her partner he seems familiar yet I can't place him.'

Bendor and Grace joined them. They had come as Robin Hood and Maid Marion. Gabriel took the opportunity to tease his best friend for wearing green hose and a tabard. Eleanor saved him by taking Bendor to the dance floor.

Gabriel said he wouldn't dance in such a crush. Nevertheless, for the first hour or so both Eleanor and Grace weren't short of partners and they left their men folk discussing a recent horse sale they'd attended. Eleanor kept her eyes on Caroline and her partner. Why did the man seem so familiar?

'Shall we see if Caroline wants to sit with us at supper?' Eleanor asked as her partner, Sir John Riddleston unimaginatively dressed as a judge, brought her back to her husband.

'Yes let's eat,' Grace said, 'I'm starving.' Grace was with child again too and as with her last pregnancy she was always hungry. They made their way across the refreshment room, but most of the tables were taken. Caroline and the pirate were sitting with Lottie, dressed as Boadicea, and Wilson who was a bishop. Another couple who were dressed identically as sailors and a group of army officers made up their table so there wasn't enough room for them.

Eleanor was annoyed the four friends were forced to sit at some distance from Caroline and her intriguing guest. She still couldn't see the pirate's face.

Gabriel bit into a chicken drumstick. 'The black wig and the beard are a good disguise.'

'I agree, though there's something about his stature I recognise. It's most annoying he has his back to us so I can't study him.'

'Well not long to wait my dear. It will soon be midnight,' Grace said finishing off her third pudding.

A gong sounded and it was announced the unmasking would take place in the ballroom. The guests began to make their way there. Everyone stood in a circle and waited for their cue. After a tantalising drum roll masks were removed. Eleanor looked for Caroline and her escort but frustratingly now they were unmasked they were heading for the terrace to watch the fireworks. The only view she got was of their backs. Then it dawned on her who it was and Eleanor knew one guest this evening would be irked by the discovery. The guests spilled down onto the lawn and the fireworks began.

'I know who it is.' Eleanor had to raise her voice above the crackles and bangs. She thought it best to warn Gabriel who the mystery man was.

'What?'

'I said I know who Caroline's escort is. It's Padraic Turner.'

'Turner? How can that be?'

'How should I know? But it's definitely him. I just saw him turn around. Look there he is. He's removed his beard as well as his mask.'

'Man alive! What does she want with *him*? I can imagine what he wants with her.'

'Oh Lord, don't start Gabriel. Don't make a scene.'

'A scene. I can't like the man, you know that and after his last encounter with you I mean to have words with him, ball or no ball. If he's trying to ingratiate himself with Caro then I'll warn him off.'

'Please Gabriel try to be nice, they're coming over.'

Before Gabriel could reply Caroline and Captain Turner were before them. Caroline beamed happily.

'Eleanor, or should I say Lady Astolat, you look marvellous and you,' she tapped Gabriel with her fan, 'look quite scary. I shouldn't like to meet you on a dark night. The ball is a great success is it not Eleanor?'

Gabriel's face was stony. Eleanor filled the awkward silence. 'You look sheepish, Miss Bo Peep, ha ha.' Eleanor's false humour rang hollow.

'Captain Turner,' Eleanor stared at Blackbeard, 'this is a pleasant surprise. When Caroline refused to tell me who her guest was I never imagined it would be you. I was sorry to hear from Papa you had resigned your post of The Whitby Lass.'

He looked from Gabriel to Eleanor and smiled derisively. 'Good evening Mrs Reynolds, Mr Reynolds. I too was sorry to leave your father's employ, but I found I had need to remove further north.' He leered licentiously at Caroline. It was a taunting look that neither Eleanor nor Gabriel missed, Caroline on the other hand smiled warmly at her beau.

'For what reason pray tell?' Gabriel's irritation was plain for all to see as he addressed the man he'd grown to dislike.

'Gabriel!' Eleanor squeezed her husband's arm in a warning gesture. 'Perhaps my husband was a cat in a previous life for his curiosity makes him forget his manners.' She'd seen the look of embarrassment on Caroline's face and wanted to spare her.

'Captain Turner wanted to move to Alnmouth,' Caroline said plainly. 'We met again at my aunt's can you believe, my cousin Arthur was in the same regiment as Padraic, it's a small world as they say.'

Eleanor noticed the use of Captain Turner's Christian name. She knew her husband would have noticed too.

'I never met him, but I remember you telling me he lost an arm.'

Eleanor was ill at ease seeing Gabriel so sullen, so agitated.

'We met again at Christmas,' Caroline added, 'and now Padraic has decided to remove here to Alnmouth.'

'You can probably guess why.' Turner smiled warmly at Caroline, then looked to Eleanor. 'The ladies hereabouts are very much to my liking I find.'

Eleanor felt Gabriel's body tense as the captain swept a look over her uncorsetted body. She knew her husband, usually slow to anger, was struggling to hold onto his temper.

'Shall we tell them Caroline?' Turner said flashing his charming smile.

'Yes of course, I'd like my dearest friends to be the first to know.' Caroline, her arm through Turner's, giggled coyly.

'We are to be married,' she announced.

For a long moment there was silence. Then Eleanor bethought herself and exclaimed: 'Congratulations! When did all this happen? You kept the romance very quiet Caroline. What a dark horse you are.'

Caroline beamed radiantly. 'Earlier this evening Padraic did me the honour of proposing. I never thought to be happy again after Father died, but I am. Very happy indeed. I know Father would be pleased for me.' She shot Gabriel a penetrating look.

'This is sudden is it not?' Gabriel was tight lipped.

'Not especially. Not as quick as your marriage to Eleanor I would venture.' Caroline's reply was terse, her voice betraying her disappointment at her one time fiancé's lack of support no doubt.

Eleanor sought to calm troubled waters. 'When is the wedding to be?'

'We've not yet decided, but I should like it to be soon. I know Caroline doesn't care to wait and neither do I for that matter.'

Eleanor gripped her husband's arm. There was an interminable silence broken at last by Turner. His easy charm was turned towards Eleanor.

'You look every inch the Arthurian lady. How on earth did you travel with the headdress?'

Eleanor explained at length in the hope of defusing the situation.

'I was tempted to bring a real sheep,' Caroline smiled, 'but we thought it would create more trouble than it was worth, so abandoned the idea.' The atmosphere crackled.

'I hope you'll be very happy together, I love weddings,' Eleanor blurted out trying to compensate for her husband's sour face.

'Will you excuse us, this is the dance you promised me Eleanor.' Gabriel's voice was intractable. He affected a stilted bow to Caroline and steered Eleanor towards the dance floor.

'What the... '

'Not now Eleanor. Please, just dance.'

R

They had arrived home in the early hours of the morning, foot sore and tired. The ball had been a great success with the exception of one thing; Caroline's announcement. From the moment she'd said she was to marry Turner, Gabriel had been morose and quiet, quiet like a volcano before it erupts.

'I don't understand why you're so angry about Caroline's news.' Eleanor flung the headdress on the floor.

'I'm not angry. I'm concerned. There is a world of difference.'

'Concerned about what? Did you not see how happy she is? Surely you don't begrudge her some happiness after all she's been through?'

'It's not her I have a grudge against; it's *that* man as well you know. He's nothing but a fortune hunter. Is it not obvious he's after her money? Just listen, hear me out.' Gabriel held up his hand as Eleanor was about to speak. 'Turner shows up in Whitby and makes a play for you, a married woman, which to my mind is scandalous. Then the next thing he's at Westshore trying once again to seduce you and behind my back, in my own house, and now, now he's to marry a beautiful *heiress*! He's a libertine and a wastrel, a womaniser with his eye on the main chance. He thought his luck was in after your father's ship was endangered. Then, when you refused him he makes a beeline for Caroline, a fatherless, defenceless heiress.'

Eleanor was frustrated with his description of Caroline but rarely had she seen her husband so animated. 'You're over reacting. She's not some heroine from a melodrama. Fatherless, defenceless indeed.'

'Very well, what has he to offer her I ask you? He has no fortune, I wouldn't think him a man of means, and he's certainly no gentleman. I doubt he's even able to make an honest living.'

'Caroline is a grown woman Gabriel. She knows her

own mind and knows *him*. Possibly better than we do.'

'Does she know he's a womaniser and a libertine? I think not.' Gabriel examined the bruise on his leg where Scrabble had tried to bite him earlier.

'Come to bed Gabriel, there's nothing you can do, nothing you *ought* to do. I agree he's a rogue but there it is. Caroline obviously thinks him a loveable rogue.'

Gabriel scowled. 'I see him for what he is. Thomas will be turning in his grave.' He got into bed, but stayed sitting up his arms folded defiantly across his chest. 'When I ended my engagement to Caro I promised her father I'd always look out for her, protect her. I keep my promises. The scales must fall from her eyes. She can't let her fortune go to that scoundrel to gamble away.'

'Is he a gambler?'

'He strikes me as the type.'

Eleanor sighed in exasperation, she knew Gabriel was too heated to be reasoned with. She blew out her candles.

'I know you feel you ought to take care of her, but she'll not thank you for interfering. If someone had tried to tell me not to marry *you* I shouldn't have listened and resented the person who tried to meddle in my affairs.'

'I'll go and see her tomorrow and tell her what a scoundrel he is. Better still, I'll go and see him, tell him I know his game, have it out with him.'

'You can't. You'll only make matters worse. I'll

speak with Caroline, woman to woman, to make sure she's certain of him. Ask her to proceed with caution. I shouldn't want her hurt either. In the meantime get some sleep, I for one am exhausted.'

Gabriel blew out his candles. Eleanor waited for him to kiss her goodnight. After a long moment she realised it wasn't forthcoming. She rolled over to him and began to stroke his chest.

'It's such a shame... '

'I agree he - '

Eleanor put her lips to his to silence him. 'You misunderstand me. A shame you're not in the mood for... you know what I mean. I've been looking forward all evening to being taken by a strong, dangerous highwayman.'

She felt Gabriel release the air from his lungs.

'I know what you're about Eleanor but I'm too wound up, too annoyed, too - oh I don't know.'

'Sir pray be gentle with me, I haven't any money I only have my honour for you to steal.'

She heard Gabriel laugh as she stroked his chest.

'Jezebel. Very well then, I shall take that.'

'Are you to take me even if I refuse sir?'

'Since when did you ever refuse me? Prepare to stand and deliver.'

R

The next morning, Eleanor tried again to persuade

Gabriel not to go to see Turner. In the end they compromised and he set off to see Caroline as early as was respectable. He'd been given strict orders *not* to lecture Caroline.

'I expected a visit from you this morning Gabriel.' Caroline was in the drawing room, the very drawing room where many years ago he'd asked her to be his bride. It seemed a lifetime ago.

'Do you wonder why I've come?'

'Not at all. You didn't exactly rejoice at our news last night.' The childhood sweethearts glowered at each other; both were ready for combat.

'Are you surprised? Before your father died I promised to take care of you. I'd be going against that promise if I didn't speak out now. Caroline, you're too good for him. This is all so sudden, you barely know the man, you're not worldly. You know nothing of his way of life, of his past.'

'I know all I need to know. He may not be conventional but I love him regardless and remember he's not all bad. He's a war hero. I've known him almost a year and as I said last night I've known him longer than you knew Eleanor when you became betrothed.'

'That was different.'

'Different yes I agree. On paper you didn't look such a good bet as Padraic. He makes me happy Gabriel. You think he's nothing to offer me, whereas you on the other hand, had a lot to offer Eleanor; a broken engagement promise, a charge of manslaughter hanging over you and a mistress you thought you'd kept hidden for years.' Caroline arched an eyebrow. 'Yes Gabriel, I knew about Libby Lawson.'

Gabriel rubbed his cheek with his knuckles.

'In comparison I think you'll agree Padraic is a shining example of what a future husband should look like.' Gabriel was temporarily stuck for words. 'I know you dislike him. He told me of the misunderstanding between you two in Whitby but for my sake please try to be happy for me. Is it so wrong for me to want what you have? A happy marriage, children perhaps? Is it too much to ask?'

Gabriel paced the room then turned, still clutching his tricorn in his hands.

'I can't like him Caro, there's something... something untrustworthy about him. He turned up in Whitby, sailed once for Eleanor's father, a trip which ended badly I might add, then throws it all up and - '

'Falls head over heels in love with me. Is that so unthinkable? Are you saying he's marrying me for my money?'

Gabriel hung his head. 'I said before any man would be lucky to have you.'

Caroline's temper flared. 'Any man but you Gabriel? Is it a case of not wanting me yourself, but resenting any man who would want to marry me? Is that it?'

In all their years together Caro had never raised her voice to him, she'd never had the need.

'I'm not so mean spirited, surely you know that. I can't help but think you're making a big mistake. I want you to have what I have but... ' Gabriel tried to calm himself. He rarely got agitated and he didn't like the feeling of losing control of his temper. 'He'll not make you happy. He's not worthy of you.'

'Eleanor is pleased for me, why can't you be? You got off on the wrong foot with Padraic. You're both stubborn. Come to dinner, just the four of us, perhaps if you got to know him better as I do you'd like him.'

Gabriel flung his tricorn on a chair.

'How did you meet him, after the first time I mean? Did he seek you out after you met at Westshore?'

'We met at my aunt's. Arthur and his wife invited me for a visit. Padraic had looked Arthur up, they'd lost touch. It was a lovely coincidence; they'd served together and were friends. It seemed like serendipity. We spent a wonderful Christmas getting to know each other and then we fell in love.'

Gabriel remembered Eleanor's warning but couldn't keep his thoughts to himself. 'I'm sorry Caro, but at present I think I'd find it hard to be in the same room as the man and be civil. If it hadn't been for Eleanor talking me round I would be having it out with *him* now instead of you. He's pulled the wool over your eyes, over everyone's eyes but mine it seems. Perhaps you're blinded by fancy talk, sweet words. You're infatuated.'

Caroline stood and faced him. Her face flushed with

anger.

'How rude and patronising you are! How arrogant. Very well, there's nothing more to be said - for the present. It saddens me you feel this way, but I know you and know I'd be wasting my breath trying to change your mind.'

'Caro I'm sorry. It's only because I've your best interests at heart that I speak so plainly. I apologise for my rudeness, but you know I couldn't stand by and allow you to make the biggest mistake of your life. I care about you, *we* care about you, Eleanor and I.'

Caroline's temper cooled at his contrition.

'I'd hoped - '

'Hoped I'd approve?' Gabriel scoffed.

'Well yes but, hoped that as Father isn't here to take the role that you would step into his shoes and give me away on my wedding day. Take Father's place and walk me down the aisle.' Caroline sat down and placed her hands in her lap.

Gabriel was overcome. He wrestled with his conscience. How could he lead her down the aisle to what he thought would be a disastrous marriage? He looked at her as she met his gaze. She'd asked for nothing since her father's death, yet he couldn't in all conscience grant her this one wish.

'Man alive Caro, how can you ask that of me? I must go before I say something more to upset you. We'll speak again soon. I bid you a good day.'

He turned on his heel and marched out of the room.

He sprinted down the drive and headed for the beach. He knew he could do no more, for now at least. His temper had subsided, he was distressed rather than angry, and now he felt powerless, powerless to change her mind. He'd hoped Caro was not quite certain about her choice and he'd be able to sway her, but he could see that wasn't the case. She was determined. He'd never seen this side of her character before; she'd always been compliant, biddable. Why couldn't she see sense? Why was she blinded to the man's faults?

He tramped the length of the beach wrestling with his principles, trying to think how to dissuade her from this folly, no not folly, this marriage would be an unmitigated disaster. The scoundrel would take her fortune, continue his womanising ways and leave Caro heartbroken and possibly poorer both spiritually and materially. He headed for Westshore not noticing menacing clouds were gathering on the horizon.

R

Eleanor and Gabriel were in the library at Westshore. Eleanor had listened while Gabriel told her about his visit to Caroline.

'I agree with Caroline. You might have guessed I would. It's her life, she's in love, head over heels in love and it's nothing to do with you or anyone else. She's had ample time it seems to get to know him, over a year she said. I still can't believe she kept it from me. I expect she thought I'd tell you and you would behave... well anyway let's not stir things up again. I can see what she sees in him. He can be very charming, I can vouch for that.'

Gabriel shot her a cool look. 'I don't admire your point of view Eleanor.'

'As I said before if someone had tried to tell me not to marry you I would have been infuriated, but look how our marriage has turned out. Are we not happy? No one knows what goes on behind closed doors. You can't interfere.'

Gabriel remained intransigent.

'Say you'll be honoured to do as she asks and agree to take her father's place and give her away. Let it be a peace offering. If the marriage isn't a success you can have the pleasure of saying "I told you so". Will that satisfy you?'

'I don't want it to end badly, surely you know me better than that.'

'Then let me ask another question.' Eleanor tried appeasement. 'If Thomas were alive would he be trying to stop this marriage?'

Gabriel thought for a long moment. 'Possibly not; she could twist him around her little finger. She always did get her own way with him.'

'Well then, if *he* would allow it don't you think you must stand back and let her make her own decision, for good or bad?'

Gabriel swilled the brandy around his glass. 'You're

right as usual my love. She knows how I feel, my ranting may have made her question her stance, but I doubt it. I'll go and see her and tell her I'll do as she asks.'

Eleanor looked at her husband fondly. 'You're a good man Gabriel. You're right also, she perhaps has given your views some thought. I know I would in her shoes, not that she'll admit it of course. But when all is said and done she'll do as her heart dictates. Let's just hope she doesn't rue the day. I know you're trying to do right by Caroline, but there's just one other thing.'

'What?' He looked suspicious.

'Try and look happy when you tell her you'll give her away. Perhaps wait a day or two until you're in a better frame of mind. A wedding is supposed to be a cause for celebration remember, your face at the moment looks like you should be chief mourner at a funeral.'

He threw a cushion at her.

19

Finally Bryony had secured employment which not only paid well, but more importantly was not beneath her standards. She had been forced to admit to herself her captain was a philanderer, a handsome reprobate who as the old adage had it, had a woman in every port. She hadn't set eyes on him for many weeks. She had decided to head back to Alnmouth hoping the competition for work was less keen than in Whitby. She'd hoped, perhaps foolishly, that he might look for her there on his return from his latest mission. Then her luck had finally changed.

Almost as soon as she returned she'd been successful in securing a position in Lesbury, a village a short distance inland from Alnmouth. She had been right to trust her instincts and was much relieved to have procured the position as companion to a Mrs Stubbs, a respectable, middle aged widow.

The advertisement had said the lady was in need of a companion for outings and travel. Bryony had liked the sound of travelling. The pay and conditions were good and the lady seemed bearable, not too old and certainly not at death's door. The last thing she needed was to secure a position only for her employer to fall off the mortal coil in the next six months.

Bryony had been in Lesbury for two weeks now and so far she didn't regret the move. Mrs Stubbs seemed amiable and easy to please. The large house was comfortable and Bryony's own quarters were generous. She even had a small clothing allowance. She felt at last things were looking up. She still thought about her boy, but what could she do? He was better off without her.

It was the lady's custom to take a morning constitutional after she'd received her morning callers. Mrs Stubbs had recently given up horse riding so a walk to take the air was the order of the day when the weather was fine.

They had been walking but a short distance when a carriage pulled alongside them. A beautiful, blonde-haired lady halloed from the lowered window.

'Susan, I was on my way to see you. It's later than I thought, how very remiss of me.'

'Caroline my dear, your time keeping has never been good,' Mrs Stubbs smiled, 'but never mind we shall return and invite you for coffee.' Mrs Stubbs and Bryony were handed into the carriage.

Once seated, the older lady made the introductions. 'Caroline, this is Miss Swift. Miss Swift allow me to introduce you to my goddaughter, Caroline Hodgeson.'

'Good morning Miss Hodgeson.' Bryony noted the

woman was extremely beautiful, but unlike her employer, who favoured modest attire, this lady was dressed in the latest style, like a fashion plate.

Back at Lesbury Lodge Miss Hodgeson explained the reason for her visit. Bryony was all ears.

'I'm after your time or your money, or possibly both if you're feeling generous.' She told her godmother about a women's charity she and her friends were trying to establish. Bryony half listened, do-gooders bored her. No one ever helped her out when she was in need.

'We're looking for ladies to sit on a committee and also of course, we need money, lots of money to start the project.'

Bryony's ears pricked up at the sound of money.

'I'm not one for committees as you know my dear, they end up taking up vast amounts of one's time and are rarely entertaining.' Mrs Stubbs patted her snowy white hair and added: 'A donation for such a worthy cause is not out of the question however.' She mentioned a sum which made Bryony's big brown eyes open wide.

'You are so generous Susan. I can assure you the money will be put to good use when we can find an establishment large enough that is.'

The two ladies continued to chatter on amiably. Apparently Miss Hodgeson hadn't seen her godmother since the widow had moved back to the area, so there was a lot to talk about it seemed.

Bryony was distracted. She was thinking of how easily her employer had offered the large donation without batting an eyelid. She stopped a sigh of envy.

'Are you from hereabouts Miss Swift?' Bryony was startled to be addressed by the beautiful, but haughty Caroline Hodgeson. She was another one cut from the same cloth as the snooty Eleanor Reynolds. All airs and graces, but no idea about the real world, no idea how ordinary people lived. Charity work was a hobby for the likes of them. It was something to ease their conscience and to make them feel better as they sat in their elegant drawing rooms.

'I'm from Embleton originally.' Bryony looked down as she knew she was supposed to do. She remembered her training. What business was it of hers where she was from? Nosy baggage! How would she like it if a relative stranger started asking questions about her life? She didn't want the likes of her poking her nose in where it wasn't wanted.

'Embleton you say? You removed here to be my dear godmother's companion?'

'I've been living in Alnmouth since my last employer died.'

Bryony smiled sweetly. She didn't intend to tell the woman her life story. Luckily this seemed to satisfy her and she moved on to discuss a tea party she was intending to host.

Bryony returned to imagining what she could do with the amount of money Mrs Stubbs had just donated so easily. For so long Bryony's existence had been hand to mouth. She was tired of counting every penny. Since giving her son away she'd felt like a ship which had slipped its moorings and was drifting further and further out to sea. But now she had another chance. She may well have fallen on her feet here, or so she hoped. After all she'd been through lately, didn't she deserve a break? Who knows what the next tide would wash up she thought as she stirred more sugar into her tea. She decided to make herself indispensible to this elderly, *rich* lady.

'Are you quite comfortable Mrs Stubbs? Shall I bring you a shawl? Are you sure you're not in a draught?'

Worry not, I can make myself absolutely necessary to your wellbeing she thought, pouring more tea for her employer.

R

'My godmother Mrs Stubbs has made a donation.' Caroline handed a bank draft to Eleanor.

'Goodness, that's very generous, thank you Caroline. Without your connections we could never have hoped to raise so much money. We shall soon reach our target at this rate. Lottie is to call on another lady this morning, she's hopeful of another substantial donation.'

'You should meet my godmother, you would like her

- she's so entertaining. She's travelled extensively in her life and was married to a judge.'

Eleanor felt the ground shift a little as she led Caroline towards the drawing room. She swayed as the dizziness overcame her.

'Are you alright? You look very pale.' Caroline took Eleanor's arm and led her to a chair.

'Yes thank you, I just feel a little... ' The next Eleanor knew Charity was thrusting smelling salts in front of her nose.

'You ought to see Dr Chaffer, that's twice this week,' her maid admonished.

'I'm fine, I just came over light headed.'

'Perhaps you need to rest. Are you overdoing things in your condition do you think? You look pasty my dear.' Caroline was peering at her.

'Perhaps I'll have a lie down,' Eleanor said resentfully.

'That's a good idea.' Charity stood over her like a goose looking after her goslings.

'Should I send for Gabriel?' Caroline asked.

'Please don't. I'll rest awhile - Gabriel will only fuss. What he doesn't know about can't hurt him.'

'As you wish, but does he not know you've fainted before?' She exchanged a look with Charity who shrugged in resignation. 'You should take more care of yourself, the charity is not so important that you should make yourself ill. When you feel better you must come to tea and meet Susan. She would be interested to hear about the charity and you explain it so much better than I.' Caroline stood to leave. 'In the meantime try to take some rest. I'll not stay, I can see you aren't up to visitors. I only came to give you the money. Goodbye Eleanor, I hope you feel better soon.'

A few days later on a fine afternoon Eleanor was on her way to Eastshore to meet the illustrious Mrs Stubbs. She was keen to meet the lady who had made such a generous contribution to the charity.

Eleanor had decided to walk as the weather was clement and it was but a short distance. Coming past the bay she had bumped into Nancy Pearson, Nat's wife, and had stopped to pass the time of day. Sally her eldest daughter was to be married and Nancy wanted to make sure Gabriel had told her they were invited to the wedding. Now Eleanor was going to be late.

'I set off in plenty of time,' Eleanor explained, 'but as usual time isn't as flexible as I imagine.' Eleanor was in the drawing room where Mrs Stubbs was already waiting. 'I apologise for my lateness,' Eleanor said before Caroline stopped her in her tracks.

'Lottie hasn't arrived either, don't fret. Tea is not yet served.'

There were three ladies present, but Eleanor's eye was drawn to a small, middle aged lady with snow white hair and plump, pink cheeks. They were introduced.

'Eleanor, this is Susan Stubbs and her companion,

Miss Swift. You know Miss Coates of course.'

Eleanor's open smile slid from her face as she looked at the woman sitting beside Mrs Stubbs. She was saved from an embarrassing exchange by Lottie's arrival. There was much chatter and fuss as everyone talked at once; all except Bryony and Eleanor who stared at each other in astonishment. As to who was the most surprised was a question of debate. It was Bryony who looked away first and smoothed the skirt of her grey day dress.

Tea was served and the chatter died away. Lottie, sitting next to Eleanor, turned and sotto voce said, 'Isn't that... ' She could see from Eleanor's raised eyebrows that it was indeed the woman she remembered cutting them dead in Northumberland Street some months ago.

Mrs Stubbs addressed Eleanor: 'Caroline tells me you have a baby girl. How splendid. The good Lord did not bless Geoffrey and I with children, so I am keen to help with this scheme of yours. I am fond of children and saw in Berwick the distress caused to young women who were left without means to rear their children when the men jumped ship as it were. Tell me more about your plans. How did the idea come to you?'

Eleanor took a deep breath. She was suddenly on edge. She prayed she wouldn't faint again.

'I'd been aware of the plight of some of the poor women of Alnmouth for some time. Then earlier this year a baby was abandoned on our property, left in our summer house.' Eleanor paused and looked directly at Bryony Swift to establish if there was any change in her demeanour. There was none. 'We notified the authorities and after a search for the mother proved unsuccessful it was determined the only course of action was to place the baby boy in the workhouse. There isn't a foundling hospital hereabouts you understand, so there was no other choice.'

'How distressing for all concerned - a boy you say? How old was he?'

'Not a new born, a few weeks old.'

'Oh, I expected you to say a new born. The mother would have had time to get to know her son in that case. How could any mother give up her baby like that I wonder? Then again she probably had few options.'

'As you rightly say, life is seldom black and white. Some women have little choice.' Lottie added her opinion to the discussion. 'Difficult decisions have to be made and quickly if the woman is to keep her reputation. The woman probably thought she was doing the best for her baby - who knows?'

Eleanor felt uneasy. She looked at Bryony to see if the discussion was having any effect. She thought she saw a slight change in colour, but her old servant kept her eyes resolutely down.

Eleanor continued: 'Fortunately the baby has been given a second chance. I had friends staying from Holland and after the baby remained unclaimed, they took the unconventional step of drawing up legal papers to adopt the child.'

'Goodness, the Dutch have a very relaxed attitude, I know from my travels in Holland, but that's extraordinary.'

'My friends are very practical people. They're also good natured and kind; they love children. They have now taken Mats, as they named him, back to Amsterdam.'

Eleanor glanced at Bryony but saw only a companion with a keen interest in her hands.

'How altruistic of them my dear, they must be very open-minded people.'

'They are, as I said it would have been the workhouse otherwise.'

Caroline poured more tea. 'It's easy to judge. Before Eleanor opened my eyes to the problem, I'd have thought the mother callous and unfeeling. Now I see these poor women have little choice in what to do with their babies. Without a man to support them they need to work, but can't if they have a baby to look after. Some girls have relatives to help of course, but most are disowned by their families. These are the ones we will try to help.'

'In a seafaring town like Alnmouth I would wager it's an all too common plight; young girls are left to pick up the pieces when the sailors leave them to fend for themselves, leaving broken promises in their wake.' Mrs Stubbs shook her head slowly then continued: 'Mats is one of the lucky ones. Had he been sent to the poor house I fancy he wouldn't have survived infancy. How exactly are you to help these women Mrs Reynolds?'

'We're looking for a large property. We intend to find caring women to run it. They will look after the needs of the women and run the place while the mothers go out to work. We propose to hire a midwife too, so the women have somewhere safe to deliver their babies.'

'What a good idea.'

'Caroline, Lottie and myself have discussed this and don't want to run some fallen woman establishment where the women will be patronised. We want it to be a home where the women can go out to earn money knowing their children will be safe, fed and cared for while they're gone. Some we hope will pay a little, depending on their circumstances, towards their upkeep. We want them to become self-sufficient eventually.'

Lottie was enthusiastic as she swept crumbs from her lap. 'In time we hope to have a schoolroom and provide education, not just for the children, but for some of the women too. It would help them to secure better paid work, better their prospects.'

'You have lofty ideals ladies. I hope you are successful. Have you a name for the charity?'

Eleanor rubbed the base of her back which was beginning to ache. 'When my husband was looking for the baby's mother he was told she was living by the bay. He didn't find her, but he did find a young girl not more than fifteen years old living in a hovel with her baby. The father, a sailor naturally, had left her without support. She had to sell her body to maintain both herself and her little girl.'

'The poor child, but it's an all too familiar tale I'm afraid.'

Eleanor realised Mrs Stubbs had a kind heart. She knew she was going to be supportive. 'The girl told Gabriel her baby's name - she'd named her Hope. She said it was all she had left. It affected me greatly when he told me of the girl's circumstances. We thought to call the place Hope House inspired by her. We have since been back and helped little Hope and her mother. How could we not?'

After more discussion the party began to break up. Eleanor was glad because she was beginning to feel dizzy again.

'I understand you walked here Mrs Reynolds, may we give you a ride home?' Mrs Stubbs stood to leave. Eleanor didn't like to admit it, but she did feel rather queasy and her back was troubling her so she gratefully accepted the offer.

Eleanor sat opposite Bryony Swift in the carriage but the companion looked down purposefully refusing to meet Eleanor's eye. As they set off for Westshore, Eleanor decided to take the bull by the horns. 'You're new to Lesbury I understand Miss Swift?'

'I'm originally from Embleton.'

'Miss Swift has been residing in your neck of the woods Eleanor.' Mrs Stubbs smiled amiably. 'She's been in Whitby. Such a coincidence is it not? It is strange how often that happens where a thread appears to connect people, it's a small world.' The carriage pulled up outside Westshore. 'What a wonderful house my dear, so close to the seashore.' Eleanor was handed down by an outrider.

'Thank you Mrs Stubbs. Gabriel's father built Westshore. We're blessed to live so near to the sea I think. Thank you again for the generous donation.'

'You are most welcome my dear. Come and call on me and bring your daughter, I should love to meet her.' The carriage pulled away leaving Eleanor staring after it and wondering what to do about Bryony Swift. If she was Mats' mother should she tell Susan Stubbs she wondered?

'Are you coming in my love?' Gabriel was standing on the terrace watching her. Eleanor shook herself.

'Did you like Mrs Stubbs? I met her once. She seems a sensible, kind woman.' He linked arms with his wife and walked her into the conservatory.

'Yes I did. She seems... ' Gabriel waited for her to continue.

'Are you alright? You seem distracted.'

'What? Oh yes, sorry. I've had a bit of a shock. Mrs Stubbs seems a lovely lady as you say. She has a new companion.' Gabriel waited.

'Her new companion is Bryony Swift.'

R

Two days later Eleanor strolled to the beach and turned her face away from the bay. While Rose slept she thought to take a walk to clear her head. The wind whipped her hair across her face as she struggled to raise her hood. A figure stepped out in front of her.

'What the... You! You startled me. What do you want?'

'Can I speak with you please Mrs Reynolds?' Bryony Swift approached cautiously. 'I need to ask you a question, if you can spare the time that is?'

Eleanor had never known Bryony to be quite so conciliatory. 'Very well. Walk with me but I can't be too long.' The young woman fell into step with her former mistress. 'Well what is it you want to ask, though I expect I can guess?'

'I want to know if you're going to tell Mrs Stubbs about my situation.'

Eleanor was surprised Bryony had come straight to the point. 'I haven't yet decided - I have to think about it.'

'Then I can save you the trouble for I've told her myself.'

Eleanor remembered the tone of voice from when Bryony had worked for her; it had changed from conciliatory to belligerent in a heartbeat.

'After the tea party I thought you would tell her of our acquaintance so I decided to confess all. She's a kind lady and an astute one. After I heard how sympathetically she spoke that day I thought to take the risk and tell her before you did.' Bryony spoke quickly and was becoming breathless as the wind whipped her words away.

Eleanor stopped and turned to face the other woman. She was astonished.

'I hoped she would understand. I thought if I explained everything honestly she'd have pity for me, recognise my plight.'

Eleanor shot her a look of contempt.

'I can assure you I didn't lie, I omitted nothing. What you suspected was true. The baby was... is mine.'

Eleanor held onto her cowl as the wind threatened to tug it from her head.

'You're either very brave or very foolhardy Miss Swift. The stakes were high. Did Mrs Stubbs say she'll keep you on?'

'She did. She's a good and forbearing lady and I'm grateful to her.'

'What I don't understand is how you could leave him?'

'Let me explain Mrs Reynolds. I don't want your sympathy, I deserve your censure.' The young woman's tone of voice had changed yet again. She looked at Eleanor beseechingly.

'Then I can't see why you need bother me. You've

probably wheedled your way into her good books, taken advantage of her kind hearted nature. You're first-rate at that, although as I remember you prefer to aim your arrows at men.'

Bryony half smiled. 'Yet you still have it in your power to change her mind. If I can just have a little of your time I hope I can persuade you to let sleeping dogs lie.'

'Very well. I'm interested in why you left your baby in the care of a woman you thought beneath your contempt, but please don't think me a fool, I've seen how you can manipulate.'

'What I say here today is the truth.' The two women continued to walk, but headed for the dunes where the wind was less fierce. 'I'm not one of the poor innocents you hope to give alms to, I'm ashamed to say I knew all along what I was about.'

Bryony had returned Eleanor thought, to the obstinate woman she knew of old. She wondered at the turmoil that these about turns took on the woman's nerves; they were doing nothing for Eleanor's own.

'After I left Westshore I found it hard to find work. I met a man, a man who said he'd take care of me. He was involved in free trading and so was often away from Alnmouth, but he left me well provided for, especially if the run had been a success. Then I didn't see him for a long while and I was forced to take a job at an inn. It was then I realised I might be with child.'

'Did you tell him about your condition?'

'I was going to, but then he told me he'd found work captaining a whaling ship in Whitby. He said he would send for me when he'd completed the first mission. I thought better of telling him there might be a baby. My idea was to trap him into marrying me, not scare him off. I reckoned if I told him what I suspected I might not hear from him again. I decided to wait until he sent for me. I miscalculated spectacularly.'

'He didn't send for you I take it?'

'It was the usual story I expect, he'd got what he came for. He was handsome and a charmer and like all Irishmen he had the gift of the gab as they say.'

'He was Irish?' Eleanor stopped and stared at Bryony.

'Yes. When I knew for certain I was with child I set off to Whitby in search of him. He'd told me he loved me, I hoped he'd marry me still. I tried to find him as I know whaling missions can be hazardous and thought to make sure an accident hadn't befallen him - fool that I was. How easily we can convince ourselves men are true to their word.'

'When you told him about the baby did he refuse you?'

'I never got to tell him because I couldn't find him. I came back to Alnmouth on the off chance he was looking for me here. Of course he wasn't. I was at my wits' end. I couldn't get work in my condition and when Patrick was born I couldn't think how we were to survive.'

'Patrick. You called your baby Patrick?'

'It's the English translation of his father's name, Padraic. I still thought he might come back for me. I expect you think I got what I deserved?'

Eleanor ignored this last jibe. She had begun to put the pieces of the puzzle together. 'Is your Irish captain named Turner?' Eleanor was astounded when Bryony nodded, a worried frown on her beautiful face.

'Dear Lord! He was working on my father's whaler, The Whitby Lass. An accident did befall him, he was shot, but it wasn't a serious injury, nothing life threatening that would stop him seeking you out.'

'I know about the incident. I saw him when he came ashore in Alnmouth. That was the last time we met. I should have told him then, but I thought I was clever and would bide my time. He still said he'd send for me when he returned to Whitby.'

'So the baby is Turner's. He doesn't work for my father now, he's here in Alnmouth. Did you know?'

'How could I? I'm mostly at Lesbury. Is it true? He's returned?'

Eleanor couldn't believe all she was hearing. 'Please continue your story. You've not explained how you came to abandon your son, though I can possibly guess. What I don't understand is why you chose us. You never liked me, you made that perfectly clear.'

'When I was in your service I was arrogant, jealous of all you had and I was selfish. I thought I deserved more in life. I'm still only nineteen and realise now

I've a lot to learn.'

Eleanor huffed. 'If my husband had been the type to bed his servants you would have taken advantage of that without hesitation. You would have tried to trick him into supporting you. You sought to come between us. You couldn't have expected marriage?'

'No, but my silence could have been bought with a roof over my head and money. That's what I'd hoped.'

Eleanor wanted to slap Bryony Swift hard across the face. 'How dare you. And yet you still tried to blacken his name and tried to come between us by accusing him of fathering your child. You left your son with us hoping we'd keep him to avoid a scandal. Had the baby been left without the incriminating note we might have taken pity on the poor child. Your spiteful action almost backfired. I think you'd better go Miss Swift, you're beneath contempt.' Eleanor's temper flared. 'I'll think what to say to Mrs Stubbs for I see she deserves a better companion than you. You're ever the schemer and are probably devising some arrangement already to part your employer from her money. You're not to be trusted.'

'If Mrs Stubbs lets me go I'll have lost everything. I'm grateful to her and believe me I want nothing more than to earn an honest living now. I've been forced to grow up fast. I did love my son, I love him still. I did what I thought was best for him when I gave him up. I stayed and watched you take him in. If you'd not found him I wouldn't have left him, I'm not heartless.'

She brushed tears away with the back of her hand. 'I love Patrick with all my heart Mrs Reynolds. You possibly don't believe me, but it's the truth, it was the hardest thing I ever had to do when I gave him away and now I'll never see him again. I knew you loved children and would do the best you could for Patrick no matter what.' She struggled to control her emotions. 'I could've lied to Mrs Stubbs and to you, pretended to be one of your wronged women, but I won't.'

Eleanor saw Bryony's pride re-assert itself.

'I take full responsibility for my actions. Nothing you can say or do will make me feel more guilty than I feel already. My need for a better life has meant I've made serious errors in judgement. I wronged you and Mr Reynolds, I see that now, but I too have been wronged. I've had to make my own way in this life, but that's no excuse. Many have been in my position but taken a more honest path than I.'

Eleanor's head throbbed. She didn't know what to think.

'I believe my job with Mrs Stubbs could be the making of me if only you will show me kindness and not blacken my name. It's a kindness I admit I don't deserve, but I'm not the woman you knew before - I've changed. I've lost the dearest thing in my life... my darling boy. If I lose this position I'll have nowhere left to go. Mrs Stubbs has been kind and said I can stay on, she believes I should have a second chance. She believes in redemption. Do you?'

Eleanor turned her face to home. She'd never expected Bryony Swift to plead. The chilly wind made her shiver as they began to walk back.

'I'm not a vengeful person, but I can't think straight at the moment. My mind is in turmoil with all you've told me. My instinct tells me you have changed, but then does a leopard ever change its spots?' Eleanor saw the imploring look on Bryony's face. 'Had the matter concerned only myself I would be of a mind to keep my peace.' They had reached the path that led to Westshore. 'But the matter concerns others. I'll talk it over with my husband as this involves him too. You wronged him most of all. He's a good man and you saw him only as a meal ticket. If you had but asked for help both of us would have tried to do something for you I'm certain of it. Good day to you Miss Swift.'

'Mrs Reynolds, I'm truly sorry. I've never been the type of woman to trust; whenever I've let down my guard I've regretted it.' She hung her head. 'Before you take your leave please may I ask one thing? It would mean the world to me. Can you tell me how my son does? I know you said he's gone to Holland with your friends. He fares well I pray?'

Eleanor stopped. She'd been worried Bryony hadn't asked about the welfare of her baby; any mother in her situation would be desperate for news. This made a difference to Eleanor. Perhaps Bryony had changed for the better? She saw the anguished look on the mother's face and her soft heart opened to her.

'He does fare well. He's a happy, healthy baby and wants for nothing. My friends are besotted with him and write to me often about how he is changing as he grows.'

Bryony let out a sob.

'I'll send a note Miss Swift, when I've spoken with Mr Reynolds.' Eleanor sighed. 'I think you may have cause to be hopeful.'

ℛ

After discussing Bryony Swift with Gabriel, both of them were in agreement that Eleanor would speak to Mrs Stubbs and tell her their version of the story. It would come with the proviso they were not seeking retribution, but they did want Susan Stubbs to know what kind of character she was dealing with. Her companion had been a cunning baggage in the past and whether she had changed her ways was yet to be seen.

Eleanor wrote a letter asking to see the lady privately. She hinted the matter concerned her companion.

'I'll go and see Caro. She needs to know about this turn of events. I knew Turner was no good.'

Eleanor knew Gabriel was furious, but on this occasion she agreed with him. 'This time you're right to interfere. If she decides to go ahead with the marriage that's her choice, but at least she'll be in full possession of the facts, yet in fairness he didn't know he'd fathered a child.'

'He led her on, he's untrustworthy. Didn't I always say so?'

'Perhaps I should come with you, don't go to Eastshore in this mood. Poor Caroline will be devastated. As you once said she's not worldly wise, she's bound to be upset.'

'I think I should see her alone if you don't mind. I'll be kind, measured in my approach. After all I'm not angry with her.'

Eleanor knew Gabriel would be honest but thoughtful. He wasn't the type of man to say "I told you so".

'In that case wait until after I've seen Mrs Stubbs tomorrow. Take the time to compose what you'll say, or more to the point how you'll deliver the bad news so as not to cause Caroline more pain than is absolutely necessary.'

The next day Eleanor was shown into the morning room at Lesbury Lodge. 'Mrs Stubbs, how kind of you to see me.' Eleanor noticed the room overlooked a beautiful rose garden.

'Not at all my dear, it's good of you to bring your daughter to see me.'

Eleanor was thankful Miss Swift wasn't in attendance. 'Ginny will remove my daughter should she become peevish, she has a tooth coming I think. I see you're fond of roses. Meet my daughter, Alice

Rose, who has become known simply as Rose.'

'I am fond of roses, but I cannot claim to have anything to do with its design, the garden was here before I moved in, so sadly I cannot take the credit.' She smiled at Rose, who smiled back confidently.

'Your daughter has your colouring, your husband is dark haired I seem to remember. She will be grateful for her hair colour as she gets older. Gentlemen are drawn to redheads I believe.' Susan Stubbs twinkled. The two women chatted easily about everyday matters. Eleanor liked the woman and thankfully Rose was on her best behaviour.

'Regarding your letter Mrs Reynolds, I was intrigued to receive it. I'm interested to hear what you have to say.'

Eleanor drew a long breath and told her all about Bryony Swift, not maliciously, but in a plain speaking, honest way.

'I see.' Susan Stubbs sipped her tea before continuing. 'When I was in Berwick I became known for taking in waifs and strays as it were - let me explain. Often the judgements my husband made affected not just the condemned men, but also their wives, daughters, sisters and mothers; all were condemned you understand not just the perpetrator of the crime. My staff consisted largely of the women who were left to pick up the pieces, women who without a breadwinner had to support themselves and their children. Often when they fell on hard times all they had to sell was themselves. To avoid this, I tried to help by foisting these poor souls upon my friends. Many of the grand houses of Berwick are staffed with the relations of convicts thanks to me.' She laughed at herself. 'However, I can assure you I'm not easily taken in. I knew from the beginning there was something not quite right with Miss Swift's background. Her letter of recommendation was excellent but there were gaps unaccounted for in her history. Her appearance also suggested a woman who had once had a good position and had now fallen on hard times. It was obvious she hadn't had a comfortable life for a while; indeed I had to provide her with suitable clothing when she first came to work for me.'

'After Miss Swift worked for us for those few months I think she picked up any work she could. Then she had to take work at an inn. At least she didn't fall so far as some.'

'So she says. I have told her she can stay on as I think she deserves another chance. After all is she not the sort of woman your charity is trying to help?'

'I suppose she is. Perhaps the world has made Miss Swift the character we see today. It can't have been easy for her. I don't know whether she had family to turn to, she was never easy to get to know.'

'She said her mother was a hard worker and her father a hard drinker. It's often the case. Aside from that she said her home life was no worse than hundreds of others. She didn't seek them out when she found herself in difficulties. To her credit she says they had troubles of their own; her father drank away any money he made. When she had regular work Miss Swift says she sent money to her mother to help with her younger brother.'

Eleanor shrugged. 'I'm beginning to hold a grudging respect for Miss Swift. She could easily have spun some hard luck story of a cruel and indigent childhood yet she didn't.'

Rose suddenly let out an ear piercing cry and then continued to bawl incessantly. Mrs Stubbs screwed up her face then guffawed. After Eleanor attempted to calm her daughter Ginny removed the fractious child.

'I thank you for coming to see me this morning, but rest assured I'm more astute than I look.'

'Gabriel and I thought you should know our point of view, but as I said we're not looking for vengeance.'

'I will keep a watchful eye although I would be surprised if she puts a foot wrong - she's on a three month trial. I think she realises this is her last chance.'

'I hope so for everyone's sake.'

'When is your baby due my dear? You will have your hands full.' The subject was closed Eleanor realised. Mrs Stubbs was indeed a kind woman, but she was no one's fool either.

'In April and you're right, I shall indeed be busy.'

'In that case please let me know if I can be of assistance with the charity; with Caroline to be married and you with your own children I think you will be in need of all the help you can get. I, and indeed Miss Swift, have plenty of time on our hands. She smiled wickedly. 'If we are to show compassion for Miss Swift it's only reasonable I think she shows some largesse to others. Have you met Caroline's intended, Mrs Reynolds?' she asked changing the subject.

'Please call me Eleanor.' She felt her heart beat faster, Eleanor didn't want to get into hot water on Turner's account.

'I've met Captain Turner. He worked briefly for my father in Whitby.' Eleanor explained the connection and how he had met Caroline at Westshore. Eleanor felt uncomfortable. She was aware this was not the whole story, but she and Gabriel had agreed to keep Turner out of his part in Miss Swift's downfall until he'd seen Caroline.

'I remember Caroline mentioned she had met her intended at your home initially. She tells me he's a very good looking man. They are dining with me today so I shall reserve judgement until then. I believe you both share the same taste in men my dear Eleanor,' she laughed a tinkling laugh, 'your husband was once engaged to Caroline I know. I met him many years ago at their betrothal party. They were both so young and Thomas was keen for the match. Gabriel would not remember me of course, but you're a lucky lady for your husband is what I call a very handsome man.'

'Thank you I am lucky but he's not just handsome, he's a good husband and father too.'

'What is your opinion of Captain Turner?' Susan Stubbs skewered Eleanor with a look. Eleanor almost choked on her tea at the bluntness of the question.

'He's a fine looking man and very charming.' Eleanor decided to err on the side of caution.

'Good looks keep a lady warm at night, but what of the captain's character? What is he like? I only ask as I think I can trust your judgement, you seem to be a sensible woman. There are those who would not be friends with their husband's childhood sweetheart yet you bear no ill will.'

'Captain Turner is... ' Eleanor stopped. Obviously Mrs Stubbs was unaware Turner was the father of Bryony's baby. Eleanor thought it not her place to enlighten her, but then suddenly thought about his visit later that day. What if Bryony were present at dinner? Eleanor became flustered.

The door opened and Miss Swift entered.

'I think Mrs Stubbs hasn't put two and two together yet Mrs Reynolds. How could she?'

Eleanor flushed and Susan Stubbs looked from one woman to the other in confusion. Bryony had clearly been listening at the key hole.

'I didn't want to influence your judgement Mrs Stubbs, but I can't let Mrs Reynolds wrestle with her conscience.'

'I'm at a loss Miss Swift, I don't understand.'

'It wasn't until I went to see Mrs Reynolds I found out the father of my son is back in Alnmouth. It is your goddaughter's fiancé, Captain Turner.'

The three women stared at each other.

'You mean the captain you told me about, the one who went to Whitby to work on a whaling mission is engaged to Caroline and more importantly to her fortune.'

Eleanor wished a hole would appear and swallow her up.

'I can see Eleanor I have placed you in a very awkward position, forgive me. I had *not* put two and two together, how could I? Miss Swift didn't mention the name of her seducer.'

Mrs Stubbs poured more tea and handed a dish to her companion. 'Well my dear, this is a pretty kettle of fish is it not? Poor Caroline.'

'Gabriel intends to speak to Caroline tomorrow. We hadn't anticipated you would be meeting him today.' Eleanor shuffled in her seat. 'She does know something of his nature. When she told us of the engagement Gabriel was very unhappy about it, he doesn't like the man. He has his own reasons for taking against the captain, reasons I don't feel I can share with you. However, Gabriel went to see Caroline and said his piece, but she, as is her right, dismissed his interference.'

'I see. Well Miss Swift I suggest you make yourself

scarce when they arrive. I will have to think carefully about what, if anything, I can do about this turn of events.'

'In his defence Mrs Stubbs as I said before, Padraic didn't know I was with child, he might have stood by me had he known. We can't know for sure what he would have done.'

'He might,' Eleanor agreed, 'yet he did treat you abominably.'

'He did. He treated you like a common prostitute if you don't mind my frankness Miss Swift.'

Mrs Stubbs didn't mince her words. Even Eleanor wouldn't have presumed so much.

Oh to be present at dinner Eleanor thought as she left for Westshore later that morning. She was not looking forward to explaining all this to her husband.

20

Two days before Christmas Eleanor rang for Ransom who glided into the morning room on silent feet. Gabriel often complained to Eleanor of this habit of being crept up on, saying it unnerved him. Eleanor simply thought the butler well trained.

'Why is the library locked?' she asked.

'Locked ma'am? I wasn't aware that it was.'

'The key is usually in the door, but I've never known it to be locked. The key is gone and the door locked.'

'I'll go to the key store ma'am to see if it's been hung there.'

He returned almost at once. 'The door is indeed locked and the key nowhere to be found ma'am. Perhaps Mr Reynolds has, er, put it somewhere.'

Eleanor knew what Ransom meant. A few days ago Gabriel had locked the scullery door, then in a moment of absentmindedness put the key in his pocket and gone to Berwick for two days.

'Thank you Ransom, I'll check with him on his return from Craster this evening.'

Over supper Eleanor quizzed her husband. 'Why is the library locked? Have you got the key? The book

I'm reading is in there and I couldn't get in earlier.'

'I might have known you would be snooping.'

'Snooping? It's hardly snooping going to get a book from the library. Oh, I see, have you hidden my Christmas gift in there? It must be big. At least it's not a horse, well I hope it's not if it's in the library.'

'It isn't a horse. I know we now have a stud farm, but credit me with a little more imagination than that. You'll just have to wait and see. After supper I'd planned to give you a little something. I wanted to give it to you privately, that is to say before our guests arrive for the festivities.'

Eleanor snorted and put her hand on her growing bump. 'You've already given me an early present... two in fact.' When Dr Sharpe had examined Eleanor last he'd announced what she already knew; she was expecting twins. He'd said two heartbeats could certainly be heard. Eleanor, and especially Gabriel, were very excited at the prospect of adding twins to the family.

'How intriguing. May we go now?'

'Eleanor you're like a child. After we've finished supper.' He shook his head at her impatience, but was amused.

Eleanor refused dessert. She was far too keen to get to the library.

'I can't imagine what it will be like on Christmas Eve when Rose is old enough to know gifts will be expected the next day. If she's as bad as you my life will be a torment every Christmas.'

They stood outside the library while Gabriel removed his neckcloth. 'I don't trust you to close your eyes so I'm going to blindfold you.' Eleanor was excited as he fastened it over her eyes. He unlocked the library door.

'Be careful, I'll guide you in.'

Eleanor knew she was close to the mantelpiece when he stopped her. She could feel the heat from the fire.

'How is there a fire in here when the door was locked?'

'I ordered it so. There are two keys to the library. I'm afraid Ransom lied to you my love.'

'Did he now! I never guessed, I'll have to watch out in future.'

'I'm going to remove the blindfold, but before I do I need to explain what you will see also required me to tell an untruth or two for which I apologise in advance.' He removed the neckcloth.

Above the mantel shelf was a portrait of Eleanor holding baby Rose on her knee. In her hair, which was loose, was a circle of white roses. She was wearing the ivory medieval gown she'd worn to the charity ball. Around her neck and wrist were sapphires and in her ears she wore matching earrings. There was a huge sapphire on her middle finger. The whole effect was reminiscent of an Arthurian legend. The pose and the jewels were identical to the ones in the painting of Alice Reynolds.

'Gabriel! I can guess who painted it. My friend Abalone has also been telling lies has she not? She always has her sketch book handy so when she sat with her pencil I never guessed it was for preliminary sketches for a painting of Rose and I. The attitude is exactly like that of your mother in this painting of you both.' She turned to him tears in her eyes. 'Oh Gabriel, you're the best man in the world to think of this. I do love it, and you. Although it will take some getting used to seeing myself hung on the wall every day.'

'There's one other thing, another lie of sorts I suppose. Well not exactly a lie, but an omission if you will. Do you remember when we were discussing my mother's portrait and I said I wondered where the sapphires went?'

'I have the other jewels which belonged to your mother in the safe, but not those.'

'I got to thinking about the conversation, and then I suddenly remembered something my father told me. Close your eyes again. Can I trust you not to cheat?' Eleanor screwed her eyes tight shut. She heard Gabriel move over to the desk and then return.

'Open your eyes.'

She let out a squeal of delight. 'The sapphires! How - where were they?' She could tell he was as excited as she was.

'Father said they were very expensive, the most precious of all the jewels he'd ever given her. Mother was always worried about them he told me, so much so she insisted they be kept at the bank. It dawned on me after that evening where they were. I'd quite forgotten. When I asked Abalone to paint you, she asked to see the sapphires as they were so well painted in the original - she didn't want them to suffer in comparison. I got them from the safe deposit box and she did all she had to do to get their likeness. She's made an excellent job I think. They look just as good, if not better than in Mother's picture. She's also captured your likeness beautifully.'

Eleanor was stunned into silence as she looked at the sparkling, deep blue stones.

'Here,' Gabriel lifted the heavy necklace from the ivory silk box, 'let me put them on for you. He kissed her neck then put the bracelet on her wrist and helped her to fasten the earrings.

'You look stunning in them. Mother's hair was so dark and yours is so red, but both of you have skin like alabaster so they look... '

Eleanor could see her husband was quite overcome with emotion. She reached up and kissed him to show him how much he was appreciated. Finally he placed the large sapphire ring on her middle finger. It fit perfectly. Gabriel stood behind his wife, his arms about her thickening waist as they both looked at the portraits.

'Mrs Reynolds,' he whispered in her ear, 'you have made me the happiest of men; one baby in the crib and two more on the way. With you beside me what man could ask for more? I always wanted to fill the house with sticky fingers and scuffed knees. Thank you my love for making it possible.'

'Mr Reynolds,' Eleanor joked, 'I hope you're not lying to me now for if you were I would be very, very upset.'

'I swear I'll never lie to you again my love, unless of course I want to surprise you.' He squeezed her tenderly and placed another kiss on her bejewelled neck.

ℛ

The Christmas festivities at Westshore in this year 1768 consisted mostly of friends, rather than family, the exception being Tomas and Cora who were in attendance. Eleanor was too large to travel to Whitby and so Bendor and Grace along with Lottie and Wilson were to spend Christmas with them. Eleanor was looking forward to hosting for young people.

'Where's my gift?' Gabriel looked expectantly at his wife. 'Everyone has opened their presents, but I don't see one from my wife.'

'I've saved the best till last,' she said. 'Here's your gift from myself and your daughter. She has no money of her own so I've subbed her.' They were all in high spirits after a wonderful dinner.

Gabriel opened the present; it was a diamond studded cravat pin engraved with the entwined letters

G and E. He thanked his wife with a kiss and set about pinning his cravat with it.

'There's one other thing. Perhaps you'll think it a strange thing to give a man for Christmas but... ' Bendor made a louche comment and Grace giggled as she nudged him in the ribs. 'As I was saying before I was rudely interrupted,' Eleanor said in mock irritation, 'it's a slightly unusual gift, but when you see it you'll understand. She rang the bell and Ransom brought it in. He placed it before his master.

'A fire screen?' Lottie looked aghast. 'Are you worried for his complexion?'

Eleanor explained the significance to their guests. 'I found this beautiful tapestry which Gabriel's mother had made amongst her belongings. It needed a little work to finish it and to make it into a fire screen.' She looked to her husband. 'I thought you would like something of your mother about the house my love.'

'Eleanor it's beautiful.' Gabriel was moved. 'Thank you it's so thoughtful of you. How you kept the secret I'll never know. She's not good at secrets is she Tomas?'

Tomas agreed. 'We too have a secret, well an announcement at any rate. Tomas looked at Cora but before he could continue Eleanor leapt from her chair and flung her arms about her brother's neck.

'You're going to have a baby?' she squealed. Everyone burst out laughing.

'Well not me in particular, but yes Cora and I are

most fortunate.'

There was chatter and back slapping and many congratulations.

'When is it to be Cora?' Eleanor asked excitedly.

'Whenever the stork has a delivery date free,' she said rolling her eyes. 'I'm glad you're excited Eleanor for I'll like the end result I dare say, but I'm not looking forward to another six months of getting fat.'

'It's not fat it's a baby.' Eleanor kissed her sister-in-law's cheek. 'It may be twins. Who knows?'

Cora tried to smile, but it looked more like a grimace. 'I sincerely hope not, one will be more than enough.'

'I feel quite the odd one out,' Lottie sighed. 'I'm the only one not with child.'

'You're not yet married, your turn will come.'

'Lord I hope not. Pleased as I am for all you ladies in waiting it's the last thing I want.'

Grace turned to Eleanor and asked: 'Is it not time for cake?'

ℛ

Lady Grace Percy gave birth on a snowy January night without any of the drama of her first birthing. Two days later Bendor rode to Westshore with the happy news.

'All done and dusted in less than six hours,' Bendor said as Gabriel shook his friend's hand.

'This calls for a celebration does it not?' Gabriel headed for the brandy decanter.

'Anyone would think *you* had given birth.' Eleanor accepted a glass of canary from her husband.

'It's almost as bad as giving birth waiting anxiously for news, I can tell you.' Bendor and Gabriel were already refilling their empty glasses.

'There speaks a man!' Eleanor rested her hands on her bump.

'I should gladly swap places if it were possible,' Gabriel knelt down by his wife, 'but it cannot be. I'm just grateful as I've said before that I'm a man.'

Eleanor ruffled his curls. 'Are you two going to have one of your infamous drinking bouts? If so shall I wait on dinner for you?'

'I'd love to stay. I promised Grace I'd deliver the news, partake of your hospitality, then head straight back. Have I told you her name yet and that she has dark hair like Grace?'

'That was to be my next question.' Eleanor waited impatiently.

'Her name is Annabelle Eleanor Percy. Would you do us the honour of being one of Belle's godmothers Eleanor? She'll have two; Jane is to be the other. Gabriel is already godfather to Flora of course.'

'I'd be honoured,' Eleanor said blushing.

They sat down to dinner. Bendor, always a cheerful chap, was even more ebullient. 'You've all this to look forward to Gabe. It's wonderful news Cora and Tomas are also expecting. Both our families are growing and prospering are they not?'

'They are indeed. We'll soon be five when the twins are born. You still have some catching up to do Ben.' Gabriel refilled their glasses.

Ransom entered and announced Dr Chaffer.

'He's checking up on me I think,' Eleanor said rising. 'Give my love to Grace and tell her we'll come to see you all in a few days. And leave off the spirits or you'll be dead in a ditch when you fall from your horse on the way home.'

When they were alone Gabriel looked at his best friend. 'Thank you for choosing Eleanor to be godmother, she'll take her duties seriously I can assure you.'

He twisted the stem of his port glass in his fingers thoughtfully. 'I envy you now the birth is over. You can relax. Bringing twins into the world will be twice the burden for poor Eleanor and I fear she's not as well as she's trying to make out. My darling wife is trying to spare me which is troubling. I don't want her to spare my feelings, I want us to share everything, the good and the bad. I grow more anxious as her time approaches. How can I not worry? I think she too is concerned though she wouldn't let on for the world.'

ℛ

Eleanor sat on the chaise at the bottom of her bed.

Wilson looked apprehensive.

'Why have you sent for me Eleanor? I know you wouldn't ask to see me unless there was a problem.'

'Firstly I know this will be hard for you as Gabriel is your friend but if I'm to confide in you - '

'There is confidentiality between doctor and patient. Whatever you say to me as my patient will go no further, of that you can be assured.'

'Thank you Wilson, you know how Gabriel worries. I don't want him fussing and staying at home so I haven't told him how I feel.'

'How do you feel?'

'I often feel light headed and on a couple of occasions I've fainted. I'm eating well and I've not felt nauseous this time. I was never like this in my other pregnancies.'

'When you say you've fainted a couple of times I presume you're under reporting. I know you Eleanor. Will you allow me to examine you?'

'If you think I need to be examined I'll ask Dr Sharpe. I'd feel awkward with you... you know why.'

He took her pulse. 'Is this allowed?' He smiled. 'Your pulse is a little sluggish.' He let go of her hand. 'Twins will put a bigger strain on your constitution. Although you're in good health you need to take more rest, slow down Eleanor there's a way to go yet. See Dr Sharpe sooner rather than later and let me know what he thinks after he's examined you. Is my bedside manner so repugnant you won't let me check you over?'

'Of course not, but I would feel embarrassed you being a friend that's all.' She shifted, feeling uncomfortable. There is one other thing... '

'Go on.'

'I feel silly mentioning it now, but as I've begun...'

'Tell me. If you're concerned about anything you shouldn't keep it to yourself.'

'As I said it's foolish, but I keep getting a strange feeling, a bad feeling as if, well as if all is not as it should be, with the babies I mean. Sometimes I'm afraid. I never felt like this when I was expecting Rose and that was my first time. I know what to expect now so surely I should feel easier. But I don't. Every time I look at the painting of Gabriel's mother... '

'It's natural to feel some anxiety especially with twins. Do you feel the babies move?' Eleanor nodded. 'As I always say to Gabriel worrying will only make matters worse. That's a man speaking I know, but also a doctor. It's such a shame your mother isn't close to confide in. I understand you not telling Gabriel, but you must. It will help to talk about your fears. Promise me you'll rest and talk to your husband?'

'I'll do the first, but the latter I'll have to think about. I'm being silly, superstitious.' She was keen to talk of other matters. 'At least you'll never suffer such anxiety as Lottie appears determined not to have children. Will you mind?'

'She's not maternal as you point out. We shall see.

We haven't set a date for the wedding yet so let's not get ahead of ourselves.'

When Wilson left, Eleanor lay on her bed but sleep wouldn't come. She still felt uneasy.

21

'As I've said so many times before it's always the woman who is left to pick up the pieces when some man turns out to be a scoundrel.' Eleanor was venting as she was handed into the carriage. Gabriel and Eleanor were on their way to Wooden House to sup with Wilson and Lottie.

'I told her what he was like,' Gabriel muttered, 'yet still Caroline refuses to see it. I've told her, Susan Stubbs has told her, you've tried to make her see sense, yet she simply makes excuses for Turner. Despite what she's been told about her future husband's conduct, Caroline refuses to give Captain Turner up. It's madness.'

'I can see it from her point of view too. He didn't know of the baby's existence or what had become of Bryony. Poor Caroline, she loves him and who's to say she's wrong to do so? I trusted you when others would have thought me foolish. I've not regretted it.'

'You did when you found out about my son, we both did. Life is all about consequences, our actions no matter how benign at the time have repercussions.'

'The tide turns and washes the beach clean, but those

footprints in the sand aren't so easily erased. Those two babies, Bryony's and Libby's, were lucky; think of the hundreds that aren't so fortunate, the ones tossed over the harbour wall at the dead of night.'

Eleanor shuddered. Both of them were still uncomfortable talking about his son in America. Although Gabriel missed him, he knew it unfair to say so to his wife.

'The wedding is still to go ahead,' Eleanor continued, 'I've tried to talk to her about her wealth, about safeguarding her fortune, but she's more conventional than I. She's happy for Turner to have her fortune. She thinks he has a good business head and will run Thomas' affairs well. I'm not so sure. If what Bryony says is true, after he was a soldier, he was involved in free trading. What if his business dealings aren't above board?'

'I always knew he was a shady character. Pity the villain wasn't caught; smuggling is a hanging offence. I knew she wouldn't pay attention to me, but I'd hoped she'd listen to you. It appears not.' Gabriel shrugged.

They arrived at Wooden House and were shown into the drawing room where Lottie was waiting. 'You might have guessed - I'm afraid poor Wilson will miss your company, he's been called away on an emergency. He said not to wait on supper as he's not sure how long he's going to be. Gabriel, it's old Mr Pepper. Wilson thinks this last bout will do for him.'

'That's a shame he was a good man. My father hired

him on The Jack and Alice until he had his first heart stroke. He's been receiving a pension from me ever since.'

The door opened and Caroline and Captain Turner were shown in.

'Oh I hadn't realised... ' Eleanor's words trailed off.

Wilson followed them in. 'I was too late I'm afraid, Mr Pepper had gone by the time I arrived.'

'Gone? Died you mean Wilson?' Caroline looked to Gabriel. 'Oh such a shame. He used to let me steal apples from his garden when I was a girl. His always tasted sweeter than ours.'

'Forbidden fruit my love.' Captain Turner bowed low over Eleanor's hand and kissed it far longer than was seemly. Gabriel sealed his lips tight shut as he saw the quelling look from his wife.

'I forgot to mention Caroline and Padraic were to join us tonight.' Their hostess smiled innocently.

Lottie knew something was amiss but hadn't been able to get Eleanor on her own to find out what juicy gossip she'd missed. Eleanor was annoyed with her friend for springing this on them. Gabriel would scowl all evening now, the supper party would be ruined.

A footman announced supper was served and everyone stood. Eleanor fell to the floor in a dead faint. She was saved by Captain Turner who was standing closest to her. He scooped her up and laid her carefully on a chaise. Gabriel was at her side immediately.

Wilson took smelling salts from his bag. 'Give her some air.' Wilson waved salts under her nose. 'How are you feeling Eleanor, is your head still dizzy?'

'I felt a little light headed that's all, but please don't make a fuss, I'm fine.' Eleanor insisted everyone went in to supper. Gabriel and Wilson waited until they were alone.

'That's the second time Eleanor has fainted.' Gabriel frowned. 'She passed out three days ago; again it was just before supper.'

'Perhaps you're not eating enough.' Wilson gave her his stern doctor face. 'Remember there are not one but two babies to feed. Do you think you could eat something now? I think it would do you good if you could try.'

'I have been eating well. I'm not off my food at all. Yes I'm sure I could eat, I'm always hungry aren't I Gabriel?'

Later on their way home Gabriel addressed his wife sternly. 'Did you know Turner was to be there this evening? Were you in on the ruse to get us together?'

'Not at all, Lottie's a scheming minx. She knows something has happened, but I'm not about to tell her about Turner's shady past, and I doubt Caroline will confide in her. It's hardly something you would want your friends to know about.'

There was a silence as the carriage rattled along on the rutted road.

'Wilson's right; perhaps you need to eat more. Take

a leaf out of Grace's book. You're eating for three as he quite rightly reminded you.'

'I eat well, but I feel uncomfortable if I eat too much, like I'm about to burst. He says it's heartburn.'

'Then try a little often. Perhaps nibble something while you're reading in the afternoon.' Eleanor had been taking life easier and resting after dinner. She leaned into her husband and bit his ear lightly.

'Food I meant, but feel free to nibble me any time.'

'That was interesting when Wilson asked if I was sure of my dates. I thought I was, but he's right I'm exceedingly large.' She looked down at her bump.

'It matters not just so long as you have a care and stay well.'

'And upright,' Eleanor said. 'Never in my life have I fainted until now.' She stroked her bump.

'There was the time when you found Bryony's baby.'

'So there was, I'd quite forgotten that. Anyway I've eaten well and now I am exhausted. I can't wait to get to bed.'

'It's such a pity. I long for you to say those words ordinarily, but tonight I know you have nothing more than sleep on your mind.' He looked adoringly at her and at her large bump. 'Boy and a girl do you think?'

'Two girls I'm certain of it. I mean to overwhelm you with an all female household.' She yawned as they arrived back at Westshore.

'I can live with that,' he said.

A week later Charity found Eleanor on the floor of her dressing room; she had fainted again. Eleanor was laid in a crumpled heap her clothes in disarray. Charity rang the bell and looked for the smelling salts. Ivy arrived almost at once.

Eleanor gasped as the smelling salts did their work. 'Hurry Ivy, go and fetch Joe or Ransom. I'll need help to lift her. Then run and fetch Doctor Chaffer, this can't go on,' she said to Ivy's retreating back. 'You fainted again Eleanor. I won't keep quiet now. That's three times this week.'

Eleanor still felt light headed, but began to try to get up. 'I'll be fine, just help me to a chair.'

'Stay still you've fallen awkwardly. Wait a moment, I've sent for help. Gabriel needs to know about the swooning, I'll tell him when he comes home. You could be doing harm to yourself or the babies. Just stay still.'

'He does know, I've told him and he was there when I fainted at Wooden House, stop fussing.'

Joe arrived and stood in the doorway looking embarrassed.

'Help me get her onto the bed, she's a dead weight. She's like a beached whale, I can't lift her on my own.'

'Remind me to sack you when I've the strength.' Eleanor glowered at her maid. 'I'm sorry Joe, I'm sure

I can manage if you just help me to sit up.' Joe moved quickly and lifted her as if she were no weight at all. 'You, on the other hand, can have a pay rise.' She smiled up at the blushing groom. When Wilson and Gabriel arrived almost together, Wilson insisted on examining the patient much to her embarrassment. He then prescribed a sedative. She feigned sleep as the doctor and her husband talked quietly at the bottom of the bed.

'I know Eleanor won't like this, but I strongly suggest she has bed rest until the births. We know this isn't an isolated incident, we both know she's passed out before and I suspect there have been other times she's not disclosed.'

'She never fainted when she was expecting Rose.'

'All pregnancies are different, especially when there are two babies. Eleanor says her mother and sister didn't suffer fainting when they were expecting and they both had twins. There could be any manner of reasons why she's light headed.'

'Dangerous reasons? She's in danger you think?'

'Only if she has the added worry of you over-reacting. Calm down. If she sees you're worried she'll begin fretting over you instead of looking after herself.'

'It's easier said than done is it not?'

'She needs calm and rest. Has she been eating well?'

'Eleanor has followed your advice on that score at least. She's been eating one potato more than a pig as

Lisbet used to say.'

Eleanor sat up in bed, a stubborn look on her face. 'You want me to stay in bed like an invalid?'

'I might have known you'd be listening. If that's what Wilson recommends then that's what you'll do. There's no arguing Eleanor. If I have to tie you down then I will.'

'I love it when you are masterful,' she said. Gabriel sat on the bed and held her hand to his lips. Wilson made to leave after giving her more of the sedative.

'I hear you've had another man in here. Are you sure all this is not subterfuge to cover an infidelity? I've seen how you look at Joe.' She knew he teased her because he was trying to cover his own anxiety.

'I'm certain. Not many men would be seeking an affair with a "beached whale". Can you believe that's how my lovely maid described me?'

'Rest my love, go to sleep.'

'I'll stay in bed for a few days if that pleases you then I'll get up.' Gabriel began to remonstrate, but Eleanor stopped him with a smile. 'I can't stay in bed for another six weeks, I should go mad.' She screwed her face up then closed her eyes.

'I'll check on you in a while. I know you don't like resting up but it will be worth it will it not when you're safely delivered of twins?' He kissed her forehead and crept from the room.

Eleanor began to doze but it wasn't a pleasant, easy rest. The painting and the diaries swam together in her drowsy head. Was this not exactly what had happened to Alice Reynolds? The thought came again like an uninvited guest. Was Gabriel's mother not prescribed bed rest for weeks before the birth of her son, the birth of a son who killed them both? Eleanor wiped the sweat from her brow and shuddered. She had a bad feeling. Her eyelids were heavy, but she fought to stay awake. She didn't want to sleep. She didn't want to die. What if all three of them perished? She held her bump with both hands as though by doing so she'd keep them safe. She couldn't leave Gabriel, he was her rock and she his. Darkness pressed in at the windows. Blackness like a veil covered her and she knew no more.

R

In the event Eleanor didn't have to stay in bed for six weeks as after the fourth day of confinement her labours began early.

Gabriel, woken from sleep ran for Joe and urged him to fetch Doctor Sharpe. Next he woke Charity and Ginny to boil water and make ready for when the doctor came. His nerves were already in shreds. The last few days had been worrying; Eleanor had been so quiet, most unlike her usual cheery self.

'This wasn't supposed to happen for weeks,' he told Charity as if she didn't know.

Perspiration ran down Eleanor's face. 'Why is this

happening now? The babies will be too small, were it just one... ' Eleanor's usual confidence had evaporated days ago. She had been listless and tearful.

'All will be well Eleanor, try not to worry. The doctor will be here soon,' Charity said as she left the room. She cast a worried look in her master's direction. 'Let me know if you need me.'

Gabriel held his wife's hand to stop himself from rubbing his cheek which was a dead giveaway to her that he was anxious. He wanted to be a help not a hindrance, but his nerves were already raw.

Another contraction swept over Eleanor. She gritted her teeth and clung to his hand.

'Don't leave me Gabriel I can't do this on my own, it doesn't feel right.' She began to cry silent tears.

'I'm here, I'll not leave you.'

Gabriel was stunned. Last time Eleanor had given birth she was at pains to put *his* mind at rest, now she was frightened. She was the one needing reassurance.

'Hey, what's all this? Come on you need your strength for bringing our babies into the world. You can curse all you like, but for now try to breathe.'

She grabbed his arm as the swell of pain gripped her body. 'It seems to be happening too fast, I think I need to... '

There was a knock on the door. Gabriel saw a dishevelled Joe standing there. 'The doctor's on another birthin' and he might be some time his housekeeper said.'

Gabriel swore under his breath. 'Then go to Doctor Chaffer. Quickly now!'

'A thought er that. A called on ma way back but he's away in Glasgow.'

Gabriel remembered his friend telling him he was going to a seminar.

'Man alive, is there a midwife hereabouts? Old Mrs Tippet is too old now I imagine. She must have trained someone up in her stead?'

'You forget master, A'm not from these parts, A've no idea. A'll wake Ivy and ask her if she knows of anybody.'

Gabriel heard his wife call out in agony and returned to her. Eleanor was out of bed and holding onto the bedpost.

'Let me hold you, lean on me.' He wiped the sweat from her face and rubbed the small of her back. 'Do you want to walk?'

'Just hold me, don't let me go Gabriel, I can't do this alone. There's something not right I can feel it.'

She leaned her head into his chest and sank to the floor in a dead faint.

'Man,' Gabriel muttered. He heaved his wife to her feet just as Ginny entered the room carrying a bundle of towels. She saw Gabriel lift her mistress onto the already stained bed and promptly fainted herself.

Ivy stood in the doorway and looked at the scene. She strode over Ginny, picked up the smelling salts from the nightstand and thrust them under her mistress' nose.

'Sir, can yer pass the towels from under Ginny? Here stick that under her nose and get her out of here, she's just in the way.' Charity, who had been pacing outside the door, helped her sister to her feet.

For the first time in her life Ivy looked her master in the eye. 'Let's see what's happenin'.' The girl lifted Eleanor's nightgown. 'Not long now, if A'm not mistaken.'

'It's been too quick,' Eleanor moaned as the next pain began.

'It's as it should be, neither too quick nor too slow. Babies come when they're ready not too early and not too late. Come now, bear down Mistress Reynolds.'

Ivy seemed to be in complete control of the birthing. Ten minutes later Gabriel watched as Ivy lifted a wrinkled, red faced baby into the air. She cut the cord and passed the boy to his father.

'Wipe him down with that there sponge,' she ordered, 'Charity get the crib from the nursery,' she shouted through the open door to the loitering maid. Ginny hadn't dared step over the threshold again.

'Have a breather Mistress Reynolds, there be a few minutes yet afore the next 'en arrives, A'll be bound.'

Ivy fussed about making Eleanor more comfortable. After wrapping the baby in a blanket, Gabriel marvelled at his tiny son. He laid him in the crib and smiled then went to the head of the bed.

'We have a son Eleanor can you hear him? He has

good lungs on him - like a true Barker.'

Eleanor looked up at him with frightened eyes. 'I can't do any more... ' The sentence hung in the air as her head fell sideways and her eyes closed. Her face was waxy and pale. Before he could register what was happening, Ivy had pushed the smelling salts under Eleanor's nose again.

'You're determined to have a little rest aren't you Mistress Reynolds. Come, try to sit up a bit then you'll not feel so light headed.'

Gabriel helped push the pillows under his wife's heavy head. He clung to her hand which despite the heat in the room felt icy cold.

'Eleanor my love you're doing so well.' He stroked the damp hair from her brow. 'Not long now and it'll all be over.'

'It's starting again,' Eleanor cried out.

Ivy once again took charge. Gabriel smiled anxiously at his wife as she uttered curses he'd only ever heard sailors use.

'I see we're at that stage of the proceedings are we? Perhaps it's just as well Dr Sharpe isn't here. You'll make poor Ivy blush.'

Despite his fears, he rallied as she squeezed the life out of his hand. Eleanor told him to leave the room in a most colourful and unladylike manner. Ivy intent on her work didn't bat an eyelid.

Another son was born and this time Ivy saw to the needs of Eleanor whilst Gabriel took charge of his second son like an old hand.

'It's another boy my love!' He beamed down at his wife who tried a half smile. 'You said it would be two girls, but they're both boys, I won't be overrun with females after all!'

An hour later when they were alone Gabriel laid both babies in his wife's arms.

'How do you feel my love?' He stroked the black hair of his nearest son.

'Better than an hour ago thank goodness. They're so tiny. Ivy says under five pounds each. They shouldn't be here yet.' She looked up at him fearfully. 'Gabriel, I thought I was going to die - I felt so strange.'

'I know, but all's well now, two handsome chaps just like tiny chips off the old block.' He grinned at his wife who at last was getting some colour back in her cheeks. 'Though God knows what we'd have done without Ivy, she was a marvel.'

Gabriel, although still worried for his wife and babies, was determined she wouldn't see his fear.

'Unlike Ginny who seemed to have caught the fainting bug from me.' Eleanor's smile turned to a frown. 'Each time I blacked out it felt like I was never going to wake again, I really thought I was going to die. It was like I was drowning. I've never been afraid of the sea, but the feeling was of heaviness, as though I was sinking and I didn't have the strength to swim to the surface. All I could think of was there must be some curse, but you my love were calmness personified. You helped me through it all. Without you I don't know what I would have done.'

'Just wait a while until it hits me and I too will probably faint.'

'Do you remember the gypsy who called at the house that day? She said something about a turning tide changing my luck. I remember as I fainted thinking of her words and I thought she was right and that the worst was going to happen.' Eleanor shuddered. 'I thought it was going to happen to you again, I thought - '

'Hush my love, I said it was all rubbish at the time. The tide *has* turned, she was right in that respect; you once survived a shipwreck remember, you're made of strong stuff and now there's nothing to fear because you've made dry land. I'll look after you and the children never fear my love.'

Later in the morning Doctor Sharpe arrived, all apologies for his lateness. 'You say your maid delivered the babies? How extraordinary. Did you know she had birthing experience?'

'Not at all, in fact under normal circumstances she blushes crimson if I as much as look at her. She's a quiet little thing, but she was unflappable. Knew exactly what to do and just got on with it. We're extremely grateful to her. I had a word with her and she told me her mother was the midwife at Beadnell; she learnt birthing at her mother's knee apparently.'

'Handy to know. She's made a good job of sorting

out both mother and babies.'

'What about my wife doctor? The birth was very different from the first time. She continued to pass out even during the labour? She will make a full recovery?'

'I cannot see why not. It is an extraordinary thing, never heard of the like before, this fainting business. I wanted to bleed her just now but your wife has a very strong mind, wouldn't let me near her. She will have to rest a while, no getting up too quickly. I know she's not one for idleness, but she must have a care Mr Reynolds. Childbed fever can never be ruled out, not for seven days after the births. Insist sir. No doubt she will listen to you.'

'And the twins are small are they not?'

'Premature, but that's not unusual with twins. A wet nurse will help ease the burden. Persuade your wife sir. It will be best for all concerned.'

R

Eleanor lay back against the pillow. 'You can go to the office Gabriel you don't have to watch over us.' It was two days later and Gabriel with Rose in his arms had just introduced her to her brothers.

'The minute I leave the house you'll get up and bribe the staff to keep quiet.' Rose tugged at his neckcloth. 'Anyway, I want to be with my family. We still haven't chosen names for the boys yet.'

'Girls' names we had in abundance although you thought it would be one of each. Two boys... I was convinced they would be girls. Have you written to my parents and Tomas and Cora?'

'Just briefly. I said one of us would write with details later, when we have names for these two handsome fellows. Look at their black hair. What shall we call them eh, Rose?'

'Mama, mama, mama,' Rose shouted as she wriggled in her father's arms.

'What about the names we thought of before?' Eleanor smiled at her daughter. 'Haydan and Ruari? Do you still like those?' Eleanor added: 'Let's call them both Gabriel like you called the puppy Scrabble after his father.'

'I see your sense of humour has returned.'

'They could both have one of your names as a second or third name, Haydan Gabriel Reynolds sounds perfect?'

'I like Ruari too - Ruari Jack Reynolds? It won't matter which baby has which name. They're identical so we'll never know which one we're addressing.'

'A mother will know, and a father too if he puts his mind to it. Everyone else will be taking pot luck.'

'You sound much brighter today, possibly as a result of the gallons of bone broth you've consumed.'

'Gabriel make Mrs M stop now. I can't drink any more of the stuff.'

'Tell me what you fancy and I'll get her to change

her menu.'

'I really fancy something light, some fish perhaps? I hope I have enough milk for both boys.'

'Dr Sharpe thinks you should have a wet nurse, you're not as strong as last time. Don't go putting a strain on yourself.'

'We'll see. So far everything is as it should be, except we have babies born in March instead of April.'

R

Hope House was open for two months before Eleanor got to see it. Lottie had generously donated a building on the edge of her land by the estuary. It had needed work, but with the money they'd raised it was soon ready and awaiting its first occupants.

Lottie had taken over during the later stages of Eleanor's pregnancy and had overseen the renovations and appointed the staff, all except a midwife. None could be found in the area, old Mrs Tippet had indeed died. It had looked for a while like they might have to look further afield.

'I want you to meet someone,' Eleanor said as Lottie entered the morning room. 'Just ring the bell for me, I can't get up.' She had the twins cradled in her arms, both were sleeping soundly.

'How do you manage? I should be laid down in a darkened room.' Lottie rang the bell.

'Nonsense, look how capable you've been in

organising Hope House. It wouldn't have happened without you. With Caroline on honeymoon and I otherwise engaged with these two you've been wonderful. We all abandoned ship it seems and left you to steer the project home alone. I'm sorry the timing was all wrong. Your life has been greatly disrupted I should imagine. Poor Wilson will be suffering neglect.'

'I've enjoyed it. Wilson barely noticed I was absent I can assure you. I simply put into practice what the committee had already decided. Please don't fret there's still plenty for you to do.'

'That's one reason I asked you here this morning. That and to show off my boys. I know how you so love babies.' Eleanor's mock sarcastic tone made Lottie pay attention to the twins for the first time.

'Very nice,' was all she could think of to say, but Eleanor wasn't at all offended. She knew her friend wasn't keen on babies. Ginny came to take the twins to the nursery and Eleanor gave instructions that Ivy be sent to her.

'When first we met you told me how much you wanted to travel. You've been well and truly becalmed of late, but I'll soon be up and about so perhaps you could go after all.'

'I think not, I've changed my mind. There's too much important work to do here in Alnmouth. I don't want to be gadding about like some empty headed chit of a girl. Wilson has been teaching me things I never knew I wanted to learn, things that will be of help at Hope House. Some of the girls need more than physical help. They've been let down, abused in some cases. I think some of Wilson's ideas will be of use in their recovery. I've been avidly reading all his medical books, they're fascinating. I want to stay and be useful.'

Ivy entered and waited for instructions.

'Ah Ivy, speaking of useful, this is Miss Lambton, you've seen her before I expect?' Eleanor turned to Lottie. 'Here's the answer to our prayers.' Both Lottie and Ivy looked puzzled. Ivy flushed scarlet at being made the centre of attention.

'I want to ask you a question Ivy. It might seem odd, but bear with me, all will be revealed.' Ivy looked even more flushed and confused.

'When I went into labour, Dr Sharpe was unavailable as was Wilson. Ivy here stepped into the breach with admirable skill and fortitude; enough fortitude to deal with twins and a mother who would insist on swooning. I'm not sure how Ivy would feel about what I'm going to suggest, but she would make an estimable midwife. Hope House would be privileged to have her. I think her talents are wasted at Westshore cleaning up after us. What do you say Ivy? Should you like to become a midwife for the charity? You would get more training from Dr Chaffer, more respect and more money. There would also be a room for you there to live in. It would be a responsible and rewarding position.'

Ivy looked first stunned and then pleased.

One week later the new midwife delivered her first baby at Hope House.

R

'Eleanor you'll tire yourself out, take some rest for goodness' sake.' She had just returned from Hope House where another young girl had taken up residence. She kicked off her shoes and slumped down on the sofa.

'I will, but until Caroline gets back from her honeymoon there's much to do.'

Gabriel huffed. 'I still can't get over her getting married in secret. Why would she do that?'

'We both know the answer to *that*, do we not? Perhaps she'll move into Hope House on her return.'

Gabriel threw his wife a sidelong look and his papers in the top drawer of his desk. He still couldn't reconcile himself to the fact his ex fiancée had married Captain Turner at all - let alone in such haste. Caroline had confided in Lottie, who had in turn told Eleanor that she and Padraic had been forced to bring the nuptials forward to save embarrassment.

'Caroline is hardly in need of a refuge,' Eleanor scoffed, 'she's happily married and in the fullness of time will have a baby - prematurely. Live and let live Gabriel. You have enough to worry about under your own roof.'

'Oh why is that, are you or the children unwell?'

'Everyone is well and thriving, especially Rose who is turning into a little chatterbox.'

'So what need I worry about?'

'Staffing problems. With Ivy at Hope House we need another maid-of-all-work. Now love has blossomed amongst the staff we are soon to be short handed. Charity and Joe's marriage will mean I'll be without my maid. I pleaded with her to stay on, but she wants to return to Whitby now her mother is unwell. I can hardly blame her. Joe of course will go with her leaving us not one, but two members of staff short. I'll miss them both, but especially Charity. I've never had any other maid - except for Bryony of course.' She pulled a face.

'Yes well, least said about that the better.' Gabriel squeezed his wife's shoulder as he passed her to pour himself a brandy. 'Can I get you anything?'

'More staff?' she joked.

'You could always ask... '

'Don't even think about it, I knew you'd say that. Actually Bryony has been a godsend along with Susan Stubbs. They're both often to be found at Hope House which is some surprise considering how Miss Swift used to behave here.' Eleanor looked thoughtful. 'There's one girl at Hope House who's drawn my attention; she might be worth training up. I shouldn't mind an unmarried mother as my maid though I'm so used to Charity. I shall miss her so much.'

Gabriel began to read a broadsheet, but Eleanor was not to be put off.

'I think I should look for an exceedingly plain maid this time.' Gabriel ignored the jibe. 'I just hope Ginny doesn't decide to leave too. I don't think she will as she's walking out with Nat's son, Greg. I think it's serious between them.'

Gabriel looked over the top of his paper. 'Love is in the air clearly. Jax is to be married soon and everything is changing. The turning tides are bringing love and prosperity to our door. Did you know something was going on between Charity and Joe all this time?'

'All this time, the last six months do you mean? Of course you ninny, why would she not tell me?'

'Well you never told me.'

'You see my love,' Eleanor moved to sit beside her husband, 'I can keep a secret.'

22

Gabriel grumbled as he and Eleanor sat at supper. 'Is it me or is this beef as tough as my boots?'

'I haven't had any of the beef, try the capon it's delicious.'

Gabriel pushed his plate away sullenly as the maid came in to clear the table. When she returned she brought syllabubs, jellies, pies, fruit and cheese.

'Polly will you ask Mrs Madison to send in the apple tart.'

'There's only gooseberry tart sir.'

Gabriel sighed heavily and cut himself a slice then proceeded to cover it in heavy cream.

'Are you in a mood my love?'

'Somewhat.'

Eleanor waited for him to finish the gooseberry tart then asked: 'Are you going to get it off your chest or sulk all evening?'

'Both possibly.' He sighed again as he put down his fork and spoon.

'Jon Jenkins came to see me this afternoon and said we've lost our contract with him. *Lost* the contract we've had since my father's day. And to whom do you suppose we've lost the contract? I'll give you two guesses although you'll need only one.' Gabriel didn't wait for an answer. 'Turner has massively undercut us. Spectacularly undercut us. He can't possibly make a profit on the bid he's tendered so why would he do it I ask you? We both know the answer to that too.'

Eleanor knew to tread carefully and weighed her remark cautiously. 'If that's the case then as you've said before he's no businessman. If he's done it to spite you then he's more of a fool than I thought. Why would his factor not sway his hand? Perhaps he tried who knows?' She shrugged. 'Why did Jenkins come to see you? Was he gloating? - he doesn't strike me as the type.'

'No, no he came as a courtesy to me. He was embarrassed I think, but as he pointed out although we've done business for years times are hard.'

'And friends it seems are few my love. I imagine Turner won't put in such a low bid next half year then what will Jenkins do and more to the point what will you do?'

'None of us can put sentiment before business, you know that as well as I Eleanor. I'll cross that bridge when I come to it.'

He stood and moved over to the side table and poured them both a glass of port.

'Shall we play a game of backgammon or would you rather read?' he asked.

'In the mood you're in I should say read, but I was

never one to play safe,' she said setting up the board. 'I won't let you win just to change your sour mood so don't expect it,' she warned him.

In truth they were evenly matched at the game and *if* she'd been counting she could have told him that he was ahead by only a single game.

Only after he began bearing off his home board and looked set to win the game did Eleanor think it safe to broach a subject she'd been meaning to address for days. Her husband's mood had mellowed somewhat during the game she thought.

'I know Padraic Turner isn't exactly your favourite person, but like it or not he's married to Caroline now and soon there will be a baby. Before then I think it would be a kindness to try to get along together, after all we're going to be mixing in the same circles. Alnmouth society is not so big that we can avoid meeting them at least every other time we accept an invitation to dine or sup out. Not to mention the balls and house parties; Caroline's friends are our friends.'

'I know it and whilst I don't mind meeting Caro, we've put all that business about her marriage behind us now I hope, I don't relish the thought of Turner's smug face sitting opposite me at the dinner table.'

Eleanor suppressed an eye roll. 'I wondered if perhaps we should offer to throw a party for them. As there wasn't a wedding in the bride's hometown perhaps if we had a reception for them here at Westshore it would show there are no hard feelings but more importantly it would be nice for Caroline to see you don't hold a grudge. She could proudly show off her new husband to a wider society. We could invite perhaps fifty or sixty of the local worthies as well as mutual friends.'

She watched several emotions play on her husband's face before he replied: 'Why didn't I think of that?'

'I could tell you,' she said smiling, 'but you wouldn't like the answer.'

'I agree it would be a splendid idea to hold a reception for them. For Caroline more than for him, she would be grateful I think. She must know there are some who would snub him, Sir John Riddleston for one. I'd wager Turner's been in his sights for a while given that it's rumoured he used to be involved in the smuggling trade.'

'As you say if she invited individuals to dine they may purport to be otherwise engaged even though they like and respect Caroline. It would be embarrassing for her. Sir John especially has cause to dislike Turner and not just because he suspects him of running goods.'

'Oh does he? Why?'

'Because Caroline turned him down.'

'Turned him down. What you mean he offered for her? The man's old enough to be her grandfather, well almost.'

'Since when was age a barrier to men's lust Gabriel? That's unfair I think, Caroline has other qualities besides her looks of course.'

'She does and she also has a fortune at her disposal that would have been an added incentive to Sir John.'

'Let's not go down that well worn path again. So are we in agreement? We will hold a reception for the happy couple in say, two weeks' time?'

'If we made it the twenty first that's Caro's birthday, we could have a double celebration.'

'Fancy you remembering her birthday, I don't know whether I should be a little jealous.'

'Why? I've never forgotten your birthday have I?'

'I suppose not but nevertheless... '

'You are funny Eleanor. On reflection I think one of us should ask them first if they're agreeable to a party. It would be embarrassing if we sent out invitations and the guests of honour didn't turn up.'

'I've been meaning to call at Eastshore for a day or two,' Eleanor said. 'I'll go tomorrow.'

ℛ

Eleanor was shown into the morning room at Eastshore where the brightness of the day was extinguished by the heavy, dark furniture and the small latticed windows. Eleanor was always surprised how Caroline didn't seem to notice how gloomy the room appeared.

'The wind is awful this morning. I'm glad of the carriage on such a day.'

'Padraic just came back from the bay and said it was

440

blustery. I haven't ventured further than the conservatory myself. Can I offer you some refreshment Eleanor?'

When the pair had exchanged pleasantries and drunk two dishes of tea, Eleanor broached the subject of the proposed party.

'How strange you should offer to host a reception for us.' Caroline beamed. 'We were only discussing holding a gathering ourselves this morning over breakfast.' She suddenly looked thoughtful. 'I wouldn't say so to Padraic of course, but I was a little worried when my husband suggested a celebration that some might give us the cold shoulder. I know Alnmouth and know its residents to be more than a little conservative in their views. They don't take to new people and especially not to *foreigners*. I'm sure that's how they see Padraic; a penniless Irish ingrate who married an heiress as a means to get on in the world.'

Eleanor thought it best not to say she and Gabriel held similar views to the good people of Alnmouth regarding her husband. 'I know what you mean; I'm still regarded as a newcomer even though I've lived here for years. So would you like us to throw a party in honour of your wedding? Shall I send out the invitations?'

'Invitations? Are you to invite us to dine? How nice to see you here this morning Eleanor.' Padraic Turner had clearly only heard the latter part of the sentence as he strode across the room to her. He took Eleanor's hand and kissed it as he always did, for too long and too ardently. Eleanor thought it bad manners especially when his new bride was sitting in front of him. She'd remonstrated with him before about the habit but he'd laughed and said it was the Irish way. In fact since she'd mentioned it she was sure he pressed all the harder and for longer.

Caroline didn't seem to notice and told him about the proposed party.

Turner smirked. 'I take it your husband hasn't heard of the deal I've snatched from under his nose or he wouldn't be making the offer.' He grinned at his wife. 'I've done a deal with Jenkins, Carla. We've the work of shipping his grain for the next half year.' He stuck out his chest proudly.

Eleanor was about to tell Caroline how he would be carrying the grain at a loss most likely, or at best at a profit that wasn't worth the effort, but then thought better of it. She bit back the retort not wanting to upset her friend.

Eleanor sat up straight in her seat. 'He does know actually Padraic and still he would ask you under his roof to celebrate your marriage which says something of his character as both a person and a businessman does it not? I always think it best to separate business and pleasure, don't you agree Caroline?'

Caroline shuffled in her seat. 'I quite agree. Would you turn the invitation down when we were thinking of throwing a party ourselves my love? As Eleanor says Alnmouth is a small place and we are none of us an island. We may need our friends one day. I for one think it a generous and kind offer and propose we accept.'

Turner didn't look quite so smug but blustered on. 'The folks of Alnmouth are small minded bigots, present company excepted of course Eleanor. They're little people in a little town with the narrowness of thought that comes about because most of them have never stepped out of the county, let alone set foot in another country. When you've seen as much of the world as I have, you've an awareness of how the world *really* works. Money talks and those who want to do business with me in future better understand that fact for certain. However, I don't of course see you in such a bad light Eleanor and as Caroline says, we would be delighted to be your guests. When is the party to be?'

Eleanor struggled to keep her own counsel. She was on the point of withdrawing the invitation. If it hadn't been for Caroline she would have told him some home truths; like she knew before his marriage he wasn't a man of means and that he certainly was no gentleman. And now, with his wife's fortune bolstering his confidence, he was here at Eastshore throwing his weight about and playing Lord of the Manor. Gabriel would be infuriated. She was angry herself but at the same time sorry for her friend. Caroline deserved better than Padraic Turner for a husband.

Eleanor had thought it best not to mention the arrogance with which the invitation had been received by Turner, and on the night of the reception was simply excited at the prospect of a party. She was pleased to see her husband was similarly disposed.

'Is this the new suit you ordered? I thought it wasn't going to be ready in time.'

Gabriel was wearing a suit of black velvet which suited his colouring. The snowy white shirt beneath it showed his tanned face to perfection.

'I gave my tailor an incentive; have it finished or I take my business elsewhere,' he joked. 'You look lovely in blue. What a handsome pair we make.'

Eleanor shook her head. 'Pride comes before a fall. Will you fasten the sapphires for me please? The catch is somewhat fiddly.'

'I'm glad you're to wear the entire set this evening, they look stunning en masse as it were.'

He fastened the necklace around her slender throat then kissed her where her shoulder met her neck and was gratified when she shivered.

'I have to wear something to distract from my non-existent waist.'

'I've said it many times. You're like a bud which blossoms when you're pregnant and afterwards when you haven't lost the baby weight you're just as comely.' He kissed her again, then looked at her in the mirror.

'When you've finished admiring me we should go down, the guests will be here any minute now.'

'Then we shall be here until the end of time for I shall never stop admiring you my love.'

'If I didn't know better I'd think you were up to something Gabriel Reynolds.'

He smiled inscrutably.

'Had you thought to make a speech?' she asked. They were standing by the door of the drawing room awaiting their first guests.

'Not a speech exactly but I thought to say something to the assembled guests. Something about the men locking up their wives and daughters perhaps and how the local businessmen should look to having the rug pulled from under them in some unscrupulous deal.'

He raised a cynical eyebrow. Eleanor frowned.

'Just bear in mind why we're doing this. It's for your childhood sweetheart and my friend and not to forget the memory of Thomas. You promised to look out for her remember. It matters not what we think of Turner so long as Caroline is happy and enjoys herself tonight. Ah here are the happy couple now.' Eleanor stepped forward to greet the newlyweds. 'You look stunning Caroline, what a beautiful gown.'

'And one I shan't be able to get into soon if I'm not much mistaken,' she whispered as Eleanor kissed her cheek.

'You have some way to go before you get to be as

huge as I was with the twins. I felt like a ship in full sail towards the end.'

'Well to my eyes you look stunning also.' Padraic Turner kissed Eleanor's hand. 'What amazing sapphires.' He turned to shake hands with Gabriel. 'Thank you for throwing this reception for us. Very decent of you Reynolds.'

'It's the least we can do,' Gabriel replied passing drinks first to Eleanor and then to his guests.

An hour into the party and when all the guests had arrived, Gabriel tapped a wine glass with a paper knife to quieten the assembled party. The room fell silent.

'I don't intend to bore you all with a long speech. I hear the band tuning up and the ladies will be keen to begin dancing I think, but I wanted to say a few words of welcome to our guests of honour.' He waited a moment and saw all eyes turn to the happy couple. He was pleased Caroline looked in such high spirits. 'I hope you will all join me in congratulating Caroline and Padraic on their marriage. Charge your glasses everyone, I give you Captain and Mrs Turner.'

When the toast had been taken Padraic Turner stood tall and smirked broadly. 'Thank you Eleanor and Gabriel. I speak on behalf of myself and my beautiful wife when I say how happy we are to be here this evening. I'm a newcomer to this part of the world as some of you may know, but my wife's family goes way back here in Alnmouth. Caroline's father was a well respected businessman and admired as a true gentleman I believe, although I never had the honour of meeting him myself.' He smiled at his wife who flushed prettily. 'I hope you'll soon hold me in the same high esteem as you did Carla's father and his father before him.'

Gabriel thought hell would freeze over first. The arrogance of the man to think he and Thomas could be mentioned favourably in the same breath.

'I've served in the Spanish war and consider myself a loyal servant of King and Country. Now I'm to take over Thomas Hodgeson's business affairs and I hope I'll get to know some of you much better. Eastshore's doors are always open to you gentlemen. And as for the ladies hereabouts,' he took his wife's hand and kissed it, 'I can only say the gentlemen around these parts are extremely fortunate for I never saw such beauties.' There was a little round of laughter from the ladies. 'I'm glad you could all join us here this evening for this celebration of our nuptials and for that we have our hosts to thank. Once again I would like to thank Eleanor and Gabriel for their thoughtfulness and especially for their hospitality. Having them accept me into the fold as it were means a lot to me and to Caroline. Raise your glasses please and drink to their good health. To Eleanor and Gabriel.'

'Do you think he meant any of that little speech?' Eleanor asked as later she and Gabriel made their way to bed.

'I know not. All I know is that we did the right thing

giving them the party. Caro looked radiant and happy and that's all I care about. That's all that matters.'

'She did you're right. Now she's with child she's put on a little weight, it suits her.'

'It suits all women.' He pinched her bottom as they reached the top of the stairs. 'There's nothing attractive about a skinny woman.'

'Ouch! When I was at Eastshore last I asked her how she felt about her pregnancy. I remember you saying one of the reasons you two were incompatible was that she wasn't maternal.'

'What did she say?'

'She said although it had been an accident, obviously, she isn't altogether displeased.'

'People change I suppose. I dare to suggest she won't be the sort of hands on mother you are my love.'

'I suspect she won't be keen to breastfeed,' Eleanor said wryly, 'but that doesn't mean she'll be a bad mother.'

'Thomas would have been a doting grandfather. He would have easily made up for any deficiency the parents may have.'

'I can't picture Padraic as a father somehow.'

Gabriel suddenly thought of little Mats in Amsterdam. 'I wonder if Turner even knows he's a father already.' Gabriel knew instantly that both his and his wife's thoughts had gone unbidden to his own son Steven. Gabriel felt a hypocrite for criticising the man.

'Well if he does he's never made any attempt to see him. Perhaps Bryony kept her own counsel, who knows? She was always hard to fathom.'

Charity came to help her mistress prepare for bed. Gabriel went to his own dressing room where he knew Walters would be waiting for him. When he returned, Eleanor was alone again and about to get into bed.

'Is that a new nightgown?'

'It is. I'm so warm in bed of late I thought to get something lighter and sleeveless thinking I would be cooler.'

Gabriel looked his wife up and down appreciatively. The gown was gossamer thin, transparent almost. 'I don't see the point, it usually comes off anyway. You always were a wanton woman.'

'And look where it got me,' she said laughing. 'Did you put the sapphires in the safe?'

'I did. Now stop trying to change the subject, I know your game.' He pushed the thin straps from her white shoulders then stared blatantly at his wife's naked body as the gown slid to the floor. Eleanor stepped out of the pool of silk that lay discarded.

'Now look what you've done.' She smiled and was about to get into bed when he stopped her.

'You're never as lovely to me as when you've just given birth my love. It's a precious thing you do bringing new life into the world; precious and miraculous. Your body is just as beautiful to me now as it was on the first time I clapped eyes on you at The

Fleece Inn.'

'Clapped eyes! If only I knew then what I know now.' She threw her head back and laughed. 'Who am I fooling; I should have let you bed me then. As you always say I never could resist you. I don't know how I escaped intact that night for I was keen to see what all the fuss was about I can tell you. You were very persuasive.'

'Wanton,' he said.

She took one of his curls in her fingers, pulled it gently and watched as it sprang back. 'Don't ever sack your tailor Gabriel. Your outfit this evening made you look quite dashing.' She cocked her head to one side. 'What I mean is it fit like a glove, showed your physique to full advantage. You said earlier that you never stopped admiring me and I feel the same about you.'

'That's just as well as you're stuck with me forever and a day.'

She ignored his comment and carried on with her praise. 'I see how some husbands change as they grow older. They turn to fat, their hair thins and turns grey, or worse they don awful wigs.' Gabriel stroked her arm and noticed the freckles sprinkled on the curve of her forearm. 'They become florid and gouty with too much rich food and drink.'

'There's time yet. You talk as if we're an old married couple with thirty years under our belts.'

She sighed suddenly. 'I feel matronly when I've

given birth. Old, fat and matronly.'

'Matronly is one word I'd never attach to you my love and you certainly aren't old. Standing here now as you are, naked as the day you were born but nowhere near as innocent, you're like a delicious peach, ripe and ready for the eating.'

'Why so poetical all of a sudden? Earlier I thought you were after something and now I'm certain of it.'

'Aren't I always poetical?'

'On occasions yes, but never quite so lyrical.'

'Well tonight is one of those occasions when I appreciate all that I have. I love you more than words can say. In fact now I think about it mere words *aren't* enough. I need to demonstrate my love.'

'I knew it; I knew you had an ulterior motive Gabriel Reynolds.'

ℛ

Caroline said: 'What a wonderful evening. It was so kind of Eleanor and Gabriel to gather together the great and the good from hereabouts to help us celebrate our marriage. It almost made up for us not getting married in Alnmouth.'

'Almost? I seem to remember when I suggested we steal away to wed you were all for it. You said it would be romantic as I recall.'

'And it was but it would have been nice to have my friends about me. Under the circumstances however it was the best thing to do, to marry in haste away from prying eyes.'

'By your friends I presume you mean Reynolds?' Ribble opened the door of Eastshore to let them in. 'Why you thought it a good idea to ask *him* of all people to walk you down the aisle in the first place beggars belief. As if I'd want *him* handing you over to me while I waited at the altar with your friends looking on and making comparisons between me and your old flame.'

Caroline had heard this speech before. She handed her cloak to Ribble. 'You can lock up Ribble. I'm going straight up.' She picked up a five branch candelabra and headed for the stairs thinking it best not to let her husband get worked up any further. Since her marriage she had witnessed how he could become heated over seemingly trivial matters, especially money matters.

'Very well Miss Caroline.'

'Mistress Turner. Mistress Turner! Is it so difficult to remember your employer's name? For the love of God, I think staffing changes might be in the offing soon enough if you aren't capable of simple changes in name.'

'Padraic! Poor Ribble has known me as Miss Caroline for fifteen years and only for a few weeks as Mrs Turner. It will take some getting used to I dare say.' She smiled at her faithful servant. 'Good night Ribble. Are you coming up Padraic?'

'And why are all the rooms lit when we've been away from home all evening? Do you know how much spermaceti candles cost a dozen?' Padraic once again turned his wrath on the bewildered looking footman.

Caroline jumped to Ribble's defence. 'Why would Ribble know the price of candles and don't ask me either for I haven't a clue. Father and I always kept the rooms at the front of the house lit whether we were at home or not. The servants are only doing what is customary at Eastshore.' She smiled sweetly at her husband trying to settle him like she was trying to calm a fraught child.

She'd noticed how off-hand her husband was with the servants, noted how he barked orders with an abruptness that bordered on rudeness. She had always prided herself on her well trained, able staff. They knew their place and were treated fairly. In return they were loyal. The staff at Eastshore were long serving, for once staff came they never left, or almost never. Caroline liked the continuity, especially after her father's death.

She reached her bedchamber where Ellise was waiting to help her undress.

'Did all go well? Did you enjoy your party?'

'It was marvellous. All the county was there it seemed. All but for Lord Riddleston I noticed, but then I don't suppose he would have come even if he'd been asked. I'm not sure that he was invited of course.'

She pondered over the matter for a moment. She was

sure he would have received an invitation being a local worthy. Had he declined because she'd turned down his marriage proposal or because he suspected her new husband had dealings with the smuggling trade? If it was the latter then the magistrate was more of a fool than she had previously thought; Padraic had no more to do with the trade than she had. She got into bed. 'Don't wake me in the morning my dear, I may be lazy and lay abed late. I think my ankles are swelling again.'

The maid left the room and Caroline was about to blow out her candles when there was a tap at the door; Padraic appeared smiling broadly.

'May I join you my sweeting?'

'Not tonight my love, I'm worn out.'

Ignoring her rejection he came in and sat on the edge of the bed.

'Are you to refuse me for the next five months? Am I to be banished to my own rooms without a second thought?'

'Of course not, it's just that standing all evening and dancing so much in my condition has made my ankles swell.'

'Everyone couldn't fail to notice you dancing my love, especially when you danced with Reynolds. Was that wise in front of the whole county?'

'It is expected that I, as guest of honour, dance with my host just as you danced with Eleanor.' Caroline wasn't keen to start another argument. She knew he was jealous of Gabriel, why exactly she couldn't say. She loved Padraic to distraction he must know that. Why else would she have married him?

'Do you expect Eleanor refuses Reynolds his bedroom rights?'

Caroline frowned. Where was he going with this line of thinking? She could feel herself blushing.

'They've been married a few years and we only a few weeks and yet already you're turning me away. She's just been with child remember. Are you to use your condition as an excuse?'

'I don't need an excuse, or at least I wasn't aware that I needed one. My love I... '

He picked up her hand and began to kiss each finger in turn. She knew this was the start of his seduction ritual. She tried to slide her hand away but he clung on. 'I bet if Reynolds kissed your fingers you'd not pull away.' He gave her a warning look. She tried not to sigh. She loved Padraic, she was mad about him but that morning she'd been sick and had felt quite ill. Now she felt nauseous again. All she wanted to do was go to sleep.

He moved closer and began to stroke her hair. He began to kiss her, slowly at first but then with growing urgency. Should she surrender? Might it not be easier?

'My sweeting you're so lovely.' He stood, dropped his dressing gown on the floor and climbed into bed. 'There now my darlin' Carla, isn't this what you wanted? You know I can't sleep without you.'

Later as he lay by her side she wondered how their marriage would progress, how would they navigate the matrimonial path in a way that made them both happy. Would it be as tonight where she'd said no and yet he'd ignored her wishes and took what he wanted anyway? She hoped as they got to know each other better they would be able to see things from the other's point of view, learn to compromise, learn mutual respect. It wasn't that he didn't consider her feelings, he did. Usually. He could be thoughtful, charming and attentive. But she saw he could also be implacable, self opinionated and domineering. At first she had seen his strength as manly, as knowing his own mind but would this come to grate on her nerves she wondered?

By nature she had always been compliant, reticent and the type to give in rather than to create discord. Padraic was a soldier, used to issuing orders and having those orders followed. She realised something would have to change if she wasn't to be subsumed in this marriage, but she hated confrontation. Feared arguments of any kind; they were alien territory to her - she had always lived peaceably and amicably with her father. Even with Gabriel she had never stood up for herself she realised. She had given way and would probably have married him if he hadn't changed his mind and jilted her.

She sighed into the cool night air. And what of her father's business empire? She knew Padraic wasn't used to handling the shipping line, the ropery, the chandlers and he certainly hadn't a clue when it came to Home Farm. Cattle and sheep were bewildering to him but instead of letting the stewards, managers and factor get on with their jobs he seemed intent on getting involved. At first she was pleased, she had no interest whatsoever in the businesses, but when John Carr the Home Farm steward came to double check that she wanted to sell their prize winning bull she hadn't known which way to turn. Both men seemed to have right on their side. What did she, a mere woman, know of bulls? It was all very perplexing. She just hoped her husband didn't run through her fortune like the plague runs through a village.

Now she was wide awake whilst Padraic lay beside her sleeping the sleep of the just. The hours dragged on. She couldn't sleep but at least the nausea had gone away. Padraic began muttering under his breath. She had noticed before that he talked in his sleep and when she'd mentioned it to him he'd grinned and said he hoped he wasn't giving away state secrets. Sometimes the murmurs were nonsensical sleep talking, at other times he seemed to get quite agitated, fidgety. Once before he'd mentioned a woman's name and her ears had pricked up but he'd never mentioned her again - Milly.

Tonight he was repeatedly saying his own name over and over again in a voice that sounded incredulous, as if he didn't believe the name was real. Padraic. Padraic. Padraic. Then his tone changed to disparaging

as if he were mocking himself. She listened as he
changed tack and said something like: 'It matters' or
'They changed it'.

'What's that my love?' she asked into the darkness.

He went back to repeating his own name but sadly,
mournfully. She touched his shoulder to try to move
him on, so he'd quieten and rest easier, but he was still
for only a minute before he began again: 'Carla love.'
He slurred a little and then called out: 'No, no, no he's
not, he's Irish like his father. You can't change it.'

Suddenly he turned towards her and still asleep
reached out for her. 'I love you Carla. My sweeting,
don't leave.' The words were clear and heartfelt.

'I'll never leave you my love, I love you so much
you know that.'

She moved closer and put her arms about him.
Padraic became quiet, at peace. She fell asleep in his
arms.

𝓡

When Caroline woke she felt more tired than ever. The
sun was trying to squeeze in through the latticed
windows but not quite succeeding. She could hear the
sea on the rocks below. She remembered Padraic's
sleep talking and it reminded her of the pounding on
the cliffs. The door opened and her husband appeared
carrying a breakfast tray.

'Carla my love, I've brought you a surprise.'

She sat up and sniffed. 'So I see.' The sight and smell of the food brought the sick feeling back again. She swallowed hard.

'I didn't know what you'd fancy so I got that moon-faced cook to put a little of all your favourites on a tray, just a little so as not to overface you. I know you were unwell yesterday morning. How are you feeling today?'

Caroline looked up at him. 'How thoughtful you are my love. Strawberries, delicious.' Her stomach lurched.

He picked one up and offered it up to her lips. As she bit it he nibbled the pointed end until their lips met. They kissed.

'You're so romantic to think of this, I don't deserve it.' She knew she couldn't eat another thing. It was taking her all her time not to vomit.

'Ah, but you do my sweet. I bring this peace offering by way of an apology. Last night I was a fool. I didn't mean to bully you into surrendering to my lust but, well I can't resist you. You know that. It's not just lust, it's more than that. More than I've ever felt for any woman before, I love you so much I just had to have you.'

'You don't need to apologise silly. You're so very tempting my love.'

'Ah, but I do need to say I'm sorry for I see that you need your rest. That's why I've brought your breakfast. Lay abed all day if you want. Rest those pretty ankles Carla and I'll wait on you hand and foot. And tomorrow we'll spend the day together, go shopping or whatever you like. I've a whim to buy you jewels, lots of jewels. What are your favourite stones? I never asked you before.'

She fingered her large, diamond engagement ring. It had been a belated gift given to her *after* their marriage. She suspected he hadn't been able to afford the ring before he'd come into her fortune.

'You guessed correctly before. Why my love, what woman doesn't adore diamonds.'

'Eleanor Reynolds for one or else her husband's not as rich as he makes out. The sapphires she wore last night were breathtaking but not as glorious as the diamonds I'm going to buy you. We could go to Spencer and Cobbs in Alnwick. I'll make the appointment.'

'But I've enough jewels already. You don't have to buy me anything. All I need is your love.'

'That you have and always will. I want to buy you all that your heart desires. Before I've finished you'll be dripping in diamonds.'

'I've all my mother's gems and more besides.' Her protestations were falling on deaf ears.

'I suspect the "more besides" are jewels Reynolds bought you?' She saw his happy mood change.

'Actually, I was going to say jewels my father gave me for my coming of age. I told you I returned my engagement ring to Gabriel after we parted ways.'

Padraic took her hand and kissed it. 'There I go again playing the jealousy card. I'm sorry my colleen. Here am I apologising for last night and making matters worse. It's just that I love you so much and it makes me unreasonable. I'll leave you to break your fast before I say something else to get me into bother.'

She thought to placate him. 'If you insist on treating me might I have a tiara? I've always fancied one.'

He roared with laughter. 'A tiara it is then! You'll be my very own princess.'

'Your queen at least,' she quipped. 'Whichever I am I'll get up soon, I can't lay abed like royalty. I intend to ride over to Westshore to thank Eleanor again for last night.' She sat back on the pillow feeling the bile rising in her stomach; the smell of kippers was too much.

'You'll be back to dine?'

'No later than two of the clock I should think.'

'Good. Take care my love, you have a precious cargo on board.' He kissed her hard then strode out of the room.

ℛ

'It were lucky A were out rabbitin' otherwise she might have laid there some time.' Joe bent double trying to catch his breath.

'What happened exactly?' Gabriel flung his tricorn on the hall table. He waited until Joe could speak.

'A were on the top of the dunes an' A saw this black hound, a big fella he were, run out onto the beach; ma gunshot probably startled him. Her horse were spooked by him and reared and she were thrown off. The tide were not long since out so the sand were hard. She fell with a sickenin' thud. The horse bolted. She's probably in Scotland now at the rate she took off.'

'Then you went to help her?'

'A went to see if she could get up or speak, but when A saw she were out cold A ran to get help to carry her in. Jonty Walters were in the yard so A yelled to him an' together we lifted the Mrs, still unconscious into the house. Mrs M said to take her to the yellow room, she could see she looked bad. Then she sent for Dr Chaffer an' he came straight away, he's still with her. The lad went for you too sir, but you couldn't be found. It were lucky he saw you comin' out of The Hope and Anchor.'

Joe followed his master into the drawing room where Gabriel poured them both a brandy. 'Thank you Joe, as you say it was a good job you were there, this is some shock.'

Wilson Chaffer, his sleeves rolled up, came into the room wiping his hands on a towel. 'Ah Gabriel, they found you. Miss Hodgeson or I should say, Mrs Turner, is still unconscious I'm afraid.'

Joe, looking out of place, made to finish his brandy and leave. 'It's a good job you were there Joe and got her inside out of the cold though at this point it's hard to see how things could be any worse.'

'A'll go an' see if A can find her horse sir.'

Gabriel thanked his groom and poured a drink for Wilson.

'You knew of course she was with child? It's lost I'm afraid,' the doctor stated baldly.

'Man, that's distressing. She was excited to be... I've just thought. Someone ought to alert Turner I suppose.' He rang the bell and ordered a note be sent to Eastshore. He explained what he'd written. 'I've said there's been an accident. I don't want to distress him too much, even though I can't stand the man.'

'Gabriel, sit down, you've known Caroline all your life - this is some shock to you too.'

'Sit down? What are you saying? She will be alright won't she? Can I see her?'

'With head injuries it's hard to tell. She may well wake up in ten minutes and be as right as rain, but on the other hand... '

'What... she might die?'

'I can't say, but there's always a chance. She was lying in an awkward position, twisted around. I would think she'll be lucky to walk again. Her neck or back could be broken. If she wakes and can tell me if she has feeling in her legs and feet that might help with a diagnosis, but until then it's all guess work I'm afraid. There was some bleeding with the miscarriage, but that seems over now. She wasn't far advanced into the pregnancy.'

Gabriel, who had been sitting with his head in his hands, stood up abruptly. 'I need to see her. Is she alone?'

'Charity is with her.'

Gabriel ran up the stairs and into the bedroom where he saw his childhood sweetheart laid as if asleep.

'She hasn't woken up?' Wilson asked. Charity shook her head.

'She looks peaceful, as if she's resting.' Gabriel looked enquiringly at the doctor.

'It may well be she'll recover herself as I say. There's nothing more I can do for her, I've made her as comfortable as I can.'

Out on the landing a commotion could be heard, the door was flung open and Padraic Turner burst in.

'What the - '

Wilson went to restrain him. 'I'm sorry to say Caroline has had a fall from her horse Padraic.' He explained all he knew. Turner sat heavily on the chair which Charity had vacated. Gabriel saw the look of anguish on Turner's face and after muttering platitudes left the man to his misery.

R

Eleanor, along with Rose and Ginny came bustling into the drawing room. 'Oh, I expected to see Caroline. Mercury is in the stableyard.' She handed Rose to her father who then began to untie his neckcloth. Gabriel kissed the top of her head and tried to stop her.

'There's been an accident my love.' For an instant Eleanor thought some mishap had befallen the twins. Gabriel reassured her and told her what had happened.

'Ginny, take Rose for her nap,' she said taking her reluctant daughter from her father's arms. Rose began to cry and struggle to get back to him.

'Let her stay. After this morning's events I'm in need of consolation.' He held his daughter close. 'Man alive, that could be you lying up there now. Bad enough it's Caroline, but I couldn't have borne it if it were you whose life was hanging by a thread.' Gabriel put his hand on his wife's shoulder and squeezed it, then explained about the fall.

Wilson came in rolling down his sleeves. 'I must away to my other patients as there's nothing more I can do at the moment. If Caroline wakes send for me immediately of course.'

'*If* she wakes?' Eleanor gasped and looked at her husband.

'I hope she will, but I can't be certain, as I told Gabriel she may make a full recovery, but we shall just have to wait and see.'

Wilson left leaving husband and wife alone with their thoughts. Eleanor rang the bell. 'Ransom take the Irish whisky up to the yellow room for Captain Turner, I would think he has need of it. Ask him if he minds if I come to sit with his wife.'

'She looks just as she did the last time she slept here, like sleeping beauty.' Gabriel tried to keep his emotions under control. Eleanor knew he wouldn't allow himself to think he'd lose his oldest friend.

'I'll go and see for myself, Padraic must be going through hell.'

'Do you think so?'

Eleanor was halfway to the door when she stopped abruptly. 'Of course! You just said how you'd feel if it were me whose life was hanging in the balance. He loves her. They're just married. They were expecting their first child. They had their whole lives in front of them, why would you not think him devastated?'

'Because I think he married her for her money. He probably finds her attractive, what man wouldn't, but I've never thought he truly loved her. Not like I love you. Her beauty was an added extra to the money and position she brought to the marriage.'

She snapped at him: 'For God's sake Gabriel I can't believe you! Perhaps you should think about that statement.' She swept out of the room. She knew he disliked Turner, but never realised quite how much.

Padraic was sitting by the bed cradling a glass of whisky in his hands. It struck Eleanor forcibly that he didn't hold his wife's hand. Gabriel's words rang in her ears.

'I'm so sorry Padraic. It's such a tragedy about the baby, but let's pray Caroline has the will to pull through.'

The captain smiled ironically. 'The luck of the Irish seems to have deserted me.'

'Perhaps on some level she knows you're with her Padraic, would you not hold her hand? It might be a comfort to you both.'

He drank off the whisky, put the glass down then reached for Caroline's hand. 'She feels as cold as death.' His face looked away in disgust.

Eleanor watched as he placed her lifeless hand back on the cover. He poured himself more whisky. 'I knew it was too good to be true, she's gone - I know it. Better she dies I think than live the rest of her life a barren cripple.'

'This is grief talking, you must have faith Padraic. Caroline needs your strength to pull through. She'll sense your love I'm sure of it, try to stay strong for her sake.'

'Love? Your husband has never hidden the fact he thinks I married Carla for her money, and her looks too of course. You possibly are in accord with him. I'm a soldier Eleanor. When you've seen death as I have many times, then you come to accept it as part of life.'

Eleanor could think of no suitable response. She knew everyone dealt with shock in different ways, so tried not to judge. She thought about her own grief after her miscarriage and how Gabriel had been her rock, her saviour. She'd come to terms with the loss only because of her husband's care, attention and love.

She looked down at Caroline and felt sympathy for her friend. In her hour of need Turner was too arrogant or too selfish to show her any real affection. Was Gabriel right after all?

'I can sit with Caroline if you prefer or perhaps you would like to be alone with her Padraic?' The captain didn't move or indeed answer. 'You know where we are if you need anything, don't hesitate to ring the bell.'

Back in the drawing room Eleanor poured herself a glass of canary.

'You look done in,' Gabriel said.

'You too my love.' She sighed and stood by the fire feeling the need for warmth. 'It sounds trite to say it, but one never knows what the next tide will wash in. How many times have I ridden out on the beach? The hound could have startled Jet and I could have left you a widower with three children to raise. I know what you're going to say, that we can't think that way, but when something like this happens is it not natural to think of the tragedy in those terms?'

Eleanor decided to unburden herself further and tell Gabriel what Padraic had said. She could hardly believe his coldness. It had struck her hard.

'As you say, it's the shock talking I bet. The waiting is agony, not knowing if she'll survive and if she does... Perhaps earlier I judged the man too harshly. I'm sorry Eleanor, I spoke out of turn.'

'You're upset my love. We both are I see that. One

of you should be able to kiss her awake like in a fairy tale.' A tear slipped down Eleanor's cheek. 'She has everything to live for - life can be so cruel. Over time I've become so fond of her, she's my friend too.'

Gabriel wrapped both arms around her and held her tight as if he would never let her go. It was a comfort.

𝓡

Two days later Caroline died. She never recovered consciousness.

23

The same church bell that tolled for her father now tolled for Caroline. Eleanor, flanked by her husband and Captain Turner, stared down at the coffin as the rain fell steadily. Lottie Lambton, Susan Stubbs, Bryony Swift and several women whom Caroline had befriended from Hope House tossed the earth onto the coffin lid below. The men in sombre mood followed suit.

Gabriel thought how Caroline wouldn't have expected to follow her father to the grave so soon; none of them had. The words "tragic accident" had been bandied about all too often during the past week. It was a salutary reminder to all who knew Caroline that no matter how rich or how beautiful you were the grim reaper could cut you down regardless. Gabriel had long banished the black moods which used to be a regular visitor, but Caroline's death had shaken him to the core of his being. His father and Thomas had had their three score years and ten, but Caroline was young and vibrant and dead long before her time. He shuddered as once again the thought flickered through his mind; the same fate might have befallen Eleanor.

He drew a long steadying breath and squeezed his
wife's gloved hand. She smiled at him recognising his
grief.

ℛ

Back at Eastshore the wake was almost over. Eleanor
saw Padraic Turner standing alone by the window. He
was staring down at the bay. She moved to stand
beside him.

'Is that the Alnmouth Boy being provisioned?' He
asked without looking away from the view.

'It is. She's bound for Holland and then back to
Whitby before returning here on the third leg of her
journey.'

'Ah, good old Whitby. Did I not hear some story of
you once stowing away to Holland in your younger
days? I bet you were a wild one then?'

'I suppose Mr Eskdale told you that tale,' Eleanor
said, 'it was his ship I stowed away on. I was sixteen
and keen to see the world. It seems a lifetime ago.'

'Tis a pity you couldn't join the navy if it was the
world you wanted to see. I once heard about a girl who
dressed up as a soldier for two years. She was only
found out when she was injured.'

'I'm a pacifist and besides, I'm not brave. My plans
involved seeing the world not killing men. War is a
pointless exercise to my mind; men playing war games
and planning their military tactics all for what?'

'Ah yes, the plans we make eh! It's funny is it not?' He still looked resolutely ahead no hint of humour in his voice. 'We think we're in control then God sticks his oar in and shows us who the boss really is. Thomas Hodgeson had plans.' He drank deeply from his glass. 'Berthed by your husband's ship sits the Alnmouth Girl, the sister ship to the Alnmouth Boy. Thomas had big plans along with your husband's father, plans that would unite two families and two business empires. The Almighty, or maybe your husband, had other ideas.' At last he turned to look at her and smirked. His flinty eyes swept over her. 'Who knows how things might change?' he sneered. 'None of us knows what the future holds. Perhaps God has plans for we two? You and I could be thrown together sometime in the future? Fate or the hand of God might intervene? I'm a good Catholic boy, yet sometimes I think God has a terrible bad sense of humour. When the tide turns there's nothing we can do to stop it. We're not masters of our own fate and we should do well to remember that. We're all flotsam and jetsam bobbing about like corks on the turbulent, unpredictable sea.'

Eleanor hoped these were the ramblings of a grief-stricken husband, a husband who had drunk too much to help him numb the pain and loss.

'What are my plans now you might well ask?' He continued blithely. 'I bet your husband would like to know. Perhaps I've plans that would involve you? We would make a good couple you and I, for we both have passionate natures and vision. Do you still have a wild streak Eleanor, a longing for adventure? We're both unconventional and hot-headed are we not? Run away to sea with me, there's a whole new world out there to explore.'

His look sent a shiver down her spine. There was the hint of something cruel which made Eleanor shudder; for the first time she saw Padraic Turner as Gabriel saw him. She was glad the black lace veil still covered her face hiding her horror. The words of the gypsy sprang unbidden to her mind. What was it she'd said - "beware the black dog" and "don't trust the rover"? Was it not a black hound that had done for Caroline? Gabriel had used the term "Irish Rover" often in a derogatory way about the captain since he came into Caroline's life. She felt the force of Padraic's words, as well as the gypsy's. Were they a curse? A prophecy? She turned her head and saw Gabriel watching her, his face was grey.

Eleanor let out a long breath. She felt a little unsteady. 'I came over to say we must be going Padraic, the twins will have need of me. Don't be a stranger. Come and see us anytime - come to dine or just call if you're passing.'

'Really? Would your husband countenance that I wonder?'

'Of course. I know you two don't always see eye to eye but no one knows Thomas' business like Gabriel; he would offer help if you need it. As you've said before you're a soldier not a businessman. I looked after the books when Caroline was away, I too could help if you'd rather?'

'Thank you Eleanor, I'm sure one day soon I'll avail myself of your services.'

Padraic Turner watched as she walked back to her husband's side.

'Shall we go Gabriel? I have a headache.' As they turned to leave, Eleanor noticed the captain move to stand by Susan Stubbs' side. He greeted her, then turned to her companion. Bryony Swift's pretty cheeks flushed becomingly as Captain Turner kissed her hand. She looked up at her old beau, but not before her eyes darted to her former employer. Eleanor leaned heavily on Gabriel's arm. She had a bad feeling.

The End

A Message from Jane

Dear Reader,

I just wanted to say a big thank you for choosing to read The Turning Tides. If you enjoyed it, I'd be grateful if you could leave a review on Amazon, or mention it to your friends and family. Word-of-mouth recommendations are so important to an author's success, and doing so will help new readers to discover my work.

It would be lovely to hear from you too, either via my website, or on Facebook, Twitter or Instagram. The Turning Tides is the second in the Reynolds Saga so I sincerely hope you will continue the journey and read Safe Harbour which will be the third and concluding episode.

There are plenty of other books to come so please join me for what I promise will be an exciting adventure.

www.janefenwick.co.uk

About the Author

Jane Fenwick lives in the market town of Settle in Yorkshire, England. She studied education at Sheffield University gaining a B.Ed (Hons) in 1989 and going on to teach primary age range children. Jane decided to try her hand at penning a novel rather than writing school reports as she has always been an avid reader, especially enjoying historical and crime fiction. She decided to combine her love of both genres to write her first historical crime novel **Never the Twain**. Jane has always been a lover of antiques, particularly art nouveau and art deco ceramics and turned this hobby into a business opening an antiques and collectables shop in Settle. However her time as a dealer was short lived; she spent far too much time in the sale rooms buying items that ended up in her home rather than the shop! Animal welfare is a cause close to Jane's heart and she has been vegetarian since the age of fourteen. For the last twenty years she has been trustee of an animal charity which rescues and re-homes cats, dogs and all manner of creatures looking for a forever home. Of course several of these have been "adopted" by Jane! Although she lives in the Yorkshire Dales Jane is particularly drawn to the North East Coast which she knows well; often visiting Whitby, Sandsend and Alnmouth for research purposes. When she isn't walking on Sandsend beach with her dog Scout, a Patterdale "Terrorist" she is to be found in her favourite coffee shop gazing out to sea and dreaming up her next plot. **My Constant Lady**, the first in the Reynolds saga, set on the North East coast was well received. Look out for the third book in the Reynolds series, **Safe Harbour,** coming in 2021.

Keep reading for an exclusive excerpt from the next in the Reynolds saga:

Safe Harbour

Jane Fenwick

Whitby 1774

Prologue

Gabriel Reynolds looked out over Whitby harbour. 'Man alive, it's heaving today; I'd wager I could get to the other side without getting my feet wet. I never saw so many ships.'

His brother-in-law, Tomas Barker, held on tight to his tricorn as he strode along beside him. 'It looks like rain and the wind's getting up. I think most are waiting to see what the weather will do before they commit to sailing on the next tide. None of the herring fleet has set sail so that tells you something. These old sea dogs can smell when the weather is about to turn.'

'Good job The Eleanor Rose isn't due out for two more days then.' Gabriel stopped and looked up at his ship. He still felt as proud of her now as the day she'd been built in John Barker's yard. The collier had arrived the day before from the Baltics and was now being provisioned to sail back to her home port of Alnmouth carrying grain and timber.

Gabriel, his wife Eleanor and their three children had

returned from Amsterdam two days ago, after they had been staying with their friends the Vissers for the best part of a month. Eleanor had been keen to see her family before returning home to Westshore, their house on the seashore at Alnmouth.

Ordinarily Gabriel enjoyed spending time with Eleanor's family at Sandsend. After almost ten years of marriage he now regarded the Barkers as his family too. On this occasion however, he was keen to get home; a large deal was waiting to be finalised and was playing on his mind. It was a deal which would see his tally of ships rise from three to six, effectively doubling his import-export business. Not that the deal was one he had sought out; indeed it had come about because of an unexpected and not altogether happy turn of events. Gabriel hoped the agreement would be completed to everyone's satisfaction but he worried there would be a problem and so he was anxious to get home and put the deal to bed.

The two men stood together, matched in height and stature, but not in colouring. Gabriel's dark curls ruffled in the breeze, his greatcoat blew out behind him. His chin had dark stubble covering it for unless he shaved twice a day it was the inevitable outcome, much to his wife's chagrin. Tomas' shorter, fairer hair barely moved in the blustery wind. After a sudden blast threatened to tear the hat from Tomas' head he'd removed it. He was regretting leaving his coat in the office and wrapped his arms about his body in an effort to keep warm.

'Never cast a clout until May be out,' Gabriel said as he saw his brother-in-law shiver.

He approached his captain, Nathan Pearson, a burly Geordie who had worked for Gabriel and his father before him. He enquired after the cargo. With a Geordie accent as thick as his biceps the captain replied: 'First lot er grain arrived not half an hour ago, the rest's not expected 'til tomorrow. It's goin' to be a bit tight to get it all loaded in time, but we'll manage. Don't we allus?'

Gabriel nodded and watched as tubs of herring were heaved on board. Crates were hauled up on pulleys and grain sacks unloaded from wagons. The Eleanor Rose wasn't the only ship being provisioned that day and so the quay was a mass of men, mules and merchandise. A stream of curses went up as a barrel toppled over and rolled back down the gangplank knocking two men over like skittles.

'Have a care Sol, if that there barrel had split it were comin' out of your pay lad.' Gabriel smiled, both he and Nat knew this to be an untruth, but it didn't hurt to keep the deckhands on their toes.

Another crate dangled precariously in the air then a sudden gust sent it crashing against the ship's hull. It rebounded making the dockers duck. A colourful stream of cussing followed, then nervous laughter rang out when they saw they were safe. Gabriel and Tomas stepped back bumping into each other in their haste to be out of range.

Tomas laughed as he slipped on a discarded fish head and dropped his hat. 'Lord, the wind's skittish today, I nearly went over then.'

'Don't for the love of God fall in the harbour for I'm not keen to dive in after you,' Gabriel told him.

Before Tomas could reply he saw Nat waving his arms over his head and yelling frantic instructions to the crew. The crate was still swaying crazily when another gust took hold of it. Gabriel saw it was heading straight for the two of them. He tried to shout a warning to Tomas but the words were thrown away on the wind. He shot a look at his brother-in-law who had bent to recover his tricorn and was about to raise his head. The crate looked lined up to knock Tomas off his feet. Gabriel hurled himself at him pushing him to the ground. That and a sharp pain were the last things he remembered.

R

Eleanor Reynolds sat by the fire opposite her mother. After their walk on the cliff top at Mulgrave House in Sandsend, she felt pleasantly tired. The weather had suddenly turned squally so they had retreated to the warmth of the drawing room. The three Reynolds children, Rose who had seven summers and twins Haydan and Ruari who had five, were playing on the rug. They were bickering with each other as children

4

who resent being confined indoors generally do.

'Your grandmama will get the impression you're badly brought up. For goodness' sake play nicely all of you.'

Eleanor's mother, Anne Barker, tried not to smile. 'They're just like you and your siblings at that age. They long to be outdoors no matter what the weather. You were all just the same.'

'I think it's stopped raining Mama, may we go out again?' Eleanor thought Rose was eager to get away from her annoying little brothers and who could blame her? The boys had begun a wrestling match and were intent on killing each other it seemed.

'Perhaps you could go and find Ginny and play in the nursery my love.' The boys stopped rolling around, leapt to their feet and dashed to the window.

'It's only raining a bit now,' Haydan hollered across the room.

His mother remonstrated with him for shouting like a docker then pointed out that even if it stopped raining they wouldn't be allowed out as the wind was now blowing a gale. 'You'll be blown off the cliff into the sea never to be seen again!'

'Good,' Rose muttered under her breath making her grandmama smile broadly.

Eleanor was about to order tea when a commotion could be heard in the hall. They rushed out to see what was happening. Gabriel, blood pouring from his head, was being carried up the stairs.

1

Dr Burns wiped his hands on a towel and bundled up the bloodied rags. Eleanor stared at her husband willing him to wake. Gabriel had been knocked unconscious and was yet to recover his senses. He lay on the bed as if in a deep sleep, except he had a livid gash to his head.

Tomas, his arm around his twin sister's waist, looked on. 'It all happened so quickly. I bent to retrieve my hat and the next thing I knew Gabriel had hurled himself on top of me. The crate was heading my way Nat said. Gabriel is injured because he tried to save me.'

Eleanor squeezed her brother's hand. 'It's no fault of yours Tomas; you don't need to feel guilty.'

'The wound looks worse than it is,' the doctor interrupted them. 'Often times a cut to the head can bleed profusely. A few stitches will see it right. Should you care to step out Eleanor while I sew him up?'

'Yes - no, when will he wake up? He's been unconscious almost an hour now.' She shot an anxious look at her brother for confirmation. He looked at his pocket watch and nodded.

'Sadly I've no way of telling my dear.' Dr Burns began to thread a needle.

The elderly doctor had been treating the Barker family ever since Eleanor and her siblings were small. He'd always had a kind, but no nonsense bedside manner. He was a gregarious Scotsman, stoutly built and jovial by temperament. He sought to calm Eleanor's fears.

'There is one blessing – at least he won't feel the stitches going in.'

Eleanor didn't share the doctor's levity. 'Perhaps the pain will bring him round?' she suggested. Dr Burns began to sew. Eleanor winced, but resolutely watched her husband's face for signs he was waking. There were none.

Anne Barker crept into the room and took her place by her daughter and son. 'The children are playing in the nursery. They're having their tea shortly, so there's no need to worry about them. I've said their father will be as right as rain in no time.'

'But will he? He's still out cold. What if ... '

Dr Burns finished sewing the gash and looked at Eleanor over his pince-nez. 'My dear I cannot be certain of course, but Gabriel will regain consciousness soon I hope. Often it's the body's way of repairing itself, being unconscious, but if by tomorrow he hasn't come around I'll bleed him.'

'Tomorrow! He may be unconscious until tomorrow?'

'It is not uncommon, but who knows he might rally tonight. If he does do not hesitate to send for me no matter what the time.' He picked up his bag.

'Let me see you out doctor. How is your wife? I heard she's been suffering with her rheumatism again.' Anne led the doctor from the bedchamber.

Eleanor sat by the bed, reached for her husband's hand and suddenly burst into tears; she could hold in her fear no longer. Tomas was quick to come to her aid.

'My love he's as strong as an ox, he'll pull through. You heard what old Burns said, it looks worse than it is.'

Eleanor wiped her eyes. 'Do you remember what happened to Caroline?' She mentioned a family friend who had been thrown from her horse and knocked out. 'She never recovered consciousness and died. She was just three and twenty.'

'That was different Eleanor, Burns says apart from the scratch to his head Gabriel has no other injuries. Caroline had broken her back from the fall remember.'

For the next few hours Eleanor continued to gaze at her husband willing him to regain consciousness. At last she was persuaded to leave Gabriel to say goodnight to her children. She returned to her husband's bedside to find her father had kept vigil in her absence.

'Papa, has there been any change?'

'I would have sent for you had there been my dear,

try to stay calm.'

'The boys are over excited, what is it with boys and blood? They've convinced themselves Gabriel has been fighting a duel. Poor Rose is distraught. She's such a daddy's girl.'

'I've sent for a tray for you my dear, you cannot go on without sustenance, you must eat.'

'I'll try, but I'm not hungry.'

A chambermaid brought steamed fish and potatoes. The smell made Eleanor nauseous. She picked at the food before pushing it away uneaten.

ℛ

Gabriel opened his eyes and tried to adjust them to the candlelight. He looked up at the unfamiliar bed canopy. Where was he? He tried to look sideways, but a sharp pain shot through his head like a bullet. He lifted his hand to his head and felt something... a dressing? Had he been shot? Carefully he tried to move his head to the side again and saw a lady asleep on a chair by his bedside. He blinked trying to clear his head. Who was she and why was she here?

Her long, red hair glowed in the light from a three branched candelabra. It was unbound and fell in waves to her waist. She had slid slightly to one side, her head resting on the back of the chair. He searched her features for recognition. Her pale face had a sprinkling of freckles across her cheeks. Her nose had a slight bump on the bridge, but it didn't detract from her looks. Who was it that watched over him? An angel? His head felt fuzzy and heavy, confused. The room began to swim and swirl. He fought to stay awake, willing himself to keep his eyes open and focussed on the red-haired beauty. He tried to lift his hand to touch her but it felt like a lead weight. He was as weak as a kitten. Once more he sank into oblivion.

www.ingramcontent.com/pod-product-compliance
Lightning Source LLC
Chambersburg PA
CBHW030141200726
48285CB00004BC/1257